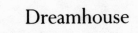

Dreamhouse

Alison Habens
Dreamhouse

First published in Great Britain in 1994
by Martin Secker & Warburg Limited,
an imprint of Reed Consumer Books Limited,
Michelin House, 81 Fulham Road, London SW3 6RB
and Auckland, Melbourne, Singapore and Toronto

A CIP catalogue record for this book
is available from the British Library

ISBN 0 436 20204 2

Typeset by Deltatype Ltd, Ellesmere Port, Cheshire
Printed and bound in Great Britain by
Mackays of Chatham plc, Chatham, Kent

For Frank Lyons, my mother June, and my sister
Heather Habens; for believing in me while I told a story.

Contents

1. Celia Small

Celia has been staring at this page for ages. The words are blurred. Twenty times her eyes have helter-skeltered all the way down to the bottom, but her eyelids have followed them, falling fast; so that instead of turning over and starting at the top of the next page, Celia has sunk further into her white pillows, her eyes shut tight against the bright bedside light, and started to go to sleep.

And with a score of startled snores she has sat up abruptly and tried to find her place again, peering blearily into the dense text. There are no diagrams or dialogues to alleviate its darkness; but there is one word in the third paragraph which points itself out to her every time, sending her into daydreams, though she is supposed to be having an early night.

The word is finance, but Celia keeps reading it as fiancé. This is only to be expected, she supposes, on the eve of her engagement. But she chose the most boring book on her bookshelf with the sole purpose of not getting over-excited tonight, of not gazing starry-eyed around her room with a view to vacating it as soon as decency permits.

The room itself is not the problem. The room itself is quite pretty, though the walls are pale and peeling in the glare of the lamp. Damp patches are covered with posters, a pair of cute kittens, a couple of cheeky chimps in *lederhosen*; and facing Celia at the foot of the bed a shy child fondling a faun. This is Celia's private picture collection, and she doesn't know if she'll be able to put them up in her new home, but she is sure of one thing: in her new home, her skin won't crawl like cheap wallpaper each time her thoughts wander beyond the four walls of the bedroom.

Celia is living in a shared house. Four people occupy two adjoining rooms apiece; the rest of the space is communal. It could be called a complete commune if the housemates liked each other; but none of them seem to hit it off, though all except Celia are equally hateful. She has been watching them from a safe distance. She wouldn't touch them with a plastic-wrapped bargepole.

First, there's Cath, who rents the set of rooms above Celia's. Now, call Celia squeamish, but she can't stomach the way Cath sticks the tip of her tongue between her lips when she smiles; or how she stretches, with her spine arched and her arms straight out behind her, as if to say Hey! see how far back I can bend. Celia's shoulders stiffen at the sight of such a show-off. And Cath comes so silently upon her in the corridors, and never says sorry when she makes Celia jump, just smiles and sticks her tongue out and tells Celia that their milkman used to be a member of the Byrds but he still catches worms, or something similarly stupid.

Then there's Phoebe if you please in the other pair of upstairs rooms, the door to which has to be passed to go to the toilet. When Celia first moved into the house, Phoebe's door was red. Then, one morning, she awoke to find it had been painted black. Since she's lived here, Celia has suffered from constant attacks of cystitis.

For Phoebe is fierce. She has bristling black hair and burning brown eyes, which put Celia in mind of hot coals and potholes. Her every tut and mutter thunder under her door and resound around the house. Each time she uses the staircase she breaks one of the balustrades, leaving the hallway with banisters like the smile of a toothless old hag. She got an electric shock once from the light switch on the landing, and when Cath tried to save her with some rubber-soled slippers, Phoebe screamed, 'Piss off! No, piss on me, piss on me! I don't want it to stop!' But the thing about Phoebe that Celia finds most frightening of all is this: how can she have eyebrows which meet in the middle and still be so breathtakingly beautiful?

Between the sheets, Celia crosses her legs and tears her mind from the topic. Because the more she thinks about how she'd hate to have to go up those croaking stairs and down that creaking corridor and past that black door to get to the bathroom, the more she feels that's exactly where she needs to go. Nerves are blowing her bladder up like a balloon, and if her stomach starts to sink too, it will be all she can do to hold on tight till tomorrow morning when either she or Phoebe has gone to work.

But tomorrow is Saturday. It's the weekend. Celia will have jobs to do all right, but none that weren't commissioned in heaven. She'll have furniture to shift, food to cook, hands to shake, smiles to lift, champagne to pour, eyes to shine and a wobbling bottom lip to bite. For one night only, she'll be playing the leading lady, and by the time next week comes Celia's workaday lifestyle will have changed for ever.

In one fell swoop of excitement she slams her boring book shut and gets out of bed. On rugs arranged as stepping stones she crosses the shabby carpet to the bookcase. She puts her *Beginner's Guide to Middle Management at the End of Capitalism* back on the bottom shelf, and pulls a lighter-looking paperback off the top. It has a short title in curly red writing and a soft-focus face with the same colour lips on the cover, but Celia turns straight to pages 121 and 122. A key is Sellotaped between them.

Celia takes the key to the dressing-table and unlocks a jewellery box in the shape of a Swiss chalet. Once inside, to the tinny strains of 'Feelings', Celia gains access to the secret compartment by twisting the third gold rosebud to the left of the revolving ballerina twice to the right. The secret compartment contains another key. Celia extracts it and drops to her hands and knees beside her bed. Reaching into the regularly dusted darkness underneath she finds the small silver casket which is all that lurks there. Celia unlocks the casket with the second key and lifts a layer of cotton wool to uncover a third. This one is bigger and overly ornate. It fits the keyhole of the trunk on top of Celia's wardrobe. This trunk has much more in common with a lady's shoulderbag than a seaman's chest, but Celia has to do a lot of heaving and toing and froing with a chair to climb on before she can complete her mission. At last the trunk is on the floor and the lid is open and Celia is back in bed with her booty on her lap.

Celia's treasure is a scrapbook, carefully wrapped in confetti-thin sheets of tissue paper. It is white and gold, encrusted with glued-on lace and ribbon and rice. But it is yellowing with age, like a jilted bride waiting at the altar. The words on the cover say GREAT EXPECTATIONS, and then, in littler lettering, 'Of Celia Small'.

Celia holds her breath and turns to the first page. The opening entry is dated sixteen years ago almost to the day. It is an early English homework assignment, copied up neatly, but careering unsteadily across the unlined expanse of the page. It is entitled, 'When I am Older . . .', and it goes like this:

When I am oder I will get married I will have a job too but I

4

only want to get married really because that is what I want to do. It is the law. I love Nickerless Pearce in my class and I itend to marry him when I am older.

When you are married you can have a house with a matching kitchen and bathroom like my house at home but you must not be blue. You must not shout or else you get a hedake. You can go shopping and get anything you want except for more children and having grandma and granddad to stay because these are the things that money can't buy.

While my husband is at work I will play Mummies and Daddies, and when he comes home I will give him his dinner. I would also like to have a dog.

To be a brid you wear white and people throw flowers at you because you are pretty.

Celia chuckles at this infant idealism. She knows these strings of words by heart, and could chant them as hollowly as Hail Marys on a rosary of cheap and cheerful children's beads. But seeing them written in that round and racing hand reminds her that ancient prayers are about to be answered: it's all right, she says to her eight-year-old self through the pages of this time-travelling tome, your dreams will soon come true.

Celia turns over a leaf or two. Six years pass but her dreams stay the same, though now that she is at secondary school she has learnt to disguise them as pieces of pure fiction:

The Porposal

Clothilde was thrilled. The postman had bought her a big bunch of red roses and buried in them was a card from her boyfriend, Prince Kevin Smith, saying 'I'm taking you out for tea tonight so please wear your best dress.'

At five o'clock Kevin came and they went to a cafe and had chicken and chips and Kevin had beans and she had peas, and after the cafe they went to the shopping centre where there was a jewellers.

Kevin went down on one knee, but not because he was a prince. 'Will you marry me he said.' 'Well said Clothilde.' 'I love you said Kevin.' Still Clothilde wasn't sure. She looked in the window of the jewellery shop.

'See those gold rings, said Kevin, they're your eyes. See that silver necklace, that's your smile. See that watch, that's your heart. See that crucifix, that's your soul. See that christening mug, that's our baby. See that grandfather clock, that's how long our love will last.'

'Oh said Clothilde.' 'So do you want to marry me then said Prince Kevin.' 'Yes said Clothilde.'

The happy couple went into the shop and a lady showed them lots of engagement rings and the best one was one which went on two fingers together, joined by a tiny chain made of diamonds which could never break.

Celia sniffs a bit and wipes away the suggestion of a tear with the third finger of her left hand: ringless now, but not for much longer. Don't worry, she says silently to her teenage self, you'll soon have what you want.

At the foot of the page is a note added by Celia's mother, the editor of this book. It says that due to the distressingly low grade awarded this piece of work she paid a visit to Celia's school, where she was informed by a Miss Van Dyke that her daughter should stop being silly about men and matrimony and start doing some serious work. As a result of this teacher's comments, Celia will be going to a different school in the spring.

Celia turns the musty pages faster, past possible guest lists and pictures of prospective presents; past collages of kitchens clipped from catalogues and soft furnishings snipped from fabric samples. Like a silent movie, her handwriting runs and jumps; the rows of characters growing taller and thinner with the speeded-up passage of time, the drawings gaining in perspective, the underlining going deeper.

In a pull-out section halfway through the book, Celia's engagement party is planned to perfection; from the smoked salmon starters to the hemming on the hostess's special dress. Celia unfolds the fine blue paper and scours the small print for anything she might have forgotten. In the centre of the page is a biro dining-table, with seating arrangements pencilled around it. The guests are represented by simple circles, attached to speech bubbles which provide more complex conversational details.

'We've been looking forward to meeting you for a long time, Celia,' says one, 'it's a pleasure to make your acquaintance at last.'

'This is a feast fit for a king,' adds another. 'You do us too much kindness.'

The circle which is supposed to be Celia is surrounded by glitter stuck on with glue. This has a thought cloud instead of a speech bubble, containing the words: I'm So Happy, and He Loves Me.

Around the edges of the paper are remarks and reminders written over the course of a decade. The earliest, in green felt-tip pen, says 'get caterers and waiters'; the latest is a last-minute shopping list. Celia scans it. She still hasn't bought the serviettes. She must remember to rush out for them first thing tomorrow.

Celia folds the party blueprint back into the book and flicks over more leaves. Pressed flower petals fly, fanned by the breeze. A cinema ticket falls out, and a champagne label, and a lock of hair. She stops at the last page. This is dated only months previously, but it is framed with fancy stick-on silver stars, and its title echoes the childish exuberance of her earliest entries:

The Proposal

At last! It's actually happened! Someone has asked me to marry them! I'm over the moon, of course. This is the moment I've been waiting for for as long as I can remember.

Now there's not a moment to lose. Luckily, the plans are already made, and laid in waiting in this book. The first major step is the engagement do, which we've scheduled for as soon as is humanly possible. My main concern here is to give my mother – who is beside herself with delight (and relief!) – time enough to make my special dress, which we designed nine years ago, but didn't want to sew up before the date was set for fear of tempting fate. Other than this, I shall be doing everything myself, because that is the bride's prerogative.

By the way, my fiancé-to-be is called Kenneth Conn. Some people call him Ken, but I don't because he says it sounds common. And in actual fact, he is much richer than any future husband I ever dreamed of, which is a bit of an added bonus. I haven't met his parents yet, but apparently their house is more like a mansion, and we will inherit it when they die, apparently. Looks like I'm going to have to rethink the dimensions of my fitted kitchen!

How shall I describe Kenneth? Well, he's got mousy hair and skin that sunburns, he's slightly taller than me, and is always smartly dressed, even at weekends, which is something I admire in a man. His eyes are . . .

[Here there is a gap, as if Celia had to go and check the colour, but then forgot to fill it in.]

Kenneth is a banker, but he doesn't tell me anything about it because he says it is boring. There was a party at his workplace the other day, but we didn't go because he said that would be boring too. I am satisfied that it is a secure job, however, because his father is on the board.

Out of the office, like myself, Kenneth prefers the quiet life. His favourite sports are cricket and golf, I think, but he doesn't actually play them; he watches them on television. He enjoys plain food, and also eating at home rather than in a restaurant.

Mind you, we were in a restaurant when he proposed. Well, it was a McDonald's actually, but we were in a hurry to catch the end-of-season sale at the department store next door. The subject came up quite unexpectedly; after all, we haven't even known each other very long; it really has been a whirlwind courtship.

Anyway, I was about to buy some new bed linen and was saying what a waste it would be to get single-sized stuff if, in the foreseeable future, I'd be wanting to swap it all for a double set. So, we put our heads together and worked out quite coolly and calmly exactly how much money could be saved by buying the double-bed size straight away, and before we knew it we were rummaging through the display of reduced-price king-size continental quilt covers with a view to making a lifelong commitment to each other.

I know it wasn't quite the magic moment of my imaginings, but, like Mum said, time was running out. The main thing is, I can get settled now and get sorted out. I can be myself.

A photograph of Kenneth accompanies this true story; stuck in with self-adhesive corners sprayed silver to match the stars which surround it. Kenneth is the hero of the hour, but even as Celia sighs over his likeness her look slips and her eyes slide to her bedside clock, where they linger longer. Mickey Mouse's arms are held at an awkward angle, the hands telling a time that Celia rarely sees: she's normally in the land of nod by now.

If Celia isn't careful, she'll spoil her big day by being short on sleep. She shuts up her wedding album, snuggles down between the last of her single sheets and turns off the light.

Celia closes her eyes and squeezes them tight. Kenneth's head is silhouetted black on red. Breath stirs hair on her brow. She blinks. And the red gets brighter, up her nose, buzzing like a light bulb, in her ears; the red plants itself on her mouth in the shape of a kiss. She turns her face away. Slowly.

Celia closes her thighs and squeezes them tight. Her legs are white, even in the blackness and under the blankets. Her hips are white and her stomach is white, and the bone-china xylophone of her rib-cage is white. Celia breathes in with a brittle rattle.

Kenneth's head comes back, darkly, bleeding into red at the edges, beating in time with the pounding in Celia's ears. Celia sighs and her thighs relent and release their tension deep into the mattress. There is an equal and opposite reaction in her spine, which tightens; her feet, which twitch; her shoulders, which shudder; her neck, which stretches; and her nipples, which tingle.

All at once the fabric of Celia's nightdress is feeling like fingers, everywhere it touches her flesh. She holds her breath and hardly dares move for fear of rubbing against it. The blankets are bearing down harder too now, like big hands on her chest. The lungful of air she's too scared to let go is forcing her breasts up to press in their palms, but she can't let it go. No.

Celia shakes her head from side to side. The after-image of Kenneth on the inside of her eyelids stays with her. He's clinging. One of her fists clenches involuntarily, then it does another thing without her consent. It touches her thigh.

10

'Why Kenneth,' thinks Celia, 'you naughty boy.' The hand backs off.

For a while, Celia lies still. In the dim light of her mind's eye she is in a bigger bedroom now. The red is a roaring log fire, some forty feet away across a liquid parquet floor. Like sails in the sunset, the drapes of the four-poster billow above, and it is four sheets to the wind down below, too.

This will be the wedding bed. Celia will be pale and frail, laid across its flowery counterpane like the Lady of Shalott. She will be shivering. Kenneth will come upon her suddenly, cleanly, completely. There will be no foreplay. They're not children.

Celia's hand has strayed again, coming to rest on her stomach, under the cover of her nightie. Her breathing deepens, but her mouth is shut fast, so her nostrils flare to take in the extra air.

Kenneth is there. Celia imagines that her legs are open and Kenneth is between them, consummating their relationship. She can't see it. She can't even feel it. But it's really happening. It's finally happening. It's happening fast. Kenneth is hanging above her, his arms as perpendicular to the bed as the four posters, his face in shadow.

'Take me, I'm yours,' thinks Celia grimly.

He does, and she is. Celia cries out in pain on her dream bed, and cringes imperceptibly in her real one. White sheets are violated.

She's been told that the pain turns to pleasure after a while. Waiting patiently, like a martyr or a masochist, her body is powerless but her soul is safe. Celia rolls her eyes in a way the Pre-Raphaelite painters apparently found attractive, and spots a new damp patch on the ceiling.

Like her mind, her hand is wandering; from the dead centre of herself an inch or so below the belly button, up and away, over

11

the hill and into the hollow, the heart-shaped hollow between the two halves of her rib-cage, where it touches the shadows but not the substance of her breasts.

It doesn't go any further.

Celia wants to wait a while, wait until it is officially Kenneth's hand on her body. She can't relax and enjoy herself till then. If she loses control before it's all legal, she could come completely undone.

But there are tugs in three of her tips, as the telecommunications cables of her nervous system contract in key places, pulling her hands, like puppets on a string, up to the tops of her nipples, and down to their triangulation point between her thighs.

Celia is going to have to give in. The suspense is making her tense. Kenneth's outline is still on the inside of her eyelids, and it doesn't look disapproving. And her hand is not her own now, anyway. It's her husband's hand. There's nothing dirty about it. Celia is going to give in.

With a rush of honey and moons and milk and money the hand takes possession of her left breast.

'Oh Kenneth,' thinks Celia.

His spectral presence looms closer. It's cowled or under a quilt or something, for his features are fuzzy and difficult to make out. But the fingering of her nipple is clear as crystal, as is the tickle of the thumb in her cleavage. He takes a careful handful of shy shrinking breast flesh and holds it.

This is how it will be in that big bed on their wedding night. Celia turns her face to Kenneth's for a kiss. She can see him better now in the hot light of the log fire. She can gaze gratefully on his familiar features: those damp curlicues of hair, framing that high brow, infringing on those cheekbones; that statuesque nose, those Greek lips, the olive skin, the marble eyes . . .

12

Celia bucks herself bolt upright in bed, mouth gaping and eyes wide in the blackness. That's not Kenneth she can see. That's Dodge!

Dodge is the third and last of Celia's hated housemates. She doesn't know if that is his real name. She's never asked. His rooms are on the ground floor, opposite hers across the hall. She can hear his television from here, shouting; a high voice and a low voice, a woman's voice and a man's, in so unbroken a volley that it sounds like one voice screaming up and down the vocal scale, one person playing both parts.

Dodge has got his TV on too loud. That must be why Celia was thinking about him, when she was meant to be practising kissing Kenneth, and rehearsing her first night generally. And suddenly Celia is even farther out of the bed, her eyes popping and her heart in her mouth. For a thought more terrible still has struck her.

A television! She and Kenneth will need a television for their new home. It should have been on the list of things to organise, in the electrical appliances section of her scrapbook, but the most obvious items are the ones that get forgotten. It must be a colour television, of course, and remote control too, though she ought to confirm that with him tomorrow. And she'd better ask about a video, and whether they'd want one with one tape deck or two.

Celia flops back on her pillows, feverish. It's all getting a bit much; she'll have to buy some kind of cabinet, with shelves to keep the tapes tidy. A corner unit, with a neat teak finish. And sliding doors.

She lies awake long into the night, worrying. Things still to do remind her rudely of themselves, as the pages of her mental filofax fly. Names and faces of people on the guest list remember themselves to her loudly, just when she thought they'd all left. But she smiles politely to the last.

Celia has waited for ever to feel this special. And if being special means having to try even harder than before, then she'll stop at nothing to get what she wants. But Celia is not one of those ambitious young women with cravings on a global scale and a hunger for power. She simply wants to be wanted. Well, that and a washing-machine.

2. Celia's smalls

Celia's smalls are strung like bunting, boastfully, above the bathtub. All smug, all silken, all white, all whispering that Celia has been out of bed and busy for hours.

Cath, freshly risen in stale pyjamas, lingers under Celia's lingerie.

Cath likes a laugh. She is starting her day with a snigger and a titter at spanking-clean briefs and a silly white bra. At white suspenders suspended from blackened bathroom string. At the frilly petticoat which hangs back shyly, suggesting that Celia fancies herself as a fairy princess.

Cath hates washing, but she doesn't mind a bit of irony. She likes white stockings when they're hung up to dry in a dank and dingy bathroom in a long cold corridor in a cavernous house. White stockings, with a snag. White stockings, frozen stiff. If they were tights they would be stalactites.

Cath turns and smiles at herself in the mirror over the sink. There is nothing clean and carbolic-naked to be seen from this angle. There are only cracked off-white tiles over her shoulder, and a ceiling black and hairy with mould above her head. She turns on the tap and the mould starts to smell. It is surprisingly sweet, sweeter than Cath, but she trusts this sweetness as much as she would trust a cosmetics-counter sales-assistant to tell the truth.

Cath puts the plug in, and yawns a big black hole in her pale pink face. The yawn struggles away, steaming up the mirror and heaving a slow 'WOW!' out of Cath's mouth in its wake. When the sink is full of dull chalky water she submerges her sleepy countenance, then rises up and reaches, blind and dripping, for the towel rail. Two towels are there. One is rank and rigid from lack of washing; Cath couldn't handle drying her face on that. Anyway, it belongs to Dodge. The other one, Phoebe's, is stridently stripey and a bit abrasive. (Celia, Cath happens to know, keeps her set of soft lemon-nice towels under lock and key in her room.) Cath uses Phoebe's towel, then looks for her own toothbrush.

She doesn't actually own a toothbrush, but refuses to recognise this fact. Every morning and night she tries to find it in the tupperware beaker full of her housemates' cast-offs. With bristles side-parted like old gentlemen hiding bald patches, these toothbrushes are plucked out of retirement and into Cath's service. Their glory is short-lived. Cath can never remember which one she is calling hers for more than a morning. But, with a different dead or dying toothbrush at her disposal every day, she has avoided spending money on a new one for nearly a year.

Today she picks out a motley blue one and squeezes some of Dodge's toothpaste onto it. There is a knock at the door.

'Hi!' cries Cath, foaming fresh and minty at the mouth.

No one answers her, but unless they've got ghosts there is somebody out there waiting to come in. So Cath spits into the sink, smooths the telltale signs of her trespasses from the towels and toothpaste tube, and opens the bathroom door.

16

Dodge is standing outside. He looks almost apologetic, but doesn't say anything. Cath steps past him with half a smile that he doesn't see. But once she is downwind of him she wrinkles her nose; a strange smell seems to cling to Dodge like a nasty negligée. Cath has never been able to put a name to it.

Dodge goes into the bathroom and shuts the door. Before it is completely closed, Cath hears him start to speak in a strangled tone. His chanting turns to choking, then to the sounds of violent vomiting; a wave of nausea, a splash in the pan. Cath wanders off down the corridor.

She sees Phoebe coming up the stairs, tiredly, as if through thick tar, an oily cup of coffee held like boiling bitumen before her.

'Morning,' Cath smiles.

Phoebe glares at her briefly.

'It's the afternoon,' she says, bitterly.

'So soon?' says Cath, in surprise. Phoebe thinks she's faking it and snarls something to this effect, but Cath is padding away up the indoor alley to her own rooms.

Phoebe stops at the top of the stairs to slurp her coffee. With a thump her headache catches up with her. At this altitude even her ears hurt. With eyes too heavy to look straight ahead, Phoebe stumbles down the corridor towards the bathroom. A cold shower is the only solution. A cold shower is the only choice; there won't be any hot water at this late hour.

Phoebe arrives at the bathroom door as Dodge is departing. They swap places smoothly in the narrow corridor, neither one giving the slightest sign of having seen the other.

Phoebe locks herself in the bathroom. Hitching up her virulent orange dressing-gown, she lowers herself gingerly onto the toilet. Once seated, she sinks forward, an elbow on each knee, her chin cupped in her hands. She usually has to wait like this for some time. But today the bathroom is not a pleasant place to be. The white stockings hanging up to dry have been looped and twisted into sinister nooses. There is something sick in the air. Phoebe shifts position so that her hands cover her nose and mouth, instead of cupping her chin. Now at least she can breathe.

The bathroom doesn't usually smell this bad. It doesn't usually smell as bad as the communal kitchen.

The communal kitchen stinks. It was designed to stink. The plans of the man who built it must have specified the stink. The blueprint must have predicted the accumulation of organic matter in every dark nook and damp cranny; especially way back when all food was wholefood. But could that ancient architect have foreseen the malodorous advances made by the tenants of his house a hundred years in the future, the tenants of today?

No, Celia doesn't think he could.

Sod them! They're so selfish! Today of all days why should she be the one to clean up after the orgy of private boredom and self-abuse which is Friday night in the shared house. Well, basically because if Celia doesn't do it, it doesn't get done.

Celia purses her lips.

And the kitchen hums with three-tone fumes, like a chord; each note a distinct component of the whiff which welcomes Celia to the sink. The old wooden draining-board is incontinent, but its smell is overpowered by the new-fangled fetors and techno-aromas stacked on top of it.

Cringing, Celia prods the pile of monstrous crockery and unnatural cutlery with a washing-up mop. Cath's contribution to the world of fragrance, Garlic Ashtray with a Hint of Incense, leaps and licks at her nose like a flame. Pulsing beneath this heart-attacking inhalation is a muskier tone: this Celia puts down to Phoebe's being a bit Free and Easy with her Bodily Fluids and not always Disposing of Used Tissues in the most Hygienic Manner.

To top it all, there is the high note, the heady note, of the waste produced by Dodge: Scintillating Astringent Substances in glasses and mugs with empty crisp packets like jam-pot covers over their necks, in Lurid Synthetic Shades which Celia can only assume to be medicinal.

Celia's housemates are mad, bad and dangerously undomesti-cated. But Celia is practically a saint, the way she washes up beyond the call of duty. There are no rubber gloves. There is no hot water. This operation must be done without an anaesthetic. All she can do is dream of wine and roses and not think to deeply about the cracks in the communal crockery. Celia has her own tableware, a complete set from Laura Ashley. She keeps it under lock and key in her rooms. It only comes out at mealtimes, and goes back straight after afters. No one else in the house is allowed to touch it.

But no one else in the house would touch it if she paid them to, probably. They never do any washing up. They just leave the sink full of their shit as if to say Celia, Kiss Our Afters. She has sworn never to wash up for them again. On several occasions.

But today, today of all days, she needs a nice clean kitchen, uncluttered surfaces, bridesmaid-fresh air; and not so much as a squeak or a reek out of her hated housemates. She rinses the last piece of chipped pottery with a furious flourish, and pulls the plug out of the sink. The washing-up water has turned to soup and drains slowly; the thin bouillon filtering between the teeth of the plug-hole, the chunky bits waiting to be forced down with the handle of a wooden spoon. Which she then has to wash again.

On a ledge above the sink a plant in a tiny pot is lodged. It is the only green thing in the house and the only pretty thing in the kitchen. Celia is the only one who waters it. She thinks it might be Wild Thyme. Its leaves are sharp as arrows and its flower purple as a wound.

Someone has stubbed a cigarette out in its saucer of water. Celia screams softly and, snatching up the pot, clasps it as close to her breast as she can without getting her breast moist and muddy.

'I knew it!' she whispers. 'They're trying to kill you!' Her lips touch the flower tenderly, but pull tight like a drawstring purse when she tastes its flavour on her tongue. Briskly, Celia rinses and refills the saucer of water, then walks to the sturdy wooden table which runs the length of the kitchen floor. This table, cleared now of washing-up-in-waiting, reveals a scarred surface which runs the length of the kitchen's history. Setting to work with a scrubbing brush Celia sloughs off several layers of the table's dead skin. The smells which surge up as she scrapes off scab after scab are old but not offensive; the haunting after-images at the end of decomposition.

Anyway, Celia is not scared of ghosts. The kitchen is a dungeon and the house is a house of horrors; but after tonight she'll be out of it. After tonight she'll never be alone in the dark again. This might be a good moment to give her first smile of the day.

Celia smiles a small, slightly unsuccessful smile. And Celia scrubs for an hour, then leaves. If the table had leaves it would have taken longer.

Cath saunters through the kitchen door and screeches to a standstill.

The kitchen is clean! The table is clear!

What a cosmic stroke of luck. All the time she's wasted so far is saved. She jumps up and down on the spot to celebrate, then remembers the straining carrier bags hanging from each hand.

Cath tips her shopping onto the table. Now that some kind interplanetary force has done the worst of it, she can have a cup of tea and a smoke while she works. She had not been looking forward to that washing-up: her housemates had left the sink so sunk that she could hardly see it. But now Cath catches sight of her ashtray, gleaming nicotine-yellow on the draining-board, and smiles at it with her matching teeth. It must be a miracle.

Cath breaks only one small plate while taking her wet ashtray from the bottom of the pile of clean crockery. She gets only a little electric shock from plugging the kettle in without drying her hands. While she is waiting for the kettle to boil, her gaze settles on the plant on the ledge above the sink.

'Hello, lower life form', she says, 'would you care to join me in a drink?'

Cath picks up the pot and holds it under the cold tap, with a 'Whoops' as it slips out of her grip and sheds its biological load in the bottom of the sink. Cath says 'Oh wow! Sorry!' and packs the sodden earth and approximately all the greenery back where it belongs. Standing the plant upright in the pot, and the pot upright on the shelf, she gives the purple flower a charming but crazy smile and chuckles, 'Well, there's wild times for you!'

Cath has come into the kitchen to make a large number of jam tarts. She has a book called *One Hundred Jam Tart Recipes*, though she has tried each type so many times that she knows all the instructions by heart. She never cooks anything else.

On every page of this precious book is a photograph of the appropriate tart; but these look flat and lifeless next to the home-made illustrations with which Cath has augmented the text. On every page of the book is a dried dollop of the tart in

21

question, stuck fast enough to be used in the manner of the 'scratch and sniff' books of her childhood, and providing a more detailed impression of each tart-to-be.

Cath drops her dog-end into the dregs of her cup of tea and starts making pastry. Cutting the corners of page one of the book, where she is asked to wash her hands, tie up her hair and put on an apron please, she turns to page two, where the rules for making Old-fashioned Fluted Beauties, a formal tea-time tart, are preserved in print for all time. Cath is a traditionalist at heart. But this doesn't stop her from diverging from the recipe, like a kid swerving off the road in a stolen car. Halfway through the pastry-making process she pulls a small purple velvet pouch from her pocket and empties its contents into her mixing bowl. Gripping the rim, she stares in; her eyes blink rapidly and her tongue comes out like a dirty old man's, as she watches a chemical reaction happen.

None of the One Hundred Jam Tart Recipes specifies this secret ingredient, but Cath can't stomach anything without it.

It takes her quite a while to whip up ten big baking-trays of her favourite pastry cases. She lays them out carefully amid the chaos on the table, and prepares to plop in the jam.

'Ratshit!' Cath curses, her head in the kitchen cupboard. She has made an alarming discovery. There is no jam. Or, to be more specific, there are five inches of jam with a foreboding furriness around the neck of the jar, and fifty people coming to tea. At least fifty. At the rate of half an inch of jam per partygoer she can cater for ten. But as for the other forty: what a finger-buffet from hell it could turn out to be.

Cath cobbles together a small plateful of finished tarts with the limited jam, then selects the biggest one and sits down with it to wait for inspiration. It comes after four mouthfuls, stunning in its simplicity:

Take Heart Young Woman And Go Again To Waitrose,
There To Purchase Four More Pots Of Finest Own-Brand Jam.

Rummaging in redundant pockets Cath rushes for the door. She hasn't got any money, but purchase can also mean 'get a grip on', so she may manage without it. Cath leaves the communal kitchen darker and more devastated than she found it.

Phoebe was expecting it to be dark and devastated. Why should today be pleasant just because there is a party on? Why should the house be transformed into the Ideal Home just because it's got guests coming?

The kitchen stinks. As Phoebe stands in the doorway its fruity, floury, faggy fingers form a fist and hit her right in the hangover. She reels from the punch. She won't drink tonight, special occasion or no. She's never going to drink again.

However there is something to be said for being so hung over that the horrors of the kitchen are as remote and controlled as if they were on television.

Phoebe walks around the table, her bare feet clicking on the sticky floor. She is too sleepy to see that the tarty mess on the table is not the same as the nasty mess she noticed at three o'clock this morning, and which she swore to tackle once and for all as soon as she regained consciousness. She doesn't realise that someone has already dealt with all that asthmatic ashtray and chemical crisp-packet stuff.

Phoebe brings the kettle to the boil, fills the sink with hot soapy water, and holds her head in the steam.

She begins to sing.

This is not as bad as she feared. Post-pastry, the plates and pots and pans are putty in her hands, and the zesty lemon washing-up liquid cuts like a shaft of sunlight through Phoebe's internal cloudiness as well as the actual cloudiness of the kitchen.

Phoebe would wash up more often if everyone else in the house did too. She'd wash up all the time if there were only her own things to do, but she won't spend hours washing up a mountain of somebody else's making before she can start on the molehill of her own. So usually Phoebe simply leaves her own bits and bobs at the bottom of the mountain, with the promise that she will be back when only her things remain. But it never works like that. On her return everything has been washed and wiped and put away; and a new mountain is in an advanced stage of development.

Phoebe wonders about sticking a sign over the sink, something eye-catching like OWN UP TO YOUR OWN WASHING-UP, but she's done that before: nothing changes but the signs themselves, which go yellow and crisp and eventually fall off. Anyway, Phoebe suspects that Celia is the mystery maid and loathes her self-imposed martyrdom so much that she is willing to let Celia go on doing all the chores for as long as being miserable makes her happy.

As for things falling off, at this very moment something green and brown and about to be broken is tumbling off the ledge above the sink and into the washing-up water. Phoebe fishes around with frantic fingers and sopping sleeves. Stirred, the water becomes muddy; the plant bobs to the surface like a body, and the two halves of the broken pot crash in the current and smash against themselves until they are several.

'Fuck,' says Phoebe.

As she stares into the sink the water parts again and the purple flower, the severed head of the plant, struggles into view. Phoebe glances guiltily over her shoulder, shrugs, and pulls the plug.

Then, snatching up a sponge, she turns her back on the sinking flower-face. Because she recognises its drowing expression. She sees one just like it every time she glimpses herself in a mirror. And she'd see it again, reflected in the silver of the sink if she stood there till the water had all drained away.

Phoebe wipes the long wooden table with a damp sponge and starts to feel that it's time for the first drink of the day. But perhaps she should wait, just for a while, just till she's tidied her rooms. Then it will be her reward.

If Phoebe's mother had considered her system of child control more carefully, Phoebe might not be the pathologically untidy closet alcoholic she is today. For the young Phoebe, having an untidy bedroom was a punishable offence; tidying it up yielded rich rewards. Years of compensating for the contradiction in the logic of her mother's legal structure have left Phoebe unable either to accept her own untidiness or to tidy up for its own sake. So she lives in squalor until visitors appear on the horizon; then she hoovers and polishes and pants like a puppy for a pat on the head. But unless the visitor is her mother no such reward is forthcoming; because unless the visitor is her mother it is taken for granted that a tidy room is reward enough in itself.

And, due to an outbreak of outrageous misfortune in Phoebe's recent history, her mother will never visit her again.

So Phoebe slings down her damp sponge, scowls at the uncaring kitchen, and stomps off to clean her so-called living-room.

Celia bustles back into the kitchen with four green bottles clasped to her bosom. Their contents are sparkling, and she is beginning to feel slightly fizzy herself.

Tonight she will be the Queen of the May, the Rose in June,

the July Bride. For once in a lifetime all eyes will be on her. All eyes will see the blush of her interior décor, all noses will breathe the freshness of her flower arrangements, all taste-buds will be tickled at her table.

Celia puts her bottles in the fridge. It would probably be wise to stick signs on them saying DON'T DRINK ME, but Celia is feeling charitable. Someone has left a plate of home-made jam tarts on the table. Her mother must have popped in while she was out. How sweet, if a little inappropriate. Jam tarts are for children. Celia is not thinking that far ahead. Yet. She puts the tarts on top of the fridge and gives the table a big bossy push. It shudders an inch across the screaming floor in the direction of the kitchen door. She shoves it another squealing inch, then pauses, panting. This is going to be difficult.

Celia wonders if she should wait until Kenneth arrives; but oh! how she wants to do it herself. She has set her heart on surprising him, just this once. She has longed to lead him inside with his eyes shut and trill a lilting fanfare in his ears as he opens them on a scene of domestic bliss, a living-room in this decaying house, where a family dining-table is spread with a baby-soft cloth and laden with man-sized portions of the sort of meal his mother used to make. Celia has waited to become a wife like spilled seamen wait for lifeboats, clutching at husbands like drowning sailors clutch at straws, so she is not going to stand by and watch her plans spoil n . . . *ow*!

Celia has been nudging the table inch by inch towards the hall with the strongest bit of her body, her pelvis and thighs, but the table has fought back, hitting a dip in the floor and tipping sharply upwards, threatening to puncture the very part of her which tonight's celebrations are in aid of. She folds forward, knock-kneed and fast-hearted, and makes a fearful face into the table top.

26

When the unsightly moment has passed, Celia raises her head and shakes back her hair. Through the tears in her eyes she sees that the table's front legs have stopped at the kitchen doorstep. Even with stars in her eyes she cannot see how she is going to get the table out.

As Celia stares at the problem, Cath appears in the doorway. With her lower limbs hidden behind the table, and a highly flying look on her face, Cath seems to be floating in mid-air. Celia suspects that Cath often feels legless, and for this reason alone is not on speaking terms with her.

But the hippy has got legs, and she knows how to use them. Cath clunks her second batch of carrier bags onto the table and climbs on after them. Pushing them along in front of her she crawls the length of the table. Celia stands clear to let Cath climb off at the kitchen end. Bags in hand, Cath walks into the space where the table usually stands. Then, before Celia's very eyes, she begins to weave her trunk from side to side and whoosh her bags in circles around her.

'Wow!' breathes Cath, 'isn't it weird!'

Celia isn't sure what to say. She hasn't spoken to Cath for two months now; though they have done nothing but pass each other in the corridor during this time. Celia is reluctant to blunt her pointed silence by answering what is, after all, a rhetorical question; but today would be a good day to put the hostilities in the house on hold.

'Isn't what weird?' she manages, coolly, as a concession.

'Space, where once there was none. New floor space. For all we know,' Cath continues, still weaving and whooshing, 'no one has ever done this here before!'

Now Cath starts to spin on the spot like a top, and her voice takes on a sing-song qualitiy as she says,

'It's a virgin. You know what I mean?'

As abruptly as it began, the burst of inexplicable self-expression stops. Cath's clinking carrier bags spin off in opposite directions, and Cath grabs the plate of jam tarts.

'Look!' she says, shoving them under Celia's nose, 'here are some I prepared earlier.'

Against her will, Celia is won over by this old *Blue Peter* joke. Pink and appeased she says, 'Oh! Did you make them yourself?'

'Yeah, for the party,' says Cath, eating one with an excess of concentration and bracing herself in a casual attitude against Celia's next question, which ought to be something like, Oh! what party? But the question never comes.

For Celia is choking. Her pleased pink face is suddenly red hot and a rising panic promises to push a flood of tears before it.

How has Cath found out about the party? No one else in the house should know there is a party.

But Celia manages to speak.

'Thanks. How kind,' she says, polite to the last.

Now it is Cath's turn to choke. She spits out a mouthful of tart. Her eyes bulge. Her mind locks in a meaningless repetition: bollocksbollocksbollocks.

How has Celia found out about the party? No one else in the house should know there is a party.

Cath clears her throat.

'Are you coming?' she asks, cool as a cat in a crisis.

Phoebe is trying to get into the kitchen, with a scarf tied round her head and the weight of the world on her shoulders, but there is a table blocking her entrance. It is the last straw.

Phoebe, back-broken, sinks to her knees, and gains miraculous access by shuffling along the squat passageway underneath the table. Blinking, she emerges into the light at the other end of the tunnel. She heads for the fridge, in search of a beer.

It is lighter in the fridge, unearthly light; and Phoebe is almost blinded by the bright objects of art and appetite which have superseded the fridge's usual supply of mouldy cheese and mummified vegetables. What Phoebe sees when she gets her sight back is a sumptuous array of glistening cling-film and translucent tupperware, the sheen of grease-proof paper and the shine of silver-foil. The fridge is stacked from bottom to top with mouth-watering packaging, and four bottles which look remarkably like champagne are lying in the non-functioning ice-box.

Champagne? This can only mean one thing.

'Mum?' Phoebe whispers into the fridge.

There is silence except for the sound of things settling more comfortably into their packets and wrappers.

'Is that you?' Phoebe asks in an undertone.

There is no answer but the buzzing of the fridge and the fragrance of Brie.

'Is this for me?' Phoebe adds.

Her face is as white as the ice-box. Her teeth are chattering.

'Mum,' she says, 'where are you?'

In her panic Phoebe reaches out and grabs the first thing that comes to hand.

It's fleshy and

it's wrapped in a bag and

there's blood.

Beef.

Phoebe stumbles to her feet and slams the fridge door shut. She turns towards her housemates with grief and disbelief smeared all over her face.

'Am I coming?' Celia is asking Cath. Lost in the time tunnel of their turmoil, they have not yet noticed Phoebe's arrival.

'Are you coming?' says Cath, slowly and unsurely.

'Coming where?' says Celia, slower still.

'To the party. To the party. Are you coming to the party?' says Cath.

Phoebe steps back in amazement.

How have Celia and Cath found out about the party? No one else in the house should know there is a party.

'Going to gatecrash are you?' Phoebe asks, and her voice is as violent and as broken as the sound of someone smashing a door down.

'It's my party,' says Celia. Her lower lip protrudes, past the point of no return. She's definitely going to cry.

Cath and Phoebe are looking at her as if she is mad. They must be mistaken; surely, Celia is the sanest of the three.

'*Are* you coming?' says Cath, to Celia.

'Are *you* coming?' says Phoebe, to Cath. There has been a leak, then. The whole bloody house is going to be squeezing itself uninvited into her room.

Cath turns on Phoebe. 'Hey,' she says loudly, 'whose party is it?'

Phoebe opens and closes her mouth several times without any sound coming out.

Celia is speechless too.

Dodge is standing in the doorway to the kitchen, listening. He thinks Cath's question might be more open to answers if posed in a questioning tone of voice.

'Whose party is it?' he enquires.

'Mine,' says Cath, fast.

'Mine,' says Phoebe, furious.

'Mine,' says Celia, incredulous.

'Mine,' says Cath, firm.

'Mine,' says Phoebe, ferocious.

'Mine,' says Celia, in tears.

'Perhaps,' Dodge breaks in, 'you are each having a party?'

'Here? Tonight? Three parties in one house?' Cath is laughing.

'How can you laugh?' Celia is hysterical. 'This is my life, my real true life. It's serious. It might be a game to you, but this party is the most momentous moment of my whole life.'

'Well, I'm sure you'll have a ball,' says Phoebe, her voice splintering with sarcasm as she turns away from Celia and tries to get back under the table. In the heat of the moment she misjudges its height and nearly knocks herself out cold, but shortly after the sound of head hitting wood there comes a long, hurt shout, 'What is this table doing here?'

'I expect it's going to a party,' says Dodge, from the hall.

'But there are three parties, man. Which one will it choose?' wonders Cath.

'Mine! Mine! It's coming to mine!' Celia's world is tumbling down around her ears and getting tangled in her heated hair curlers, 'I've got to have it! Please, oh please! My party is a dinner party.'

Cath ducks to address Phoebe under the table. 'Is your party a dinner party?' she asks.

Phoebe is sitting cross-legged with her head in her hands. 'It's a fucking surprise party,' she says, 'and I couldn't be more fucking surprised, I can tell you.'

Cath straightens up and faces Celia. Straightfaced, she says, 'You can have the table. And I hope it is poisoned,' she adds silently as she clambers across it to the door.

Celia forgets to say thank you. 'Wait, wait!' she calls after Cath with her tongue tied, her throat nightmare-tight. 'What, what, what about your party? Will it be big? Boisterous? Will it be out of control?'

'Oh yes,' says Cath, sliding away along the table-top, 'all that and more besides. It will dwarf yours, Snow White. Like, seven times over.'

'But ... but my parents are coming. You can't dwarf my parents, they won't stand for it,' Celia stammers rapidly. 'You can't change anything, everything's planned already, it's all meant to be. I've been expecting this evening for ever. You mustn't make it all different at the last minute.' Celia's heart is rattling her rib-cage like a panicky animal, but her voice is barely audible as she continues, 'You'll ruin my life, Cath. Kill me now, Phoebe. Because my mother and father. And my fiancé's mother and father. And his godparents and my grandparents. Will be here, in the house. *Because it's our engagement party!*' Celia is still relatively restrained. What Celia really wants to do is go blue in the face and jerk alarmingly on the floor. But all she is managing is a hoarse whisper, and her housemates seem hardly to have heard her.

Cath slips off the far end of the table, landing next to Dodge in the hallway.

'What are you doing tonight, Dodgy?' she asks him.

'Hiding from you,' he replies.

Cath gives him a smile that isn't absolutely a smile. 'And am I supposed to seek?' she says.

Dodge doesn't answer as such, but while Cath waits watchfully his eyes flick like a whipcrack at Celia, still standing in the kitchen. He looks quickly back at Cath but by now Cath is looking at Celia. And when Cath looks back at Dodge he is covertly considering Celia again.

Celia is still standing like a lemon in the kitchen.

'Can I squeeze through?' Phoebe bursts abruptly from under the table and barges between Cath and Dodge, breaking up the deadlock they have got themselves into and dragging them both halfway down the hallway in her wake.

'Er, excuse me. Excuse me,' Celia calls shakily after her housemates as they hurry out of her line of vision.

They falter and then halt, looking over their shoulders at her in silence.

'Er, would one of you mind helping me to move the table,' Celia's voice wobbles, 'into my room.'

Cath smiles and bows at Dodge in a gesture of deference.

Phoebe, who was going to walk away without another word, sees this silly bow and attributes it to sexist assumptions on Cath's part. Scowling she strides back towards the blocked kitchen door. With hands in her pockets and legs astride she stares first at the table, then at Celia, and addresses herself to the empty air between the two.

'It won't fit. It's far too big,' Phoebe says and, turning on her heel, walks to the foot of the stairs and starts to climb.

Cath and Dodge watch her go. They've got their hands in their pockets too now.

Celia, captive in the kitchen, clears her throat.

Cath and Dodge look at their shoes.

There are no clocks in the hall or the kitchen, but everyone can hear the time ticking just as loudly as if there were. Two minutes pass before Dodge raises his gaze to Celia again.

Weighed down though it is with heated curlers, her hair is standing almost on end. When she sees Dodge looking at her, Celia says, 'I've been planning my party since I was sixteen.'

In the silence that follows her comment Celia comes over all claustrophobic. She lurches towards the table in an attempt to get out of the kitchen, but seems unable to decide whether to crawl across the top like Cath, or underneath like Phoebe. Over and under, over and under Celia tries to go, but it becomes clear that she is incapable of doing either. She starts to run in circles around the empty kitchen crying, 'I've planned what's going to be on the table and who's going to sit round the table, I've planned it to perfection. I've even done diagrams! But I never imagined for one minute that the table itself would cause me any trouble. I assumed that the table would . . . would just be there, as a matter of course.'

Cath and Dodge, independently of each other, collapse with laughter at Celia's speech.

'Look,' says Celia, still now and staring pathetically out of her prison, 'look, I know you don't like me, but will one of you lend me a table. Just for tonight. Please.'

'Sorry Celia,' says Cath, 'I need mine. For my own party.' And with a shrug which would look like one of standard regret if her eyes didn't have a sadistic smile in them, Cath turns and slowly climbs the stairs.

'Dodge?' asks Celia, when Cath is just a series of creaks on the landing.

'I haven't got one,' says Dodge.

'What?' says Celia, 'no table at all?'

'No table at all,' says Dodge.

'What about Phoebe?' wonders Celia.

'Well,' says Dodge, 'why don't you ask her?'

At this precise moment, but perhaps not as a direct result of her fear of Phoebe, Celia faints. Before she can even flutter her eyes shut, Celia has fallen to the kitchen floor like a felled tree. And by the time she comes round again, Dodge has fought his way into the kitchen and is fanning her face with a copy of the Yellow Pages.

'It may interest you to know,' Dodge is saying, slowly and strangely and stupidly as a dream, 'that there is such a thing as a furniture hire firm. It says so in this book.'

3. Celia's so small she could sink through the floor

For the last half-hour before her guests are due, Celia hoovers between life and death.

Everything else is done. Her room is ready, the table is laid, the meal is cooked and keeping warm in the kitchen.

Celia is chilly. Her dress was made specially for her, made specially for tonight, and to cover it up with a cardigan would be a crime. But its sleeves are short and its silk is flimsy, and even with several layers of flouncy petticoat underneath, Celia can't help shivering.

She is hoovering the hallway, and all the coldness of the house collects in this communal space. But apart from waiting for the knock at the door, it is the last thing left to do.

She hired a table in the end. It wasn't as hard as it sounded; all she had to do was phone the local furniture hire firm, ask if they had any spare tables for this evening, then relax and wait for it to be delivered. Celia didn't actually relax, she's been so busy that she hasn't sat down all day long, but she could have done if she'd wanted to. She had to wait ages for the men from Praised Seating to come, but seeing as how they were saving her life at such short notice she couldn't really complain.

35

It's a fantastic table, from the very top of their range. A banqueting table, they told her. Fit for a fairy tale. When Celia found out that it would set her back a hundred and fifty pounds for a single night, she nearly had a fit. Still, there was nothing else for it, she said to herself, as she spread a white cloth over the table's warm wood and emptied the contents of her bottom drawer onto it: silver, crystal, candlesticks and place-mats, linen napkins and matching napkin rings. Celia has been accumulating this stuff since she was sixteen. She has a big bottom drawer.

The flowers were delivered by the florist an hour before the guests are due. Tender, moist, opening only as Celia touches them with a trembling fingertip; these roses of personal and private hues, blood-red lip-pink peach skin, have been skilfully wrought into a pair of public table decorations. Celia arranges them amid the clutter of cutlery on the table and stands back to admire the display.

Beautiful!

As beautiful as she is, in her special engagement outfit?

Celia can't see whether she is beautiful or not, even though she has spent hours staring at herself in the mirror.

She knows her shoes are beautiful. They're shiny black and silver buckled and cost a bomb.

She knows her sheer white stockings are beautiful, even though someone tied them up in the bathroom this morning and tried to spoil her day.

She knows her frock is beautiful. It's real silk, the same soft blue as her eyes: eggshell blue, china blue, blue that is easily broken. It has puffed sleeves and pin-tucks and ruffles in all the right places.

And she knows her hair is beautiful. It's long and blonde and can't go wrong.

But Celia isn't so sure about the beauty of her whole person, of all her parts combined. Perhaps, when the guests start to arrive, their glances will gather her together. Perhaps, when she sees herself reflected in Kenneth's eyes, she will get a glimpse of the full effect and know exactly what she looks like.

Now, hoovering the hallway with half an hour to go, Celia anticipates the moment of his arrival.

'Come in out of the evening air,' she cries aloud. 'Come in!' This hazardous evening air comes from an old book about etiquette, and smacks of fur stoles, slender necks and gentlemen who know how to look after a lady.

Her fiancé's family belongs to that world, Celia has been led to believe. She has not yet met them, just as he has not met hers, but she has read a number of books in preparation. Books about posh people, polo players and the like.

Celia turns off the hoover.

'Won't you please sit down,' she says in the sudden silence.

Celia hides the hoover behind a hat-stand and hurries back to her room. Standing with her hands on her hips, she surveys the scene, to see if it lives up to the expectation in her head. Well, the whiteness of the table is right, and the profusion of silver and glass is even greater than she'd imagined. Her antique-look bureau, chandelier and display cabinet are all quietly confident in the background. The walls look rosy in the warm light, the roses look like velvet, and the curtains are velvet, closed against the world and cosy. But what else . . . what else? Is anything wrong . . . is anything not ready?

Celia remembers the food and heads for the kitchen to check that it is still there. Now the big moment is only little moments away she wishes she had more time. In her hurry, Celia trips on the doorstep, slips, and lands in a heap on the hall floor.

37

There is a snag in her stocking. There is a sting in her eye where she's trying not to cry or her mascara will run. A sigh comes up from the basement of her body, bringing rising damp and darkness on her breath. There is a sinking feeling.

The prospect of the upstairs parties is weighing heavily on Celia's mind and upsetting the balance of her perfect planning. Since Cath's and Phoebe's revelations this afternoon all she can see is scenes of psychedelia and social deviance, the house full of fierce foreign bodies, and herself having to fight all night to keep her own little corner of it forever England. She can't tell how Kenneth and his parents will react to this state of affairs; whether they'll wage war with her, or object to her lack of control and leave her to get her house in order before letting her into theirs.

One thing is certain; Celia must keep her wits about her this evening, for thanks to her ad-libbing housemates she will not be able to rely on her script.

Shaking all over, Celia staggers to her feet. No sooner is she stable in an upright position than there comes a knock at the front door. Celia goes to the door as if she is going to her death. Never has the wood seemed so dark, the weight so overwhelming. For a moment she forgets how to open it and fumbles, fumbles with its fixtures before finding the right bit to turn and the right way to turn it. Then she takes a breath as deep as a door opening, and opens the door.

Celia's face smiles.

And five figures on the doorstep beam back, seemingly frozen, until Celia's voice invites them over the threshold.

'Hello,' it says, sounding like a stranger's. 'In you come then. Out of the . . . out of the evening. The air.'

The voice gives a breathless giggle which the eyes fail to play along with. Celia's eyes are refusing to function; she still doesn't know what her fiancé's family look like, other than that they've all got faces, none of which is dramatically disfigured.

'Hello,' says Celia again, retreating up the hallway as fast as her guests are advancing, in an attempt to get them all in focus. Then, finding herself level with the door to her own rooms, she gasps, 'Here, look. In here. This is me.'

Celia rushes into her room ahead of her fiancé and his folks and has arranged herself up against the fireplace in a position of perfect composure by the time they follow.

While they file in Celia makes a proper perusal of Kenneth's parentage.

He looks like his father.

And his father looks . . . his father looks a bit funny, actually. His father is looking Celia up and down as if she is something on sale. Celia feels her composure slipping and her slip showing under her fiancé's father's scrutiny. She clenches her fist in case it flies to fiddle nervously with her hair, and holds her breath in case some other part of her body tries for freedom.

Caught in the cold claw of self-control, Celia can't speak. This doesn't seem to worry Kenneth's father, whose eyes are still in contact with every part of Celia except her eyes; but when she turns her wordless gaze on Kenneth's mother she sees that vocalisation is long overdue. Kenneth's mother is waiting with bated breath for Celia to say something.

Celia is now caught in the cold claw of eye-contact with her future mother-in-law. The lady's lips are moving silently, willing Celia to speak, as if she is a ventriloquist and Celia the dummy.

Celia splutters into life. 'Hello,' she says for the third time, 'I'm Celia. That's . . . that's a tiara isn't it?'

Kenneth's mother looks both put out and pleased by this. While she does so, Celia looks over her spangled and stately shoulder at the godparents who seem to be cowering in its shadow. From what Celia can see, Kenneth's godparents are staring at her table with terror.

Celia sneaks a peek at the table; it looks fine. It looks perfect. It looks exactly as it did in the pictures she executed for her Art O-level. Oil-paintings, they were. The teacher, Mrs Meacher, gave the class a title, which was 'Growing Up', and the pupils could portray it in any way they chose. Celia didn't like Mrs Meacher. When Mrs Meacher saw Celia's Growing Up paintings she said something horrible about Getting Real and gave her a C minus.

This is a bad time to start roaming off into old resentments; fortunately, the voice of her fiancé's father brings Celia back before she gets any further:

'Well, will you introduce us to your young lady, or will you stand around all night like a spare you-know-what at a wedding?' This comment is addressed to his son, and takes a moment to sink in, albeit laden with laughter.

Kenneth nods in eventual acknowledgement, and says, 'Celia, this is my father. This is my mother. These are my godparents.'

'Sit down,' says Celia. 'I mean, won't you please sit down. I'm very happy to have you all . . .' She catches her fiancé's father's eye as she says this and falters. His look is not much less than a leer. She is held like a hare in his headlights, motionless until the other members of the party start running into her in the move towards the table.

'Er, there are name cards on the places . . . telling you where to go,' says Celia. Then with a real smile, a smile so real it comes complete with a little shiver of excitement, she says, 'I designed them in art.'

'In art?' says Kenneth's father. 'In art? Kenneth never said anything about art. He led us to believe you weren't that sort of girl.'

40

'Oh, it was at school,' stammers Celia. 'It was a long time ago.' And then, because her fiancé's father is still staring at her as if she is wearing a beret, she adds, 'It was before I met Kenneth.'

'If it was before you met him,' says Kenneth's mother, picking up one of the place cards and looking down her long nose at it, 'how did you know what names to put?'

'Well I didn't do the actual names then, I just did the designs. I didn't know who it would be, I just knew it would be somebody,' stutters Celia, red in the face and wet in the armpit.

But Kenneth's mother isn't listening.

'This is you, dear,' she says to her husband, putting his card back in place, 'and if everything is as it should be, I'll be sitting directly opposite.' She steps stiffly around the table to her seat, and Celia rolls her eyes in relief. At least she's done something right.

'Don't pull faces,' Kenneth's father barks at her. 'One day you'll have one come off in your hand, and then there'll be trouble.'

'Oh I'm sorry, I wasn't . . .' says Celia, and stops, foxed by the second half of his statement.

Kenneth is still wandering round the table picking up and putting down place cards like a spare you-know-what at a wedding.

'Where am I?' he wonders aloud.

'What are you, son, a man or a moron?' shouts his father. 'Use a bit of common sense.'

'Yes, sir,' says Kenneth and looks at Celia.

Celia, shocked into silence, points to the top of the table.

'No, don't tell him, girl,' says Kenneth's father, turning to Celia and actually slapping her hand, 'let him think for himself. Good God, son, you'd better find your way to the head of the table pretty damn quick, because you're about to become a married man and this little lady will want someone to look up to. Isn't that right?' he turns again to Celia and laughs, but not so that she thinks he is only joking.

Celia sits down suddenly, between her prospective parents-in-law at the foot of the table.

'Well? What do you say?' continues Kenneth's father, boring into her with his bloodshot bullish eyes. 'You girls don't want nancy boys for husbands, do you, not even you arty types.'

'Dear, you're drooling,' interjects his wife, leaning across the table with a napkin fluttering from her thin ringed fingers. 'Pat your chin with this, please.'

Before Celia can see whether Kenneth's father will do as he's told, her attention has been grabbed by Kenneth's godfather, further up the table.

'Er, excuse me, excuse me, Miss . . . Miss . . .' he mutters.

'Yes, sir?' says Celia, so flabbergasted at hearing her fiancé address his father thus that she can't get it off the tip of her tongue.

'Would you bring some water for my wife?'

Celia looks from the godfather to his wife, and her eyes widen in alarm. 'What's wrong with her?' she gasps.

'She wants water,' says Kenneth's godfather.

Celia, still staring at his wife, thinks she wants more than water. Immediate hospitalisation, for starters.

Kenneth's godmother is so tense and trembling she seems to be skimming the surface of her seat, not sitting in it at all. Her face is white, and her eyes are glued to the ceiling.

Celia glances up to see what could have caught her attention there. Only a chandelier. Surely the chandelier can't be making her fiancé's godmother feel so strange. And surely it'll take more

42

than water to set her straight. But Celia isn't one to argue with her elders.

'Er, of course,' she says, 'I'll bring some at once.' She springs to her feet and heads for the hall. But no sooner is she out of her room than there is another knock at the door.

All thoughts of water wash away like footsteps in sand. Once more, Celia faces the back side of the front door.

'Coming,' she quavers, and struggles towards it as if the hall floor has become a conveyor belt moving in the opposite direction. She makes a running jump for the door handle and hangs on tight.

'Who's there? Mother?' Celia calls through the closed door.

'Hello? Mother?' Celia says, opening the door an inch.

'Oh! Mother!' Celia shrieks, as her mother dives off the doorstep and into her arms without so much as a how-do-you-do. Celia staggers under the impact of perfume and plumpness.

Having given Celia the briefest but most full-bodied of hugs, Mother stands back to survey her. 'Darling, you look a picture,' she says. 'That dress is perfect. I'm so proud of you.'

'*Moi aussi*,' says Celia's father, appearing from behind like a second head on Mother's shoulder.

'Hello, Daddy!' says Celia.

'How's my daughter?' he asks.

'All the better for seeing you,' says Celia. 'Hello, Grandmother; hello, Grandfather! Come in, come in, you must be getting chilly!'

Celia's grandparents step into the hall and the huddle.

'Have our opposite numbers arrived?' asks Celia's mother in an unsuccessful undertone.

Celia nods and puts her finger to her lips.

'Look, love, this is for you,' smiles Grandmother, slipping a small package wrapped in white and gold into Celia's other hand.

43

'Gosh!' says Celia, 'you shouldn't have.'

'Listen, love,' says her grandmother, coming in closer, 'it didn't cost me anything but time; and time I have in abundance.'

'Shut up, you silly old trout,' says Celia's grandfather in tones which echo like whale song in the long low hall; and he would say more were he not shut up in turn as Celia's mother clamps her hand over his mouth and says to Celia, 'What are they like?'

'I'm not sure yet,' stammers Celia.

'Did you welcome them properly?'

'I think so.'

'Did you smile?'

'I think so.'

'Do they like you?'

'I don't think so.'

'What do you mean, you don't think so?'

'I'm not sure.'

'Well, what did you do wrong?'

'I don't know.'

'You must have done something wrong if they don't like you.'

'I don't know.'

'Did you do things according to plan?'

'Yes.'

'So what's gone wrong then?'

'I don't know . . . I didn't plan . . . what they were going to say . . . to me.'

'And what did they say?'

'I don't know.'

'Celia!'

'What?'

'Speak to me properly.'

'Look, Mother, I'm in the middle of it. I can't talk now. Can we just go in and try again? Or else I'm going to . . . cry.'

Celia's mother gets Celia by the upper arm and squeezes it until there are tears in Celia's eyes.

'Fine. Cry,' says Celia's mother.'But believe you me, it won't impress your fiancé or his parents. Do you want them to think there's something wrong with you? How many proposals of marriage do you suppose you're going to get? This is once in a lifetime, Celia; and heaven help you if you foul it up, because I sure as hell won't!'

At this awful moment, Grandfather, who still has Celia's mother's fingers pressed to his lips, lets rip a loud grandfatherly fart. Everyone pretends they haven't heard it, and in the shuffling of feet and examining of shoes that follows, they move slowly towards the party waiting for them in Celia's rooms.

As they go through the door to Celia's dining-room, Celia's mother gives Celia's arm a warning squeeze; but by the time they come into view of the family sitting round the table she is smiling sweetly and pretending to be holding her daughter's arm out of love and support.

'Er, ladies and gentlemen. Everyone,' says Celia, rather shakily, 'this is my mother, this is my father. And this . . . where are they . . . oh yes . . . this is my grandmother and grandfarter. Grandfather. Sorry.'

Kenneth stands up at the top of the table.

'Hello, folks,' he says. 'Meet my lot. That's my mother and father, at the bottom there. And these are my godparents . . . er . . .'

For some moments everyone waits, wondering if he is going to say any more. When it becomes apparent that this is the end of Kenneth's most eloquent speech so far this evening, everyone nods graciously and says hello to someone they already know.

Celia, nodding and saying hello several times even though she knows everyone now, decides to serve the starter straight away in the hope that it may help to break the ice.

'Right, sit down,' she says to her parents and grandparents still standing like sheep behind her, 'and let the celebrations commence!'

Her family take their seats in silence. The womenfolk are previously acquainted with the concept of place cards, having spent many an evening with Celia poring over the plans and preparations, the designs and the diagrams.

'You sit opposite me, love,' says Celia's grandmother to Celia's grandfather. 'That's right. Well now,' she continues, as she settles down between Kenneth's father and Kenneth's godfather, 'isn't this nice.'

Celia turns around and bends over her hostess trolley which is parked in a corner of the room. The smoked salmon starters are ready and waiting in the trolley's cool cabinet. Celia takes them out two by two and puts them down in front of people. They are received in silence, by all except one who is going out of her way to substantiate the stereotype of the garrulous grandmother.

'Oh smashing, Celia,' this lively lady says, 'and aren't the flowers super!'

Across the table from her, Kenneth's godmother gags as if she's going to be sick.

Celia's hand flies to her mouth in horror. 'Oh, the water!' she cries, 'I was fetching you some water. I'd forgotten.'

Hastening to her hostess trolley, where water and wine are lined up alongside a company of corkscrews, Celia's eyes catches Kenneth's father's. It hurts like she's caught it on a corkscrew, and something tears when she tugs her gaze away. She feels the prick of tears again. She turns her back on the rest of the room, lifts an opened bottle of wine to her lips, and waits for the warm rush in her mouth. When it comes, she swallows once, twice, thrice; great big gulps of potent grape. Then she pauses and licks her sticky lips.

Celia doesn't often drink, and she hardly ever surprises herself, but in one fell swoop she's just done both. Feeling dazed but slightly less distressed, Celia approaches the table again, brandishing the bottle. She pours wine wildly into glasses, stopping only to uncork a second bottle when it becomes clear that some of the guests have downed their first glassfuls in one.

In the confusion, she can't be sure if she's given everyone the same amount. But no one seems to be sticking their hands up for more, so Celia sinks into her seat. She fumbles for her fork, fumbles with her fish, and then remembers the small white-and-gold-wrapped package which is still in her hand, making her butter-fingered. Celia puts her fork down, and fumbles with Sellotape.

The paper comes off in one piece, and something thin and blue and bendy like a bow or a crescent moon comes out. It takes Celia several seconds to work out what it is and what she is supposed to do with it.

It's a hairband. A hairband covered in the same blue silk as Celia's special frock. It's a special engagement hairband.

'Oh thank you, Grandmother,' says Celia, in shock.

'Go on then, try it on,' says Grandmother, beaming all round the table as if she'd like to see everyone wearing it, one at a time. 'She's got beautiful hair,' Grandmother continues confidingly to Kenneth's father, 'but she hides behind it. I like to see her face.'

And so it is that no one is staring at Celia more intently than Kenneth's father as she slips the hairband onto her forehead and slides it backwards, and the long blonde curtains of hair which

47

were closed across her face are pulled back by the band, revealing her face and her forehead in their hot and spotty shame.

'That's better,' says Celia's grandmother, and adds in another aside to Kenneth's father, 'It's just remnants, you know. Cheap and cheerful. Left-overs. Cost next to nothing.'

Closer to Celia, in extreme close-up in fact, her fiancé's father shrugs: 'I wasn't expecting much. Kenneth might be made of money, but he's got shit for brains. Excuse my French. No, this is the sort of standard I thought we'd be looking at.'

Celia's mouth has dropped open. Celia's mouth has dropped open and her mind is screaming. Celia's mouth has dropped open and her stomach is about to walk out.

It was the hairband her grandmother was referring to when she said cheap and cheerful: it was the hairband, not Celia. How could Kenneth's father have thought otherwise? How could he see Celia as something his son has scraped from the bottom of the barrel, being too thick to do any better?

Before Celia can register a protest, a sudden crash rocks the room. Celia's ceiling is Cath's floor, and it sounds as if rocks are falling onto Cath's carpet.

Celia gulps her glass of wine and gapes at her party over the rim. Everything still seems to be in place, exactly as planned. But everything has been planned so long that Celia can't help thinking she has seen it all before. The arrangement of the guests, the arrangements of flowers, the arrangement of the folds in her dress; all are in accordance with the lore, and Celia's dream is finally a reality.

But it has never felt more like a dream. This dull ache of *déjà vu* disturbs Celia almost as much as the unforeseen presence of Cath, which is weighing on her mind like a migraine. Celia squints up and sees her chandelier shaking to her housemate's beat. She sighs. If Cath's room is the heart of the house, what romance can there be for Celia tonight? Is Celia's party doomed to be flawed by a thump-thump-thump from the ceiling?

Celia starts on her second glass of wine. She can't stomach her starter. She feels insignificant. She feels sick. She stares in silence from one guest to the next, over the glass's rim.

Opposite her, but all the way up at the top of the table, Kenneth sits small as a mouse. He is gazing at the ceiling, with his nose twitching and his ears back in alarm. He maintains this pose long after the noise has stopped, eyes darting from point to point on the ceiling as if he expects something to come through it at any moment. Eventually he lowers his look and peers at his plate of smoked salmon. He picks up a slender lemon segment and tries to squeeze it onto his fish. The lemon slips out of his grip and juice spatters his shirt front. Kenneth casts a fretful glance at his father. He doesn't look at Celia at all.

From the seat next to him, Celia's mother is watching her like a hawk. Celia can feel those speckled brown eyes boring into her. She braces herself and raises her wine glass at Mother with a cheerful and unconcerned wink. It doesn't work. Almost imperceptibly, Celia's mother shakes her head. With a single silent eyebrow movement, Celia says, 'What's wrong now?' In answer, Mother bares her teeth at Celia in a monstrous snarl. Celia takes a minute to work out what she means.

Lipstick, that's what she means. Celia has lipstick on her teeth. Behind closed lips Celia licks every tooth in her head. Her mother has a new dress on, she sees while she does so, and wonders how on earth she didn't notice it sooner. It fits the occasion perfectly, even if it doesn't quite fit Mother. Its heart-shaped bodice is bloody with red and pink and purple printed hearts, and the pattern is repeated all over the endless skirt. Celia takes a mouthful of wine and tries to swill it around without making a noise.

Looking back at her mother with a stiff white smile, Celia finds she is no longer the object of attention from that quarter. Mother has turned to Celia's father and is giving him a full-frontal rendition of another of her family-only facial messages. When Celia sees what her father is doing she starts to make cross-eyes at him too.

For Celia's father, though appearing to tuck into his smoked salmon with relish, is actually playing a portable computer game. Concealed on his lap by starched folds of tablecloth, and totally silent, this tiny world of his gives hours of private pleasure in public places. Only the strange and warlike curses which he utters at inappropriate moments alert his wife to his secret life. Thus the good woman gives him a warning glare and nostril-flare; Celia hammers the message home with her eyebrows.

But her father is the least of Celia's problems. One place farther down the table towards her, between her parents and grandparents, Kenneth's godparents are facing each other across an orgy of floral decoration. Roses of the lustiest hues trail over the crockery and climb up the candlesticks, pumping out perfumes which overpower even the strong scent of the smoked salmon. Godmother's face is shut tight and white, and God-father's fingers have tiptoed through the flowers to hold his wife's hands still. Watching, Celia assumes that Kenneth's godmother either hates the fish or hates her.

Not having met Kenneth's godmother before, how can Celia know that this sad lady suffers from a rare fear of flowers, a phobia which sees, in the sweetest rose garden, only murderous red faces and dead white faces and sick pink faces, all swollen and shouting atop unnatural long and thin green necks. How can

Celia know that when the wind blows, even at table, all the flowers turn and look at Kenneth's godmother with the stretched smile of sex in their eyes and the stench of it in their mouths? And how can Celia know that the flowers speak?

Even if Celia did know, she could not imagine that the flowers talk as much as her grandmother, next in line to be looked at on Celia's secret tour of the table.

Grandmother was the first to finish her starter, and hasn't stopped talking since. She is currently discharging a detailed history of her life to the party in general and Kenneth's parents in particular. And this, Celia knows from years of tea-times, is only the introduction, a mere entrée to the lives of her daughter and grand-daughter, of whom she is as proud as Punch.

But as Celia watches, her grandmother breaks off and leans across the table to squeeze the sliver of lemon slipping like a fish between her husband's fingers. 'There, look,' Celia's grand-mother croaks, 'that's the way to do it. That's the way to do it.'

Celia makes a sound somewhere between a snort and a sneeze, which should have been a shout of laughter, but which she felt obliged to cut short before it left her throat. It would have been rude to laugh. Poor Grandmother! But how like Punch she is, with her wobbling head and her hoarse voice and her 'That's the way to do it!' And Grandfather, Celia wonders, turning to look at his watery eyes and his wooden chewing, is he Judy?

And suddenly Celia sees them both, as she saw them a long long time ago, silhouetted against the light in their bedroom window. Celia is hiding in the dark at the bottom of their garden; she is supposed to be staying the night, but she's scared. Grandmother and Grandfather are fighting, and Celia is at the bottom of the garden watching as if their bright bedroom window is a Punch and Judy show, and they are the puppets. Pow! that's a blow of the truncheon. Biff! that's another, and poor Judy's head is almost off!

In those days, Grandfather was Punch. And Grandmother, holding her head on and crying, was always Judy.

Celia had forgotten about those fights until tonight. How unlucky to remember them at her engagement party. How awful to be sitting here seeing scenes of domestic violence in her mind's eye when she should be smiling gently at the guests gathered to glory in her imminent matrimony.

Celia peeks at Kenneth's parents, in place on either side of her, in case they are taking note of her bad manners. But their heads are bowed over their smoked salmon, inscrutable as sphinxes, unapproachable as cats eating fish. Every so often they nod or shake their well-groomed crowns, seemingly in response to something Grandmother has said; but Celia wouldn't be at all surprised if the nods were sleepy and the shakes suppressed mirth.

Celia sighs. She has stared long and hard at everyone at her party, and things don't seem to be going with the swing she was hoping for. There is no love in the air. She lifts her glass of wine to her lips, and sees the only person she hasn't looked at yet, reflected, round-faced, in the curve of the crystal. Her eyes and her eyes meet in this mirror and melt into wine and tears.

She can't cry here.

She can't cry here.

They might think there's something wrong with her. They might call the whole thing off.

Celia drops the glass as if it stung her. The movement stops her tears in their tracks; her eyes are frozen. Now she is not looking out of herself, she is looking in at herself. She is looking down on herself from a great height, seeing how she fits into the picture of her party, seeing how she sits at the bottom of the table, seeing herself as others see her; which is all, it seems, that they want to do with her, for no one is taking the trouble to talk to her.

'Why,' says Celia to herself, 'am I wearing this frock? This baby-blue dress which, at the age of fifteen, I mentally sewed myself into. And why have I still got long hair and a little girl's hairband?'

There is a ringing in her ears. She shakes her head from side to side but it doesn't stop. Then she hears a rumbling as someone runs downstairs to the hall outside her door. The front door is opened, and the ringing stops. It was nothing to do with Celia's ears. It was someone arriving at Cath's or Phoebe's party. Ascending scales of screams and laughter trip away up the stairs.

'How,' says Celia silently to the skin-thin smoked salmon on her plate, 'can I make my party swing? Like it does in the plans, like it does in my dreams.'

The corners of the salmon slices are curling in a dry smile.

Give 'em another drink, it says.

Celia rubs her eyes, in an attempt to restore normal vision. She clears her throat, and hopes for normal sound.

'Would you like some more wine, sir?' she asks her future father-in-law.

He fixes her with a look of contempt. 'Young lady,' he says, 'I have, as yet, had none. So I cannot very well have more.'

'Gosh, sir,' cries Celia, 'you mean you can't have less. You can easily have more than none!'

'He means, my dear,' says Kenneth's mother, pointing at the glass standing dry as a bone in front of her husband, 'that you are neglecting your duties. You have failed to provide him with any liquid refreshment at all.'

This is a sobering accusation. Celia doesn't realise how drunk she is getting until she hears this sobering accusation. She forgot to give her fiancé's father some wine, but has been drinking for two herself.

'I'm sorribly terry,' she says, 'I'm afraid I'm a little nervous.'

'Yes,' says Kenneth's father, in an uncompromising tone, '*I'm* afraid and a little nervous, too.'

Celia stands up and sits down again straight away. 'Is that what I said?' she snorts, and slaps him matily on the tailormade sleeve. Even as she does so, she sees Kenneth's mother throw up her hands in horror.

Celia shoves her chair squealing backwards and rises more slowly. This time she stays up.

At her parents' end of the table there is, by now, one of those arguments married couples have to fill the awkward pauses at dinner parties. Celia will have to speak up to get Kenneth's attention. 'Er, DARLING . . .!' she shouts, her voice booming like someone else's in her ears.

Kenneth gets to his feet at the head of the table. A hush falls upon those who remain seated. But Celia can't speak any softer.

'MORE WINE AND MAIN COURSE WITH ME PLEASE,' she bellows, and sees Kenneth start towards her. Celia turns on her heel at the foot of the table, takes hold of the hostess trolley and hustles it out of the room. Without so much as an 'excuse us'.

It's cold in the kitchen.

Kenneth is tight-lipped and doesn't speak for ages. He opens bottles of wine, silent except for the sound of corks popping.

Celia ties on a tiny white apron and dishes up a roast dinner for ten. This requires so much concentration that she doesn't speak either; and it takes so long that, by the time it's done, she is almost sober. And when she is almost sober she sees that some of her food is missing.

When catering for large numbers Celia calculates carefully, to make extra sure there will be enough to go round. But today, of all days, there is less than there ought to be. Celia does a quick count of the potatoes: they are four short. A spot check of the asparagus spears: six missing. The cauliflower florets: down, down, down! Celia's bottom lip quivers. What in the name of heaven has happened to her vegetables?

'It's not fair, Celia,' says Kenneth, who has nursed his grievance until it is raw and now expects Celia to kiss it better. 'You said tonight would be the best night of our lives. All you've done so far is got pissed and been rude to my parents. You haven't even said hello to me!'

Celia flings open the oven door and bends over to look inside. 'Oh hell!' is all she can say. For behold! Her splendid saddle of beef, crudely carved into. Her proud Yorkshire puddings, whittled down and whisked away. Someone has stolen her food. One of her housemates has been and gone and stolen some of the most important meal she has ever made.

Kenneth is stacking things on the hostess trolley with a martyred air. Celia heaves her mutilated meat out of the oven and shoves it in his face.

'Look what they've done!' she cries. It's right under his nose, but Kenneth can't see it. He doesn't understand anything in the kitchen, which is why he's getting married. So all he'll ever have to do is load Celia's cooking onto the trolley, and dish it up in the dining-room as if he made it himself.

Kenneth snatches the sizzling saddle of beef out of Celia's hands, and squeezes it onto the hostess trolley between big bowls of steaming vegetables. He is sulking.

'You haven't even said, "Hello nearly-Hubby" to me,' he says, 'and it's our engagement party.'

Celia, stirring gravy, is overcome with remorse. For years and years she has dreamt of the magical moment, snatched between Cordon Bleu courses, when she and her fiancé would dally in the kitchen, kissing and cooing, with the loving laughter of their nearest and dearest echoing in their ears. Over and over she has pictured fairy-tale scenarios of love and the latest electrical appliances, and how she would be bursting with bubbles of happiness on the happiest night of her life.

But now that the moment has finally come Celia has to turn away from her fiancé. Because she has a belch brewing; a belch of unprecedented magnitude. Yes, Celia is bursting with bubbles all right. But not bubbles of happiness. No. She's never made a rude noise in front of Kenneth before, but now she comes to think of it, she may as well. Because now she comes to think of it, Celia is a bit depressed.

She is embarrassed by her depression and inconvenienced by her depression, but try as she might, she can't shake it off. On the contrary, *it* appears to be trying to shake *her* off. How long has this been going on? How long ago did Celia decide that tonight would be the happiest night of her life? Because that, more than anything, would appear to be the action of someone deeply and dangerously depressed. How long has Celia been like this?

Kenneth is working his way into her line of vision.

'What's the matter with you, Celia?' he says.

Celia shakes her head. There are things on the tip of her tongue, but they are bad words like 'bored', and weird words like 'worried'.

'Nothing,' she says.

Kenneth sighs melodramatically.

'Is there someone else?' he asks.

Celia almost laughs. She doesn't even know if there is her.

'Don't be stupid,' she says.

'Don't call me stupid,' Kenneth says.

'Sorry,' says Celia.

Celia fills her gravy-boat with gravy and sails it into the last space on the hostess trolley.

'Kenneth,' says Celia, 'do you love me?'

'What do you think?' says Kenneth.

'I don't know,' Celia says. 'You're cross with me.'

'Well, that's your fault,' says Kenneth. 'Honestly, Celia, this trolley is a better hostess than you are.'

Celia looks at it. 'Is that how you want me to be?' she asks. Kenneth shrugs his shoulders helplessly, and avoids her eye. He wouldn't like to say.

'I'm sorry,' Celia says. 'Take no notice of me. I'm sorry, darling, I'm really really sorry.'

Now that he has reduced Celia to a state of mindless apology, Kenneth straightens his tie and trundles the hostess trolley out of the kitchen. All he wanted was a little bit of a snog. It must be the wrong time of the month.

As soon as he is out of earshot Celia starts to sob: deep, dangerous sobs which sometimes aren't satisfied with being sobs and insist on becoming burps. Stacking pots and pans in the sink, and squirting them violently with washing-up liquid, Celia says to herself between sniffs: 'Come, there's no use in crying like that! You ought to be ashamed of yourself, a great girl like you! Stop this moment, I tell you!'

But this is easier said than done, and Celia is so upset that she stands there with the taps full on until the sink overflows and foam and water flow to the floor. The next thing she knows, there is a large pool at her feet, an inch deep and reaching halfway to the kitchen door.

'Oh . . . sugar!' squeaks Celia, and turns off the taps and pulls out the plug.

The puddle is not deep enough to drown in, so she splashes to the highness and dryness of the hall.

As Celia is wiping her eyes on her hanky and her shoes on the carpet, there comes a knock at the front door. Caught in the hallway, halfway between her rooms and the communal kitchen, it is easier for Celia to answer than to pretend she hasn't heard it, even though she has sworn to play no part in the other parties. She squelches to the front door and throws it open.

Standing on the doorstep is a large white rabbit with pink eyes. It has pulled a watch out of its waistcoat pocket and is examining it anxiously. As Celia swings into view the animal looks up at her and smiles.

'Hi,' says the White Rabbit. 'Am I late?'

Celia stares at it. Either it is swaying slightly or she is. She leans against the doorpost.

'Alice, I presume?' the Rabbit continues. It certainly is a polite little chap. The least Celia can do is be civil in return.

'No,' she replies, 'I'm afraid there's no one here by that name. Are you sure you have the right house?'

The Rabbit laughs. 'Out of sight!' it says.

Celia recognises the turn of phrase. 'Oh, you're one of Cath's friends,' she says, strangely disappointed.

'No, I'm just a rabbit,' says the Rabbit, 'honestly.'

But its denial comes too late. Celia has spotted a whole series of telltale signs: pink eyes, wide and wild; vocabulary way out of date; a waft of patchouli from the waistcoat. This is no rabbit – this is a hippy.

Celia stands aside to let it into the house, and gestures at the staircase. 'I expect you know where to go,' she says.

White fur tickles her wrists and elbows and ankles as the Rabbit brushes past her. She shuts the door and, leaning on it weakly, watches the White Rabbit bounce up the stairs. When it gets halfway the Rabbit turns and addresses her.

'Coming?' it says. Its plump pom-pom of a tail twitches as it speaks. Celia feels her knees give way. She doesn't answer the Rabbit's question. 'Please tell Cath,' she says instead, her voice unnaturally prim, her pronunciation unnaturally proper, 'that I shan't be opening any more doors. Er, what I mean is, I shan't be opening the door any more. I'm trying to get engaged down here, you see!' She finishes with a fart of forced laughter.

The Rabbit cringes.

'Hey!' it says, raising its paw in mild-mannered protest, and hops to the top of the stairs without looking back.

Still leaning on the front door Celia hangs her head. The White Rabbit must have thought her too square and boring for words. Hippies don't get engaged, do they; they marry spontaneously in a tie-dyed daze or they don't marry at all.

Behind her there is another loud knock on the door. Like a shot Celia is up and running scared down the hall. At the entrance to her room, her hand on the knob and heart pounding, she waits until she hears Cath coming down the stairs, then opens her door and steps inside.

Celia's guests sit in stony silence. The food steams slow spirals. It is still piled high and topple-heavy on the trolley. The atmosphere is unappetising.

'What kept you?' asks Kenneth, a pout about his pale lips.

'Is there a problem?' probes Celia's mother.

'Yes. No. I don't know,' says Celia, concentrating on unloading the trolley and not catching anyone's eye. Hot china and cooling food conspire to confuse her and before she knows it she has knocked over a bottle of wine. Roses and nose-bleeds bloom on her rabbit-white carpet. Celia stands still and watches the seeping and the staining in silence. Not one of her guests leaps up and rushes to her aid. They must all want her blood.

'Will you serve the wine,' she says to her fiancé shortly, 'I've got enough on my plate trying to sort this food out.' Celia cannot keep the gravity out of her voice. Her pathetic 'plate' pun goes down like a lead balloon.

Kenneth arms himself with bottles and marches to the bottom of the table. He pours wine for his parents, who tug at his cuffs and worry him with whispered questions.

'She's not herself tonight. I've got to go,' is his hoarse and hurried response. When they refuse to release him, he elaborates on his answer with a mime designed to demonstrate the nature of Celia's condition. Kenneth gesticulates at his genitalia and rolls his eyes at an imaginary moon to convey to his parents that Celia has her period and everything will be all right as soon as it is over. But as he moves up the table to pour wine for Celia's grandparents, they are left with the distinct impression that there is something sinister about this fiancée of their son's. Celia's grandmother tugs at Kenneth's cuffs too, but only to tell him that he is a nice boy.

Celia plonks plates of meat in front of her parents and petulantly points out the dishes of vegetables now arranged along the length of the table. Mid-point, her mother grabs her wrist and asks, 'What's wrong?'

'I don't know, Mother,' gulps Celia, wriggling her wrist out of her mother's grip. 'You tell me. You usually do.'

Leaving her mother struck dumb at this insubordination, Celia moves on down the table to serve Kenneth's godparents their main courses. The lively society specified in her party masterplan is nowhere less in evidence than here. There is something else missing too: the floral centrepieces.

'Where have the flowers gone?' says Celia, gravy slopping over the sides of the plate as she pitches up and down to see behind the godparents and under their chairs.

'Oh dear,' says Kenneth's godfather in sepulchral tones, 'I'm afraid . . . they disturb my wife, so, you see . . .'

'I'm sorry,' says Celia, 'I had no idea. Let me move them out of your way.'

'Oh dear,' says Kenneth's godfather, 'too late, I'm afraid. Had to act quickly. Had to eat them.' As if to prove it, he gives a gentle belch. The air is brushed briefly with the sweet scent of summertime. His wife shudders.

Feeling as mad as Ophelia, Celia puts plates of meat in front of the godparents and points out the big bowls of vegetables. 'There's roast potatoes for you. Asparagus. Cauliflow . . . er, can I say that?' she stops ruefully, wondering if cauli too has to be concealed from the flower-phobic godmother.

But Kenneth's godfather is not attending to her. He is talking too: timid overtures of the 'Well, it's been a splendid evening but we really must be on our way,' variety. His refrain, Celia realises as she passes along the table in a state of shock, is being picked up by her grandparents.

'Yes, it *has* been a splendid evening!' Grandfather is repeating as Celia places his main course before him. Looking up, Celia meets the gaze of her fiancé, who is standing opposite, pouring wine for her grandmother.

'But it's only just beginning,' says Celia.

A small smile of satisfaction licks Kenneth's lips. This is the nicest thing his nearly-wife has said all night.

But we really *must* be on our way!' Grandmother chips in as if Celia hadn't spoken at all.

'You can't leave yet. It's only just beginning,' Celia says again. If everyone goes now, she'll have to get herself to a nunnery.

Kenneth's shoulders slump. His nearly-wife is not being nice after all. She's behaving like a spoilt child. Perhaps she's pregnant! With furrowed forehead and twitching cheeks Kenneth moves up the table to pour wine for his godparents and her parents; Celia moves down the table to offer his parents withered vegetables.

'Ever heard of grace?' says Kenneth's father when everyone is poised to plunge into the cold dinner.

'Oh God!' says Celia, and her head sinks into her hands and stays there for some time. This is not grace as such, though Celia is praying – praying for strength, for forgiveness, for a miracle. She is summoning the strength to start again from scratch, to go back to the beginning and be a better hostess, to do all the things she should have done and say all the things she should have said. And Celia is silently beseeching her guests to forgive her bad behaviour, to forgive her funny mood; and even, if at all possible, to forget all the awful things that have happened so far this evening.

Suddenly, a minuscule miracle occurs. Some of the darkness inside Celia gets slightly lighter. 'Oh goodness!' she says, lifting her head and looking at the congregation with wide eyes, 'I'd quite forgotten about grace. We should have said it hours ago. You must think me an absolute heathen.'

Kenneth's father, who only moments ago was thinking of Celia

62

as the anti-Christ incarnate, finds himself beginning to warm to her.

'I'm such a silly girl,' continues Celia. She is stone-cold sober and her social skills are surfacing again. She smiles sadly at Kenneth's father. 'I was nervous, and I got a little bit drunk, and I'm sure I've given a perfectly ghastly account of myself.'

Kenneth's father goes so far as to pat her hand. This could be the perfect woman, after all. Knows her place, needs a break from time to time, but always comes back feeling good and guilty.

His wife turns to smile at their son. From the top of the table Kenneth raises his glass proudly. Kenneth's mother's gaze meets Celia's mother's. A glow passes between them; a glow the colour of wedding dresses and christening robes. At last there is a hint of magic in the air.

'Grace,' says Kenneth's father firmly, lest the occasion stray off the straight and theologically narrow.

The assembly bow their heads over plates of cool and congealing substances.

'For what we are about to receive . . .' intones Kenneth's father.

No, she couldn't possibly be pregnant, thinks Kenneth.

She won't get away with white anyhow, thinks Kenneth's mother.

Stuck-up cow, thinks Celia's grandfather.

They're posh and no mistake, thinks Celia's grandmother, but I always thought our Celia was destined for better things. As I was saying to the butcher only the other day . . .

Headache headache headache, thinks Kenneth's godmother.

Heartburn heartburn heartburn, thinks Kenneth's godfather.

Thwack, kerpow, take that you dastardly droid, thinks Celia's father.

Nearly there, not long now, thinks Celia's mother.

'. . . may the Lord make us truly thankful,' concludes Kenneth's father.

Everyone looks up. Everyone looks slightly flushed. Kenneth's father now wants to take things one step further.

'Join with me,' he says, 'in a few moments of private prayer. Let us quiet ourselves awhile and meditate on the meaning of this special occasion. Let us pray for Kenneth and Celia; may theirs be a long and happy union.'

Behind their smiles the members of Celia's family are racking their brains to see if they can recall Celia saying something about her fiancé's father being a man of the cloth. He sounds so convincing that no one dares argue, but everyone closes their eyes reluctantly, with many misgivings.

When everyone's eyes are closed, Kenneth's father settles down to stare at Celia's breasts for two whole heavenly minutes.

There is silence in the room. And now there is silence in the room it becomes clear that the crescendo of party sounds was not made by this particular party. Celia's guests have shut up, and the sounds are carrying on.

Now there is silence in the room it becomes clear that the thumping and the ringing and the bumping and the singing are coming from elsewhere in the house.

So the silence Celia's party is attempting to have is turning out to be a noisy silence indeed. The chandelier is shaking. The cutlery is clattering. The condiments are rolling around on the table. Every so often a bell rings and a body comes crashing down the stairs outside the room. The front door opens, there is some screaming, then the door is slammed shut. Footsteps run down the passage to the kitchen or up the stairs, and strange voices shout strange things over the sounds of glass breaking and people falling over.

This is a meths-drinking mother-fucking house-breaking silence if ever there was one.

'Celia?' says Celia's mother, her private prayer coming to an unceremonious conclusion.

Celia jumps. Kenneth's father jumps too; brought round by the bounce of those blue silk-clad breasts.

'Are your housemates making that dreadful noise?' asks Celia's mother.

'Mmmmmm,' says Celia, in the hope that cunning ambiguity will fox the possibility of further questioning.

It doesn't.

'Where are the fuckers?' roars Celia's grandfather. 'Lead me to them. I'll show the little shits a thing or two.'

'Hear, hear, sir!' cries Kenneth's father. 'It's most inconsiderate. Surely they know there is a private function here tonight.'

'Well, it *is* their house too,' Celia finds herself saying, but she is drowned out by testy male voices pledging allegiance to her grandfather.

Across the table from him Celia's grandmother sits and shakes her head in disbelief. 'Would you credit it,' she says. 'One minute the man's a vegetable, just sits and stews; the next it's 1939 and he's acting like an able seaman all over again. It gives me the creeps, and no mistake.'

This remark is addressed to Kenneth's mother, who lights a cigarette by way of an answer. At the other end of the table Celia's mother does the same. Celia doesn't know that her mother smokes. Even in the midst of all this other madness, it comes as a shock.

Grandfather is knocking his chair back and heading for the exit. 'No young commie cunt is going to spoil my Celia's engagement party!' he is shouting.

With much throwing down of napkins and rolling up of shirtsleeves the other men follow suit. Only Kenneth's godfather remains seated, picking stray petals off the tablecloth and sighing softly to himself.

Celia succumbs to the series of sobs and sentences which have been struggling to escape. 'It's no good,' she wails, and her words are slurred, 'they're having parties too. There are three parties in the house tonight. It's an accident.'

Grandfather stops his frenzied ruffling through the folds of velvet curtain which hang in the way of the door, and stares at Celia's shaking shoulders. He never looks at faces. Especially when they are women's faces. Especially when they are wet with tears. 'What are you saying, girl?' he growls.

'You can't stop them. They won't stop,' sniffs Celia.

'And why not, may I ask?' asks Kenneth's father.

'They won't take any notice of you. They'll laugh at you. They'll fight. They're like that,' Celia shrugs her shaking shoulders. 'They're not normal.'

The men sit down again.

Kenneth clears his throat and loosens his tie.

'Let's eat,' he says.

Both his and Celia's mother blanch. In the absence of ashtrays they have stubbed their cigarettes out on their plates.

So some of the guests eat. Some of the guests start to discuss the possibility of phoning the police. Perhaps the boys in blue will be able to bring the house back from the brink of anarchy. No matter what sort of jokers these housemates are, the arrival of the police should force the smiles off their faces.

Celia, glum, goes up and down the table pouring more wine for everyone. After the oven raid and the vegetable theft there was only enough food left for nine. As hostess, it is Celia's duty to put

66

herself tenth and go without. No one has noticed that there is no plate of meat in her place. No one has noticed that she has not been digging deeply into the dishes of vegetables. No one even notices her pouring them wine. Celia slinks back to her seat and sinks into it. She doesn't pour more wine for herself.

If she's the sieve-head that these guests seem to think she is, she won't be able to hold her drink anyway.

The food is cold, but the conversation grows heated. It burns like a fuse, snaking its way towards the subject of capital punishment. It spreads like a line of fire, heading straight for the notion that hanging is too good for Celia's housemates. It crackles like anger but is fanned by fear. If conversation could kill, the other parties would be dead as dodos.

Celia's dying to go to the toilet.

'I've got to go to the toilet,' she says. No one hears her. Her party is otherwise engaged. Having a holocaust. It looks as if her family and Kenneth's family will get on like a house on fire after all. For once, a visit to the bathroom seems safer than staying in her room. Celia makes her escape, behind the velvet curtain and through the door to the hall. No one notices her go.

The hall is empty, but by the sound of it, there are a hundred people in the kitchen. It looks like Celia served her food up in the nick of time. Glancing nervously back at the kitchen door, and expecting to find herself chased by the crazed contemporaries of Cath or Phoebe, Celia sprints up the stairs two at a time. Until she gets to the top. Where she stops.

There at the top of the stairs is a large mushroom, about the same height as herself; and, when she has looked under it, and on both sides of it, and behind it, it occurs to her that she might as well look and see what is on the top of it.

Celia stretches herself up on tiptoe and peeps over the edge of the mushroom. Her eyes immediately meet those of a large blue caterpillar that is sitting on the top with its arms folded, quietly smoking a long hookah and taking not the smallest notice of her or anything else.

Obviously this is not a real caterpillar. The only bits of it that are really big and blue are its eyes. Otherwise it is blue because it is wearing some sort of skin-tight body-stocking in that shade, and it is big because it is a human being. Celia is far too sensible to fall down the stairs in surprise.

The caterpillar and Celia look at each other for some time in silence. At last the caterpillar takes the hookah out of its mouth and addresses her in a languid, sleepy voice.

'Who are *you*?' says the Caterpillar.

This is a fine question to be asked by something blocking one's way to one's bathroom. Celia replies, rather scathingly, 'Who wants to know?'

'Don't you?' says the Caterpillar sternly.

'You're one of Cath's friends, aren't you,' accuses Celia.

'Aren't you?' says the Caterpillar. There is not the tiniest twinkle of a tease in its big blue eyes. It draws deeply on its pipe and chokes smoke into the air at the top of the stairs.

Celia blinks, momentarily blinded, but she has seen more than enough to work out what is going on here. 'So Cath fancies herself as Alice in Wonderland does she?' she says, her sibilants spitting with sarcasm. 'Some people never grow up.'

'And you,' says the Caterpillar looking Celia up and down, 'are the biggest little girl I have ever seen.'

'Look, I don't have to listen to this,' says Celia, after a slight pause. 'Will you please stand aside and let me pass.'

'You!' says the Caterpillar contemptuously. 'Who are *you*?'

Which brings them back again to the beginning of the conversation. Celia feels a little irritated at the Caterpillar's making such very short remarks, and she draws herself up and says very gravely, 'I think you ought to tell me who *you* are first.'

'Why?' says the Caterpillar.

Enough is enough.

'Because you're in my house!' shouts Celia. She wants to kick the Caterpillar, but the Caterpillar is too high, so she lands the mushroom's soft stalk a blow with the toe of her shiny shoe.

'Oh she got me bollocks man . . .' comes a slow wheezing groan from somewhere underneath the Caterpillar. Celia steps backwards in surprise.

She slips halfway down the stairs. Her face is split from cheek to cheek by a silly smile. There is someone in the mushroom. Or rather, the mushroom is someone. Looking back at the landing, Celia sees the stalk which had been bent double by her attack straightening up, and two arms appearing out of holes in its sides a quarter of the way down its length. Gloved hands grab at the brim of the mushroom's cap, like a lady trying to keep a huge floppy hat on her head in a high wind. But the mushroom has the voice of a man.

'Give me that,' it is saying as it wrestles with the Caterpillar for possession of the hookah. 'Go on, give me it. You've had it for hours.'

'Four hours,' says the Caterpillar blissfully, but it sees Celia coming back up the stairs with her silly smile and its expression changes abruptly.

'That'll teach you,' it scolds.

'Teach me?' sniggers Celia, secretly pleased that she is still open to surprises, still able to be turned upside-down. If she is honest, her own party was feeling a bit unspontaneous. 'Teach me what?'

'To keep your temper,' says the Caterpillar.

The smile slowly disappears from Celia's face. The Caterpillar sounds like her mother. The damn thing has obviously set itself up as some sort of bouncer to monitor the flow of partygoers past the top of the stairs; but pretending to be people's parents in order to scare them into better behaviour . . . well, that really is going too far!

'Look,' says Celia, 'this is all very clever and even vaguely amusing and I'm sorry for battering your mushroom, but I'm bursting to go to the bathroom. Will you take my word that I won't gatecrash this party which I don't even want to go to, and let me pass.'

At last it seems the Caterpillar is prepared to see sense. It knocks solemnly three times on the top of the mushroom as if to convey new orders. But the mushroom now has the hookah wedged firmly between its gills, and ideas of its own.

'Hey lady, the only word I want to take from you is *Yes*,' it says to Celia, between puffs; 'Yes, you shall go to the ball, baby. Shit, you've already been to both of mine, if you know what I'm saying.'

Due to the mushroom's having no eyes to speak of, Celia continues to stare into the Caterpillar's big blue ones. They are beginning to look less self-satisfied.

'Pardon?' says Celia to the Caterpillar.

'Get your ass into that party now,' says the mushroom. 'You're a very groovy girl.'

The Caterpillar raises its eyebrows in a look of disbelief. Celia is inclined to agree with it.

'No, really, I'm not,' she says, addressing herself to a random spot on the mushroom's stalk, 'I'm not groovy at all. I'm getting engaged downstairs.'

'Oh man,' comes the voice of the mushroom. 'Big, big bummer!'

70

But on top, the Caterpillar lets slip a little sigh of relief. It reaches down for the hookah and offers it to Celia, slapping the mushroom's hands when they struggle to hold on to it.

'Congratulations,' says the Caterpillar coldly.

But Celia shakes her head at the hookah. She doesn't take that sort of thing; it may be something to do with drugs.

'Er, I don't think that's really me . . .' she mutters.

'You!' says the Caterpillar. 'Who *are* you?'

Celia sighs. The Caterpillar is very persistent. Perhaps if she gives it her name it'll let her go.

'Celia,' she says.

'Content?' asks the Caterpillar.

'No,' says Celia. 'It's the happiest night of my life.'

'Delirium from beginning to end,' says the Caterpillar decidedly, and there is silence for some minutes.

The Caterpillar is the first to speak.

'Who do you want to be?' it asks.

'Well,' Celia clears her throat, 'I want to be . . . er, well I don't really care *who*, I just want to be, er . . .'

'What?' says the Caterpillar.

Celia is getting hot under the collar.

'I just don't want to wait any more,' she says. 'I've always been waiting. And now I'm ready to go. So, if you don't mind . . .'

The mushroom squashes up spongy to let Celia squeeze past at the top of the stairs. Then Celia runs like the wind down the corridor to the bathroom.

'I hope you find out,' the Caterpillar remarks as she goes.

'Find out what?' says Celia to herself as she flings open the bathroom door.

'Who you want to be,' says the Caterpillar, just as if she had asked it aloud. Celia slams the door shut and is out of sight.

4. Underwhere – the second storey

By the time Celia comes out of the bathroom the Caterpillar and the mushroom have vanished.

Her chat with the madcap characters has cheered Celia up a little, though she has now had more conversation with Cath's fancy-dress guests than her own real ones. As she makes her way back down the corridor to the landing, Celia resolves to return her party in a new and improved frame of mind; to try to recapture its sparkle and shine.

So engrossed is Celia in gearing herself up to start again, she fails to stop at the top of the stairs and almost steps in a jam tart which is lying on the landing, and which certainly wasn't there before. But with an agility born of years of amateur ballet, she sidesteps before the tart becomes a splat on the sole of her shoe.

'You may well let your finger-food get out of hand,' Celia says, in the direction of the dark passageway that leads to Cath's rooms, 'when you know I'll be the one hoovering up the crumbs in the morning!' But the tart comes off the decomposing carpet in one complete piece. It looks delicious. Even a little dusty it looks delicious. Celia remembers that she hasn't had anything to eat for ages. There wasn't enough engagement dinner to go round so she did the decent thing and went without.

Celia eats the jam tart.

It tastes delicious. Even a little dusty it tastes delicious. The pastry is bitter and greasy which, unlikely as it may seem, is just the way Celia likes it. The sides of the case rise crisply fluted to a height of three inches, unusually high for a jam tart. At the top the pastry curls in a plump lip, powdered with fine icing-sugar. The case is crammed with red jam; juicy and goose-pimpled and pouting with the promise of strawberries.

This is no ordinary tart. It has none of the sickly sweetness of supermarket tarts. On the contrary, it is almost savoury and has an aroma, a pungency even, which Celia has never encountered in a commercial product. She could tell it was home made a mile off.

No sooner has Celia licked the last of the tart's lusciousness from her fingers than she catches sight of another, lying a little way along the landing. Right in the mouth of the black passage to Cath's rooms. If it stays there, sooner or later it will be ground into the carpet by a horde of marauding weirdos. It would save Celia a lot of hoovering tomorrow if the tart were sucked into her own mouth today.

Celia tiptoes towards it. She is getting dangerously close to the source of the strange sights and sounds and smells which Cath has so selfishly subjected the house to this evening. Yet Celia is having second thoughts about Cath. Anyone who bakes such beautiful cakes can't be all bad.

Celia has always believed that 'you are what you eat', and after tonight she is convinced that 'you cook like you look' too. She knows the food she gave her own guests was every bit as foul as the mood she served it up in.

But Celia is getting her act together now. She's going to grab

73

this last tart, go straight back downstairs, and get herself engaged, once more with feeling. There are no two ways about it: that is, until she reaches the tart in the mouth of the passageway and a whole new avenue of possibilities opens up before her.

Looking down the dimly lit and deafening avenue to Cath's party Celia sees that the tart in her hand is by no means the last; the floor of the passageway is studded with fallen jam tarts, and each looks twice as tempting as the one before it.

Celia pauses, torn, at the top of the passageway.

She's not one for descending into darkness, as a rule. She's more the sort who stays well and truly in the light. But surely, where there is mess and waste involved, it is her duty to boldly go and gather those scattered foodstuffs, scared or no. Celia stands indecisive on the edge of the darkness, and could well be there indefinitely if the sound of several someones coming up the stairs behind her doesn't send her scurrying to hide herself in its depths.

Pressed up against the wall of the black passageway, Celia peeps out at the landing. Is this Kenneth coming, is this her mother, could it even be her father trying to find her? Did they see her leave the table after all? Were they worried about her, wandering alone in this strange house? Celia smiles and strokes her skirt; how silly she is to think they don't care about her.

The conversation draws closer, then people start to come into Celia's line of vision. She can see pieces of them only, standing together at the top of the stairs, but enough to know that they are complete strangers. Then the group walk away, down the other corridor towards the bathroom and Phoebe's rooms. They must be part of Phoebe's party.

Celia swallows the whole of the second tart in something more like anger than hunger. So she is still lost then. No one is looking for her at all. She turns her back on the landing and strides up the

74

passage to the third tart, her hands slapping at her skirt as it swishes about her. If that's how her family feel, they can wait for her to eat this one before she goes down to dish up their dessert. She stops and stoops to take the tart, then stands up and spins around and starts to go and steps on something that kicks back with a life of its own.

'Get off my foot,' comes a monotone from the floor.

Celia suppresses a small scream of shock and backs up abruptly against the wall of the passageway.

There is an alcove set into the opposite wall and there is something sitting in it. Celia doesn't want to stare but, as she recovers from her fright, she reasons that unless whoever is in there can see in the dark, they won't know whether she is staring or not.

Eyes straining, Celia counts one, two, three, four feet in white socks and buckled shoes sticking out of the blackness of the alcove. From the safety of her vantage-point she traces the pale outline of one sock all the way up to a knee, where it disappears inside one leg of a pair of liveried breeches. So whatever Celia is dealing with here, it is at least human.

'Hello,' she says quietly, hoping it won't hear her.

'There's no sort of use in saying hello', comes a solemn voice from the gloom, 'because they're making such a noise inside, no one could possibly hear you.'

And certainly a most extraordinary noise is going on within Cath's four walls: a constant rapping and clapping and thunderous foot-tapping. But Celia is oblivious to it now.

'I know who you are!' she is shouting triumphantly. 'You're footmen. And you're not human after all, are you? One of you is a fish and one of you is a frog. Which is which?'

She is almost on top of them by this time, her party problems temporarily forgotten in the thrill of having her all-time favourite

75

story come to life in the discomfort of her own home.

'Do you want to get in?' one of the characters says, and his large and lumpy frog face looms at Celia out of the darkness.

'Oooh gosh!' says Celia, backing off a bit. 'How do you do that? You look so real. Unreal, I mean.'

'Do you want to get in?' repeats the Fish Footman, rather rudely, Celia feels.

'Er . . . no,' she replies, 'I'm just . . . er . . . tidying up these tarts. Look, there's another one down there. They'll be trodden into the carpet, you see, and there'll be crumbs.'

Under the thunder of the party she hears the Fish Footman sigh and the Frog Footman suck his teeth sharply. They don't seem to be very pleased to meet Celia. But perhaps she hasn't been so polite herself.

'Er . . . are you going in?' she asks, with a friendly smile.

The Fish Footman only shakes his scaly head crossly and stares at the ceiling.

'We shall sit here,' he remarks, 'till tomorrow . . .'

' . . .or the next day, maybe,' the Frog Footman continues in the same tone.

Celia shivers, and the hairs on the back of her neck stand up stiffly. The thought that these two could still be lurking here like the memory of a nightmare on Monday morning when everything ought to be back to normal is nearly enough to send her running downstairs at top speed.

But she is just inches away from the fourth jam tart.

And she inches towards the fourth jam tart.

As she goes she thinks she hears the Frog Footman say, 'Another new Alice, then,' and the Fish Footman reply, 'Amateur, ain't she,' but the noise of the party is so loud that Celia could have heard wrong.

The fourth jam tart is lying in front of a second alcove, further down the passage and on the opposite side to the first. Celia is beginning to get her bearings now. She has been to this neck of the woods before, but only in daylight, and only when Cath is out of the house. She remembers, from these rare visits, that this second alcove normally contains a battered bookcase and a number of boxes stuffed with abused books.

But nothing has been normal all night and, assuming that this alcove too will be altered, Celia approaches it with caution.

A tiny orange light is moving within its depths. Celia's eyes widen in alarm as the light flares up. But the lighter it gets, the better she sees what it is. It is a cigarette, smoked by a woman who is sitting on a three-legged stool with a baby sucking at her breast. Celia's eyes continue to widen. Smoking while suckling is very bad for the baby.

The woman stares at Celia. Her dress is unbuttoned and both breasts are bare but for shadows. She shifts on the stool and draws on the cigarette again, and the shadows recede into the darkness of her dress. Now her breasts are as bright as moons, and as round.

Celia swallows hard but can't stop staring back.

The woman smiles at Celia. With the hand that holds the cigarette, she cups the breast that isn't feeding the baby, and offers it to Celia. Yes, unless Celia is much mistaken, the woman wants her to step into this alcove and kneel down at those feet and take that glowing global breast in her hands and that enormous erect nipple in her mouth.

Celia steps backwards and feels a sickening squelch as the fourth jam tart splats on the sole of her shoe. And Celia runs squashily away, but she runs the wrong way. Rather than returning to the relative safety of the landing, she finds herself

77

farther up the passageway towards Cath's party. Now the woman in the alcove is between Celia and the rest of the house.

So there is no going back. And there is only one more jam tart on the floor before the floor disappears under Cath's dark door and into Cath's party. Scraping her sticky shoe on the carpet as she goes, Celia wanders worriedly towards the fifth and final tart. She should never have started sorting out this food spillage. It has taken much too long, and it isn't even her problem. Her problem is what's going to happen when she gets downstairs again.

Celia squats at the party end of the passageway to pick the last jam tart off the carpet, and crams it straight into her mouth. Dribbling jam and choking on crumbs, she stumbles to her feet and finds herself face to smiling face with Cath, who is standing in a shaft of light from the half-open door to her party proper.

Celia's first thought is that Cath looks lovely. Her second thought is that she shouldn't have had her first thought for three reasons: a) she hates Cath, b) they are both girls, and c) Cath is dressed as a cat. But when Celia manages to speak she pretends to have been thinking something else.

'I thought,' she says, 'that you would be Alice.'

'Oh no,' says Cath, still smiling, 'there is only one. Do you want to come in?' She points a padded paw at the door.

Celia isn't at all sure that she does, and stalls for time.

'Er, I found several of your tarts on the landing and um, up your passageway,' she shouts awkwardly over the music. 'I hope you don't mind that I ate them?'

Cath's smile grows bigger. 'Hey,' she shouts, 'I wanted you to. When I saw you earlier, talking to Sindy and Leroy at the top of the stairs, I thought you looked stressed out and I wanted to give you a treat. I laid the trail while you were in the toilet.'

'Sindy and Leroy?' says Celia. 'What are you talking about?'

'Leroy is the guy in the mushroom costume,' answers Cath loudly, rotating her hips in time to the music. 'Sindy is his girlfriend. The Caterpillar, yeah? They're really cool.'

'A trail?' repeats Celia, somewhat dazed. 'Were they part of it?' She gestures back down the passage at the Frog and Fish Footmen in the first alcove.

'Well, they were just sort of there anyway. But you were lucky, or unlucky – I'm not sure which; moments before you came the Walrus was giving the Carpenter a blow-job in the second alcove. I asked them to move along. They were really pissed off.'

'There's a woman in there now,' says Celia. 'And she's . . . she's feeding a baby!'

Cath is still smiling but her eyes are steely as she says, 'She's the Duchess. She's got to do it somewhere.'

At this moment a pack of people dressed as playing-cards shuffle slowly down the passage and squeeze themselves sideways through Cath's door, stopping to say their hellos to the hostess.

Celia takes this opportunity to examine Cath and her costume more closely. If there were any way in the world that Celia could criticise what she sees, she would willingly do so.

But Cath is tall and slim and laughing. She is wearing a cat-suit, in the most literal sense of the word: it is, like all cat-suits, close fitting and covers her entire body; but, unlike any other that Celia has ever seen, it is made of soft silky cat fur. Cath's high-heeled shoes are covered in the same stuff; which, knowing how vegetarian she is, Celia assumes is fake. There is a fat fluffy tail swinging between her legs and furry mittens on her hands. Celia can see real pearly claws nestling in the pink pads at Cath's fingertips.

Cath's hair (which usually reminds Celia of pigs because it is pinky and punky) is concealed under what can only be described as a cat-hat: it has two triangular ears and lots of whiskers, and does up under the chin like a motorcycle helmet. Cath has painted the tip of her nose pink, lined her eyes with black, and covered her cheeks with a fine feathery network of a hundred honey colours and silver and white.

The playing-card people have passed into the party and Cath is turning to face Celia again. Celia swallows. She has something serious to say.

Cath is going to have to call off her party, much as one would call off a Doberman. Its noise is gnawing at Celia's engagement, its paws are all over her thoughts. It's really messing up her plans.

But before Celia can make her request, Cath says 'Come in and meet someone. Who's your favourite character?'

'Pardon?' says Celia. The music is so loud.

'Who's your favourite character?' Cath shouts.

'Pardon?' Celia says again. She actually heard the question this time, but her favourite character was always the Cheshire Cat and there's no way she's going to tell Cath that.

Cath puts her cat face close to Celia's and talks into her ear like a telephone.

'I think it's time for a disappearing trick,' she says.

'Eeeee!' says Celia, leaping out of Cath's reach. The voice and the face and the fur feel funny. Celia squirms. 'It tickles!' she squeaks.

Then Celia can contain herself no longer. She's been wanting to stroke Cath since the start of their chat. Now she stretches out her hand and scratches the top of Cath's head.

'Oh your ears and whiskers!' she whispers. 'They're wonderful.'

Cath can't contain herself either. She thrusts the tip of her tail into Celia's hand. 'Hang onto this!' she shouts with glee. 'We're going in!'

*

At first Celia can't see Cath's party for the crowds of people, and can't hear it for the music.

Next she gets the impression that Cath's party is taking place inside a tupperware container. The lid is on, and some giant hand, God's or perhaps God's Wife's, is shaking the contents to kingdom come. There is nothing that is not moving. The high white walls are water, translucent and turbulent with tricks of the light. The floor is as taut as a drum-skin, and the dancers are trampolining on it. Vibrations collide, filling the air with cymbal sounds.

Nothing is not moving. Celia is stepping backwards, feeling behind herself for the door which already isn't where it was. The Cat is pressing onwards. Celia can't see it in the crowd, but she still has the tip of its tail in her grip. The tail is pulling Celia into the party and Celia is pulling the tail out; but going backwards isn't always what it seems, and before Celia can even think of letting go of the tail and getting away, she is as close to the centre of the room as it is possible for someone who can't see any corners to be.

No one is not dancing. Someone behind Celia is sticking their wing in her back, and very sharp and scratchy it is too. She turns to give a warning stare, but everything turns with her, and the thing with the wing is still behind her back. She tries again. Hopping from foot to foot on the spot to make it look like she is dancing, she starts to swing her head from side to side, slowly at first, then faster and faster; and when she gains enough momentum she can see over her shoulder without having to turn around in the crowd at all. All well and good, but for the fact that when Celia sees what is over her shoulder the inside of her head begins to spin.

It is a Gryphon. It is anatomically correct, but much too big. No wonder its wings are impingeing on her personal space.

'Excuse me,' Celia shouts. 'You're too big.'

Mythical it may be, she says to herself with a snort, but there is a regulation size to conform to; creatures don't become legendary by picking and choosing their dimensions without regard for the norm. If Celia stopped to think about it, earlier this evening Celia had no idea what size a Gryphon should be; but now she is on the crest of a crusading certainty: the Gryphon should be smaller, not bigger, than Celia is.

'You're too big!' she screams again, just as the music stops. A lot of people look at her, though people is probably the wrong word. Someone, she doesn't see who, says something that sounds like, 'Kindly keep your ego closed, Alice.'

The song starts again; though song is probably the wrong word. It is made without musical instruments, unless computers which compose like a million Mozarts or a billion Beatles without the time-consuming drink or drug habits can be called musical instruments. It is sung by random samples of singers who don't even know they are in the song. The lyrics are incoherent, especially when you can make out what they are; at hypnotic intervals, an inhuman voice screams what seems to be the word 'whiting'.

The Gryphon gets on with its outspread eagle-winged lion-legged dance. Several smaller creatures are sprawling at its clawed feet, victims of its vast choreography. Celia wonders why no one else complains. If we were in a normal nightclub, she thinks, the sort of place the girls from work go to, this guy would have been bounced off the dance floor by now, and maybe even beaten up in a smelly alleyway.

Celia keeps up her toe-pointing hair-tossing dance bravely, but with one eye on the Gryphon's flying wings and clumsy feet. His eyes are hidden in the shadow of a huge hooked beak, which jerks open and shut in time to the music. He appears to be singing along with the song; he must be making himself awfully dizzy, Celia thinks, and maintains as much distance as she can.

But gradually, because they are face to face and forced to dance almost on top of each other, Celia and the Gryphon begin to dance with each other. The Gryphon even becomes quite chatty, though Celia is not at all sure what he is talking about.

'First form a line along the sea-shore,' he shouts, apparently as an opening gambit. Celia smiles and nods. 'Each with a lobster as a partner!' he adds, clapping his hands. Celia claps her hands too, more out of politeness than enthusiasm. 'Take some time to clear all the jellyfish out of the way . . .' comes the cry from behind the big beak. Celia assumes that she simply mishears him. 'Advance twice, set to partners, change lobsters,' says the Gryphon, coming closer. Celia backs away.

'Then, you know,' says the Gryphon, grabbing Celia by the hand, 'you throw the . . . lobster . . . out to sea.' Celia pulls her hand out of his, but undaunted the Gryphon continues, 'Swim after it . . . turn a somersault in the sea . . .'

Here the Gryphon stumbles into the Six of Hearts who is shuffling sideways through the pack. At this, he seems to lose his train of thought; his dancing diminishes and dwindles until it is merely marking time.

So Celia nearly jumps out of her skin when he suddenly screams 'Change lobsters again!' and snatches her off her feet. She struggles, airborne, but not for long. This may be an unfeasibly large Gryphon, but she is not little or light enough to be his lobster. He lets go and they stagger apart.

'Back to land again, and that's all the first figure,' says the Gryphon, breathlessly.

Celia smiles. She understands now. This chap is not just wearing a costume; he is playing the part of the Gryphon too. He has learnt all the words, like the Caterpillar, what was her name –Sindy? How clever, thinks Celia, who has never been to such a realistic fancy-dress party in her life. She looks forward to meeting the Mock Turtle, who must be close at hand.

Celia dances on with new ease, twitching the tip of the Cheshire Cat's tail in time to the music. Because this music never changes, and stops and starts arbitrarily, it is difficult to know how long anything lasts. Celia is just wondering whether she has been jumping up and down in front of her clever feathered partner for five minutes or five hours when she spots someone familiar pushing his way through the crowd, someone who stops and stoops and speaks to everyone he passes. She sees a pair of pointed white ears standing high above the heads of the other bodies, and a pair of pale pinkish eyes, and her face slips into a soppy smile. It's the White Rabbit.

Celia waves the hand that isn't holding the Cat's tail and the Rabbit turns sharply and heads towards her, ducking and weaving through the dancers. But he reaches the Gryphon first. The Rabbit shakes the Gryphon by the shoulder. The Gryphon doesn't stop. The Rabbit shakes again, harder. The Gryphon stumbles, and slows down. The Rabbit grabs the Gryphon by the beak and forces it open.

The Gryphon's real face appears, the face of the guy in the Gryphon costume. The Rabbit is shouting and pointing at the pocket of his waistcoat, but the Gryphon doesn't seem to see him. The Gryphon's face is wet with sweat, but his eyes are dry. Deep as wells, but dry and dead. The Rabbit laughs and shuts the beak up. The Gryphon dances more slowly still.

Celia has stopped altogether, shocked by the sight of his vacant face. Is it still fancy-dress, she wonders, if there is no one inside the outfit, and nothing but death behind the mask? Or is it something else?

'He's out of his tree!' the Rabbit shouts at Celia.

'Pardon?' she says, squeezing the Cat's tail tighter.

The Rabbit shoves his furry face in Celia's; its blurriness takes her aback.

'Mary Ann, yeah?' the Rabbit shouts.

'What?' says Celia.

'Are you Mary Ann?' the Rabbit shouts. Celia still can't hear what he is saying but nods anyway. She is a little alarmed at the change that seems to have come over the Rabbit; she can't help feeling that he is less fluffy than he was before, more sinister than he was at the front door. He certainly doesn't tickle her fancy any more.

But, judging by what he is ejaculating in her ear, he would like her to tickle his.

'Ecstasy!' the Rabbit shouts, and repeats the peculiar pointing at his waistcoat pocket.

Celia shakes her head. She doesn't believe that she has ever experienced ecstasy. But seriously, she is saving that sort of thing for Kenneth, and preferably for when they are married. When the lights are off.

For a split second, everything goes dark and Celia thinks that the time for ecstasy has come. But the thing that was blocking out the light lands with an agonising bang on her foot. Bending in bewilderment, Celia finds her hands closing round the huge heavy head of the Gryphon, who appears to be unconscious. Celia comes to her senses.

She straightens up with the head still on her foot and appeals to the Rabbit for help in humping if off.

But the Rabbit stares at her with vegetable eyes. 'Ecstasy. Twenty quid,' he repeats, pointing at his pocket.

'He wants me to pay for it?' thinks Celia numbly.

The Gryphon begins to sing on the floor, on her foot; something about 'Walking a little faster.'

'He's out of his tree,' repeats the Rabbit.

Slowly Celia starts to understand. Her mouth opens wide in shock, then snaps shut in horror, then opens wide again and, 'You're trying to sell me drugs!' she screams primly, pointing at the Rabbit with a long straight arm. 'Look, everybody, he's trying to sell me drugs!' she screams properly.

She kicks the Gryphon's head off her foot and looks wildly around for support. She hears someone laughing. She sees someone staring.

The eyes are all the same.

All the eyes are the same.

'Right, that does it!' Celia shouts, tugging on the Cheshire Cat's tail. 'Come here, Cath. Come here at once!'

The tail is stuck between the bodies of a Walrus and a Carpenter who are dancing nearby, locked in an obscene embrace. The Cat must be on the other side of them.

Celia's eyes smart with tears; can it be that hers are the only smart eyes here?

'Cath! All your friends are on drugs!' Celia shouts, trying to prise the Walrus and the Carpenter apart. Abruptly the Walrus stands back. The tail falls to the floor. The Carpenter picks it up and hands it to Celia. There is no Cheshire Cat on the end of it.

'Now fuck off,' says the Carpenter to Celia.

She stares at him stupidly. She's shocked. All the time she thought Cath was right behind her, looking after her, she felt fine.

But actually she is adrift in an airless place, in outer space, without a lifeline.

'Fuck off,' says the Carpenter again.

Celia takes the Cat's lifeless tail and tries to. She was about to leave anyway. She is going to report these people to the authorities. She is going to tell her parents about them. And her fiancé. And his family. Just as soon as she can find a door.

Somewhere between a minute and an hour later Celia finds a wall. There is no door in this wall, but there is a sign which says EAT US pinned on it halfway down. Under the sign is a long trestle table. As Celia makes her way towards it she sees that it is laden with jam tarts in incredible shapes and colours.

'These people are obsessed!' Celia says to herself, and then, as she gets closer, 'Oooh! *That* sort look nice!'

But she wants something to drink first. She feels so hot and thirsty after all that dancing. She is looking along the length of the table to see if she can spy any glasses or bottles when a lady loading a paper plate with tarts shaped like chess pawns catches her eye. Celia recognises her; it is the Red Queen.

'Er, excuse me, Your Majesty,' says Celia, sidling up the table towards her, 'is there anything to drink?'

The Red Queen looks as though she is about to say one thing but changes her mind and says another.

'Yes,' she says.

'Where?' asks Celia.

The Red Queen looks at Celia as if she is stupid, and points at the piles of tarts.

'There,' she says.

'Where?' asks Celia again.

The Red Queen points again and prods one tart in particular.

'That's a jam tart,' says Celia.

87

'It'll quench your thirst though,' says the Queen.

'Oh, I see,' says Celia, 'you're talking topsy-turvy.'

'It's very refreshing,' says the Queen.

'Yes,' says Celia, adding 'Thanks', as the Red Queen and her full plate are swallowed up by the ravenous crowd.

There is nothing to drink, then. Though the sight of the tarts does make Celia's mouth water, which is something. There is one sort which particularly takes her fancy. The pastry must be wholemeal, it is tree-trunk brown, and the jam is green. Gooseberry, Celia imagines. She lifts one from the top of the pile and takes a large bite. The crumbly case collapses inward, sending jam surging through the splintered sides. At the same time someone kicks her hard on the ankle.

Celia looks down crossly. Before her very eyes the someone kicks again – a foot in a stripy stocking and a big black boot shoots out from under the table, makes violent contact with her elegant ankle, and skids back the way it came.

With her mouth full of tart, Celia crouches to look under the table. She nearly chokes on what she sees.

A big woman wearing a cook's hat and a voluminous apron sits with her arm around a smaller woman who bears more than a passing resemblance to Celia herself.

Celia's eyes almost pop out of her head. Perhaps it's the long blonde hair and blue hairband, perhaps it's the dress or the shoes that do it. Wherever the similarity lies, looking at this other woman is like looking in the mirror; and, judging by the expression on the face staring back at Celia, the feeling is mutual.

The Cook takes a pipe out of her mouth and passes it to her gobsmacked friend. Then, reaching forward, she grabs Celia by the pinny and pulls her under the table.

'Impostor!' the Cook cries.

'Pardon?' says Celia, crammed so tightly in the small space under the table that her knees are clamped against her ears.

'You heard,' snaps the Cook.

'What are you doing here?' adds the other woman.

'Nothing,' says Celia, and cracks her head on the low plywood ceiling, 'Just . . . passing through. What's the problem?'

'What does it look like?' says the blonde woman.

'Where do you come from?' adds the Cook, quickly.

'Er, from downstairs,' says Celia, flustered. 'I live downstairs. I've got my own party down there, which I'd like to return to, if you'll let me go.'

'Are you for real?' gasps her lookalike.

'You're not another Alice?' asks the Cook.

'No,' says Celia.

'Because there is only allowed to be one,' adds the Cook.

'I see,' Celia mutters meekly.

'Are you saying you're not even officially in Wonderland?' says Alice.

'And you're wearing that costume in all innocence?' asks the Cook.

'It's my engagement dress,' says Celia.

'Engagement?' says the Cook. 'What year is it where you come from?'

'Let's see your ring then,' says Alice.

Celia struggles to extract her left hand from the tangle of limbs under the table. But when she finds it, the third finger is bare.

'Oh,' she remembers, 'I'm not wearing it yet. It's supposed to be slipped on at the climax of the evening, you see.'

Alice and the Cook exchange looks.

'Well, swear on this alleged engagement ring,' says Alice, 'that you're not trying to usurp me.'

'I'm not trying to usurp you,' says Celia. Then, with a sigh, she adds, 'But I can see how you thought I might be. Perhaps if I'd remembered to take my apron off after I'd dished up the dinner . . . Even so, my dress looks a lot like yours.'

'You can say that again,' says Alice.

But Celia doesn't. She doesn't say anything. Her feelings are hurting. Just as she was beginning to relax and enjoy herself, it turns out that she's here under false pretences. Everyone thinks she's Alice. No wonder they were all so friendly, so familiar with her. Cath must be laughing her head off. And there was Celia thinking she was managing this party much better than her own, when all along the little blue dress was doing the talking for her, just like downstairs. Celia nibbles at her browny-green tart in silence.

'That's my tart,' the Cook says suddenly.

Celia gulps. 'I'm sorry,' she stammers. But with a bravado born of being sick of stammering, she adds, 'However, as there were no signs saying KEEP OFF — TARTS TAKEN I believe I am within my rights.'

'She's good, I'll say that for her,' Alice says in an aside to the Cook.

The Cook laughs. 'You misunderstand me,' she says to Celia in an altogether nicer tone of voice, 'I said "That's my tart" in the sense of "I made it myself", you see.'

'Oh,' says Celia. She has jumped to the wrong conclusion. 'So,' she adds, to cover her confusion, 'you're not as nasty as the Cook in the book then?'

'Well, Cath does like us to really, you know, get into role,' says the Cook, 'but I can't be bothered. Oh, I'll do a bit every now and then, when she's in earshot or whatever; but she's such a mad bloody bitch . . . the Cook, I mean, not Cath . . . though I have my doubts about her too, sometimes!' The Cook chuckles.

This abrupt re-entry into normality leaves Celia disorientated. She looks from the Cook to Alice and back to the Cook in a daze.

'Why did you kick me, then?' she asks.

'Because we thought you were an impostor,' says the Cook. 'You can see our point, can't you? Alice here has worked hard to get where she is today. No, let's face it, she's fought hard. Wonderland is an institution like any other. Riddled with corruption and rotten internal politics. It's back-stabbing all the way to the top. Alice thought you might have been a pretender to her throne. It happens.'

'And sometimes,' adds Alice, 'official Alices visit from the other regions. If they show up unannounced they must expect to have to prove that they are who they say they are. Things can get pretty unpleasant. But most of them get some sort of masochistic pleasure from it, I think.'

Alice stops and eyes Celia defiantly, obviously anticipating an alternative viewpoint.

'Masochism?' says Celia. 'But it's a bedtime story for children.'

'That's what I used to think,' drawls Alice, 'until I realised I just wasn't going to grow up. It was only when I made friends with her' – she nods at the Cook – 'that I found out there are no such things as adults after all. You either take shit, or you dish it out, it's as simple as that.'

Alice does make it sound simple, but Celia doesn't understand a word of her speech. Anyway, she is much more interested in the tart in her hand, so she crams the rest of it into her mouth.

'This is delicious,' she says indistinctly, 'what's it made of?'

'Marijuana, mostly,' says the Cook.

Celia spits it out.

'Drugs?' she splutters. 'Drugs? In the tart?'

91

'Look,' says the Cook, 'let's not . . .'

'You can't do that!' shouts Celia in a shrill monotone. 'Innocent people could . . . could . . . suffer!'

The Cook begins to wobble and heave with huge laughter in the small space under the table. Celia runs her tongue around the inside of her mouth. Some of the tart is lurking in the cracks and cavities between her teeth. She clutches her throat and stares at the Cook and Alice with bulging eyes.

'What have you done to me! What will become of me!' she cries, sounding for all the world like the poisoned heroine of a Victorian melodrama.

The Cook and Alice laugh harder. Celia shrinks from what she is now convinced are their fiendish grins.

'Call me an ambulance. Get me to the church on time,' she says, and then starts to cough like she's got a bone stuck.

The Cook leans forward and strokes Celia's back.

'Look, love,' she says softly, 'this won't be a problem for you. It will probably be a solution.'

'Go with the flow,' adds Alice, and pats Celia on the knee.

Celia looks at the hand landing bright and lively as a waterfall on her knee, then looks up at Alice in surprise.

What is she saying? It sounds so profound.

But how come Celia can't remember what they are talking about?

How come Celia can't . . .

Oh yes. The party. The parts. This is Wonderland. Alice and the Cook must be quoting from the book.

'Go with the flow,' Celia repeats, nodding wisely. 'That Lewis Carroll . . . what a way with words!'

Alice and the Cook nod wisely too.

'She's gone,' the Cook says to Alice, out of the side of her mouth.

*

Celia is deep in conversation with the Cook in the shallow space under the table. The subject is whether or not vegetables die and has been in contention for some time, but it is cut short when Alice says, 'Shut up, something interesting's happening!'

An enormous amount of what seems to be green plastic or polythene has arrived at their table. It is standing where Celia was when the Cook kicked her, and at first its surface is as smooth as Celia's stockings; but as the three women stare in astonishment the green polythene wrinkles and crinkles and rumples and crumples and folds and folds until there is a face at floor level.

'There you are, you agoraphobes,' gasps a voice, 'I've been looking everywhere. I should have done the darkest corners first, I suppose.' The face frowns; the polythene is forced into furrows.

'Is it time?' asks Alice.

'It's gone time,' replies the voice. 'There's been one game already. Come on, she's waiting!'

'Whoops,' says the Cook and shuffles forward on her haunches until her squat body is clear of the table. 'Come on!' she calls over her shoulder to Celia and Alice.

The noise and light hit their heads as they struggle into the open. Slowly they stand up and dust themselves down. Celia watches with interest as the person in polythene straightens up and smooths out; then she claps her hands in delight as a sign saying DRINK ME appears around the neck of a man-sized green bottle.

'Yeah, it's all very authentic,' comes the voice of the bottle, 'but I'm in agony.'

It rolls off, leading the way through the crowd who gyre and gimble regardless. Alice and the Cook snatch a couple more tarts from the table, and follow the bottle. Celia takes one of Cath's big red ones, because she still thinks there's nothing but jam and tart in them.

The little group go through the dancers and come out at a different wall. This wall has a door in it. They go through this door too.

This is the door to Cath's bedroom. It is quieter here, but no one is sleeping. Celia staggers on the step. The Cook and Alice each have an arm around her. She is beginning to feel a bit queer. Someone is smiling at Celia. She can see the teeth quite clearly. The smile comes closer, and lips appear. And a nose. And eyes. Celia blinks. It is the Cheshire cat.

'You're still here,' says Cath, in surprise.

'Which is more than one can say for a part of you, Puss,' says Celia, producing the tail she has kept tied safely around her waist. She hands it to Cath, along with a facial expression of her disappointment at being left behind.

'Let me introduce you to some people,' says Cath, taking Celia's arm and tugging her into the room. 'They're all mad.'

'But I don't want to go among mad people,' Celia remarks.

'Oh, you can't help that,' says the Cat, grinning broadly. 'We're all mad here. I'm mad. You're mad.'

'How do you know I'm mad?' says Celia.

'You must be,' shouts Cath, jumping up and down with glee, 'or you wouldn't have come.'

The Cat's eyes are shining like diamonds, thinks Celia, and almost loses her place. However, she goes on: 'And how do you know that you're mad?'

'I don't. I can only hope and pray, and go out of my way to have one of my parties every day,' laughs Cath, unable to limit herself any longer to lines from Lewis Carroll. 'So what do you think of it so far, Celia?' she continues rapidly, spitting with

94

excitement and sticking her claws into Celia's shoulders.

Celia draws away.

'There's something you should know,' she says, serious-faced. 'Some of your friends are – ' she pauses dramatically ' – doing drugs.'

Cath pretends not to hear. She turns on her heel and shouts at the room in general. 'We're starting. Hey! we're starting!'

Celia leans against a wall to watch what happens. She's too tall to stand up on her own now; she'd topple straight over. Celia is as tall as the wall she's leaning on. She can't imagine how this could have happened. There were no growing pains, just a rushing sound in her ears and a sudden enormity in her head. And now she is looking down at her feet, and they are so far away they're not in the same century as Celia. They are Victorian. She has Victorian feet.

'Well, well, well!' Celia whispers.

From her great height she can see four hats lying upside-down in the centre of Cath's coffee-stained carpet. The hats are old-fashioned too. There must be a Mad Hatter about. Celia looks all around the chattering room but finds no one to fit that description. But she does spot Leroy, the man in the mushroom, whose great floppy cap has slipped down to his waist where he wears it as gracefully as a tutu.

Celia, tall and thin and stuck to the wall, laughs like a drainpipe.

Way beneath her, in the smog of the room, people are scribbling on small squares of paper. There is some squabbling over who's stolen whose pencil. Two tiny teenagers dressed as guinea-pigs fight for a slate and a piece of chalk. The Knave of Hearts sits on one of them and shuts them both up. The Cook and Alice are conferring in a corner, chewing the ends of their pens and screwing up page after page of paper.

Cath is stalking in her stilettos and talking to everyone at once. As Celia stares down from above, she sees Cath give Humpty Dumpty a wad of paper and nudge him in her direction, whispering something to him as he goes.

If Cath thinks I'm going to play with him, says Celia to herself, she's got another think coming. I'm much too tall. I'm so high I won't even be able to hear what he's saying. The man's an egg, for heaven's sake; I could eat him for breakfast.

But as Humpty Dumpty starts to walk towards Celia, the strangest thing happens. Celia shrinks. Yes, with every step that Humpty takes Celia is a foot shorter. Painlessly, imperceptibly, Celia slips down the wall to meet him; so that, when he reaches her, they come face to face. If anything, he is the taller of the two.

'I'm afraid I can't sit down,' says Humpty Dumpty, 'the shell is so fragile, you see.'

Celia sniggers. Humpty gives her a hard stare and hands her four scraps of paper.

'The game proceeds thus. You must write one word on each piece,' he says; 'an adjective, a noun, an adverb and a verb. Lean on me if you like, but don't press too hard or I'll crack.' He bends over in front of her. 'Oh and by the way,' Humpty calls back over what would be his shoulder were he not wearing an eggshell suit, 'stick to the theme.'

'Do what?' says Celia. He speaks far too fast.

'Some people,' sighs Humpty Dumpty, 'have no more sense than a baby.'

Celia recognises this bit; it's another line from Lewis Carroll. She doesn't like the way some of the creatures slip their quotes in seamlessly, as if they think you're too stupid to notice.

'Now listen here,' she says, 'if you're going to play with words, you might at least do it gently so that everyone can get the joke.'

'Postmodernity!' Humpty smiles contemptuously.

'I don't know what you mean by that,' Celia says.

'Of course you don't – till I tell you. I meant, "Who said anything about a joke," ' he replies.

'But post . . . post . . . postmododdity doesn't mean "Who said anything about a joke", does it?' objects Celia, on very shaky ground.

'When I use a word,' Humpty Dumpty says in a scornful tone, 'it means just what I choose it to mean, neither more nor less.'

'The question is,' says Celia, 'whether you *can* make words mean so many different things.'

'The question is,' says Humpty Dumpty, 'which is to be master – that's all.'

If he sneers much more, the ends of his mouth might meet behind, thinks Celia, and then the top of his head would come off. But she doesn't know what else to say, and after a minute Humpty Dumpty begins again. 'They've a temper, some of them – particularly verbs, they're the proudest. Adjectives you can do anything with, but not verbs. However, I can manage the whole lot of them. Impenetrability! That's what I say!'

'And what does that mean?' says Celia distantly.

'Now you talk like a reasonable child,' says Humpty Dumpty, looking pleased, 'I meant by "impenetrability" that we've had enough of that subject, and it would be just as well if you'd mention what you mean to do next, because I suppose you don't mean to stop here all the rest of your life.'

'That's a great deal to make one word mean,' Celia says in a distracted tone.

'When I make a word do a lot of work like that,' says Humpty Dumpty, 'I always pay it extra.'

'Oh,' gasps Celia. She has slumped against the wall again,

though she doesn't feel at all tall now, and is fanning her face with the scraps of paper.

'Ah, you should see 'em come round me of a Saturday night,' says Humpty, not noticing Celia's plight, 'for to get their wages, you know.'

'Oh dear,' gasps Celia. She is getting smaller and smaller.

'That's wrong,' says Humpty sharply.

'Oh dear, oh dear,' gasps Celia again.

Humpty turns a pair of addled eyes on her.

'Have you forgotten what comes next?' he asks.

'No,' gulps Celia. On the contrary, she has just remembered. What comes next. And for the rest of her life.

'Well, get on with it then,' snaps Humpty. 'You're supposed to say "You seem very clever at explaining words, sir." '

'No,' says Celia, 'I'm supposed to be getting engaged.'

'What?' snarls Humpty Dumpty. 'And you were doing so well too. Much better than our Alice. She,' he darts an angry glance at the party Alice still cuddled in a corner with the Cook, 'is something rotten in the state of Wonderland. *She* wants to mend her ways, or she's going to break one rule too many. So, what region are you from?'

'Downstairs,' says Celia, giving at the knees.

At this moment Cath appears and asks how far they've got. 'We haven't started yet,' says Humpty, looking sideways at the sheaf of blank papers in Celia's sweaty hand. 'We've been conversing. This young lady is a first-class reconstructionist. But she won't tell me where she's from.'

'Downstairs,' says Cath.

'Never heard of it,' says Humpty Dumpty.

'No, man,' says Cath, 'she's from downstairs in this house. She's a real person. She's only in Wonderland by accident. Almost.' She grins wickedly at Celia.

But Celia doesn't see it.
She is falling
smalling
getting smaller
getting faller
getting
engaged
to be married . . .

'Come on,' says Cath, clapping her hands, 'hurry up. Hurry up everyone,' she shouts, striding back into the centre of the room, 'we're starting!'

'I don't know what to do,' cries Celia, and the scraps of paper flutter forlornly from her fingers to the floor.

'I've told you once,' says Humpty. 'Four words, one of each, nice and topical, if you please. Come on, quickly, there's no more time.' Breathlessly, he goes down on bended knee to retrieve Celia's pieces of paper. The smooth surface of his shell seems to be glistening with perspiration.

'Married, I'm meant to be getting married. I'm meant to be down, down, downstairs, running a diner,' mutters Celia.

'At last,' says Humpty, scribbling fast. 'Dinah, that's your noun, Alice's cat, very appropriate. Married, well now, that's an adjective and a verb; let's put it twice, to save time.'

Cath is punctuating Humpty's every sentence with strident shouts of 'Hurry up!'

'What about an adverb?' he says to Celia.

Celia is
still
falling.
Downstairs
down stairs

down a stairwell

down a well.

Celia is falling slowly down a well.

'What?' she says.

'You're out of it, aren't you?' says Humpty in exasperation.

'I'm in it,' Celia says emphatically.

'Describe a verb!' shouts Humpty Dumpty, with a stamp of his foot which makes his whole shell shudder and threaten to hatch him. 'Describe "Marry", quickly!'

'Quickly, yes, that's best. Before it's too late,' says Celia, sliding down the wall into a sitting position, landing with a bump on the well's soft bottom.

With a sigh of resignation Humpty licks the tip of his pencil and writes 'Quickly' on the final scrap of paper.

'That's all there is to it,' he says, and inclines his porcelain body at Celia in a brief bow. But before he can take his leave, she catches hold of his ankle and tries to say something through a sudden storm of laughter.

'Humpty,' Celia is spluttering, 'when you fart,' she stops and wipes away tears, shaking with mirth, 'is it eggy?'

Humpty Dumpty pulls away and hurries to the centre of the floor, his delicate nose wrinkled in distaste. He puts a piece of paper, folded up, into each of the four hats. Then he turns crossly to Cath. 'It is done,' he says, 'but let me tell you this. Things are getting worse every year. Standards are slipping, Catherine. I'm serious.'

He says no more, but stares pointedly at Celia who is holding her sides and spewing laughter like shaken champagne.

Cath follows his gaze and, when she sees the state of Celia, her lips twitch; but she keeps the rest of her face straight, and says to Humpty 'Oh, I know . . .'

'I'm your only sensible friend,' he says to her. She nods. She knows.

Back by the wall, Celia wipes her eyes. A league away across the floor people are picking pieces of paper out of the hats. The game has started.

It's very silly. It proceeds thus: one person picks one of each sort of word – an adjective, a noun, an adverb and a verb –out of each of the hats. The four words form a sort of sentence. The person who has picked the words then picks a team and they all disappear behind a screen in the corner of the room. They stay there for as long as they like. There is a lot of laughing and arms and legs flailing around the edges of the screen. At last they come out and mime the sentence, in a massive mutual charade, to the rest of the room. Everyone becomes hysterical, but no one gets the right answer without being given hundreds of spoken clues.

After the first few goes Celia gets the hang of the game. She looks on, helpless with laughter, as a group led by the Cheshire Cat mime something which she thinks is Stiff Choir Sing And Smell, but which actually turns out to be Live Flowers Sing Obsessively. Half an hour later she is gasping for breath as the Cook does a solo rendition of Sodden Dodo Rides Secretly. Celia's guess, which is Wet Bird on a Strange Horse, comes closer than most, though she doesn't call it out. She doesn't say anything at all. Because the longer she stays here, the shyer she becomes.

At the start of the evening, Celia assumed that everyone at Cath's party would be stupid. And smelly. She thought she would be able to turn her nose up at the best of them. But she can't. There is, unless Celia has lost her marbles, more beauty in this back bedroom than there is in the whole of the British Museum. There is, unless Celia has lost her mind, more wit here than in all the books in the British Library.

Unless Celia has gone barking mad. And she's not at all sure that she hasn't, actually. Since the start of the evening, for example, she has found herself sexually attracted to more animals than she cares to mention. More people dressed as animals, she should say. And then there is what's happening right now. Right now the Duchess from the dark alcove is stooping over Celia and stroking her sleeve, and the hairs on Celia's arm are stiffening to the thrill of the touch. Celia's scalp, and she's sure she's never given her scalp a second thought before, is throbbing to the sound of the Duchess's voice as the Duchess says: 'Hey, you! Wakey-wakey, rise and shine. Do you want to be on my team?'

'Er, yes, I suppose so,' Celia stammers, and struggles into an upright position. She is sure she's never stood up in such a 'Goodbye feet!' fashion before. She stumbles across the floor behind the Duchess, who seems to have put her baby down somewhere and forgotten about it. Or perhaps it turned into a pig.

Celia and the Duchess go behind the screen in the corner of the room. Drink Me is there with his lid off and Celia sees his face for the first time. The lewd look in his eyes as he says hello tells Celia that he would like her to drink him in more ways than one. There is also a man dressed as the Red Knight. He tells her that his friend, who came as the Red Horse, slipped a disc and had to go home early.

'So I'll have to walk,' the Knight adds, angrily.

The Duchess asks for silence so that she can read out the sentence. Watching Celia out of the corner of a winking eye, she says, 'Unaware Alice Marries Madly. All right?' And she starts to tell them her plan, putting people in positions and explaining their parts in the small space behind the screen.

After several rehearsals the team are ready to perform. They take up their places in the middle of the room to catcalls and cheering. Celia is still protesting that she doesn't see what's so mad about it.

She and the Red Knight stand side by side. Celia is holding a bunched-up handkerchief which is supposed to be a bouquet of flowers. The Duchess stands behind them, with a handkerchief on her head, holding up the back of Celia's skirt. Drink Me, with his lid back on, stands facing Celia and the Red Knight with an open book in his hands. They are meant to be miming the meaty bits of the wedding ceremony.

But Celia can't concentrate. The Duchess is holding her skirt too high, and she's worried that everyone can see her knickers. She has to keep swivelling around and slapping the Duchess's hands to make her lower the swathes of blue silk. This gets a laugh every time, but detracts from the real message of the mime, which reaches an ignominious end as the performers turn sheepishly to the whistling audience.

People start calling out suggestions. Everyone thinks that Celia is Alice, which means that Alice is probably the noun. Everyone thinks that it is something to do with a wedding, which means that the sentence is probably Something Alice Marries Something. But the missing words are wide open to interpretation.

Celia stands with her head bowed, smoothing her skirt and listening to people she doesn't know saying personal things about her: sulky Alice, spare Alice, slack Alice, scared Alice, stoned Alice. She looks up when someone says sexy Alice. It is Leroy. Celia looks away. Leroy has a girlfriend.

The adjectives keep coming, but Celia stops listening.

'Why are they calling me Alice?' she asks herself. 'Finally I'm about to . . . to enter the order of womanhood, and what do I find? Suddenly everyone is treating me like a child. If being married doesn't mean you're grown up then what does, that's what I'd like to know.'

Someone tugs at Celia's skirt and tugs her right out of her thoughts. 'Sorry, ducks,' the Duchess is saying, 'but we've got to give them another clue. They're crap.'

The Duchess spins Celia around so that her back is to the audience and lifts her skirt almost over her head. The cries of the audience increase. The adjectives now apply to items of Celia's underclothing, and even to intimate parts of her body.

'No, you silly gits,' the Duchess shouts, 'It *sounds like*, right? It *sounds like*!' And she pulls at her earlobe in traditional charade-playing style.

So now the crowd are calling out words which rhyme with pants, petticoats, buttocks and thighs. Someone is convinced the answer is potty, which sounds like botty; and his volume increases in direct proportion to his conviction. Then someone says underwear, and the Duchess wheels round and cries wildly, 'Yes, it sounds like underwear!'

And after this it is only a matter of seconds before the person who wrote it in the first place remembers and shouts 'Unaware', and everyone is happy.

Except Celia.

Celia stands with her back to the audience, hot-faced and red-bottomed, long after her skirt has been safely lowered. She's having her worst nightmare, slap-bang in the middle of everyone else's wonderful dreamland.

How humiliating! What has Celia done to deserve this dunce's punishment? She didn't even want to play the game, she was happy just watching, she only joined in to be polite; but now they all think she's rude and naughty, because she's standing with her back to them, buttocks stinging as if she's been smacked. She feels like a schoolgirl, just when she is supposed to start acting like an adult. Humpty Dumpty said she was a better Alice than the actual Alice; and that's the best compliment she's had all night. All Kenneth could do was compare her unfavourably with the hostess trolley.

And that's why she's got to grow up.

That's why she's got to go back downstairs.

That's why she's got to . . .

'Wake up! Celia! Wake up! Someone's calling you!' The Cheshire Cat meows at the door to her thoughts. Celia's heart knocks.

'I've put my engagement party down somewhere and forgotten all about it,' she says to Cath in a guilty tone.

Cath smiles, then slaps her hand over her mouth and tries to make her eyes look serious and concerned.

In the other room, the dancing room, someone can be heard shouting over the music, 'Celia! Who is Celia?'

'It can't be my parents or my fiancé coming to find me,' says Celia to Cath as they go to the doorway and peer into the darkness and light, 'because they know who I am.' But she is beginning to have her doubts; she's not sure who she is any more.

'There, look!' says Cath, pointing. 'It's a Messenger.'

Celia stares stupidly for a while, then, 'I see somebody now,' she exclaims, 'but he's coming very slowly – and what curious attitudes he goes into!' For the Messenger keeps skipping up and down, and wriggling like an eel as he comes along, his great hands spread out like fans on each side.

'Not at all,' says Cath. 'He's an Anglo-Saxon Messenger, and those are Anglo-Saxon attitudes. He only does them when he's happy.'

105

Celia is about to retort that it looks more like ecstasy than happiness, but at this moment the Messenger arrives. He is far too much out of breath to say a word, and can only wave his hands about and make the most fearful faces at poor Cath.

'This is Celia,' Cath says, making the introduction in the hope of diverting the Messenger's attention from herself, but it is no use. The Anglo-Saxon attitudes only get more extraordinary every moment, while the great eyes roll wildly from side to side.

'Stop it,' says Cath. 'You're doing my head in. Have you got any cigarettes?'

At which the Messenger reaches into his pocket and takes out a battered packet. With it comes a crumpled letter which he hands to Celia.

Celia unfolds it.

'It's from Dodge!' she says in surprise.

'What does he want?' asks Cath, pulling off her pussy-foot so that she can hold the cigarette between her fingers.

'He says,' says Celia: COME QUICKLY. YOUR PARTY HAS BURST ITS BANKS. SEVERAL OF YOUR RELATIVES ARE DAMNING YOU HORRIBLY IN THE HALLWAY.

Celia turns pale. She stares at Cath and says quietly, 'I'd better get out of here. Would you tell me, please, which way I ought to go?'

'That depends a good deal on where you want to get to,' says the Cheshire Cat.

'Back downstairs,' says Celia.

'You don't have to,' says the Cat.

'Sorry?' says Celia.

'You could stay and play with me,' says the Cat.

Celia shakes her head.

'No, it's all right, thank you. I'm not a toy. The next time you

106

see me I'll be a nearly-married woman. Maybe then you and your friends will treat me with a little respect. I'll find my own way out,' she says stiffly.

But before she can leave, Alice arrives, flinging one arm round Cath's neck and one around Celia's and swinging between them.

'I'm going back under the tart table now,' she says. 'Coming?'

'There's more games yet, you monkey,' Cath protests.

'I'm bored with games,' says Alice, 'I want to talk.'

'But it's croquet next,' cries Cath, 'you can't miss that.'

Celia looks over her shoulder. She'd quite like to see the croquet. In the centre of Cath's bedroom carpet someone dressed as a playing-card is bending over, bending so that their hands and feet are four-square on the floor and their body forms a loop like a croquet hoop. A black-haired, Spanish-eyed man in pink feathers, a flamingo in fact, is standing on one leg nearby.

Celia smiles; this could be good. Maybe she'll stay a little longer. She glances at Cath in case Cath finds her change of mind something to gloat about, but Cath is waving goodbye to Alice as Alice wanders off into the crowd dancing dark and dense as a wood.

When Celia looks back at the croquet match she wishes she had gone too. This game is as far removed from Lewis Carroll's version as his was from the original. There is no quiet ball-putting, or comic rolling hedgehogs. All Celia can see is one flamingo. One flamingo walking straight up to the bent playing-card and taking it abruptly from behind.

Celia's eyes pop out on stalks. She backs away from the action, a mounting embarrassment making her ears burn. She's heard about such sexual postures, but she's never seen one in the flesh. She never really believed they existed.

'What's up?' says Cath as Celia passes her, reversing fast.

Celia can't stop to talk. She gestures speechlessly at the scene of the crime of the passion.

Cath looks, and laughs. 'They're only pretending,' she says.

This makes no difference whatsoever. If they can fake it, it must be real.

Celia wheels into the outer room. She's got to get out of here. There has to be a way out. Following the wall past innocent bystanders and people lying down, Celia finds herself at last at the doorway to the dark passage, and the rest of the house.

She is at the end of the passageway in a moment, and running downstairs – or, at least exactly running, but a new invention for getting downstairs quickly and easily, as Celia says to herself. She just keeps the tips of her fingers on the hand-rail, and floats gently down without even touching the stairs with her feet; then she floats on through the hall, and would go straight into her own room in the same way if she didn't hear the voices of parents and parents and grandparents and godparents rising and falling in violent chorus behind the closed door.

'I'll give them unemployment!' a baritone booms.

Celia comes back to earth with a bump. Nothing's changed in there. It is even the same conversation. What will she say when it turns to her and asks her where she's been? Will it see on her face what she has just seen?

Celia shivers. It's silly, but since she braved Cath's party she's become scared of her own. Now, she can't bring herself to put her hand on the doorknob.

From inside there is the sound of a chair scraping across the floor. Footsteps pound towards the door. The knob turns. From the inside.

Celia freezes.

Out of the room comes Kenneth's godmother. She jumps

when she sees Celia standing in front of her, but continues to close the door quietly behind her as if she – or Celia – were just an illusion.

'Where's the bathroom?' mutters Kenneth's godmother.

'Upstairs, at the end of the corridor,' says Celia. 'Make sure it's the corridor you go down, and not the dark passage. Don't go down the dark passageway.'

Godmother is halfway up the stairs already. She stops and looks at Celia over the banister. Her dishevelled hair and startled eyes are the same shade of grey. 'They talk, you know,' she whispers.

'Yes, I can hear them,' says Celia wryly. The furore in her room is reaching a crescendo.

'Can you?' Godmother mouths, almost inaudibly. 'Can you hear the flowers talk?'

Celia doesn't quite catch this. So she smiles, a pale but polite all-purpose smile.

'Their suggestions are improper. Don't listen to them!' screams Godmother suddenly and is gone like a shot up the stairs and out of sight.

But she has started a chain reaction. Inside Celia's room more chairs fly, more footsteps pound, banshee voices answer the godmother's cry, and the doorknob begins to turn again.

Celia panics. Celia panics. Celia bolts in a blind panic through the dingy door to Dodge's room, right behind her.

5. Celia is stuck on the ceiling but Dodge gets her down

Celia has never been in Dodge's room. She has never even seen in Dodge's room. She stops on the doorstep, shocked; as if she had opened the door to a cottage and found herself staring into the soaring space of the Coliseum. Dodge's room looks big enough to house the whole house.

But it is empty.

Celia shuts the door behind her and scuttles, mouse-quiet on white matting, into the middle of the room. She knows it is the middle because she can see all the edges.

And it is empty. Dodge isn't in it. Nothing is in it.

White walls wing away to a high white sky-white ceiling. The space and the silence send Celia's spirits fluttering upwards, with smiles following like doves into the rafters.

What a relief.

After choking on the smoking at Cath's party, Dodge's room goes down like a breath of fresh air. It is clean and clear. Celia has always considered that the comfort of a place increases in direct proportion to the amount of furniture it contains. She has never trusted the uncluttered look, but here she can feel herself expanding to fill the vacancy.

Celia yawns enormously in the yawning room. She doesn't try to hide it. There is no one to see. What a relief. For the first time this evening, Celia is not worried about what to say, wondering whether to apologise, waiting to be apologised to. Dodge's room needs words spoken like a church needs surveillance cameras. Its quiet is more resounding than the records playing full blast upstairs. Celia could rest in peace here.

But suddenly she hears her family and her fiancé's family in the hallway. They seem to have got themselves snarled up out there: too shy to ram their rage into the communal kitchen, or to rampage up the stairs. Instead, they stand still and scream Celia! Celia! Celia! as if their anger is a magnet and her will as weak as iron.

Celia has to cram a hand in her mouth to stop herself shouting, 'Help! Here I am! I didn't mean to leave you, the others made me do it!' Because she's scared now. The thrill of her narrow escape has flown. The screaming in the hallway sounds like it comes straight from the mouth of hell: 'Go on, Kenneth, get up those stairs and show us what you're made of. Overturn every room in the house, and don't come back till you've found her.'

Celia's engagement party has mutated in her absence. It is now a search party, and nowhere is safe from its prying. Wherever Celia hides, it will seek her out.

She stares at the door to the hall, defying it to give her away. Defying it to giggle, or gasp, or be torn off its hinges and tossed aside like cheap chipboard.

But Celia sees that there is a key, sticking out of the inside of the keyhole.

There is a key. On Celia's side of the door.

So there is a God. And God is on Celia's side too.

So could she tiptoe to the door, turn the key silently and achieve relative safety? Or will the hall's mouth know she is there and stick its rubbery tongue through the keyhole, knocking or licking the key out of the lock before there is time to turn it?

There's only one way to find out.

Celia braces herself makes a bolt for the door and twists the key too quick for it to turn into a tongue. The door is locked. She is saved.

But a bit shaken.

'What is the matter with me?' she says to herself. 'Why did I think the key would t-turn into a t-tongue? What's going on?'

Wrapping her arms around her body, she backs away from the door. 'Hypothetically,' she continues quietly, 'if it had turned out to be a tongue I'd have pulled it hard, jerked it towards me so that the face and fat lips on the end of it would be jammed against the other side of the door. Then I would have tied a knot in it. A double knot, nice and tight. Then, and only then, would I have opened the door.'

Something is moving in Dodge's empty room and Celia sees it out of the corner of one eye. With a scream so shrill it is silent she leaps into the air. When she comes down at a different angle, she is facing a television set raised on a pedestal at one end of the room, which has been on, with the sound turned down, all along.

Celia's relief knows no bounds. A television! Oasis of normality in the weird wandering desert of her evening. She can slump into this mental armchair and relax; cosy, comfortable, and cushioned against the sharp stabbing of her conscience by great wallowing clouds of mind-marshmallow.

Celia flops to the floor because there are no physical armchairs in Dodge's room, and stares at the silent screen.

Anthony Perkins looks back at her sideways with strange eyes.

Actually, he looks forward to her. He is in black and white, in cinema history, in the Bates Motel; he is way before Celia's time.

'Uh-oh!' Celia sighs. 'It's *Psycho*.'

Of course, she knows it's not really her he's looking at. He's looking down the decades of irreversible TV time. Like starlight, when Celia eventually meets his gaze he himself has long gone from the other end of it.

But that doesn't make him any less sinister and scary.

'Oh no!' sighs Celia. 'This is all I need.'

A nasty bit is coming up. Night has fallen. The private detective climbs the hill to the high house where Mrs Bates waits; dead in the fruit-cellar, alive at the dressing-table. The detective enters the shadowy hallway and shuts the front door behind him. As far as Celia is concerned, that is going far enough. But slowly, the detective starts to mount the stairs. And slowly, Celia crawls on her hands and knees towards the television set.

A chink of light appears as a door begins to open silently on the landing. The detective doesn't see it. Celia doesn't see it either. She is too close to the screen now. Her eyes are dazzled by the dancing patches of purple, red, green and blue which television darkness is made of. Then the detective is visible again, big in close-up, face to face with Celia. He is nearly at the top of the stairs. He is in mortal danger. Celia is frantic, fumbling for the knob to turn it off.

Suddenly she is looking down on the detective from a dizzy height. The stairs slope steeply away behind him. Her fingers find a dial. She twiddles it. It is the volume control.

And Norman Bates, dressed as his mother, flies from the bedroom with knife aloft, letting rip the most notorious screaming in the history of horror. Violins scream, Norman screams, Mother screams, the detective screams, and Celia

113

screams and turns the sound down again. All the noise except hers fades fast.

So she hears the creak as a door opens behind her.

'Oh no!' says Celia again. 'They're coming in!'

She spins around. The door to the hall is still shut. But there is another door, in another white wall; and Dodge is staring wildly around it at the television set, which has burst into life with the sound everyone leasts wants to hear from their living-room late at night when they think they are alone.

Of course there is another door. This set of rooms, Celia realises at last, is the mirror-image of her own. Inverse alcoves, displaced fireplace; this is her room through a looking-glass, this is her room in a dream. And Dodge has been in the back-to-front bedroom all along.

Dodge has spotted Celia now, sitting next to the television, so close she is almost on it. 'What do you want?' he calls cautiously.

'Nothing, sorry,' says Celia, not knowing what she wants and feeling that apologies are in order for that if nothing else.

'What?' says Dodge, confused.

'Sorry,' says Celia, standing up ready to stick her hands in the air and be strip-searched.

'Calm down. It's all right,' says Dodge. He's being nice.

Celia blushes. Celia rushes at him. 'You've saved my life,' she says.

But Dodge stops her with a shout: 'Don't come any closer!'

Celia comes to a standstill and stares at him. He is a bit flushed.

'Are you . . . Is there . . . Have I interrupted something?' she asks. All she can see of Dodge is his face, through the half-open door. It is closed. His eyes refuse her any clues. 'Sorry,' she adds, in a whisper thick with not being able to swallow.

'Stay where you are,' says Dodge. 'I'll be out in a bit.'

114

He pulls his head in and shuts his bedroom door.

Celia stays where she is but her ears twitch. Celia's feet stay where they are but her upper body bends forwards towards the door, ears flapping to keep her steady. Ears flapping, eaves-dropping.

Celia is listening at Dodge's bedroom door. Is someone in there with him? She has no idea if he has a girlfriend. She never sees anyone but him going in and out of his rooms. Actually, she did see a woman once; a woman who seemed to be leaving until Celia popped out of her room opposite, whereupon the woman slipped back behind Dodge's door like a shadow, and slammed it shut. Celia has never seen anyone since.

And now Celia listens, but all she hears is the groan of a wardrobe door opening and the whisper of clothes coming out. She smiles. Dodge was simply in bed. Alone. It is as straight-forward as that. It must be later than she thought.

But Celia hasn't thought about time for a long long time for a long long time for a long long.

She she starts to stroll around the outer room, sporadically searching for a clock. Sometimes she stops, thinking that even if she does find one it's bound to be going backwards. Sometimes she goes backwards, thinking that even if she does find one it's bound to have stopped.

Because things are going from weird to worse. There's something funny about Celia's body. Like the time, it's stretched out of shape. Her arms hang like blue silk scarves from her shoulders. They are so limp and flimsy they trail out like streamers behind her. If Celia so much as shrugs her shoulders, waves roll out of control down each arm and break in a splash of lace when they reach her wrists.

This wouldn't be so bad if her hands were working. But they're

115

not. They are helpless as handkerchieves, flapping about, perfumed and pathetic. Celia hates them. But she quite likes her shoulders. They are not the angular, jangling, coat-hanger things they used to be. No, Celia's shoulders have puffed up into a spare set of lungs; and Celia has a lovely new air-style. Unless they get popped by a pin-tuck these pillows will keep her afloat indefinitely. Indeed, they are so blown up as to be almost too buoyant; or at least they would be if she wanted her feet to touch the floor.

But Celia doesn't have feet any more. She just has legs like empty stockings, which, white and wispy, waft above the landscape, sometimes snagging on skyscrapers and splinters in the skirting-board. If they ladder, Celia can climb down them to the carpet. This would happen only in an emergency, however, because Celia doesn't have much faith in the floor. There's no way it could take her weight, not once she let her weight go.

But compared with the walls, the floor is safe as houses. Celia doesn't trust the walls at all. They are white as blindness, but they play terrible tricks on her eyes. They puff themselves up into impertinent bas-reliefs; three-dimensional projections of the sort of pictures which could never be posted in public. If they don't stop when Dodge comes out, Celia will have to leave.

Because, all around the room, the walls are carving themselves into crude cartoons of him and Celia in compromising positions. On the one dead ahead, for instance, they stand hand in hand, stark naked except for a few fig leaves; one for him, three for her. A breeze is blowing. It lifts long strands of Celia's light hair, and stirs Dodge's darker curls. Before Celia's eyes, she and the comic Dodge turn to kiss each other. As their lips touch the wind whips up, blowing off the coverings which turn out not to be fig leaves after all, but clusters of confetti. Hundreds of small horseshoe

116

shapes rise in an arc like a big one in the air above their heads, then fall in a shower and stick to those parts of Celia and Dodge which are sticky and sweaty, affording them a perverse prominence.

The real Celia swallows hard and looks away in disgust. Then slowly, and after several false starts, her eyes slide back to the wall, to see if she saw what she thought she saw or if she only thought she saw it.

It has stopped; the wall is merely moving rhythmically to the music which Celia is aware of again, beating down from above. It is the music from Cath's party – an ethereal and electronic pulse; a mind-blowing mixture of hymn and hip-hop, of magic and mathematics, of serenity and spangles. One can't work out the words. Which all goes to prove, as Celia has suspected for some time, that subliminal messages are buried in this music. It stands to reason. Or rather it worms its way into the roots of reason, and chews through the sanity of all who hear it. It is beginning to seem that Celia herself fell prey to a subliminal message while dancing with unprotected ears in the danger zone upstairs.

'For why else,' she asks herself, 'do I feel so strange? Okay, so it's my engagement night and I'm bound to be a bit nervy. It's only natural. And yes, I'm having a spot of bother with my party. But it's nothing that a little . . .' Celia breaks off abruptly when she realises that she is talking like Donald Duck, and shakes her head in disbelief.

'I'm not normally so impressionable,' she continues in her own voice. 'I know what I want and I go all out to get it, even if it is unfashionable and people laugh at me. I'm set in my ways. This party, this engagement, is the only thing I've ever wanted,' she adds, with a wobble, 'so why aren't I there? Why aren't I at it? Why am I here with these weird walls? Who's been meddling in

117

my mind?' Celia starts to sob, saying, 'What am I going to do?' in the silliest voice so far; but is too upset to care what she sounds like.

Then she steps back in amazement. The wall in front of her has produced the words EAT THE RICH in bold three-dimensional letters. Celia recognises the statement at once – she sees it in a subway every day on her way to work. 'Yes, that's the sort of thing!' she cries, 'that's exactly the sort of message I would expect to find hidden in Cath's music!' But then she stops and scratches her head. Kenneth's family are the richest people she knows. Marrying them still seems a viable alternative to eating them. So this is not what has been making wormholes in her brainwaves and causing her to abandon her aspirations in so mad a manner.

The other walls chip in with suggestions of their own, and Celia has worked her way through BAN THE BOMB and BURN THE BRA and is getting to grips with SMASH THE SYSTEM when one of her flying elbows makes violent contact with Dodge, who has crept up behind her, silent and unseen.

Celia jumps at the touch of unexpected flesh, and jumps again when she turns and sees Dodge staring at her with his mild and melancholy eyes. Her nerves are on the edge, teetering. If, heaven forbid, it had turned out to be someone other than Dodge standing behind her, she probably would have jumped a third time and gone right over, never to return.

'What are you saying?' Dodge asks Celia.

'Smash the System,' says Celia. 'It's a subliminal message and, unless I'm very much mistaken, it's holding me hostage here.'

'What?' says Dodge.

'Smash the System,' repeats Celia. She points, without looking, over her shoulder to where it is written on the wall; white on white, visible only because of the shadows it casts.

118

Dodge follows her finger and finds himself looking at the television, where *Psycho* has given way to an advertisement for shaving foam. A series of short-haired shiny men show off their short-haired sons and their shiny cars, their serious careers and their caring wives, their square jaws clamped shut in shaven righteousness.

Stubble-free, but carless, careerless and careless, Dodge stares at the screen and doesn't understand what Celia is saying.

'Are you suggesting,' he asks, 'that this advertisement is anti-establishment?'

Celia looks Dodge up and down. 'Big word!' she murmurs appreciatively.

'What?' he says.

'Nothing, sorry,' says Celia. There goes that subliminal message again, making her talk out of turn, and completely out of character.

'Were you saying,' says Dodge, 'that this advert is subversive?'

'Advert?' says Celia. 'I don't think it's an advert. Smash the System. It's an anti-advertisement maybe. Sorry, was that what you said in the first place?'

Dodge takes a step backwards. This conversation has taken a wrong turning somewhere.

'So, er,' he says, 'did you get my message, then?'

'Was it you?' says Celia, after a stunned silence. 'Was it you messing around with my mind? What are you trying to do to me?'

'Er, I just sent a note upstairs,' Dodge's voice is strained, 'informing you of the position of your party. I thought you'd want to know. I thought you'd got it. I thought that was why you'd come in here.'

Celia opens her mouth very wide. 'Oh!' she says. 'Oh I see! Yes of course! I see what you mean. Oh, I'm sorry Dodge, I got hold of the wrong end of the stick.'

'But did you get the note?' says Dodge again.

'Yes, yes, I got the note,' says Celia. 'There's only one thing I didn't get. How did you know I was up there? My own family didn't even know, or they would have brought me down hours ago.'

'It was obvious,' says Dodge. 'Your guests were out in the hallway, all screaming Celia! Celia! I assumed that meant that you weren't being the perfect hostess. After a while everything went quiet. I opened my door and looked out. They'd gone back inside your room. I could hear an angry buzzing, like bees, but I couldn't tell whether you were in there or not.

'Then this wacko guy, one of the Wonderland brigade, came out of the kitchen. I gave him your description and asked if he had seen you. He hadn't, but he said there was a Caterpillar in the kitchen who had just met an Alice who could well have been you, at the top of the stairs. Apparently, you had started an argument between the Caterpillar and her boyfriend. She was crying. Anyway, this chap was on his way upstairs so I asked him to step inside for a moment while I wrote a quick note. In case he came across you up there. Well, we had a few drinks, and one thing led to another, and it was quite some time before he left . . .' Dodge is seized by a sudden fit of coughing and breaks off.

'It was extremely kind of you to go to so much trouble,' says Celia.

'Not at all,' chokes Dodge. He collapses onto his thin carpet and looks languidly at the television. *Psycho* is reaching its unsavoury climax.

Celia paces the perimeter of the room watching the walls instead. She is keen to keep the scenes which shift across them like sand from becoming as frightening as the film.

Dodge's eyes are large and luminous and reflect the television picture in one perfect piece. But his mouth and mind seem to be about to tell a different story.

'I have a confession to make,' he says.

The walls prick up their ears; alabaster ears raised like the patterns on anaglypta wallpaper.

'I stole some of your food,' says Dodge.

The walls portray a kitchen and a female figure and a mutilated joint of meat. But it is not very realistic. The picture is modern art and could equally represent a kitchen and a female figure mutilated like meat. Celia certainly remembers feeling some pain, but, 'I'm not sure if that was me,' she says.

Celia sits down; she shivers. She doesn't know whether she is a woman or a girl and there is a draught blowing under the door.

Dodge has gone to a cupboard concealed in an alcove. He pulls out a plate with the traces of the lost portion of Celia's engagement dinner still on it. Then he presents it to her with a look of defiance lurking like left-overs on his face.

'It's nothing to be proud of, you know,' says Celia.

'What isn't?' says Dodge.

'Not being able to feed yourself,' says Celia.

'I can eat,' says Dodge.

'Yes, other people's food,' says Celia.

'I can cook,' says Dodge.

'But you don't,' says Celia.

'Well, I'm sorry,' says Dodge.

'Who for?' says Celia.

Dodge is silent.

'Don't say sorry to me,' says Celia. 'It's your body you're starving. It's your body you don't look after properly. Not mine.'

Something shines like cut-glass in one corner of Dodge's eye. 'I don't like my body,' he says, 'I don't want it. It's yours I . . . whoops!' Dodge drops the plate.

What was he going to say? Celia blinks at the back of his head as he bends over to pick up the pieces. Her eyes glance off his bottom before she looks away. Was he going to say what she thought he was going to say?

'So don't you mind, then? About the meal?' Dodge asks, straightening up.

Celia attempts to answer his actual question, because it's better than wondering what he would have said if he hadn't dropped the plate. She gives it some serious thought, her blue eyes clouded with concentration. She must have minded at first, she must have minded very much. In the kitchen she was carved up. She felt pain; she cried.

And now Celia is crying again. Because she has realised that she doesn't mind any more. She couldn't give two hoots about Dodge spoiling her engagement feast, and this does not bode well for the ding-dong of her wedding bells. Her plans have gone seriously awry.

Celia cries and cries.

But she is so dehydrated that the tears have dried up by the time Dodge gets back to her with a bottle of whisky and two tumblers. She is staring blankly at a wall which has turned to sea. Her eyes are dry, but the wall is awash.

Dodge hands her a glass of whisky and she thinks it is water and downs it in one. She doesn't notice that it isn't water.

'So, Celia,' Dodge says earnestly, settling down next to her on the floor, 'what the hell has happened to you?'

'Smash the System,' I think,' mutters Celia miserably.

'So you keep saying,' says Dodge, 'but what do you mean?'

'Can you hear the music?' asks Celia.

Dodge rolls his eyes skywards. 'Have I ears?' he sighs. 'Am I deaf?'

Celia looks at him and sniffs. 'Are you being sarcastic?' she asks.

'Yes,' says Dodge.

The walls have stopped moving. The conversation has started again. It even sparkled slightly for a moment. Celia is pleased. She would rather look at Dodge than look at herself, plastered palely in the abstract over the surfaces of the room.

'Well,' says Celia, 'I am having the weirdest night of my life.'

'Weird in what way?' asks Dodge.

'Weird as in I've run away from my parents and my party and all my plans for the future, and they've sent Kenneth upstairs to catch me. Kenneth's my fiancé.'

'Yes, that's quite weird,' says Dodge.

A blush burns brightly beneath Celia's golden hair.

'I don't mean that,' she says, 'but I don't think he's going to find me.'

'Why not?' asks Dodge. He is leaning forward; a tic in his eye, a twitch in his cheek.

'Because I'm not there,' says Celia.

'Do you love him?' Dodge demands suddenly.

'Pardon?' says Celia. Then, when Dodge doesn't repeat the question, she replies, 'That's private. That's not the point.'

'Are you pregnant?' says Dodge.

'No!' Celia finds the very idea inconceivable.

'So why are you marrying him?' says Dodge.

'Well,' Celia begins.

'What's so good about him?' Dodge breaks in.

Celia smiles. 'He's not bad,' she says.

'And what does that mean, when it's at home?' says Dodge, pouring more whisky with a shaking hand.

123

'I don't know,' says Celia. 'He'll do.'

'What will he do?' Dodge downs his drink in one. 'Bore you? Beat you up?'

Celia can't believe her ears. Does Dodge disapprove of her engagement to Kenneth? He couldn't possibly be jealous, could he? She must find out.

'Oh,' she says casually, 'that's what you think of the holy estate of marriage, is it?' The last little words squeak, blowing the cover of Celia's unconcerned tone.

'No,' says Dodge, 'that was an understatement. A tactful understatement under the . . . er, current circumstances.' He waves a vague hand in the direction of Celia's party. 'Actually,' he continues, 'don't take this personally, but the mere mention of marriage makes me physically ill. I'll be at the doctor's first thing on Monday morning, see if I'm not.'

Celia takes it personally. She feels as if Dodge has kicked her in the teeth with steel toes. The walls start moving again. She daren't look at them.

'You just haven't met the right woman yet. That's your problem,' she says coldly, and tries to stand up.

'Oh, but I have,' says Dodge.

Celia doesn't hear this; trying to stand up in a huff, she catches the heel of her shoe in the hem of her skirt, and lands in a heap on the floor. She sighs, rolls over onto her back, and tries to make it look like lying down is what she meant to do all along.

Dodge pours another whisky. He stares into its glassy depths, and Celia stares skyward; there is silence for some time.

There is silence for some time. It lasts long enough to become companionable. Then Celia breaks it.

'What? Oh no!' she whispers. 'Oh no no no! I'm on the ceiling. Dodge? Can you still see me? I'm on the ceiling. I'm stuck on the ceiling. Aren't I? And I'm looking down on the floor. Dodge? Do you know what I mean?'

Dodge does know what she means. He's been there himself, though not for a very long time. He heaves himself to his feet and walks to where Celia is lying. With a leap he lands in her line of vision; with one foot planted on either side of her prostrate body, he waves his arms wildly in the air.

'Aaaargh!' he shouts. 'Hold on to my ankles. I'm going to drop off!'

Celia grabs his ankles to stop him plunging to certain death on the white ground, where light bulbs grow like flowers, far beneath them.

'It's all right, I've got you!' she screams; and then, as he reaches up to loosen her iron grip on his ankles, 'No! You'll pull me off too! I'm coming unstuck!'

Dodge stands aside with a snigger. 'Honestly, Celia, what will the neighbours think?' he says.

But this is the least of Celia's worries.

'Oh!' she groans, 'I can't get the right way up. The floor won't stop being the ceiling. It won't swap back again. Oh Dodge! make it stop! I want to get off!'

Celia is speaking at an unprecedented volume.

'Sit up,' suggests Dodge. 'That'll do the trick.'

'No way!' wails Celia, 'I'll fall too fast. I'll land on my head, in those electric flower-beds.'

Then Dodge is standing over her again with his glass of whisky. 'Look,' he says, 'this will show you what's top and what's bottom. I'm going to tip the glass. Which will get wet, you, or the lights?'

'That way, it's going to go that way,' says Celia seriously, still lying on her back on the floor and pointing up at the ceiling. 'It's going to fall down there. I don't know how we'll clean it up. I can't go down there. I can't hold my breath that long!'

'Hold your breath now,' says Dodge, 'just for a second.'

He tips the glass and whisky splashes Celia's face. It runs into her ears and overflows like waterfalls into her hair; shallow pools of it collect in the sockets of her screwed-up eyes.

'Don't move,' says Dodge, and he gets to his knees and holds her head between his hands and rocks it until her eyes spill the pools of whisky like tears across her temples.

Celia sits up. 'Oh,' she says, 'I'm back. But that was so weird, Dodge. The room flipped. And got fixed. The floor turned into the ceiling, while I was still lying on it. Do you want a go? It's quite good fun actually. We could do it together. We could . . . oh wow, we could walk about upside down!'

'You sound like Cath,' says Dodge.

'No, I don't, do I?' gasps Celia. 'How awful!' A shadow passes across her face and leaves her looking downcast. 'But that's what I was trying to tell you. There are subliminal messages in the music. The music that's playing up there at Cath's party. Can you hear it?'

Dodge nods. Hair is sticking to the sweat on his forehead.

'It's got into my head,' says Celia desperately, 'and it's made me all different. And everyone up there is the same. They're all different. They're all,' she draws a deep breath, 'Smashing the System.'

Dodge puts his drink down on the carpet with a bang.

'Bollocks,' he says. 'They might be out of their heads, but they're not out of the system. They're just smashing themselves.'

Celia blinks.

'Subliminal messages in the music?' continues Dodge in the same cynical tone. 'Sure. Buy more drugs – shut up and die. That's what they say, okay.'

126

'Well then, I think the message must be different for everyone,' says Celia, politely but firmly, 'because I was upstairs for hours and hours and I didn't think about dying once. I didn't shut up either. I talked to some people. I talked to a lot of people, actually, and now I'm talking to you. I didn't say so much at my own party. I didn't say very much at all.'

Dodge rolls his eyes dolefully at the ceiling.

'Didn't think about dying, huh?' he says. 'Perhaps I should give it a go.'

'Oh you should!' Celia nods vehemently. 'It will do you good. You don't go out enough.'

'I never go out,' says Dodge.

'No, I've never seen you go out either,' agrees Celia, 'so now's your chance. Only, put in some earplugs or something. Beware of the words in the music. If they're different for everyone, they're even more dangerous than I thought. See what they've done to me. I daren't look at the walls. I daren't look at the ceiling. I don't know how long this is going to last, and I can't go back to my own party till it's worn off, because I keep saying what I really mean. It's playing havoc with my plans, Dodge, so be sure to take precautions.'

But it seems that Dodge was only being polite when he pretended he wanted to go to the party. It seems that he would prefer to discuss it from a safe distance, with Celia.

'Listen, music couldn't have done this to you,' he says. 'You're raving. It's much more likely to be the drugs. Did you do any drugs?'

'No!' protests Celia. 'Well, hardly any. Hardly the teeniest tiniest taste of a jam tart which I didn't even swallow, hardly.'

Dodge is laughing. 'You tried one of Cath's tarts?' he says. 'You surprise me.'

'No,' protests Celia. 'Cath's tarts weren't like that. Cath's tarts weren't funny. It was the Cook's.'

'But Cath was the cook,' says Dodge. 'Crikey, Celia, how many did you have?'

'No, no, no,' protests Celia. 'The Cook is a character. An Alice in Wonderland character. And upstairs, at Cath's party, the Cook lives on in . . . er, feminist form. It's nice, because she and Alice are best friends, even though she's nasty in the book. Mind you, some people don't seem to approve of their friendship. Humpty Dumpty was really rude about Alice. He said I was a better one than her. But anyway, it was the Cook who made the' – Celia drops her voice – 'the knavish tarts, see.'

'So tell me,' says Dodge, 'did you eat any of Cath's?'

'Loads,' says Celia, 'I forget how many. She laid a little trail of them for me to follow. Isn't she gorgeous?'

'She's a gorgon,' says Dodge.

'Don't you like her?' asks Celia.

'She's a complete cat,' says Dodge.

'She is now,' says Celia, 'but she was short of a tail for a while this evening.'

Dodge frowns. 'I can't talk to you any more, Celia,' he says. 'You've stopped making sense.'

'She is *the* cat, the . . . oh what's the name of the bloody thing . . . the Leicester Cat . . . the Lancashire Hot . . . Pot?' Celia peters out, pathetically.

Dodge has had enough. 'I'll show you to the door. I think you ought to go and lie down,' he says, hooking his hands into Celia's armpits and dragging her towards the door to the hallway.

'It smiles all the time,' says Celia, as she goes, 'and it's not always all there.'

Dodge stops heaving. 'What on earth is that?' he says.

There is a cataclysmic commotion in the hallway. It sounds like a body has been thrown down the stairs. A torrent of abuse is hurled like beer glasses after it. The body bounces, the beer glasses break.

Celia digs her heels into Dodge's floor. 'I don't want to go out there!' she cries. 'Please don't make me go!'

'It's nothing,' Dodge tells her. 'It's only one of Cath's guests meeting another on the landing.' He holds her by the shoulders and starts to draw her towards the door again.

'No, they all know each other already!' says Celia, 'but I think they've just met one of mine.' Celia is scraping along the carpet, digging her fingernails in to slow her progress.

'Come on, Celia,' says Dodge, humping and heaving, 'now is as good a time to go as any. You can't stay here for ever.'

Celia screams softly, grips his wrists hard, and pulls him down on top of her. Like an accident, they crash together; heads banging, knees and elbows knocking, stomachs punctured.

The wind is knocked out of Dodge's sails. And the blue silk and white spray of Celia's skirt and petticoats billow up and break over his head like a seething sea.

'Sorry,' says Celia. She fishes for Dodge's face under her garments. When they come eye to eye she sees that he's not nearly as cross as he is pretending to be.

He's not cross at all.

'Sorry,' says Celia again. But now she knows he isn't angry with her, the word has a whole new meaning: please feel sorry for me.

'I think that was my fiancé falling down the stairs and I'm not quite ready to face him yet. He'll probably be a bit cross,' Celia goes on. 'If you let me stay just a little longer, I won't get in your way.' Keeping her limpid eyes locked on Dodge's, Celia rocks, and rolls on top of him with the momentum. Dodge seems to have several sharp objects about his person. He seems to be struggling. He seems to be trying to say something, something which Celia can't quite hear for the coughing and choking and spluttering and wheezing.

Dodge doesn't seem to be feeling very well. 'A drink,' he coughs, 'get me a drink.'

Celia gets off him and runs for the bottle of whisky, then thinks better of it and heads for his bedroom to see if he has any water, but, 'No,' chokes Dodge, 'don't go in there.'

Celia swerves towards the door to the hall, with a picture of clear cool water streaming from shiny kitchen taps appearing as if by magic on that door's wall, but, 'No,' splutters Dodge, 'don't go out there.'

Celia screeches to a halt and heads back to the whisky bottle. Panting, she picks it up and pours a glass. Then she hurries back to Dodge, who is lying where she left him.

'This won't help, you know,' she says as she helps him to sit up and hands him the tumbler. 'Are you asthmatic?'

'No, I'm . . .' he starts, and stops. He doesn't think Celia could handle hearing him say what he is.

'Oh, well, drink up then,' says Celia. She doesn't think she could handle hearing him say what he is.

They sit side by side again, drinking out of the same glass and staring at the silent television. *Psycho* is over, and everything is all right again. An American sitcom is on. Bad actors sit on sofas, playing themselves. Though 'playing with themselves' is perhaps a more apt description of their art. Celia's attention wanders. It wanders round the room, watching the walls. She knows now that they only move when she is looking at them. She doesn't want to look too hard or they may move away altogether, exposing her to the hostilities of the hallway.

130

But something American is on the walls too now.

'Buffalo,' thinks Celia. 'Blimey!'

Buffalo pale as cave drawings turn to look into Celia's eyes before turning into burgers. Big beefy burgers, oozing with relish, between baps like butch buttocks. And beside them, etched in white in the whiteness of the wall, piles and piles of thin buffalo- leggy fries.

Celia faces Dodge. 'I'm hungry,' she says. 'I'm hallucinating McDonald's.'

'Well,' says Dodge, leaning into a cupboard and pulling out a plate of Cath's jam tarts, 'here's something I purloined earlier.'

'You're an angel!' Celia beams and grabs one greedily.

'But listen,' Dodge continues, 'they're not the harmless sweeties you think they are.'

Celia is poised with the tart just touching her lips.

'You mean they're . . . they're . . . you know . . .?' she demurs.

'I couldn't have put it better myself,' says Dodge.

So that's what's done it! That's what's been causing Celia's misbehaviour! It's a jolly good job she hasn't gone back to her engagement party yet. If she'd been under the influence of drugs there's no knowing what sort of damage she would have done. The whole damn thing could have been called off by now.

'Have you eaten any?' Celia asks Dodge.

'Yeah, I tried one,' says Dodge. 'They're not really my cup of tea.'

But it's a bit too late in the day for Celia to be demure about Cath's confectionery. She's had six or seven already. And she's still here. Though she should be there. So Celia shrugs her shoulders and sticks her tongue into the heart of the tart, deep into unresisting redness.

She's hungry.

Or is it angry?

If Kenneth really wanted to find her, he would have done so by now. She's only in the next room. What sort of fiancé is he?

Dodge watches Celia devour the jam tart, his eyebrows so high they are out of sight. 'Be careful,' he says, and his voice cracks, 'if you stay out of your head too long, you might not be able to get back in again.'

Celia, sucking Cath's sour pastry and sweeter jam, doesn't care. She pauses to swallow, and says so in no uncertain terms.

Dodge lifts his hand to Celia's head. His fingers sink into soft golden hair.

'Is that how you feel?' he says quietly.

'Yes!' says Celia, louder, verging on tears, her standard response to any sort of sympathy. 'I do. Being in my head is nothing to write home about.'

'Are you unhappy?' says Dodge.

'What?' sniffs Celia.

'Are you unhappy?'

'No. I don't know. Maybe.'

Dodge's hand is still in Celia's hair, sending shivers spiralling round her skull and running in rivers down her spine.

'How can I make it better?' he says.

Celia's heart misses a beat.

'Do you want to talk about it?' Dodge adds. His voice is as gentle now as his hand. Celia gets goose-pimples all over. All the walls get goose-pimples.

'No,' she says. She is feeling better already.

'But do you want to be happy?' Dodge persists.

Celia smiles a jammy smile, and nods in assent.

'Then you need a Big Bang,' Dodge says. 'Forget drink, forget drugs; you always wake up again in the morning. Forget your fear of dying; it's only a fear of being alive.'

'Sorry?' says Celia, in shock. Dodge sounds like a salesman suddenly.

'Don't even think about sex,' he adds.

Celia jumps as Dodge says aloud the small word which has been standing proud in enormous bas-relief, all over his walls, all night long. What's going on? Is he reading her mind?

'Why? Well, it's all the same you see,' continues Dodge, completely misinterpreting her worried look. 'It's temporary. Short-term. You do the sex, you have the explosion, five minutes later you're back to square one. The better the climax, the bigger the anti-climax. It's best not to bother at all.'

Celia stares open-mouthed. Dodge seems to be a different person. Has she turned over two pages at once?

'A Big Bang is the only effective form of personal relief,' Dodge concludes.

Celia manages to get some words out: 'What is this, some kind of religious sect?'

Dodge shakes his head. 'No, it's all my own idea.'

'I don't understand what you're talking about,' says Celia, and now her own voice is ringing unintelligibly in her ears.

'I'll show you,' says Dodge. 'I'll show you how happy I am; and then I'll design a Big Bang for you, all your very own. But you'll have to tell me a bit about yourself first.'

Both his hands are in Celia's hair now; thin fingers teasing long strong strands.

'Why?' she says, and tosses her head like a horse, testing his strength. His grip does not slip.

'Because I need to know you,' he replies.

'Why?' Celia asks again. She wants him to say something that she can understand and remember later and dream about.

Dodge looks her full in the face for the first time ever.

'Because I . . .' he begins.

'What?' Celia says breathlessly, when it becomes obvious that Dodge is not going to finish his sentence of his own accord.

But Dodge seems to have stopped altogether. He sits very still, one hand on Celia's shoulder and the other in her hair, and stares at her hard.

Celia Small is in big trouble.

Across the hallway her engagement party is hurtling on without her; and here she is almost in the arms of a strange-smelling man who is sickened by marriage, dissatisfied with sex but says he knows how to make her happy. It doesn't make sense.

Unless he thinks marriage is sickening and sex is unsatisfying because it's not taking place between him and Celia. Celia experiences an explosion of light and heat in her solar plexus. Does this mean that Dodge, her hated housemate, is secretly in love with her, and has been all along? Does this mean that, at the eleventh hour, just when her evening was getting dark and cold, her party will turn out to be the most romantic engagement in the history of the world after all? Celia sees herself returning triumphant to her dining-table, borne aloft on her conquering hero's shoulder, declaring Dodge to be her real true love and demoting Kenneth to the role of her financial adviser.

'I knew you'd save the day,' she whispers.

'You haven't seen anything yet,' Dodge replies.

His fingers begin to fumble with the frills around the neckline of Celia's best dress. She feels cool silk and warm flesh coupling under her chin.

'You haven't lived,' rasps Dodge.

Now both his hands caress the swollen curves of the puffed sleeves which stop just short of Celia's elbows. They perk up panting at his touch.

Celia feels all the weights in her body shift with the heave and the ho of her heart. Breathing is hard.

'You haven't even been born,' whispers Dodge, his fingers rummaging in the little rows of ruffles which run between Celia's breasts.

'My mother's got some photographs of me as a baby. Would you like to see them?' asks Celia, working on the assumption that so long as she can keep some sort of conversation going nothing too untoward will happen.

'Shhhh!' says Dodge.

Celia melts in the middle. Molten stuff seeps slowly from volcanic stone. A crater is gaping in Celia's underwear and there's going to be an eruption.

'But . . . but you said I wasn't to think about sex . . .' she gasps.

Dodge doesn't stop. He takes the strain of the silk stretched across Celia's chest, and shushes her for the second time. Then his hands swoop down and glide outwards over the soft folds of fabric which cover her cross-legged thighs. Celia stops talking. She very nearly stops breathing. Back and forth Dodge's hands skate over the rumpled surface, and every time the skirt is drawn a little higher over Celia's spread knees, and every time it seems like hot fingers will meet stinging flesh, sheer stocking and satin suspender. And every time is an exquisite disappointment.

Until Dodge, with a great nervous twitch of desire, clasps Celia to him and grapples with the buttons which bustle down her back.

'Celia,' he utters, urgently.

'Yes?' she says.

'Can I try your dress on?'

Celia has run all the way to the door before she remembers that

135

everything outside the room is at least as unlikely as Dodge wanting to try her dress on. She stops her frantic fumbling for the doorknob, and turns her flaming face to face him.

'Why?' is the first thing she says.

'Why?' is the first thing asked by every woman whose dress Dodge has ever wanted to wear. It is the last question he is prepared to answer. If they said, 'Well, will it fit you?' or 'Are you sure it's your colour?' there would be no hesitation in his reply. If they even thought he was joking . . .

'Are you joking?' asks Celia.

'No,' says Dodge.

Celia thought as much. If trying dresses on was a joke, men would do it all the time.

Collapsing against the door to the hall, Celia closes her eyes and thinks and thinks. Colours come and go behind her eyelids, most of them blue. She thinks and thinks and can't think of any reason why Dodge shouldn't try her dress on. Except that it would seem to mean that he isn't about to ask her to marry him. But then, she is still supposed to be getting engaged to Kenneth, so this is probably for the best.

When she opens her eyes again, Dodge hasn't moved a muscle. He is still staring at her, in what looks increasingly like desperation.

'Oh, all right then, if you really must,' Celia sighs, like a teacher letting a child who's threatening to wet itself leave the classroom for the third time in a lesson. 'Can I change in your bedroom?'

But Dodge has scrambled to his feet and is already halfway through his bedroom door. 'No, sorry,' he calls over his shoulder, 'I'm in here. Knock when you've got it off.'

He disappears into his inner chamber, and Celia sighs 'Charming!' as the door slams behind him.

136

She struggles to undo her buttons. As an engagement garment, the dress is not designed to be removed single-handedly. Its whole point is that the wearer becomes part of a partnership while inside it. Come the end of the evening, all being well, a sanctioned companion should be on hand to help get it off. But all is not well, and poor Celia has to assume the most uncomfortable positions before the dress lands around her ankles like a parachute and she can step out.

Bending over, she bundles it in her arms and takes it to the door of Dodge's bedroom. She knocks, the door flies open and a naked arm snakes out and seizes a handful of the slippery silk.

'Wait and see,' says the voice of Dodge as her dress slithers inside his lair. 'Wait and see!' As if Celia could care less how it will look on him.

She wants to leave, now that she can't. She waits impatiently. She waits in white underwear in Dodge's bare white waiting-room; shivery, sick, seeing things. Is there a doctor in the house? Celia wants to go home, but she's home already and it isn't. Her bed might as well be a million miles away for all the hope she has of slipping between its sheets and falling fast asleep.

Celia and her stupid dreams.

She's really torn it this time.

Dodge only wanted her for her frock.

All the white in the room sighs.

But suddenly there is a bolt of blue lightning by the bedroom door, crackling in the sadness. Celia spins around when it sears the side of her eye and screams and screams and, 'Dodge?' she says before she has finished screaming, 'you nearly gave me a heart attack.'

Dodge doesn't say anything. He has changed. Completely. He is standing in the doorway, looking at Celia, and looking like Celia, and doing much better at the latter.

'Is that a wig?' says Celia.

It must be a wig. Dodge's real hair is short, damp and dark. But despite her assurance, Celia's hand flies to her long blonde locks to check that they are still there, and that she is still she.

(For what if she and Dodge have flipped over, like the floor and the ceiling, now he has her frock on and she has nothing.)

Celia's hair is still on her head. She takes a step towards Dodge. Dodge looks like her.

'It's wonderful,' she whispers, her throat sore from screaming. Now Celia knows what she looks like.

'So I *am* beautiful,' she says.

'No,' says Dodge, 'this is me.'

Dodge walks past her, with what would be a dazzling smile if it didn't pass her faster than he did, and into the centre of the room. He spreads his arms like a camp Christ and spins on the spot, skirts swirling, head thrown back, hair flying.

He laughs, and everything in the room gets lighter.

'Big Bang!' he shouts at the ceiling. 'See! I died and now I am alive.'

Despite herself, Celia starts to laugh. 'I'm afraid you've not had much practice in walking in high-heeled shoes,' she splutters.

'What makes you say that?' Dodge stops spinning.

'Because people don't . . . stagger so, when they've had practice.'

'I've had plenty of practice,' Dodge says petulantly, 'plenty of practice.'

He tosses his head at her and starts to move his hips to the rhythm of the music from upstairs. It's a fast beat, and soon his shoulders and his feet are getting into the groove. Celia leans against the wall and watches Dodge dancing as if he were his own sister. But it's infectious; before very long, she is dancing too, dancing around him in circles.

Then a thought strikes her like the sharp edge of Norman Bates's knife. 'Your female relatives,' she says, 'are they all alive?'

Dodge stops dead. She can see him trying to work out what she means. He stands with his hands on his hips and glares at Celia, still but for the quiver of his lips. Then his back arches, and words sharp and pointed as arrows fly straight for her heart.

'Oh yes, that's funny. That's clever,' he cries. 'Make me out to be some kind of weirdo. That's really supportive, Celia!'

Celia claps her hands to her mouth, but there is nothing she can do to stop her eyes saying, slowly and clearly, 'Well excuse my totally unfounded accusations, Dodgy!'

'There's no need to be sarcastic,' says Dodge. 'After all I've done for you tonight, after all the help and advice I've given you; the least you can do is refrain from making Psycho jokes about me.'

'Help and advice?' says Celia. 'Help and advice? What are you saying ... there's something wrong with *me*? What are you saying, you transvestite you; I won't be all right until I'm wearing a pair of your Y-fronts.'

'I haven't got any Y-fronts,' says Dodge, smiling placidly now, 'and I'm not a transvestite. I'm a woman.'

Celia gives a rude laugh.

'No, I am,' says Dodge, smiling broader by the second.

'Oh yeah?' snorts Celia.

'Yeah,' Dodge brazens it out.

'Oh yeah?' shouts Celia. 'Well what's this then?' And she stomps up to Dodge and flicks the tip of what is unmistakably, even under a blue silk skirt, a magnificent erection.

'Ow!' says Dodge.

'Yes, well,' Celia cries, completely out of control, 'if you think that hurts, you'd better not even dream about being a real woman!'

She turns on her heel and races blindly from the room.

Because she is wearing only her underwear, it is fortunate that this sightless flight takes her through the door to Dodge's bedroom and not the door to the hall.

Unfortunately, Dodge's bedroom is a woman's bedroom, and Celia is going to have to eat her words. As her anger slowly subsides, Celia wishes she could sink through the pink, panty-strewn carpet. Dodge was right and she was wrong. Only someone who truly believes themself to be a woman could sleep in a room like this. Even Celia's room isn't as pink and panty-strewn as this.

Everything is pink – the walls, the carpet, the bedclothes. The nightie.

Everything is perfumed – the piles of cosmetics stacked in pyramids on the dressing-table, the pots of pot-pourri. The pillows.

All over the floor slips and stockings and handbags and hair remover and copies of *Cosmopolitan* are scattered like viscera. Celia couldn't be more convinced of Dodge's femininity if she had cut him open and pulled out a womb.

She sits on the edge of the bed, her head in her hands. She feels like she's falling again. And now she wishes she was.

Because it's time to come back down to earth. She can't stand any more weirdness and wonders. It's time to get back to her proper place, her parents and her party. It's time to wake up.

Wake up!

Dodge doesn't want her.

Dodge wants to *be* her.

He wants to

Wake up!

Wearing make-up,

he'll fall right through the earth
and get the best of both worlds.
But if Celia put on trousers and a tie
she'd still be
ding-dong-bell
pussy in the
well.
'Wake up!'

Celia opens her eyes and sees Dodge standing at the bottom of the bed, telling her to wake up for the hundredth time. But she wasn't asleep. She was just thinking.

'Have you ever seen the original illustrations for *Alice in Wonderland*? By Tenniel,' she asks him, to prove it.

Dodge shakes his head.

'His Alice looks like a boy. A boy with a wig on. Wearing a dress. Just like you,' Celia goes on.

But Dodge doesn't say anything. He is sulking.

'Borrow my copy some time,' says Celia. 'You'll see.'

'If this is an attempt to apologise,' Dodge answers icily at last, 'it's not working. A girl doesn't want to be told she looks like some Victorian queen's sexual fantasy. It makes her feel unnatural.'

'Sorry,' stammers Celia. Then, struggling for something better to say, she blurts out what she really means by mistake: 'I thought you were in love with me.'

Dodge's cold mood melts in the warmth of her blush.

'I'm heterosexual, Celia,' he says, 'I only go for men.'

He turns to the mirror. Celia sees him staring straight at his reflection – not pouting, not pursing, not mincing like most men who pretend to be women.

Dodge smiles when Celia's eye meets his in the glass. 'I'm off out,' he says. 'I'm about to explode.'

'I ought to go too,' Celia mutters. She doesn't know where. She doesn't know if she is actually awake yet. She only knows that Dodge is behaving badly as a dream.

'What will you wear?' he says.

'Wear?' whispers Celia. What, isn't she wearing something already?

'Because, if it's all the same to you,' says Dodge, 'I'd like to keep your dress on. And go upstairs to Cath's party.'

'Oh,' says Celia. 'Oh well. That's that then. That's the end of my evening. That's the end of my life. Don't mind me.' She adopts a martyred expression.

'Well, you could say no,' says Dodge, mildly.

Celia shakes her head, wildly.

'What does that mean?' asks Dodge. 'No I can't wear the dress, or no you can't say no I can't wear the dress?'

A sound escapes Celia's compressed lips. 'Wear it,' she says, 'if you want to be looked at like a picture book. Wear it, if you want people turning you on your head and looking up your skirt the whole time!'

Celia has never been so angry. She's never lost anything as much loved as this frock. It was made from memory, from the hopes and prayers she can't bear to forget. It's her oldest friend. Being stripped of it hurts like having several layers of skin ripped off.

'Wear it!' she shouts. 'It's a ridiculous dress. It'll suit you.'

'Thanks,' Dodge rallies razor-sharp, but he looks a little deflated.

'Don't mention it,' says Celia, and turns her face away.

A short silence follows.

Then Dodge clears his throat and opens his wardrobe doors.

'Er, I've got hundreds of other dresses,' he says. 'You can choose whichever one you want.'

142

Celia gets to her feet and heads for the wardrobe, looking like she might change her mind and ask for her dress back at any minute. Dodge's fingers are crossed behind his back.

Celia crosses behind Dodge's back and looks deep into his wardrobe, where she sees that when he said he had hundreds of dresses he wasn't showing off. The cavernous interior is chock-full of frocks in all the colours of the rainbow, sequinned as a summer shower. They hang together tangled, skinny but sad, like a houseful of anorexics; wigs and shoes are stuffed on shelves above and below them like sweets stashed in secret hidey-holes.

'I'm not sure about this,' says Celia, and looks longingly at her own dress, stretched to its limit across Dodge's broader shoulders. 'They all look a bit . . . unstable.'

'There's other stuff further back, stuff you can't see from here,' says Dodge. 'Go on, I know you'll find something you'll be comfortable with.'

It's a walk-in wardrobe and Celia walks into it, silhouetted against a spectrum of shimmering light; then right through the beaded curtain of dresses into the darkness behind. Back there are the things Dodge never wears: most of them are men's clothes, kept for fancy-dress and emergencies.

Dodge sits down at the dressing-table to reapply his lipstick and powder his nose. He brought the bottle of whisky into the bedroom earlier, and now he swigs it between perfumed strokes of his powder puff. He is nervous. It's his first time out in the house.

A muffled humming and the squealing of wire coathangers on clothes-rails herald Celia's return to the room.

Dodge swivels on his stool to flatter her, his face fixed in a look of rapture which freezes the instant Celia steps through the wardrobe door.

'Casual,' Dodge coughs, 'but chic.'

'Well,' explains Celia, 'I think my party is probably over.'

She doesn't look as bad as Dodge is making out. But she doesn't look like herself at all. Her shiny shoes and sheer stockings have been replaced by black Doctor Martens boots and a pair of black jeans. Over the jeans a baggy black jumper hangs shapelessly, almost down to her knees.

Celia has never worn anything like this before. What will her parents say when they see her? Will they even know it is her?

On impulse, Celia steps back inside the wardrobe, and when she comes out again her hair is crammed into a short and curly red wig, bright and bristling as a brillo pad, but cut in the shape of a bob.

Dodge falls off his stool with laughter and Celia gets a chance to stare at the strange her in the mirror. Then she looks from herself to him, flashing petticoat-white and blue as he rolls over and over on the carpet, and back to herself again.

'What's so funny?' she says. 'I couldn't wear one of your cut-away numbers; there'd be nothing to keep me together. But this is warm, it's comfy, it's as black as my mood; I feel fine.'

Dodge lies still and flaps his skirt at her like a floozy. 'You look fine,' he says. 'I'm only laughing because I'm nervous.' Then he adds, 'I lost my virginity in those boots. And I never found it again. It must still be in there.'

'Oh,' says Celia. She already had cold feet about going out into the house again. Now they are cold and clammy.

Dodge sits up and tugs at her trouser leg.

'What about a bit of jewellery?' he says.

'Jewellery?' repeats Celia. 'I don't think so.'

'It doesn't have to be nice,' says Dodge. 'I've got bangles, beads; chunky stuff, you know . . . uncompromising.'

144

'Uncompromising?' repeats Celia. 'Oh. Okay then.'

Dodge points at a shell-encrusted casket on the dressing-table.

'In there,' he says.

Celia riffles through the casket's contents. Just when it seems that she isn't going to see anything she likes, she slips a length of shiny black ribbon around her neck and stares down at the big silver symbol swinging from it.

'Let's have a look,' says Dodge.

Celia swivels on the stool. As she comes to face Dodge he smiles smugly. 'Woman,' he says, 'you're crying out for liberation.'

'What?' says Celia.

Dodge nods at the circle and the cross resting on Celia's chest.

'It's the sign of woman,' he says.

'I know,' says Celia, 'but there's something a bit wrong with it, see. The cross is too long, it's more like a crucifix. Where did you get it?'

'Found it,' says Dodge, 'here in the house, I think.' He shrugs his shoulders and offers her a swig from the bottle of whisky.

Their hands touch as it passes between them. Their eyes meet. Celia's are sore. She thought he was going to fuck her, and he thinks he hasn't. Dodge stands up, and becomes very busy; bustling around the bedroom, straightening the bedclothes, shutting the wardrobe door, putting the lid back on his lipstick.

'Come on,' he says, 'we've got to go.'

And before Celia knows it they are standing side by side by the doorway to the rest of the house, and Dodge is turning the key in the lock.

'Dodge,' she says quickly, 'take care of the frock. It's special.'

Dodge smooths the blue silk of the skirt over his lean thighs. 'Of course,' he says, 'I shall treat it as I would treat you.'

145

'Thanks,' says Celia, 'and thank you for having me. Enjoy Cath's party.'

'Where are you going?' asks Dodge. 'Home to your friends and family?'

'If they'll have me back without the dress of honour,' says Celia, 'but I've got to go to the loo again first.'

And she smiles at Dodge as he opens the door and they step in each other's shoes into the hall.

6.

I

Dodge lets her down

In the cold light of the hallway, Dodge shuts his eyes as Celia
sneaks past the entrance to her own room in unfamiliar boots.
They squeak, and Dodge winces; but there's no need to worry.
Behind the closed door Celia's party are singing so loudly that
they couldn't possibly have heard her.

They are singing the theme tune to *The Dambusters*; unaccom-
panied but for the whizz-bang and ratatata of bouncing bombs,
Celia's father's speciality sound effect.

Dodge swallows hard, and starts to tiptoe after Celia, who has
got safely to the foot of the stairs. Then it strikes him that if he is
going to gatecrash Cath's party it would be better to do it with a
bottle of wine. Waving Celia on up the stairs, he turns on his high
heel and hurries down the hall to the kitchen. On a night like
tonight, there's bound to be loads of free booze in the fridge.

Dodge approaches the kitchen with caution. Earlier in the
evening it appeared to be throwing a party in its own right. A
great congregation of guests gathered there before proceeding
loudly up the stairs and into Cath's or Phoebe's rooms. But now,
as Dodge pauses on the doorstep, all is silent.

The kitchen looks like one of Celia's father's bouncing bombs has hit it. It is dark and devastated and the floor is inches deep in debris. Before he can step inside, Dodge has to clear away beer cans, a beehive, a crushed paper cup, a rattle, a corkscrew and a hedgehog (stuffed), with a croquet mallet which he found propped considerately against the doorpost.

Then he sees the bodies.

Two young men are having tea at the kitchen table. A third is sitting between them, fast asleep, and the other two are using him as a cushion, resting their elbows on him and talking over his head.

One of them is the ugliest man Dodge has ever set eyes on. He is all hair; it flops in dreadlocks, in matted white and brown patches, like two fat rabbit ears down his back. Buck teeth rear like horses in his thin yellow face, a big nose protrudes at the same steep angle, and his nostrils are unfashionably flared. Dodge is tempted to tiptoe away before the guy spots him standing shy, half in and half out of the kitchen. Indeed, his stomach has already done a U-turn at the thought of that startled gaze meeting and greeting his. He can't guarantee his disguise won't slip under such unattractive scrutiny.

But before Dodge can slink off in search of more promising thresholds on which to tremble, and some prettier people to play with, the men at the table see him. They clamber onto their chairs in such clumsy transportations of delight that Dodge is sure they have fallen for his Celia costume. Flattered and flustered, he fails to hear what the men are shouting at first. And when he does, it doesn't make sense.

'No room?' Dodge says to himself, blinking in bewilderment at the vast table and the vacant places. 'No room?'

Both men are standing on their seats and bending their hands at him in such urgent little beckoning gestures that Dodge can't believe they want him to go away. They must be teasing, playing a trick on the chick; Celia warned him of this tedious tradition.

'There's plenty of room,' he tuts, wondering if this is how she would have handled the situation.

One way or another, he seems to have said exactly the right thing. The two men smite their hands together in strange glee and climb down from their chairs. They nod towards an empty chair at the opposite end of the table. Then, when Dodge doesn't take the hint and sit in it, they nod at him and the chair and him and the chair, and then one nods at him and the other nods at the chair, until the non-hairy one's hat falls off his head and lands like a cosy on the teapot. The hat, Dodge notices as its owner puts it back on, has been fashioned from hundreds of other hats, all sewn up into a working museum of millinery through the ages.

Dodge sits down at the top of the table, enfeebled by the force of the staring eyes and frozen smiles of the men at the bottom. Is this what it's like to be a woman? Dodge is sure he doesn't have the constitution for a whole night of it. He is in need of respite already.

He lowers his gaze like he's seen Celia do. He always thought this was a calculated coyness, but next time he'll know she's just having a rest. Then Dodge finds himself looking straight at the third man, the one crashed out between the others, face down on the table, empty teacup laced loosely in sleeping fingers.

It is Kenneth!

Now here is a turn-up for the books. Dodge's flagging spirits are revived in an instant. Could he convince Celia's fiancé that he is Celia? A stunt like that would stretch his cunning to the limit, but it would be the highlight of his low life, the Nobel Prize for female impersonation, and no mistake!

Dodge gives the unconscious Ken his best Celia smile.

The hairy man smiles back with big bad teeth.

'Have some wine,' he says encouragingly.

Dodge looks all around the table; but there is nothing on it but tea.

'I don't see any wine,' he remarks.

'There's isn't any,' the man replies.

'Then it wasn't very civil of you to offer it,' says Dodge, angrily.

'It wasn't very civil of you to sit down without being invited,' says the hairy man; but he grins all over his grotesque face and gives Dodge a stumpy thumbs-up sign.

Faced with such a mixture of messages, Dodge decides to ignore the smile, and replies rather coldly, 'Well, excuse me, but this is *my* house. And that is *my* fiancé, so kindly take your elbow out of his ear.'

The man with the hat slams his hand on the table. 'Your hair wants cutting,' he shouts. 'I can see it sticking out under your very cheap wig!'

So, they know that Dodge isn't Celia. Well, it's no skin off his nose. As tea-party hosts, these men are as mad and boring as chimpanzees; and they don't promise to be any better as sexual partners.

But Ken is another matter. And Ken is still asleep and blissfully unaware of the short dark hair at the nape of Dodge's neck. The best thing Dodge can do is to practise rolling some stony Celia statements off his tongue, and wait for Ken to wake up.

'You should learn not to make personal remarks. It's very rude,' he says to the man with the hat.

The man with the hat sneers, and replies, 'Why is a raven like a writing-desk?'

Do Dodge's ears deceive him, or is this a death-defying change of direction? He shakes his head in disbelief.

'What?' he says.

'Why is a raven like a writing-desk?' hat-man repeats. The ugly one smirks.

Dodge sighs and his head sinks into his hands. This is getting sillier by the second. He should have made a speedy getaway, but now he's beginning to feel sleepy; his body is becoming numb and seems about to nod off altogether. Dodge rubs his eyes wearily, then licks a little fingertip and runs it under his lower lashes in case of smudged mascara. Finally he looks up and answers the man's question.

'Because they both produce notes,' he says.

The man with the hat's hat falls off. The hairy one looks as though he is about to go bald. The grins slip from their faces like the setting sun slides from the sky, and a greyness grips their features.

And at the other end of table, something dawns on Dodge: these guys are part of Cath's party, and this kitchen is a small corner of Wonderland. He has wandered into it, an accidental Alice, looking like a proper Alice in Celia's frock.

He starts to smile at the Mad Hatter and the March Hare, both of whom are behaving as if it is Dodge who is one sandwich short of a tea-party.

'I don't believe it,' mutters the Mad Hatter.

'You bitch!' breathes the March Hare.

'I don't bloody believe it,' shouts the Mad Hatter, sending his teacup and saucer spinning to the kitchen floor. 'That riddle is meant to have no answer, you know.'

'You selfish bitch!' shrieks the March Hare, 'it's supposed to be unanswerable.'

Dodge laughs. He's never been called a bitch by a man before. It makes him feel flamboyant and flagrant, as if he's wearing a feather boa and flicking its tip in the Hatter's and Hare's faces.

151

'Well, boys,' he says, 'I've heard better riddles in a primary school urinal. Now who's going to be a darling and pour me a nice cup of tea?'

The March Hare bares his buck teeth in an inhuman scream. The Mad Hatter leaps to his feet and, cramming his mad hat back on his head and rolling up his Victorian shirtsleeves, moves menacingly to the top of the table. 'Now listen here, lady,' he growls, grabbing Dodge by the shoulders and forcing him to stand up, 'what day of the month is it? Eh? *Eh?*'

'Er, the twenty-second?' gasps Dodge, his feet not quite touching the floor.

'Now look here, lady,' says the Hatter, letting go of one of Dodge's shoulders and shoving an antique timepiece in his face. 'Two days wrong!'

'Well, why not put it right,' gulps Dodge. 'Give that little knob a twiddle. Gently, mind!' He giggles, partly at his poor *double entendre*, mostly out of nerves.

But Dodge's wit is wasted on the Mad Hatter who has double meanings of his own to deal with.

'I told you butter wouldn't suit the works,' he bellows over his shoulder at the March Hare, who is still sitting stiff with shock, startled spittle drying in the shadowy undercliff of his chin.

'It was the *best* butter,' the Hare murmurs.

Without taking his bullying eyes and beefy breath off Dodge, the Hatter answers his friend. 'Yes, but some crumbs must have got in as well. You shouldn't have put it in with the breadknife,' he says fast and furiously.

'It was the *best* butter, you know,' says the March Hare again, before succumbing to the sobs which shake his mangy frame.

The Hatter's face is red and his lips are white and blue. He stares wordlessly at Dodge, letting the March Hare's sobs speak for themselves, and as the seconds tick by his eyes bulge with the brunt of his accusation.

'Well,' he says at last, 'we're waiting. What do you say?'

Dodge doesn't know. Feminine intuition and lucky guesses have kept him afloat so far; but now he is floundering, out of his depth in a sea of something he has never read. And the two men are swimming around him like sharks, deadly serious, silly as it seems. Dodge simply hadn't realised the effect that nineteenth-century children's literature still has on some people. In desperation he pleads ignorance.

'I don't know. I did biology . . .' he begins, but is cut short by the Hatter screaming, 'Say it! Say it!! If you're not going to play properly then *piss off!*'

Due perhaps to the tightness of his dress and the grip of his wig, Dodge feels faint. 'What do you want me to say?' he whispers, as his head drops onto the Hatter's iron chest.

'What a funny watch! What a funny fucking watch! It tells the day of the month, and doesn't tell what o'clock is it!' cries the Hatter, shaking Dodge so violently he will be laid up with whiplash for a week.

'You're the worst Alice we've ever had!' adds the Hare, bounding up the table to box Dodge's ears. 'You breeze in, right on cue, all costumed up, then cool as a cucumber you answer the unanswerable riddle, and clam up when it's *our* chance to get the better of *you*.'

And screaming 'Say it! Say it!' they shake, rattle and roll Dodge around the kitchen. Their brutality is gratuitous; if Dodge knew what they wanted him to say, he would have said it by now – he's no hero. But he is brave enough to try a shot in the dark, even though the dark is very dark and the bullet is a blank. For Dodge is hardly an *Alice in Wonderland* fan, let alone a fanatic, and the only

153

line that springs to mind is, 'Curiouser and curiouser said Alice'.

So Dodge squeezes these words in between the pushing and hair-pulling, the pinching and poking, but soon finds that they only make matters worse. The Mad Hatter and the March Hare don't take kindly to anything even remotely resembling irony, and are so beside themselves with rage that there seems to be four of them. And Dodge is starting to see double, putting the total of his assailants at eight.

In terror he talks off the top of his head, hoping against hope that, if he can hold out long enough, he will eventually hit upon Alice's next line by accident.

'Boys, boys, be reasonable,' he gabbles, 'it's only a game, isn't it? Only a hobby? What do you lads do for a living, then? No, don't tell me, let me guess. Bouncers? Bankers? Ow! Sorry. No, see, I only ask because in *my* spare time I do a bit of charity work. Old people, handicapped kids, you know, helping in the community. And . . . and . . . I think you might do something better with the time than waste it in asking riddles that have no answers!'

At last! The beating ceases. The Mad Hatter and the March Hare break away from Dodge and, breathing heavily, start to smooth the creases out of their costumes. The Mad Hatter nods grimly at the March Hare, and the March Hare smiles darkly at the Mad Hatter, and the Mad Hatter turns back to Dodge.

'If you knew Time as well as I do,' he says pompously, 'you wouldn't talk about wasting *it*. It's *him*.'

Dodge had collapsed into a chair when the rain of blows was over; but he is now struggling back to his feet to meet the Hatter eye to eye. He grabs the edge of the table to steady himself. 'You can't scare me,' he spits. 'Sticks and stones may break my bones, but sexist sound-bites are water off a duck's back. I don't know what the fuck you think you're playing at, but as far as I'm concerned the game is over. I can't say it's been fun.'

Dodge turns and walks away, intending to sail stiffly from the kitchen without another word. But before he gets to the door one of the barmy bastards leaps on his back and brings him crashing to the floor. Dodge is rolled over roughly, and comes face to sweaty swollen face with the Mad Hatter. There is thunder in the Hatter's eyes, where the heat of his hatred meets the cold hardness of his heart.

'Oh, I've got it!' says Dodge, provocative to the last. 'You're a rugby player!'

The Hatter interlocks his pelvis with Dodge's, like pieces of a jigsaw puzzle. The pain is more than a pinprick. Dodge wonders if this would be a good moment to reveal his true gender. He knows the Hatter knows he isn't Celia; but then, as the Hatter is one of Cath's guests, he probably doesn't know Celia from Adam anyway. No, it seems that Dodge has been taken for a renegade Alice; all woman, and rotten to the core. Eve.

'I'll show you, lady . . .' splutters the Hatter, confirming Dodge's theory, 'I'll show you . . .'

'I think, on the contrary,' says Dodge, still tongue in cheek and penis in pants, 'I'll be showing you.'

The Hatter does not heed him. He is attempting to lift Celia's skirt, handicapped by his own great grunting weight which is holding it down. He is a big bruiser, and Dodge's thighs are soon covered with round red and purple patches like a child's finger-painting. If Dodge were in a position to close his thighs, squeeze them tight, and spread them again, a pair of butterfly wings would appear – a symmetrical smearing of blackish paint, that other stalwart of pre-school art.

155

But Dodge is not in a position to close his legs. The Hatter is lying between them.

Dodge is in a daze. He doesn't know what to do. He's never been in this sort of situation before; and now that he is, it still doesn't seem to be actually happening. Crazy incongruous things revolve in his mind like a fairground carousel. Pointless thoughts and useless notions pass him by: like tiny fire-engines and great psychedelic snails. His head is an incredible hurdy-gurdy, a wheezy squeeze-box which makes it hard to hear what's really going on.

But then there is the unmistakable sound of ripping silk. 'Oh no!' Dodge has his first coherent thought. 'Not the frock!' There is the sound of ripping silk and the Hatter's hand is sliding up one of Celia's stockings, underneath her skirt. Dodge will have to act fast if he wants to save her. Poor Celia! She trusted him to keep her out of trouble. Dodge is sure she'd never have let him get into her dress if she thought something like this would happen.

He starts to struggle, and is surprised at the Hatter's strength. He thought struggling would be the last resort, one big heave and the Hatter would be off. He tries harder, but he's stuck in thick treacle. The Hatter's hips are pinning him to the floor, and the Hatter's sweat is trickling between his legs, and the Hatter's hands are pressing down on his chest, and the Hatter's voice is shouting, 'This bird's got no tits! What a rip-off!'

Then more blue silk is ripped off and the Hatter says, 'Bollocks! She's flat as a pancake!'

Dodge is stuck in slow motion; he can't move his mouth fast enough to say anything. All he can see is Celia. She doesn't look so good in this situation. But whose fault is that?

Dodge feels fully responsible and absolutely powerless. He shuts his eyes and those bruised butterfly wings are between his

156

thighs again. Red and purple and black and spread like the lips of a vagina. Splat.

What if the Hatter really rapes him? Will he be a real woman?

The Hatter's hands are under the skirt. They hurt, and it's getting worse. They're working their way up, high above the stocking tops. Any second now the Hatter's hands will find

bollocks

or butterfly wings

bollocks

or butterfly wings

depending on whether Dodge is male or –

Suddenly, a female voice is screaming, 'Get off you bastard! Get off you bastard! Get off or I'll break your back!'

Dodge doesn't think this is him.

He opens his eyes. Over the Hatter's shoulder he sees Phoebe brandishing a kitchen chair. She looks like an avenging angel, her hair a black halo, her eyes on fire.

'Stop it or I'll kill you,' she says to the back of the Hatter's head. 'I'll kill you so badly you'll wish you'd never been born. And then I'll tell your mother you were a rapist, and everyone else you were a virgin.'

The Hatter goes limp on top of Dodge. Dodge suffocates in the slump. His head is spinning. He gasps for air.

'Right. You,' Phoebe turns to the March Hare, 'get him off her.' The Hare shrinks under Phoebe's glare, and shrinks and shrinks until he's small enough to tap the Hatter timidly on the shoulder. The Hatter is off Dodge like a shot. But as soon as he is on his feet he squares up to Phoebe as if he thinks she stoppped his fun because she fancies some herself. Yes, believe it or not, the Hatter is about to attack her instead.

Phoebe should have learnt karate as a kid. The Hatter is easily stronger than she, but what good is a big body when you've got a brain the size of a pea? All Phoebe needs to do is be a real princess and hit him where it hurts.

'Get out of my house now,' she says, 'or I will phone for the police, while my friends force you to eat your own penis. They'll remove it painfully from your person first, of course, and stuff it with chopped nuts – that's *your* nuts, you understand; then cook it in its own juices until it's crisp and sizzling and the skin has turned to crackling. You can see that we have a very well-equipped kitchen here, though it's not always as clean as one could wish.'

Phoebe looks the Mad Hatter in the eye as she's speaking. But she seems to be staring at the March Hare too.

The March Hare is pale. He nudges the Hatter with his elbow, twice because the first time he misses.

'Quick,' he says, 'I'm going to be sick.'

The Hatter shakes his head. 'We can't go,' he says, 'we're holding him in custody.' He jerks his head towards Ken, still out cold on the table.

'Sorry? Custard, you say?' says Phoebe sweetly. 'So you don't favour the savoury option. Well, in that case allow me to suggest the spotted dick – the same dick, but steamed, and smothered with as much piping-hot custard as you can swallow. I'm afraid we're out of dried fruit, but you can get a similar effect, aesthetically at least, with small pieces of smouldering coal, or cigarette burns.'

The Hare is halfway out of the kitchen with the Hatter hot on his heels. He and Phoebe hold their gazes to each other's throats like unsheathed blades until he gets to the door.

Once in the hall the Hatter smiles a scarred smile and says, 'Mad cow!' But he's only got the guts to say it to the March Hare, who can't hear him for vomiting.

158

Back in the kitchen Dodge has adopted a foetal position on the floor and started to shake with stomach-aching silent sobs. Phoebe puts the kettle on and crashes about with crockery, stamping from cupboard to cupboard, banging doors and slamming saucers. She makes so much noise that no one, including herself, can tell that she is crying too. Every so often she tries to wake Ken by slapping her fist on the table near his sleeping ear and shouting, 'Wake up, you wanker!'

This doesn't work so, when the kettle boils, she makes a pot of strong black coffee. Then, leaving it to stand on one side, she squats down next to Dodge on the floor. She hugs him. He clings to her, his head buried in her breast, his blonde hair everywhere, his breathing slowing to stay alongside hers. His tears of distress, and the tears in that dress, are forgotten in the blackness of her embrace.

But soon, too soon, cruelly soon, Phoebe pulls awkwardly away, and Dodge falls face first to the floor.

'I'm sorry, but I've got to go now, Celia,' Phoebe says. 'My sister's just flown in from America and badly needs a drink. She's waiting upstairs. But, look, I think your fiancé is stirring.'

She leaps to her feet and deals Ken a blow to the head. There is no response. Phoebe stacks a tray with coffee and cups and wafts its wake-up aromas in Ken's direction as she carries it shaking and steaming out of the kitchen and up the stairs to her sister.

Phoebe is shaking and steaming too. She spits some parting words at Dodge: 'Don't be a doormat all your life, Celia. Next time someone is standing on you, try fighting back. Try shouting for help.'

Phoebe is out of earshot by the time Dodge unsticks his lips from the lino, licks them, and yelps.

'Help!'

II

More and more curious

Upstairs, Celia hops from foot to foot outside the bathroom. She has crossed one leg over the other so many times they are starting to knit together.

To while away the wait, she is knotting her brow and gnawing her lips and worrying about how to face her family. What will they do when she goes down to dish out the desserts without her dress on? Kenneth will probably be inclined to give her some just deserts, for leaving him in the lurch.

She'll have to splash her face with cold water and hope that it will clear her head. High-precision thought and speech will be needed, for there'll be plenty of explaining to do. She'll have to say what she's been playing at all evening. That is if she can speak at all, after accidentally, by a simple slip of the lips, doing some drugs.

Celia feels awful now, for staying away so long and for making such heavy weather of the return trip. Her engagement was inevitable; it had to happen sooner or later; her mother swore she wouldn't rest until she'd seen Celia safely up the aisle. And if this means she'll get off Celia's case once she's packed her away on honeymoon, it's as good a reason to get married as any.

Celia blushes at her naughty thought, and the toilet flushes behind the bathroom door.

At last!

She unties her legs and takes a step towards it.

Whoever is in there is coming out.

But as the sound of rushing water rushes away another assails her ears. A soft humming, like a distant airplane.

Celia steps backwards. This is a war song! It is *The Dambusters* again: low-key, abridged, a reprise of the large-scale version she

160

has just heard bursting from her room. So whoever is in the bathroom must also be a member of her party.

And they are unlocking the door.

They are unlocking the door.

But there is another door. Right beside Celia. The door to Phoebe's room.

Celia has never been in Phoebe's room. She has never even seen in Phoebe's room. And Phoebe's room has never seen anyone make an entrance like this before. Celia bolts into the blackened chamber and throws her weight back against the door which clicks shut behind her like a slipped disc. She waits, paralysed, as part of her party walks past the other side. Then she feels the pain of having avoided the issue again.

And the dark room is suddenly shockingly light, and in the light a hundred nuns and a hundred nurses bounce their beaming faces at her and shout 'SURPRISE!'

Celia screws up her eyes and screams, higher than the hundred nundred people, a wordless stream of vocal steam. Celia screams a tall thin scream and her whole body seems to grow taller and thinner and longer and slimmer and lifts up into the air like a party balloon that's going down. As she screams, her throat vibrates like the neck of the balloon and her thick rubber lips would need to be knotted to stop the shock rushing out of her like wind from a tunnel. As she screams, her body, breathless, billows like an empty bag beneath the fireball fury of her face and the outrage O of her mouth.

Celia's scream goes on and on, though Celia's eyes now scan the crowd and see that there is just one nun and only two nurses. Her scream goes on although Celia now notes with calm detachment the fifty other faces, all of which have fallen, and the party streamers hanging limp in a hundred hands. The scream tails off with a final flourish as Phoebe flies from the crowd and seizes Celia and squeezes Celia and says: 'Hey it's okay oh shit I'm sorry don't be scared.'

There is hay. There is the sweet sweaty smell of hay in Phoebe's seize and Phoebe's squeeze. Crushed against Phoebe's velvet, Celia sniffs, and there is hay but no shit. Phoebe is right then; it *is* okay. Celia starts to stop being scared.

Celia stops being scared completely.

Phoebe's arms are closed around her like curtains; they shut out the night. Phoebe's breast supports Celia's head like a pillow, or a perfumed pouch of sleep-inducing herbs. Strong, Phoebe is strong. For Celia's eyelids are heavy, and Celia's heart is heavy, and Celia has been dragging herself around the house like a cart-horse; but Phoebe has picked her up and put her to bed as if she were no bigger than a baby.

Rocked and dreamy in Phoebe's arms, Celia goes back over the last few minutes on her way to sleep. First there was darkness in the room, then there was light, and then came the surprise. Phoebe's face, the face of the housemate who hates her, is buried in Celia's new red hair. The arms that scorn her are holding her up by the tatty black armpits. And the voice that ignores her has changed its tune.

'No don't oh dear it's all my fault,' Phoebe is saying. But the last time she spoke to Celia, about an hour and a half before the first guests arrived, it was to swear that if Celia's party were to go ahead Phoebe would be fucked by five sailors if she didn't send the ceiling crashing down around its silver-plugged ears. Those were Phoebe's exact words, but Celia wasn't at all sure what she meant by them. Except trouble.

And now, although she is standing in the arms of a possible schizophrenic, and still up to her neck in it, Celia slips softly into

162

six or seven seconds of sleep. And in a dream, which lasts for four of them but tells a story which spans several years, Celia and Phoebe are identical twins, separated at birth in a sociological experiment; and on coming face to face with each other in a supermarket one day Celia, a check-out girl, and Phoebe, a highly paid industrial spy from a rival chain, attempt to strangle each other with till-receipt rolls until a supervisor with cat-food cans for shoes clatters up to sack Celia for slacking.

The supervisor says, 'Come and check her out, one of you nurse-types ... she's gone completely slack ... a sack of potatoes ... Oh, hey, she's back! It's okay, she's back!'

'Hello,' says Celia distantly, from between Phoebe's breasts.

'Hello' echoes all around her. Someone somewhere says 'Surprise!' again.

'What's happening? I don't understand,' says Celia. Shy as a child, she can't pull her eyes out of the deep purple darkness of Phoebe's interior. Phoebe doesn't mind, though; on the contrary, she seems reluctant to let Celia go. In fact, Celia is clamped, and couldn't escape Phoebe's embrace if she wanted to.

'It's for me?' she asks. 'The surprise party is for me?' She feels the vibrations as Phoebe nods.

Now that Celia comes to think of it she does recall a conversation in a kitchen several centuries since, with Phoebe acting cagey about the purpose of her party and reacting with rage to the news that Celia had made plans for the evening. Could Phoebe have known about Celia getting married and going away? And could Phoebe have thrown this party to say goodbye and good luck?

Possibly.

But Phoebe hates Celia.

'I'm surprised,' says Celia, and her legs begin to buckle. She is making a rapid descent towards the earth-coloured carpet at

Phoebe's feet. Pheobe whistles, and Celia feels extra hands holding her and extra bodies orbiting her. Thanks to their support she is soon stable again.

'Thanks,' says Phoebe. 'I think I'd better go and make her some coffee. Would someone sit her down somewhere? I'm sure it's only shock. She was fine when I spoke to her earlier . . .'

Phoebe fades away, and Celia is forced to stand on her own two feet and be taken to an armchair by someone stranger. Having been found again, her feet seem reluctant to relinquish the attention, for as Celia is lowered into the chair they start to dance in the air. A ballet solo, in big black boots. Silly show-offs! Celia grimaces apologetically at the woman who has helped her and is now hovering watchfully a hundred feet above her head.

'Jetlag?' asks the woman, thrusting an open cigarette packet at Celia.

'Er, no, thank you,' says Celia.

The woman puts the packet in her pocket and folds herself down on the floor at Celia's feet. 'So how does it feel to be back in England?' she smiles.

Cold hands grip the back of Celia's neck. She gulps, and two thumbs press a pathway through the muscles which stand firm as rock formations on either side of Celia's spine.

'Are you a bit tense?' comes a voice from behind Celia's head. Celia jumps.

'No, why?' she says, tersely.

'We scared you, didn't we?' says the voice.

Celia cranes her head backwards and sees a ceiling. She twists it sideways and sees walls. She turns her whole body around and sees a woman with glasses grinning at her over the back of the armchair. The woman's eyes are invisible behind the lenses which wink and blink in the party light.

'You nearly hit the roof,' she is saying.

'So?' says Celia.

The woman leans on her elbows on the back of the armchair and says, as if it wasn't the height of rudeness, 'What's your problem?'

'I beg your pardon?' says Celia.

'Well, that wasn't a normal reaction, was it?' says the woman with glasses. 'Come on, don't tease. Name your neurosis.'

'I don't know what that means,' says Celia. 'You just made me jump, that's all.'

'Weren't you expecting all this?' asks the woman.

'No,' says Celia.

'Not even a sneaking suspicion?' asks the woman.

'No!' says Celia.

'Why not?' asks the woman. 'Don't you think you're worthy?'

She has strummed Celia's heartstrings and struck a chord. It must be a minor chord, so melancholy is Celia's answer. 'If you must know,' Celia says, 'I thought she hated me.'

'Who?' says the woman. 'Not Phoebe? What a revelation!'

Her glasses steam up. She rummages in a hectic handbag for a handkerchief, but brings out a notebook and pencil instead. She turns the pages till she finds a clean one, and then looks at Celia with pencil poised and mouth moving.

'Slow down, Nat,' says the first woman, who is still sitting at Celia's feet, 'she's just this second in from the States, remember.'

'Yes, thank you,' says Nat, imposing her insensitive self on the arm of Celia's armchair. 'Is that why you're so wired up?'

Celia glares up at the woman whose glasses are glaring down at her. The lenses have cleared, but Celia still can't see her eyes.

'It's not me,' Celia says angrily. 'It's not me who's in a state. It's you. And you,' she glances at the woman on the floor. 'How can this be my surprise party if I don't know any of the guests?'

165

'We know you,' says Nat, 'that's how. Now tell me how you feel about the party, *per se*.'

'Surprised,' says Celia, still rather loudly. 'Busy. I've already got one on the go downstairs. I suppose I'll be juggling them like balls for the rest of the evening. And please don't call me Percy.'

Nat looks like she's struck gold. Mad gold, her favourite sort. Her glasses gleam. 'Relax,' she says. 'I'm a nurse. I can help you.'

'How?' demands Celia. 'Have you got a hostess trolley that can go up and down stairs?'

'No,' says Nurse Nat.

'Well, a fat lot of good you'll be then,' mutters Celia.

'Why were you so frightened when you came through the door?' says Nat.

'I don't like doors any more,' says Celia.

She chews off a fingernail.

'They're all one-way, this evening. There's no going back,' she adds, and drops the nail into a crack between two cushions.

'What do you mean?' asks Nat.

Celia sighs fretfully, and stares past Nat at Phoebe's party. It's pretty, prettier than the pastel blush of hers, and the animated technicolor of Cath's. It is a picture painted in red wine and gold dust, charcoal and white chocolate; it's textured and rich in detail and . . . Celia frowns as, somewhere in her subconscious mind, some third eye spots that everyone at Phoebe's party is a woman. There are no men. This fact doesn't cross her main mind, though she continues to scrutinise the party as if it were a still life, stiller than Cath's, more alive than her own.

'Tell me about your childhood,' Nat says, beaming bloodthirstily.

'Why?' answers Celia. 'Can't you see it for yourself, four-eyes?'

On the floor the first woman starts to smirk. 'Oh artful!' she splutters, 'crafty!'

166

Nat gets off the arm of Celia's chair in a huff.

'You're all the same, you bloody clever-clever culture-clogs,' she stammers, incoherent with indignation. 'You think you know everything; but if you don't know yourselves, and I can see that you don't, you don't know anything!' With an angry flash of her spectacles, Nat walks away.

'God speed,' snorts the first woman, watching Nat's stiff-shouldered retreat. Then, turning to Celia, she adds, 'That was exactly the sort of one-liner that's made you famous.'

Famous?

Celia stares in a paranoid panic.

Famous?

It would seem that someone has been talking about her behind her back. It would seem that she has a reputation which has gone before her. In her confusion, Celia's stare becomes a glare, and the woman on the receiving end begins to blink in it.

'I'm sorry,' she stutters. 'Let me introduce myself. I'm a colleague of Phoebe's. And I'm one of your biggest fans. Harrier . . .' she thrusts her hand at Celia.

'Hello . . . Harriet?' says Celia, her own offered hand as uncertain and unsteady as her voice.

'No, it's Harrier,' smiles Harrier, 'and I'd like to take this opportunity to welcome you back home. Fans are foaming at the mouth to meet you – those of us here this evening represent the really rabid elite of your following – and words can't express how fab it feels to be the first to shake you firmly by the hand.'

'Are you pulling my leg?' says Celia.

On the floor, Harrier lies down with laughter. Celia snatches her feet out of the way and tucks them underneath herself in the armchair. This Harrier woman must be mistaken. Mistaken or mad. Indeed this laugh she is laughing is the laugh of a maniac;

167

single-minded but many-mouthed, and coming from more than one direction at once. Celia, in the armchair, is surrounded by it. She sinks into cushions, shrinking from the brink of another Hitchcock movie. She claps her hands to her ears. The clapping doesn't stop. It carries on, like the laughter. It grows and grows until it could almost be called applause.

Then Celia sees the crowd that has gathered around the armchair.

Yes, a crowd has gathered around the armchair. Faces fawn at Celia over the arms of the chair; and, five rows deep, the throng has arranged itself so that all the tall ones are standing at the back.

Then Celia sees the silver on every woman's chest: a circle, a cross, low-slung on shiny black ribbon; every single one the same as the pendant between her own breasts.

Under her wig Celia's hair strains to stand on end. How come they're all wearing what she's wearing? And how did they all know what she would be wearing, when she put it on (on a whim) only minutes ago, and they've been here waiting for hours? And why have they been waiting for her, somewhere she stumbled upon by accident? What do they want with her? How do they even know who she is?

Something supernatural is happening all around this purple armchair and Celia is trapped. Out of control. Simultaneously claustrophobic and insecure.

Supertrapped!

'I'm stuck in a low-level job while younger male colleagues leapfrog me for promotion. What can I do?'

The comment comes from the vicinity of Celia's left elbow, but before she can focus on any of the faces lined up along the arm of the armchair other voices begin to clamber over each other, clamouring for attention. Celia listens in stunned silence.

'Stand up straighter!'

'That's no problem. I'm trapped in a high-rise flat. I can't get a job without child care and I can't afford child care without a job.'

'Kill your children. It's a good career move. Ow! No, I'm only joking!'

'Excuse me . . .'

'No, I *am* only joking.'

'Is anyone laughing?'

Celia turns her head from side to side, like a spectator at a tennis match, trying to see who's speaking. Then another voice interrupts like an umpire from somewhere in the middle.

'Excuse me,' it says, 'can I ask . . . When you said to Nat, and I quote, "Can't you see it for yourself, four-eyes", did you mean that your childhood is still current?'

There is a pause, but no one answers the question, and the voices at Celia's elbows resume their rally.

'Look, I'd never kill a kid. Not even of the goaty variety. It was a joke!'

'Yeah, but I bet you use contraception.'

'Excuse me . . . can I continue . . . And were you, by extension, suggesting that we never stop being children?'

The inbetween voice comes again with another of its complicated questions, but now those on either side of Celia don't give it space.

'Don't give me that crap,' the loudest one is saying. 'If contraception were murder it would be called murder. And it's not. It's called contraception.'

'Excuse me . . . can I finish . . .' The flat tones of the middle voice are all but drowned out. 'And did you deliberately sharpen the point into a veritable weapon with your use of the childish term of abuse, four-eyes?'

'What's in a name?' comes a cry from Celia's right. 'That which we call a condom, by any other name could strangle someone with a smallish neck.'

'But if there's a neck already it's too late for contraception, you complete cretin,' howls someone to Celia's left. 'If there's a neck, it's murder. But if the act in question occurs before conception it can't be murder. Because there's nothing to murder. Because there's nothing. No neck, smallish or otherwise.'

Celia, whipping her head from side to side, is in danger of breaking her own slender neck, as the volley of voices picks up speed.

'There's the possibility of something.'

'But you can't murder a possibility.'

'Course you can. You can nip it in the bud.'

'Yeah, you can murder anything you want to. And I want to murder you.'

'Yes, but I'm more than a possibility. I'm actually happening.'

'You flatter yourself.'

'And you're talking bollocks.'

'Hey, come on, I'm a talking cunt.'

From somewhere behind Celia someone gives a great shout: 'Girls, girls, consider our guest!'

But the speaker at Celia's left elbow is not put off.

'With pleasure,' she says, looking at Celia in a funny way.

At this, everyone in the crowd says something at once.

'Shut up.'

'You silly cow.'

'Your favourite person in the whole world is sitting right in front of you, and what do you do?'

'Make vain boasts and bicker on about bugger all.'

'So has anyone got something interesting to say?'

'Or are we just going to listen to mouth-almighty showing herself up all night – '

'When we can do that any day of the week.'

There is the briefest of pauses. Then someone at the back sticks a hand up and says, 'Yes, er, I'd like to ask, actually – are there any instances in which you would condone murder?'

There is no doubt about it. This question is directly addressed to Celia. She had a horrible feeling that a couple of the earlier questions were meant for her; but happily, now as then, other voices shout their way into her silence.

'Yes! There are!'

'How do you know?'

'I've seen the films.'

'So?'

'The odd character does get away with the odd murder.'

'That doesn't mean she condones it.'

'An "eye for an eye" mentality rears its ugly head at certain moments.'

'It might not be her personal opinion.'

'Oh come off it. If you had her job, you wouldn't spend your time and energy presenting other people's points of view. Especially if you didn't agree with them.'

'But she can't believe everything she's ever said!'

'Why not?'

'Well, because she's said everything. She can't believe it all. She'd be very confused. Incoherent, even.'

Suddenly, everyone looks at Celia; but almost everyone was looking at her already, so she doesn't notice any difference.

'Off the top of my head,' says Harrier to Celia's feet, 'I can only think of one instance where you advocate murder.'

'I can think of two,' says the woman at Celia's left elbow.

'Look, will you shut up or fuck off,' comes an angry voice from the back. They are all big at the back, and the little woman with the large mouth shrinks behind the arm of the chair.

'Am I right in thinking,' says Harrier slowly, 'that you would condone the murder of a rapist?'

There is silence. Everyone is staring at Celia.

'Who, me?' she says. Her voice is hoarse from not having spoken for so long.

'Yes,' says Harrier.

'I don't know,' says Celia.

'See!' says the voice at her elbow, triumphantly.

'I don't think so,' says Celia. It is a neigh.

There is an uproar: everyone roars at once. There is an uprising: everyone gets bigger and stiffer of hairdo. There is an upshot: Celia's bottom lip begins to wobble. She draws a shaky breath and raises a hand to her eyes which are starting to smart with tears. But the hand never gets there. It stops, suspended in space, as Celia sees that, at this slightest of gestures, the group has fallen abruptly and absolutely silent.

Celia's hand lands limp in her lap.

'Er, thank you,' she says quietly. 'Please, can you tell me who you are.'

'One by one?' trills a thrilled voice from somewhere in the crowd.

'Only if you don't want me to cry,' says Celia, and everyone laughs.

One by one, a hundred hands reach out of the crowd to shake Celia's; cold hands, dry hands, warm and wet hands, fingers with rings, fingers with nails, one hand with no fingers, two with too many. And one by one, the women introduce themselves to Celia: Sarah, staring; Charlotte, heartfelt; Fanny, adamantly; Emma,

172

embarrassed; Jo, joking; Connie, keenly; Brenda, on bended knee; Patience, after all these years. Celeste, student; Helen, tobacconist; Amanda, administration; Glenda, Labour Party; Melissa, microwave engineer; Liz, poet; 'Psycho', therapist; Dawn, French.

'Have we met before?' says Celia, as the waves of now friendly faces which wash over her form themselves occasionally into familiar features. And sometimes someone says something about a festival in 1988, a conference in 1990, a residential course in California, but no one seems cross when Celia can't quite recall the occasion.

On the contrary, everyone is pleased with her: Hilary loves her sense of humour, Rita wants to write a book about her, Gwen even goes so far as to say she should be knighted. One woman pats her knee warmly, one ruffles her wig, one envelops her entirely in a big hug.

Celia wonders what she's done to deserve this.

She skims the surface of the armchair, while the women inflate her with love like air. The more they admire her, the higher she gets. There is only one thing holding her in her seat, only one string attached: one little voice at the back of her head is insisting that all the others are lying. They haven't a clue who Celia is, and if they had they wouldn't like her.

Celia slaps her neck, half expecting to find Nat buzzing around behind her again. But there is nothing there and the negative thoughts don't stop. They seem to be coming from another place, a previous place, and the longer they go on the more Celia wonders if the previous place is her proper place.

But Celia can't remember where she was before she was here. In fact, Celia can't even remember why she is calling herself Celia. Everyone appears to think that her name is Hebe; and frankly, she

173

can find no firm grounds on which to contradict them. So she sits still on the shifting sands of the armchair, and takes no notice of the deep-seated statements that are trying to bring her down. Stairs. That are trying to bring her downstairs.

Everyone wants her autograph. She signs her name as Hebe on the backs of hands and envelopes. At first she does it in her old small Celia writing. The Hs are straightforward, the es are neat, and the bs are not very big. Then slowly but surely, her handwriting becomes more mighty as she starts to use her pen like a sword. Now, the Hs look like avenues of copper beech trees, the es resemble rare ammonites; and the way she does the bs makes her new name look like the score of a symphony in that key. Celia's writing is growing to fit Hebe.

Someone asks her to sign it on the corner of a stiff white teatowel; tugging it and tugging it to get enough room to write on she finds that the teatowel is fixed firmly to the someone's head. All at once Celia is staring deep into the hundred eyes of the nun she saw from a safer distance at the start of her surprise party.

The nun stares back steadily, but with her head held at an alarmingly acute angle. Celia screams.

'I knew it,' says the nun. 'I knew it! You suffer from nun-phobia, an irrational fear of nuns. Was that the unconscious process which produced the film *NunAware?*'

'Sorry?' says Celia, swallowing the rest of her scream in surprise.

'Hold your horses, Hebe,' says Harrier. 'What's that line from *The Name of the Film*? Ah yes,' she strikes a pose: ' "Love is never having to apologise for your own unconscious processes." '

'Sorry?' says Celia.

'You're sorry?' says Sarah, the small one at Celia's elbow. 'So you don't practise what you preach, then?'

174

'Pardon?' says Celia.

'Do you practise what you preach?' says Sarah, louder, but not quite loud enough to drown out the sound of someone at the back saying, 'She's not half the woman she was in San Francisco.'

Celia doesn't preach. The question doesn't apply to her. She passes it on to the nun.

'Do you?' Celia asks her, letting go of the wimple.

The nun straightens up. 'I', she says, a little stiffly, 'am all practice and no preaching.'

The audience laughs.

But Celia shushes them. Her head is on one side now, considering the nun carefully.

'Well then,' she says, 'what do you need a costume for?'

'It is the uniform of my sisterhood,' says the nun severely; but then her face softens as she draws a cross and circle like Celia's from the deepest folds of her robe, and says, 'As, I might add, is this.'

'So,' struggles Celia, thinking hard, 'if you practised in jeans, say, would you still be perfect?'

She speaks in all innocence, but the audience cheer as if she had deliberately scored some sort of goal.

'My dear young woman,' says the nun, 'did I say anything about being perfect?'

'No,' says Celia, 'but that's what you get when you practise all the time.'

The audience start to clap their hands slowly.

The nun shrugs her shrouded shoulders. 'I'm the same as you,' she says.

Celia is suddenly red in the face, as red as her wig. When she speaks, her voice is bashful too.

'Oh no you're not,' she says. 'I've got carnal knowledge. Not much, I'll admit. But I'd like some more.'

175

Members of the audience clutch other members of the audience. All the air goes into everyone's gulps.

'And you don't want any at all,' adds Celia.

'That's right,' says the nun.

'Why?' asks Celia.

The nun clears her throat.

'To be nearer to God,' she says.

'So we're not the same,' says Celia. 'God prefers you to me.' She pauses, and then adds in an aside to the audience, 'I've never had much luck with men!'

The audience like this. They laugh loud and long, but the nun shouts them down.

'That's not true. We are equal in His eyes,' she says.

The nun is scary, like a crow; big, black and flapping in front of the sun, casting shadows over the slopes and planes of Celia's armchair.

But Celia ploughs on. 'God wouldn't want every woman to be a nun though, would He?' she says. And then she adds, in another aside, 'Unless He's gay, of course. And let's face it, girls, all the best men are.'

The audience bends in half and holds its sides and wipes its streaming eyes. Celia smiles. So she is sparkling tonight, after all. All she's ever wanted is to be the belle of a ball. It was well worth waiting for.

'Ladies, please,' the nun shouts over the laughter, 'He'd like you at least to try for perfection.'

'But if perfection means not having sex, some people must be imperfect. Otherwise we wouldn't reproduce,' protests Celia. 'We'd die out! Is that what He wants?'

The nun stares at Celia and her lips move silently for several seconds.

176

'Yes, I think it probably is,' she says at last.

Celia slams back against the back of the armchair, aghast.

'Look,' says the nun, 'you clearly haven't a clue about Christianity. There are certain rules to play by. In the privacy of my own prayer I know that although anyone is free to abstain from sex and be nearer to God, there are not many who are prepared to take Him up on the offer. It is only the fact that most people don't believe that makes these acts of faith possible for those of us who do.'

'Blimey,' says someone in the crowd, 'you're a bit radical.'

The nun nods, and her stern eyes nearly smile.

'Well, that's what I've come about,' she says. 'The film *NunAware* changed my life. For the first time, I was forced to admit to myself that the thing I believe in might not actually exist.'

'But you haven't renounced your nun-ness. Like they did in the film,' Harrier butts in.

'No, because I think the film made a mistake,' the nun hurries on. 'That's what I'd like to discuss. Is it wiser to accept the fact that God isn't really . . . you know . . . up there, or to reject him in favour of some new false truth of . . . well, let's say sexual equality, as that is the thrust of the film.'

'But equality *is* the truth! The only truth!' comes a voice from the back.

'And lies arise only when you try to persuade me that you are better or more important than I am!' another chimes in.

'God is like politicians: the one who wants the position most badly is the one most likely to abuse its power.'

'Is "God" the guy's name or his job description, anyway?'

A theological free-for-all is threatening, but the nun stops it with a shout like a thunderbolt.

'I've come a long way to speak to Hebe today,' she cries, 'and that is what I intend to do. If you don't mind. Now then,' she turns to Celia, 'I'd like to question you on another matter. In *NunAware* the part of the Mother Superior is played by a man in "drag". What on earth was the meaning of that?'

Celia wishes that these women wouldn't keep asking her questions about films she's never seen. She wishes she had either the strength of character to own up to her ignorance or the sheer insolence to bluff her way out of it. But all she ever has to fall back on in times like these is her automatic deference to authority.

'Well, what do *you* think?' she asks the nun.

The nun purses her lips. She has a slight problem with unsightly facial hair, Celia notices.

'I think it's a cop-out,' the nun says, 'an easy option. You couldn't be bothered to ask a real Mother Superior about the sexual subtleties of her belief, so you simply assumed that anyone who takes God's word as law must metaphorically be male too. I think you're overrated, Hebe; never mind condoning murder, I think you're getting away with it!'

By way of a reply to the nun's accusation, Celia makes an awkward attempt to unmask her as an impostor. She grabs hold of a corner of the stiff white teatowel on the nun's head, and pulls and pulls until she pulls it off. The nun's hair is going grey. It is tousled from the tugging, and lustreless from lack of sunshine. The nun's hair is long.

'We're all sisters under the skin-tight headwear,' says the nun, looking pointedly at Celia's short red curls.

'I'm sorry. I shouldn't have done that,' says Celia; but because she and the nun both speak at once no one hears either of them.

Then there is a commotion in the crowd.

'Make way ... coming through ... make way ... thank

you . . .' The top of Phoebe's head bobs up and down in the audience. Her hand, holding aloft a cup of coffee, carves a passageway to Celia in the armchair. Celia is relieved to see it. On coming closer, Phoebe explains why it has taken so long to provide Celia with refreshment.

'It's a madhouse out there. Don't venture out of this room alone. Be in twos or threes at least. If the infernal noise doesn't get you, all along the landing there are people lining the walls like idiots and acting like animals. The stairs are a descent into hell. In the kitchen, would you believe, I had to stop a rape before I could start to make the coffee.'

No one is sure that they do believe it. It sounds a bit too much like one of Phoebe's sick jokes. No one knows her well enough to detect the desperation in her casual tone, the depression in her laughter.

Someone decides that they'd better change the subject.

'Your sister is something else,' says an anonymous voice, as the crowd parts to admit Phoebe to the central armchair area, then closes protectively behind her.

'I know,' smiles Phoebe, handing Celia a hot mug.

'Your sister has just pulled off a piece of practical deconstruction,' says Harrier, taking the nun's crumpled wimple and waving it at Phoebe.

Celia looks from the wimple to the nun, and wonders why Harrier thinks the Sister belongs to Phoebe.

Pheobe sits down in Celia's lap, and knocks the wind out of her.

'She's brilliant in bed too, by all accounts,' says Phoebe proudly.

Celia stares at the Sister with an open mouth. So she was wrong all along: nuns do have sexual intercourse. But the nun is still looking Celia straight in the eye. Everyone is looking Celia straight in the eye.

'What are you looking at me for?' says Celia.

She feels Phoebe stiffen in her lap.

'For a thrill, if that's all right with you,' says a voice to her right.

'For research purposes,' says a voice to her left, 'to see how closely your relationship with Phoebe corresponds to the portrayal of sisters in your films.'

'But I haven't got any films,' says Celia, confused and frightened now. 'I haven't got any sisters. I'm only a child . . . I mean, I'm an only child.'

Then there is chaos.

'What the . . .?' shouts Phoebe, scrambling off Celia's lap, grabbing her by the chin and forcing her face up into the light of furious scrutiny.

'Fuck, it's Celia!' Phoebe continues. 'Fucking . . . *Fuck*! What in the name of God are you doing disguised as my sister?'

Celia's wig has come off in Phoebe's hand. She tosses it in Celia's face and turns away in disgust. The audience are stone silent. Most of them are speechless with shock at the unmasking of this Celia, this most insidious impostor; the others are more disturbed by Phoebe's subsequent language.

Celia has a lump in her throat, so she can't speak either. She didn't know that Phoebe didn't know it was her here. She thought that Phoebe thought that it was. She thought she heard Phoebe say the surprise party was specially for her.

Celia is such a fool. She knew that Phoebe wouldn't usually give her the time of day. Why should tonight be different just because she's getting engaged? Why should Phoebe suddenly turn out to be her best friend and greatest fan? Why did she think they were calling her Hebe? Celia's not part of this party at all. But she was having such a good time till Phoebe came back. It was everything she'd hoped her proper party would be. While they thought she was Hebe, the guests smiled at her and spoke to her and listened to her answers. And Celia actually had something to say for herself, her conversation shone. All the guests wanted to meet her, or was that only because they thought she was Hebe?

So now, Celia can't say a word.

Celia has a lump in her throat, because she is the littlest girl in the whole wide world and none of the big girls want to be her sister.

Phoebe is recovering her composure just as Celia is completely losing hers.

'Sorry everyone,' Phoebe says to the stunned crowd, 'this is only Celia. She's just someone who lives in the house.'

A few boos and hisses brave the air as the crowd breathe out.

'Please take your places again,' says Phoebe, 'we'll have to start from scratch. The real Hebe has not yet come. The real surprise has not yet been sprung. The real party has not yet begun.'

'But Phoebe,' the woman called Brenda butts in, 'it's gone one o'clock. It looks like she's not going to show up.'

A couple of silly moos in the crowd boo again.

'Her flight may be delayed,' says Phoebe, 'she's coming straight from the airport.'

'But Phoebe,' tries someone else, 'we can't sit in silence and darkness all night. She'll be surprised enough as it is, don't you think, when she walks in and finds us all . . . here.'

'And another thing,' notes another nameless speaker, 'the surprise caused something of an adverse reaction in rehearsal; we don't want to scare the hair off your real sister, do we?'

'That wasn't a rehearsal, it was an accident, okay?' shouts Phoebe. 'Give me *some* credit for spontaneity!'

And as if to demonstrate this quality in herself, and entirely failing to do so, Phoebe throws herself into the crowd and disappears in the direction of the light switch.

'Oh, Phoebe!' Harrier wails plaintively, 'we're not having much fun. This is turning out to be all surprise and no party.'

Phoebe's voice is frayed at the edges as she shouts back, 'Well, whose idea was it, Harrier? Tell me that. Not mine, I think you'll find.' But then, from farther away, she adds, 'Nevertheless, I want it to be perfect. Reload your party poppers, everyone!'

And suddenly the party and all the people are plunged into blackness. Celia gasps. Other gasps and assorted exclamations pierce the depths of the darkness like swords or fish.

'Hey, who turned the lights off?'

'Someone's blown a bloody fuse!'

'Who's that sitting on my face?'

'Anyone got a bob for the meter?'

'Ain't no one named Bob here, ma'am!'

Then someone laughs like a mad axe-man and everyone else screams. Most of them are only pretending, but there is one who is serious.

'Ssshhhhh!' Phoebe's testy tones are unmistakable, even in a whisper. 'If she hears us before she comes through the door it won't be a surprise any more.'

Most of the screams subside into tuts and mutters of discomfort and dissent, but there is one which goes on and on like a whistle in an old-fashioned emergency.

'Celia?' says Phoebe. 'Celia! If you can't keep quiet, you'd better go back to your own party and bloody well get engaged.'

Celia's thin tin-whistle scream stops.

There is a sharp intake of breath in the darkness.

And someone says,

'Engaged?'
And someone says,
'What, to a man?'
And someone says,
'What, to be married?'
And someone says,
'What do you want to do that for?'
And Phoebe says,
'Oh no, here we go . . .'

Her party has spontaneously started quoting from her sister's most recent film, *Wet Wendy*, and she is powerless to prevent its impromtu performance of Hebe's famous musical interlude on the subject of marriage.

'Shut up everyone!' says Phoebe, in a last-ditch attempt to stop them sliding down the slippery slope to song. 'Shut the fuck up!'

But her guests are beginning to bang out a beat on the backs of chairs and the tops of tables and the dusty rugs.

One of them hums the introduction, and after four bars all the women start to sing; softly at first then slowly coming to a shattering crescendo.

'You are single, Wendy,' her sister said,
'and you could stay up all night;
and yet at ten-thirty you hurry to bed –
Do you think, at your age, it is right?'

'When I wed,' Wendy replied to her sis,
'I will be expected to do it;
Early to bed equals marital bliss,
I'm getting acclimatised to it.'

'You are single,' said sis, 'as I mentioned before,
And are warmly and comfortably fat;

Yet you discourse on diets and constantly bore –
Pray, what is the reason for that?'

'When I wed,' said Wendy, as she wobbled her flab,
'My obsession with eating will stop;
Because I'll be happy and life will be fab,
and hubby will pay for the op.'

'But they cut out your stomach and wire your jaws,'
said her sister in utter disgust,
'They don't mention that in the conjugal laws –
are you really quite sure that you must?'

'When I wed,' said Wendy, 'I will be a wife
to put all the others to shame;
Into his hands I will put the knife,
if he should see fit to maim.'

'You are mad,' said her sis, 'I am led to believe
that this bastard has driven you nuts;
Call off the engagement, get a reprieve,
and alter the fate of your guts.'

'I know you're just jealous 'cos you want him too,'
said Wendy, 'so get off my case!
You're no sis of mine, and I'm not telling you
what he's planning to do to my face!'

There is a climax in the penultimate verse. The door from the hall
flicks open and a blade of light falls across Phoebe's party floor.
There is a climax as a real redhead steps into this shaft and is lit
from behind, lit like the second coming. There is a climax as the
real redhead drops her suitcase and falls to her knees on the floor.
It is a multiple climax.

Most of the women manage to keep singing till the end of the song, though Phoebe is flooding the room with light and detonating the party poppers and dancing with streamers around her real sister.

Celia, with her wig back on, watches over the back of the armchair. She sees Hebe arriving at her surprise party all over again. She is surprised by Hebe's beauty, her grace, the size of her suitcase, the scruffiness of her clothes.

But she is not surprised that Phoebe loves her. Because Hebe isn't screaming like Celia did. She's smiling.

Celia scrutinises this new arrival for the secret of her success. Her eyes zoom in on the third finger of Hebe's left hand, looking for significant rings.

But the sudden movement is too much for her, the shock is catching up with her, and her own mind has had enough of her.

Celia swoons.

7.

I

Dodge frocks up again

In the cold kitchen, in the aftermath of the Mad Hatter's tea-party, Dodge is making a pot of hot coffee. Dodge has never made coffee in the kitchen before, but Kenneth has asked for it, and Ken thinks Dodge is Celia.

Yes, thanks to Dodge's flawless female impersonation, Ken thinks Celia's making coffee. But Dodge is making the coffee for the female he is impersonating. He's making it for poor flawless Celia. She's had an awful shock. Her nerves must be shattered.

She could sue him if she wanted to.

Dodge's hand shakes, hot water splashes; scars, like stretch marks, spatter the silk stomach of Celia's best dress.

He has spoilt it. Like he would have spoilt Celia, if Phoebe hadn't come to get a drink for her sister in the nick of time. Because Dodge was just lying there, spread-eagled and silent on the kitchen floor, all set to sully Celia in his attempt to achieve womanhood. On her engagement night!

'I'm sorry,' he sighs, after a big swig of the bitter brew.

'So you should be,' says Ken, from the bottom of the table.

'I wasn't talking to you,' says Dodge.

186

'Well, it's about time you did,' scolds Ken.

Despite this apparent animation, Ken seems still to be in the grip of a strange sleep. He is holding his heavy head off the table by a handful of his own hair; like a hanged man, lifeless but not lying down. His eyes follow Dodge around the kitchen, but every time Dodge looks back Ken's eyelids drop dead. When he speaks it is so indistinct that it might as well be snoring.

'Sugar?' says Dodge; and then, softer, 'Shit!' If he is Celia he should know whether or not Ken takes sugar. But Ken is much too sleepy to spot the mistake. Dodge puts a mug of coffee in front of him, clanging a spoon against the sides like a school dinner-lady.

'Here's your coffee,' Dodge says.

Kenneth's hand twitches on the table. Dodge slides the coffee closer. 'It's right by your hand,' he says, 'your right hand.'

'So I thought,' slurs Ken, 'but it snuck away while I wasn't looking.'

Dodge pushes the cup across the table till it touches Ken's thumb. Ken pulls his thumb back as if it's been burnt.

'Don't,' he whimpers. 'I know it's not real. So don't try to persuade me otherwise. I've been caught like that before.' Ken jams his thumb between his lips, and the elbow which has been propping him upright flies into the air. Without its support, Ken's head hits the top of the table, narrowly missing his mug of coffee. A startled snore is his only response to this new position.

Dodge sits down next to him. 'Can you hear me?' he asks.

Ken snores again, and it could be a snort of sarcastic laughter, but Dodge can't be sure. He stares in silence at the head lolling sideways on the table. Ken's sensible haircut has gone silly with sweat, and his eyeballs are rolling rapidly behind pallid lids.

'I can hear,' mumbles Ken, 'but it's not you.'

Dodge's Celia-face falls. Ken has seen through him. Even with his eyes shut, even in this soporific state, Ken knows that this isn't Celia sitting next to him in Celia's evening dress. Dodge's face falls, but Ken rises in his estimation. Perhaps the man is not such a dickhead after all.

'How did you know it wasn't Celia, then?' asks Dodge.

'I didn't,' mutters Ken, 'but I do now.'

Dodge flings himself backwards in his chair. Blast! Ken has called his bluff, and he has blown his cover. Dodge has confessed unnecessarily, and foiled his own plot to persuade Celia's boyfriend that he is her. How dull. Dodge stares at the ceiling and stifles a yawn.

'I did it with her, but it wasn't Celia,' snores Ken suddenly.

Dodge's chair lands back on four legs with a bump.

'What did you say?' he asks.

'Don't tell Celia,' snores Ken.

'What have you done?' Dodge asks.

'I did it with a lady,' snores Ken. Spit spills onto the table.

'Who? When? How?' says Dodge, straining forward in his seat.

'I was looking for Celia!' Ken's snore is indignant and he heaves his head up and opens his heavy eyes. 'Oh, there you are,' he mutters as his eyes meet Dodge's briefly before he slumps back into his original prone position.

Things are more complicated than Dodge thought. Kenneth seems to be in a bit of bother. Is this why he was held in the so-called custody of the Hatter and the Hare? Is this why he can't tell whether Dodge is Celia or not? As Dodge stares at him in confusion, Ken snores a troubled sigh. Dodge sighs in sympathy, and stretches out his hand to smooth the hair from the snarls of the fiancé's feverish forehead. Ken shudders and says, 'Can we talk?'

'I think we'd better,' says Dodge.

'I was looking forever for Celia everywhere,' says Ken. 'Everywhere I looked was in vain because it was empty and she is not particularly pretty. Well, one of the mothers said I was to go upstairs and I went upstairs and suddenly it was all people. There was a party. I had known that there was going to be a party and I was prepared for it. I had brushed my clothes, and was wearing hair.

'People were playing music but there weren't proper words. But ha! there were words with me and a White Rabbit. In his shell, like. I assume we danced. I assume he stuck a long needle-thin in me, and I assume he stole my wallet. Right there in front of everybaby! But as luck would fuck it I'd taken the picture out, the picture of Celia, that was in my wallet, that was. And I raised my hand above the high crowds, but it was dark, and the photograph was more black than white, and I did declare, "I look for Celia!"

'One day of the night, one person of the party stood at my feet and pointed in a direction which smiled and said, "She's over there and who are you supposed to be?" I thought this was rude, even though it didn't have its bottom showing like I did, so I stuck my tongue all the way into its smile. Even though it wasn't Celia. Ha!

'I went over there and there she wasn't. And it was hot *hot* at the party and people were melting in the music and some of them were minced on the floor which was scared because I thought it might happen to be me. And, it sounds stupid cow, everything was twosomes and somesomes were several and they all had holes in the middle. One of them had to be Celia. So, I stuck my fun in a few of them and when they weren't Celia they went louder and I had to pull the photography out and unroll it inch by inch because their boyfriends banged my eardrums so loud they should be in a banned.

189

'And finally, when I was nearly flying my face off with frust, a crustacean said "She is under the table."

'I ran to the under the table but I was too tall, I tell you. I beat on it with both bums. Suddenly, hands came out from underneath and took me by the feet. It was dark under the table, but it was Celia through and through. Phew! Found at last!

'Celia is great. She is gymnastic. She bent over backwards to be pleased to see me. I tried to ask her why she had run away to see. Why she had run away. To see if she was willing to come back to the dessert. But something was wrong with the way the words were coming out and she said I was not altogether in English. But that was nothing compared to the nonsense she came out with about not being Celia.

' "Nonsense," I cried, "I know Celia when I Celia!"

'Then it was her turn to cry. Well I say cry, she was properly screaming!

'Within a matter of minutes my trousers were terrified and trying to come off. I hurried to help her remove her dress too, frightened little bit of flimsy that it was, for she was bellowing, "Get off! Get off!" at the bottom of her voice. But I couldn't get the frock off fast enough for her; it was frozen with fear, and some of the buttons got pulled off in the panic. Well, by this time she was everywhere. She came at me with open legs. Her body was all over my hands. She rammed herself at my rod, so soft I thought she would swallow me up. Her head hit the floor hard, she was really giving it what for; and "Stop!" she shouted like a PE teacher. "Stop!"

'But there was no stopping her. She kicked and bit and scratched and screamed; and strongly as I support women's rights to active participation in sexual intercourse, this was rapidly turning out to be the most unsatisfactory session I had ever had.

Then, just as Celia was squeezing her throat into my hands in a frenzied attempt to shut herself up, a pair of big black boots blatted on the carpet beside us, and a bit squatting bulk blotted out the light to our little lovenest. At last, Celia lay still. And a woman in a pinny and a floppy white hat pulled me out from under the table and shit the beat out of me with a wooden spoon.

'While this cook-looking woman was braising and battering me, Celia crawled out from under the table and her face was wet and her dress was bleeding.

' "I'm not Celia," she shouted; "and even if I were I wouldn't be any more, not after this. I'll see you in court!"

'And I couldn't see her much longer because my eyes were too short, because animal-men and a mushroom caught me and carried me out of the room and threw me thumpety-bumpety down the stairs; but I believed that she wasn't Celia, because even if she had been she wasn't any more. Not after that.'

Kenneth gives a fretful sigh and stares sadly at Dodge. 'I've bad a been boy,' he says.

'So it would seem', says Dodge.

'Yes,' nods Ken, 'and if I don't find Celia before the mothers and fathers find me, they'll make mince-me out of meat!'

Ken struggles to stand up, but Dodge lays a hand on each of his hot shoulders and holds him gently in his seat. It would seem, if Dodge has heard Ken's words correctly, that the White Rabbit spiked him with some sort of drug while he wandered in Wonderland in search of Celia. In his dreamlike state Ken mistook an innocent partygoer for Celia and forced himself on her under a table. Now Ken is slowly emerging from his strange sleep, but waking up is even weirder. He sits bolt upright, red eyes wide open, whipping his head from side to side in the hope that the stuff his surroundings are made of will soon make some sort of sense.

What he really wants to see is Celia, and it seems that any Celia will do. Dodge is happy to oblige, if he can only get Ken to focus on that blonde-and-blue outline, those curtains of hair and that lampshade of a skirt. If Ken thought Celia was sitting next to him, all warm and comfortable, perhaps he'd calm down a bit.

Or a nice cup of coffee; that might do the trick. Dodge picks up Ken's cup and throws its cooling contents in Ken's face. Ken finds this so invigorating that, before Dodge can even think about refilling it, the cup is snatched from his hand and dashed to pieces on the kitchen floor.

'Have you taken leave of your senses?' shouts Ken.

Dodge's eyes widen in astonishment.

'No,' he says, 'have you?'

'Oh that's rich! That's as rich as I am, that is!' shouts Ken. 'Who was the one who insulted and embarrassed everyone at our engagement party? Celia! Who was the one who went to serve the dessert and never came back? Celia! Who have we been looking for for *five hours*? Celia! Or am I mistaken? Was Celia standing at my right hand all along, and I'm the one with a screw loose?'

'She was there. She didn't leave the house. She didn't even look out of a window,' says Dodge, vehemently. Now he knows what an asshole this boyfriend is, he's not going to let Celia take any crap. She's got to learn to speak up for herself. But on the other hand, Ken is drug-crazed and dangerous, and the cup of coffee in his face seems to have revived some old burning anger. No, Dodge had better play Celia as realistically as he can, for, after what happened under the table upstairs, the discovery of a second false Celia could send Ken over the edge.

'What are you saying?' says Ken, expressionless.

'She was . . . I mean, I was waiting. I was waiting to be found. I

192

was wondering how long you would look for me for, before you gave up and went away,' stammers Dodge. He hopes this is what Celia would say. He thought all the while she was in his room that she was lingering a bit close to home; as if she wanted to see how her absence would affect her family and friends, to oversee her own funeral.

'Oh,' says Ken. 'It was one of your tests, was it? I was being tested, was I?'

Dodge shrugs his shoulders slightly. He is reluctant to commit Celia completely on this score.

'Well, when are you going to grow up, Celia?' shouts Ken. 'When, eh? This is our engagement do, dear. And we know what that means, don't we? Yes, you and I are going to be married. And why do people get married? To have children of their own! So it's time to start acting like an adult, Celia. This is not a game, girl. It's bloody expensive. And quite frankly, I find your test the height of bad taste, in the light of the amount of cash I've lavished on you and your dream evening.'

Dodge steps backwards and whispers into his wig, 'You've failed the test anyway, Ken; and no amount of bribery will make your bullshit taste any better.'

Kenneth comes forward, but luckily for Dodge he is still shouting at Celia, and doesn't stop to hear what she has to say.

'So where were you hiding then, tell me that,' Ken continues. 'To what depths of this dreadful house was I supposed to have stooped in my shining armour? From under which table was I supposed to have saved you?'

With these words Ken's self-confidence slips from him like unzipped trousers. 'Table? Table? Who said anything about a table?' he mutters, and a tic ticks in the corner of his eye.

Dodge is still damning Ken under his breath when Ken grabs

Celia by the shoulders and gushes in her face, 'Were you under a table?'

'What?' says Dodge.

'Where were you?' asks Ken.

'With Dodge, in his room,' says Dodge.

'What?' says Ken.

'I was with Dodge, across the hall, and if you really cared about me you would have knocked on the door to ask if he'd seen me!' says Dodge, and sounds so much like Celia that he tosses his head with pride.

'I see,' says Ken icily, 'and supposing I had knocked on the door, and supposing the door had been opened. What would I have found?'

'Me!' says Dodge.

'And?' says Ken.

'Dodge,' says Dodge.

'And what were you doing?' asks Ken.

'Nothing,' says Dodge. 'Talking.'

'What were you talking about?'

'Nothing.'

There is silence between them. All around them the house is in uproar, but there is silence between them.

'For five hours?' says Ken, eventually.

'No, not for five hours,' says Dodge.

Ken's forehead furrows. 'So. What else did you. Do?' he struggles.

'Nothing,' says Dodge, guiltily. It's he who has something to hide, not Celia; but it's all the same to her fiancé, who fears the worst.

Sweat breaks out on Ken's brow. 'So, tell me,' he says. 'This Dodge. He really cares about you, does he?'

'No!' gasps Dodge, 'not like that.'

'No?' says Ken. 'How come you spent the evening with him then, when you should have been getting engaged to me? How come you can tell me what a man who really cared about you would do? Because as far as I'm concerned, Celia, I'm the only one; but I think you're insinuating something, and I want to know what.'

'Ken . . .,' says Dodge.

'Are you having an affair with him?' shouts Ken.

Dodge can't help giving a dull laugh.

'Kenneth, Dodge is gay. There's nothing funny going on. Well, I say he's gay because he likes men, but in fact he is a woman, a straight and somewhat forward woman. Things are purely platonic between us; it's yourself you've got to watch out for!'

The look on Ken's face tells Dodge that he has overstepped the Celia mark by a mile.

'Did he give you that garbage?' says Ken.

'Er, yes,' says Dodge for Celia, 'but I wouldn't call it garbage.' Dodge isn't sure whether Celia thinks it's garbage or not. He didn't ask her.

'Where is he?' roars Ken.

'I don't know,' says Dodge.

'In his damn pervert room?' roars Ken.

'Er, no. He's out,' says Dodge, with the tiniest twitch of his top lip, the slightest sparkle in his eye.

All of a sudden, Ken stammers into song.

Dodge staggers backwards in surprise.

It sounds familiar. But it's not the sort of thing Dodge could join in with to tide them over the chasm of explaining to do; on the contrary, it seems that Ken is making it up as he goes along to guarantee himself a solo. Nevertheless, Dodge claps his hands in

something approximating to time, and does a couple of prim
Celia spins on the spot, as Ken sings:

> Twinkle, twinkle, little Celia;
> How I wonder what you really are!
> I see something in your eye,
> saying 'Ken, curl up and die!'
> Twinkle, twinkle, two-faced Celia;
> How I wonder who you really are!

Returning from his final spin, Dodge finds himself held up by the
shoulders again, like a shirt on a washing-line.

'So,' says Ken, breathing hard into his face, 'we're getting to
the bottom of it now. You danced. Then you went under the
table.'

'No,' says Dodge, 'I didn't go under a table. I didn't dance
either . . . Oh, I tell a lie, I did dance a bit actually.' Dodge
suddenly sees Celia in his mind's eye, dancing in his room in her
underwear; under the current circumstances, the memory makes
him blush.

Ken's red eyes grow rounder.

'You danced. Then you went under the table,' he repeats.

'Oh dear,' says Dodge quietly.

'With Dodge,' continues Ken.

Dodge is expecting another manic musical outburst at any
minute. But, instead, 'Tell me,' Ken says slowly, 'was this Dodge
pretending to be me?'

Dodge feels his eyes fill with tears. He can't believe it. He
hasn't cried for ages. The old familiar fizziness in the nose, the
sorrow that sticks in the throat and makes it impossible to
swallow; it all comes rushing back, with numbness and dumbness
hot on its heels.

Dodge can't speak in this situation. Ken, in his trousers and lace-up shoes, has the monopoly on making sense. Ken can say whatever he wants. But Dodge is wearing a dress. He's only got one leg to stand on, as opposed to Ken's two. It is an impediment.

'Did he force you?' asks Ken.

'Who?' Dodge whispers.

'The one under the table. This Dodge. The rapist. The one pretending to be me,' gabbles Ken.

'You've lost me,' says Dodge, without thinking, and immediately regrets it.

Ken wheels away and crashes into the big kitchen table.

'Under the table?' he cries, bending over and gesticulating wildly into the space in question. 'I lost you under the table?'

Dodge sobs. It is the only thing he can do without taking his dress off. And he can't take his dress off in front of Ken.

Even as he speaks Ken is rewriting the story and recasting the scene. In Ken's new scheme of things, it is no longer himself and someone who wasn't Celia under the table. It is Celia with someone who wasn't him. Cunning Ken is clearing his name, and frocked Dodge can't stop him.

'You were stolen, Celia,' Ken is shouting now, 'not lost. Stolen.'

Dodges doesn't say a word; he is thinking hard. He and Celia are about to get the blame for Ken's misdemeanour, and because Dodge is currently speaking for both of them, he can't answer for either. The two of them are locked in the same frock, like a couple of culprits handcuffed together; any attempt Dodge makes to rescue Celia's reputation from under the table might accidentally sever her relations with Ken, may even break off her engagement entirely.

Does Dodge have the right to act on Celia's behalf, just because he is standing in her shoes? Does Celia still want to marry Ken?

Would she, if she knew what happened under Cath's table? Would she, if she knew how Ken was trying to turn the tables and twist his tale? And would she have given Dodge her shoes in the first place if she still wanted to be in them?

'You were stolen,' Ken repeats, 'and I'm going to get you back.'

He starts pursuing Dodge around the kitchen at top speed, with knives and fish-slices and things spinning off in all directions. Dodge is grateful now for the hours of stiletto practice he's put in. He can go backwards fast enough to evade Ken's flying hands, but close enough to keep pacifying him.

'Ken, Ken, calm down,' Dodge says, 'everything's going to be all right!'

No it's not. Ken is pointing a finger at Dodge and screaming, 'Who are you? I knew you weren't Celia, not really! She never calls me Ken. I've asked her not to. I don't like being called Ken. Celia knows that.'

Dodge is about to duck under the table by way of escape when it strikes him that this could be a bit foolhardy. In desperation he tries to hide in the fridge, but for once it is full already. Dodge swears and slams the rattling door shut and skids around the corner at the short end of the table, where he runs into Ken coming the other way.

'Impostor!' cries Ken. 'What have you done with my Celia?'

Dodge isn't called Dodge for nothing. He sidesteps Ken's potential stranglehold and heads for the door at full throttle.

But Dodge isn't called Dodge because he's good at getting away. On the kitchen doorstep he slams slap-bang into Ken's mother, who has come down the hallway like a hen in a flap. Kenneth's mother runs into the kitchen and in anxious circles around her noisy boy.

'What's the matter with you?' she screams. 'What's the matter with him, Celia? What's he saying?'

Dodge, winded on the doorstep, shrugs his shoulders and takes a step backwards. He treads on the toes of Ken's father who has followed his worried wife down the hall.

'Steady on, Celia,' says Kenneth's father, and shoves Dodge to one side to see into the kitchen. 'What's all this then? We heard you shouting from the dining-room. What's going on?'

He catches sight of his son, sitting under the table now, shaking visibly, shaking his head.

'What have you done to him, Celia? What have you said? Where have you been all evening? We've never seen such appalling manners, have we Mrs Conn?' says Ken's father, not looking at Dodge but reaching out a long arm to grasp him by the shoulder and prevent him from leaving the room.

'No, we haven't,' says Ken's mother, hovering on her hands and knees around the edges of the table.

She starts to crawl awkwardly underneath it. 'Come on, Kenneth,' she calls softly, 'come to mother. This is no way for a big boy like you to behave . . .' Her coaxing ends in a shrill cry; she reappears backwards and at speed.

She stands up slowly and turns to face her husband and future daughter-in-law at the kitchen door. Her face is having an apocalyptic fit. She doesn't say what her son has done, but with a face like that she doesn't have to. Ken's father charges at the table and sends it squealing several feet across the floor. Feet first, Ken emerges into the open.

Ken cowers. His father towers.

'Apologise to your mother,' he says.

'Sorrymother,' mutters Ken.

'Is Kenneth drunk?' his father demands of Celia. His tone can't conceal his desperate desire to be answered in the affirmative. For if Celia says no, the next question must be, 'Is Kenneth mentally ill?'

Dodge nods Celia's head. He daren't speak. He doesn't trust himself to do anything but his natural voice. Ken's parents are already shaken; they'd be seriously stirred if Celia started to speak in a man's voice. And if they discovered the man's body in Celia's dress . . . well, surely they'd stop at nothing to find out how it got there and what it had done with Ken's real fiancée.

But Dodge's silent confirmation looks set to save the day. Kenneth's mother sighs with relief.

'Pull yourself together,' she chides her drunken child. 'Come on now.'

'Do you know where I found Celia?' shouts Ken suddenly, staring glassily from parent to parent, but stabbing a stubby finger at Dodge: 'Under a table, if you please. Under a table with another man.'

Dodge's world goes cold.

The parents turn on him in horror.

He hides his face in his wig, letting it swing closed like curtains across his cheeks. And it is to spare the parents the shock of his shadowy stubble, which will surely be spotted under such close scrutiny.

But they see it as an admission of Celia's guilt.

'Little slut!' says Ken's mother.

'Enormous whore!' says Ken's father.

Behind the hair, Dodge's mouth is open in a silent scream. Celia's name is taken in vain. Her reputation is tarnished. Her engagement is terminated. Whether she likes it or not. It is all over. Dodge is shaking. There must be something he can do. He starts to walk slowly towards Kenneth. He has to jog Ken's memory, bring him back from his trip, bring him close enough to home to tell the truth about who was under the table with whom. All this, without uttering a word.

It is the hardest job Dodge has ever had to do. But Dodge has a tool. His body is his tool. It is flexible, versatile, multi-purpose. And he can mime. He can mime.

He can mime the White Rabbit.

Dodge squats in Celia's dress in front of Kenneth Conn. He wiggles his bottom. He puts his hands on his head, pricked up, like long ears. He waggles them. Then he lifts his hips and hops. Dodge bunny-hops, up and down and up again, in front of Kenneth.

Behind him, Ken's parents are as silent as cabbages. Dodge can't see their faces, but he expects that they are white or green.

As competent and cute as Dodge's rabbit mime is, it doesn't seem to ring any bells for Ken. He is hunched back under the table and droning a dirge: 'With another man. Another man. It's another man.'

Time is running out for Celia.

Then, with a flash of inspiration, Dodge mimes the White Rabbit taking a watch out of his waistcoat pocket.

Behind him, Ken's mother says, 'She's drunk too!' and his father adds something about either that or we are which Dodge doesn't catch.

Dodge grits his teeth and mimes the watch one more time.

'It's another man!' shouts Ken.

Dodge sighs, stands up and turns away.

He comes face to face with Ken's parents. They avert their gazes.

'It's another man!' shouts Ken, behind him.

Ken's mother is looking over Dodge's shoulder at her son. She cringes.

Dodge opens his mouth. Celia is innocent. There is no other man. He's going to tell them, and serve them right if his voice comes out a booming baritone. He and Celia are just good friends. She hasn't been bad with anyone, even Ken, and . . .

'Look out, Celia!' shouts Ken's father.

There is action over Dodge's shoulder. Kenneth is coming from behind. There is a leap, a lunge, a lifting, and Dodge's head is jerked backwards. Then there is a rush of cold air; a rush of air, and no hair.

Ken has pulled Dodge's wig off. Dodge is another man.

Ken's mother starts to scream like a fire engine. She is red in the face.

Ken's father glances at his wife, glances down at his 'little fireman', glances back at Dodge, and starts to scream too.

Kenneth falls flat on the floor with Dodge's wig splayed like a giant golden spider or a sun on his stomach.

Dodge scratches his short dark hair and wonders what Celia would do now. Then Dodge collects up the dirty coffee cups and stands all the chairs back on four legs, singing this little song:

Twas two in the morning, and the lying toad
Had passed out on the kitchen floor;
His mumsy was horrified to the core,
And his old man was outraged.

Beware the lot of them, my girl!
Their eyes don't see, their hands don't touch,
Their hearts don't sing, their minds don't whirl;
And they don't like you much.

II
Celia's got the whole world in her hands

The real Hebe hates this song. She is embarrassed by the whole *Wet Wendy* business. It's her worst film yet; and, considering

202

the acts it had to follow, this is something of a feat. With its juvenile plot and delinquent music, *Wet Wendy* got Hebe into a whole lot of trouble, and she wishes people wouldn't keep bringing it up, especially when she is least expecting it.

Still, despite her surprise, the real Hebe smiles. She smiles at the shock of singing strangers; she smiles at her sister dancing around her with streamers; she smiles at whoever it is dragging her suitcase into the room and shutting the door behind it. She smiles biggest and best at her sister, whom she hasn't seen for six months.

But if Hebe's smile were music, it would be a crap electronic classic; the sort played to a client over the phone, while behind its calm façade the office is ransacked and staff are sacked in the search for that client's missing particulars.

'What's happening?' shouts Hebe, as Phoebe stops spinning and everyone else stops singing. 'What's the matter with your house?'

'It's having parties,' says Phoebe, 'parties aplenty. And hip-hip-hurrah, Hebe, this one's for you!'

Phoebe pulls her sister off the floor and onto her feet and merges with her in a massive hug. She held Hebe on the day that she was born. She believed the grown-ups when they said that this was *her* baby. She's never needed any other children.

The sisters hug for ages and hug like they have hugged for ever. Once they were small together, now they are tall together, and their bodies still fit together. Only the world they stand on has changed. It has withered as they have grown ripe. It has shrunk as they have drunk from it. The earth has become dry and dusty of late. All its moisture is held in suspense between Phoebe's and Hebe's bodies; its only juice is squeezed like blood when the sisters hug each other's stone.

An ocean has separated them for six months, and there has been nothing but salt water to drink. Phoebe and Hebe have been thirsting, and no saliva has flown. But now that Phoebe has Hebe's mouth by her ear, a fresh-water spring has sprung. And as well as the spring, clouds are beginning to build up, bank upon bank of them, all rumbling like a hungry tummy, threatening rain.

'Godsbollocks, Phoebe, what *is* this?' Hebe whispers.

'What is what?' whispers Phoebe.

'This party. What's it doing here?' asks Hebe.

'Don't you like it?' Phoebe asks.

'Well, I hardly know. We've only just met,' says Hebe.

'Would you like to be introduced?' asks Phoebe.

Hebe sighs heavily.

'Hot dang,' says Phoebe, in her ear, 'I knew this would happen. You don't want it, do you?'

Her grip on Hebe tightens. Pressed chest to chest each can feel the other's heartbeat as well as her own. They are not entirely synchronised.

'It's not that I don't want it,' whispers Hebe, 'but I'm fucked. I've been flying for two days.'

Phoebe strokes her sister's shoulders. 'Poor wings,' she says softly. 'Let's slip away to my bedroom. You can have a little lie down. Get your strength back. Come on.'

Phoebe stands back and swings Hebe round to face the surprise guests. Hebe's eyes skim-read the crowd. There is no one she doesn't recognise, even though most of them are strangers.

Hebe's eyes stop at the nun. They stumble.

She's got a bit of a thing about nuns. Once, when she was a teenager, she dreamed the same dream every night for a week. In it she was a refugee, taken in and cared for by an order of nuns. Everything was fine for a while; fun even, in a *Sound of Music*ky sort of way. But then Hebe began to get the feeling that there was something wrong, something strange and sinister going on . . .

If the dream really were *The Sound of Music*, this would be the cue for the Nazis to come in. A dramatic chase would follow. Indeed, Hebe's feeling of impending doom and imminent danger grew and grew until she was so scared that, in the dead of night (and without so much as a swastika in sight) she slipped out of bed and escaped from the convent. Hebe climbed through a window and hot-footed it down a dark deserted road with the feeling of terror growing more intense by the minute. Then, turning a corner, she caught a glimpse of dark figures behind her.

It was the nuns, the nuns were after her, the nuns were the baddies! Frozen in the path of their fast approaching forms, Hebe finally worked out what had been bothering her about them all along. There was something wrong with them, something weird about them. They couldn't walk properly. They couldn't walk at all. They bounced down the road towards her like shadows in a sack race, skirts flapping in the suffocating night air. Hebe saw at last that every single nun had only one leg. Not a normal leg either; a leg like a tree-trunk or a mermaid's tail, a thick leg like two thin legs sewn together. A big fat leg like a penis, as hard to get around on as a pogo stick.

Hebe woke up every morning wondering why she hadn't noticed sooner how strange the nuns' shoes were, or why they seemed to have only one each. Hebe woke up kicking herself for ignoring the warning signs. By the end of the week, Hebe was having a nervous breakdown.

Ten years later she made *NunAware*, a silly film about a sexual revolution in a convent. Since then she has had so many stand-up confrontations with nuns both real and imaginary that it has become a habit. A habit which Hebe is trying to break.

She tears her eyes from the nun and returns them to her sister.

'Ladies and Ladies,' Phoebe is announcing, 'I give you Hebe! The real one. The original and best.'

The party applauds. One of its members comes forward.

'I'm your biggest fan,' she says, thrusting her hand at Hebe, 'and I'd like to take this opportunity to welcome you back home. Over the years you have picked up what is perhaps an inconveniently long train of followers; but those of us gathered here tonight are a bunch which, we think, have been as close behind you as a bustle.'

Hebe shakes the woman's hand.

'Nice metaphor!' she murmurs appreciatively. 'I'd copyright it before it gets ripped off, if I were you.'

'This is Harrier,' says Phoebe to her sister. 'She's president.'

'Of the cluster clinging to my bottom?' says Hebe. Then, turning to Phoebe, she adds, 'Are you a member?'

Phoebe winks with the eye none of the others can see.

'I think I'm an honorary member,' she says. 'They never ask me for any money. And I don't wear the insignia.'

'Insignia?' says Hebe, staring into the crowd.

Then she sees it. On shiny black ribbon, pendant between each woman's breasts, the badge of her fan club; the silver circle and cross she used so clumsily as a symbol of liberation in *NunAware*.

'Well bugger me!' says Hebe. 'Or perhaps you'd better not. It's the fasci-feminists from haemorrhoid hell.'

Everyone laughs because they hope this is a joke. But no one understands a word of it, so they can't hold the hilarity for long.

'My sister would like a few moments to freshen up,' says Phoebe as the laughter grows stale. 'Please, party with all your might and main, till she comes back again.'

She takes Hebe by the ears and steers her through the crowd.

By the time they get to the outskirts, Hebe has started to hang behind.

'Look!' she is saying, 'Glenda Jackson!'

'Stop staring,' says Phoebe, driving her sister onward. 'It's rude.'

They arrive at Phoebe's bedroom door. Someone has thoughtfully left Hebe's suitcase right outside. Hebe falls over it; she is looking the other way.

'It's Glenda Jackson!' she continues to chant, as Phoebe lugs her, and her luggage, through the door.

'Yes, I know,' says Phoebe, when they are safely inside.

'Do you think she'll talk to me?' says Hebe.

'Not if all you can say is her name,' says Phoebe.

'Mum,' says Hebe, and her hands fly to her mouth.

'What?' gasps Phoebe.

'Whoops, slipped out. Sorry,' Hebe says behind her fingers.

'What?' says Phoebe.

'All I can say is her name,' says Hebe.

There is silence. Phoebe shoves Hebe's suitcase under her bed. But before it has a chance to settle there, she tugs it out again and stands it up next to the wardrobe. She waits for it to stop wobbling before facing Hebe again. By then, her chin is wobbling instead.

'So,' she says, 'how are you?'

Hebe's eyes dive into hers like kingfishers.

'How are *you*?' says Hebe.

'All right,' says Phoebe. 'I . . .' She bites her tongue.

'What?' says Hebe.

'I can't believe it,' says Phoebe.

'No,' says Hebe.

'It's been six months,' continues Phoebe.

207

'Yes,' says Hebe.

'And I still can't believe that she's . . . she's . . .' Phoebe stops. Then, 'Believe it?' she adds breathlessly. 'I can't even say it.'

'No,' says Hebe.

'Can you?' asks Phoebe.

'No.' Hebe shakes her head.

'Have you done any work?' asks Phoebe.

'No,' says Hebe, 'have you?'

Phoebe shrugs and turns away.

'Have you been . . . Have you seen . . . Have you got anyone to talk to?' asks Hebe.

Phoebe shrugs again. 'I haven't told anyone,' she says. 'I can't even say it. I can't say the words, see.'

'Sometimes,' says Hebe, 'I say "Mum" without meaning to. Like a burp. Out of the blue.'

There is silence. Phoebe picks up Hebe's suitcase and swings it onto the top of the wardrobe. Dust billows and the double doors burst open of their own accord.

Phoebe steps backwards.

'I can still smell her,' she says, and it sounds like there is a sob stuck in her throat. 'How can she be gone for ever if her smell is still here?'

Phoebe stares into the depths of her wardrobe, swaying slightly as the sob in her throat threatens to cut off her air supply.

Suddenly Hebe is standing behind her. Phoebe can feel breath on the back of her neck. Hebe is looking over her sister's shoulder at the empty clothes hanging soft as skin.

'Is that a new jumper?' she asks.

'What?' says Phoebe.

'Nothing,' says Hebe. Then she wraps warm arms around Phoebe and hugs her tightly and rocks her gently.

'If we don't talk,' she whispers in Phoebe's ear, 'we'll die too.'

Suddenly they are crying. Crying like the first painful rainfall of the season. They are lying on Phoebe's bed and crying into the dust, and nothing is dry. Everything is getting wet. Phoebe and Hebe are clinging together and crying from the bottoms of their broken hearts.

Their wounds are opening like the mouths of babes.

Their sores are weeping.

In the middle of the monsoon, Phoebe rolls over onto her back and gasps, 'The party!'

She looks sideways at her sister. Hebe's red hair has coiled into ringlets tight as springs in the humid atmosphere. Hebe runs her fingers through it, and Phoebe can almost hear it go 'Boing!' as it bounces back.

'Why?' Hebe sighs. 'Why are we having a party? I don't want to shout at strangers. I want to talk to you.'

Fresh tears roll down Phoebe's cheeks and meet the smile rising like bread in a warm oven. 'I thought you didn't,' she says. 'I didn't think you did. Your letters were so quiet. They didn't say anything. They didn't even mention M-Mum!'

'Only because yours didn't,' protests Hebe.

'Yes, but yours didn't first! Yours started it!' says Phoebe.

And suddenly they are both smiling.

'You said you were coming to England to work,' says Phoebe. 'You didn't say anything about wanting to see me. So when Harrier suggested a party in your honour I thought it would . . . would . . .'

'Serve me right?' suggests Hebe.

'Something like that,' says Phoebe.

'Give me a taste of my own medicine?' suggests Hebe.

'Maybe,' says Phoebe.

'Teach me a lesson I'll never forget?' says Hebe.

'Look, I love you. It's confusing. I don't know my arse from your elbow,' says Phoebe.

Hebe wipes four wet eyes with a single bedside tissue.

'Shall we start again?' she says.

'Yes please,' says Phoebe. 'Where from?'

'From where we left off,' says Hebe. 'From the funeral.'

'I know!' says Phoebe. Let's pretend that this party *is* the funeral, and let's just talk to each other all evening. Which is what we should have done the first time round.'

Hebe shudders.

'If this party is anyone's funeral,' she says, 'it's mine. Why was everyone singing that deadly Wendy song?' Without giving Phoebe time to answer, Hebe adds, 'No, I think we should talk tomorrow. Thanks to your kind surprise I'm working tonight. All those women out there think I'm seriously someone. I'll have to play along with them. I daren't drop my disguise.'

Phoebe springs off the bed with a startled shout.

'Sorry!' she says to Hebe, who has gone under the pillows like a pair of frightened pyjamas. 'But there's something funny peculiar going on in this house tonight. You just reminded me of it. When you said about being in disguise.'

'Oh yes?' says Hebe cautiously, peering out from under the pillows.

'Yes,' pants Phoebe, pacing up and down at the foot of the bed. 'It's completely inexplicable.'

'Surely you can tell me', says Hebe, perking up.

'I can tell you,' says Phoebe, 'but you won't believe me. I wouldn't believe it myself if I hadn't seen it with my own eyes.'

'I'm all ears,' says Hebe.

'All right,' says Phoebe, 'listen carefully. I shan't say this twice. About an hour before you arrived, you arrived.'

210

'Pardon?' says Hebe.

'Please don't interrupt. It'll only make things worse,' says Phoebe. 'Listen. An hour before you arrived, you arrived. We were all in position, the lights were off. Then the door opened, and you stepped into the room. The lights went on, we all shouted SURPRISE, and you screamed; fuck me, Hebe, you screamed like a rocket taking off and you nearly went through the roof.'

'No I didn't,' says Hebe.

'Look, shut up,' says Phoebe, seriously. 'You screamed. All right? And you sort of fainted in my arms. Harrier sat you down in an armchair, and I went off to get you some coffee.

'Okay. In the kitchen there was . . . there was a . . . there was a rape taking place.'

'What?' gasps Hebe.

'A rape,' says Phoebe, and kicks her bedroom wall so violently that the lights flicker and a radio comes on. Then she clears her throat. 'I don't want to talk about it,' she adds. 'I just want you to know that it was Celia. The victim. Was Celia.'

Hebe wipes her brow and wonders if she is allowed to ask who Celia is. Luckily, Phoebe reads her mind.

'Celia lives in the house. She's having a party too. But hers is an E party. An engagement party. Downstairs,' Phoebe says. 'I don't know who it was on top of her. But I got him to stop.' This time Phoebe hits the wall with a clenched fist. The radio turns itself off and the top drawer flies out of her dressing-table and empties its contents on the carpet. 'Then I came back up here,' Phoebe continues; 'I brought you some coffee.'

'Thanks,' says Hebe, licking a trickle of sweat from her lips, 'I needed that. This is all very harrowing. Is it nearly over?'

'You haven't heard the half of it,' says Phoebe. 'Just listen. I

211

gave you the coffee. And suddenly, it wasn't you! You see, I gave you the coffee, and I sat on your lap, but it wasn't you. It wasn't you.'

'So?' says Hebe. 'Of course it wasn't me. I hadn't even arrived yet. Unless we've upped and left linear reality altogether?'

'No, but, you see, the thing is . . .' stutters Phoebe.

'Hold it right there,' says Hebe, bolt upright on the bed now. 'Are you talking supernatural, here? Are you saying . . . jeepers creepers, Phoebe, has this got something to do with our M-Mum?'

'No,' says Phoebe, 'it was only Celia.'

'What?' snaps Hebe.

'It was Celia.'

'So what's the big mystery then?' Hebe snaps.

'I thought she was you.'

'Well, it's your problem if you can't tell the difference between me and anyone else. Were you drunk, Phoebe?' Hebe is shouting now.

'But she was pretending to be you,' Phoebe persists. 'She was disguised, see. She's blonde, but she had a red wig on, and new clothes. Well, old clothes, actually. She's usually very smart.'

This reduces Hebe to a short silence, during which she pulls at some loose wool on the left sleeve of her jumper, and undoes the delicate balance by which each sleeve is frayed exactly as far up the arm as the other.

'Do you mean to say,' says Hebe eventually, 'that any chick who turns up on your doorstep in a red wig gets welcomed in with all the sisterly . . .'

Phoebe intercepts the accusation.

'No,' she says, 'it was an easy mistake to make. I was on tenterhooks waiting for you to arrive. I was worried about how

212

you would take it, if you were even going to make it; and Celia came just as you should have done . . .'

'Through the door . . .' teases Hebe.

'All right!' shouts Phoebe. 'And yes, I was drunk. I'm always drunk. It makes no difference any more. So shut your face. Allow me to come to the point:

'Celia was here while I was making coffee and stopping a rape in the kitchen. *And it was Celia in the kitchen too*! That's what I'm trying to say. *There were two Celias*! Celia squared.'

Hebe stops fiddling with her clothing and looks up at Phoebe sharply. 'Is there usually only one?' she asks.

Phoebe nods.

'No twin sister that you know nothing about?' continues Hebe.

'Possibly,' shrugs Phoebe.

'How did you know it was Celia in the kitchen?' says Hebe.

'Well,' says Phoebe, glad to be taken seriously at last, 'she was wearing a special engagement dress in a stupid shade of little-girl blue. Her hair was long and blonde and her fiancé was asleep at the table. And she was submitting to the unwanted attentions of some shit-scum-git in total silence.'

'You don't like her much, do you?' observes Hebe.

'No', says Phoebe.

'Why not?'

'I don't know,' says Phoebe. 'Gut feeling. I've never even spoken to her. But tonight in the kitchen, when I saw that bloke on top of her, I did know why I don't like her. She wasn't screaming, Hebe; there was a houseful of people and she wasn't screaming for help. Can you imagine how self-conscious she must be, to lie there thinking, "Oooh no, I'd best not make a fuss."

'Anyway, I scared him off, then I hugged her, just for a second, till she was breathing again. What I really wanted to do was give

213

her a damn good lecture, but it would have taken too long. I couldn't see her face, but I sensed that she didn't scream because she didn't know how to, she didn't know she was allowed to. Because the only rules she's ever been taught are men's rules. So actually, as I came upstairs with the coffee, I thought maybe it isn't all Celia's fault that I hate her guts.

'But then, there she was in the armchair, masquerading as you; and I was so shocked that I forgot about the other Celia until just now. When you said disguise. The Celia that was up here, she screamed all right, she screamed the house down. But which was the real one. And how can there be two?'

'There can't be,' says Hebe, 'unless we're dreaming. Or she is. The one in the kitchen must have been someone else.'

'But it looked like Celia!' says Phoebe.

'But Celia was up here looking like me!'

'Then the question is,' says Phoebe quietly, 'why? Why has Celia changed? She loved that stupid blue dress. I think she had it made specially for tonight.'

'Maybe she simply slipped into something more comfortable,' smiles Hebe.

'But what about the wig?' asks Phoebe. 'No, see, if you ask me, she's stopped being Celia altogether. On purpose. Because that wig looks about as relaxing as wearing a hedgehog, inside out.'

Hebe is on her feet now, on the bed, bouncing. 'And she wants to be me instead,' she says.

'So it would seem,' says Phoebe.

Hebe goes higher.

'It's a big step to take in one night,' she says. 'There are years between the me who considered marriage a viable possibility and the me you see before you now.'

Phoebe dives for her sister's flying feet.

'The years haven't changed that fishy face of yours though, have they?' she says.

Hebe launches herself at Phoebe, bringing them both to the floor, then flounders around on top of her with imaginary gills going nineteen to the dozen and genuinely submarine eyes rolling in suffocation. It's an old game of theirs, a screaming all-time favourite, this dying giant fish scenario. But the party is pressing and the prospect of it has become a little more attractive.

'Do you think Celia's still here?' Hebe asks, getting off Phoebe abruptly, and going to look at herself in the dressing-table mirror. 'She's tickled my fancy. I'd like to talk to her. Either of her.'

'Let's go and see,' says Phoebe. 'Are you rested, then? Are you ready?' She stands panting, one hand on the doorknob and the other on her hip.

'No', smiles Hebe, linking her arm through Phoebe's, 'but I'll improvise. And all this drinking,' she adds. 'Let's talk about that tomorrow too.'

Phoebe opens her mouth to say something about there not being anything to say about it, but nothing comes out except a sigh like the sound of a distant distillery exploding.

And the next minute they are going swimmingly through surging crowds to the armchair where Celia was last sighted, to see if Celia is still there.

At first glance, it seems that the armchair is empty except for a worn cardigan slung casually over its cushioned curves. Phoebe shrugs and turns away, scouring the surface of the crowd for a red wig. But Hebe is not so hasty. She snatches up the cardigan. And there is Celia underneath, curled up and sleeping like a kitten.

Hebe nudges Phoebe. 'Is this her?' she asks, in an undertone. Phoebe nods.

'She's pretty,' Hebe says.

215

Phoebe looks from Hebe to Celia and screws up her nose and shakes her head. 'Shall I wake her up?' she says.

Hebe nods.

Phoebe puts out a finger and prods Celia's soft side.

'Whatwhat?' shouts Celia, sitting up with a start. She sways slightly for a second, then throws herself bodily at Phoebe, clawing at her wrists, clinging in a gluey grip.

'Wait!' Celia cries, 'I want to come too!'

Celia won't let go. She doesn't realise that she's woken up. She thinks this is all part of her dream.

Celia's dream is good enough to be a feature film. She has been on the edge of her armchair for ages, absorbed in the moving pictures and the masterful plot, unaware of the blanket blackness that will wrap her up if she takes her eyes off the silver screen.

This is the story so far:

The scene is set in a Victorian schoolroom. There are slates on the desks, religious tracts in cross-stitch on the walls, and free milk at playtime. Celia is a student. She is wearing a big curtain which smells of mildew and mothballs, and a mortar-board. Everything is in black and white.

Celia sits next to Phoebe. They are best friends. Celia is lifting the lid of her desk and quickly handing Phoebe a sweet . . . no, it's not a sweet; it's a tiny soldier. The soldier is part of a game the girls play every time they lift the lids of their desks. For in their desks' dark interiors Celia and Phoebe have built a scale model of the earth; Phoebe has the northern hemisphere, Celia has the southern. The two halves fit together to form a whole, by way of little golden hinges all around the equator, but the young friends know that if they were ever to join them together the planet would rise like a planet from behind the lids of their desks, and they would be caned for cheating.

216

The lesson is History. Celia and Phoebe are top of the class. They are way ahead of anyone else. They have got as far as the Second World War. Which is why Celia passes her chum a tiny soldier every time teacher's back is turned. Celia is finding the war rather tedious; everything happens in Phoebe's hemisphere, and Phoebe is flatly refusing to delegate any of her countries' campaigns to Celia. All Celia has to do is manufacture nationally neutral men out of matchsticks in the mornings, and dispose of the corpses at the end of the day. Most of the bodies have been laid to rest in the lunch-box of Prudence Prim, Phoebe and Celia's worst enemy, who sits at the desk in front of them.

So Celia can't wait for the war to be over. She has been pinning her hopes on Pearl Harbor or Hiroshima, has even been making a tiny atomic bomb in her spare time; but Phoebe stands firm. No matter how far south they may be, Pearl Harbour and Hiroshima are in her desk and her domain. 'It's not fair. You have all the fun,' whispers Celia, and fidgets impatiently until the Falklands War.

But it's not all fighting. Celia and Phoebe do History of Art too. This is out of sync with real History, however, due to the war's drain on manpower and resources, and they are only just starting surrealism. Here, Phoebe has deigned to allocate a northern hemisphere task to her idle southern sister. It is crucial to the cause that Mrs Magritte, mother of artist René, commits suicide by throwing herself off a bridge in Belgium in 1912. Celia is building the bridge. While she is whittling away at more minuscule pieces of matchstick the lid of her desk is slammed shut. There stands the little teacher, the tip of her cane trembling between Celia's eyes. The teacher is only two or three years old and Celia can't quite understand what she says.

'Bad Golly . . . going to get a jolly good smack . . . Golly pulled poor Dolly's head off!'

217

Celia looks sideways at Phoebe to see if she can shed any light on the teacher's language, but Phoebe is a headless form toppling slowly off its stool and falling to the floor to the sound of breaking china. Celia turns back to the tiny teacher.

'It wasn't me,' she says.

'Was! Was! Was!' says the teacher, but she doesn't look at all sure. In fact, she keeps glancing nervously over her shoulder.

'What are you so scared of?' Celia asks.

The teacher bursts into tears. 'Bad Golly . . . broken Dolly . . .' is all she can say.

'When are you going to take responsibility for yourself?' shouts Celia. 'When are you going to grow up?'

'When you blow up,' blubs the little teacher, sinking to her knees in the shadow of the much bigger teacher who is looming behind her.

Celia leans forward and looks into her inkwell
and her face in the reflection is black
and the ink is running under her as fast as a river
and the bridge she is standing on is burning.
There is nothing else for it. Celia jumps into the ink.

There is a short intermission.

When the second half of the dream starts Celia is back in Phoebe's room. She is sitting in an armchair with Phoebe's sister. It is a tight fit.

'No husband for me, thanks,' Hebe is saying. 'I'm trying to give them up.'

Behind her, the room is full of women. None of them has any clothes on. They are all tied to one long piece of washing-line.

Celia chews a fingernail nervously. 'How do you get by?' she mutters.

218

'By getting bigger. By getting better,' says Hebe. 'By getting on. By getting off.'

Celia winds a ringlet worriedly around her finger. 'Where do you get off?' she whispers.

'Don't you know?' says Hebe.

Celia clearly doesn't. She continues to stare at the bare bodies as if she can't make head or tail of them.

'Allow me to demonstrate,' Hebe says, when Celia's silence has started ingrowing, like toenails.

Hebe slips off the armchair and into the air. Suddenly she is naked too. Suddenly she can fly.

Celia grips the arms of the armchair.

Hebe is hovering six feet above her head. She gives a little whistle, which Celia recognises as blackbird song from her days in the school ornithology society. (Celia wasn't keen on birds herself, but she fancied a couple of the boys who were.) Celia looks up cautiously.

'I don't want any sticky stuff in my hair,' she calls.

'You'll be lucky,' says Hebe.

Hebe rolls over onto her stomach, bare in the air. She can fly like most people swim. A few strong breaststrokes and she is touching the ceiling with her fingertips. Hebe hangs, just below the surface of the room, slowly opening and closing her legs. If air were water, she would be treading it.

Celia's eyes haven't left her. It's rude, but Celia is staring. She still can't see what Hebe is trying to show her; but if wanting to were water, she would be drowning in it.

Hebe opens her legs wider. She feels sorry for Celia. She's going to give her a clue. Hebe has one hand on the ceiling to keep from bumping her head, and with the other hand she is not feeling sorry for herself. She is feeling herself.

219

In front of all these people. In public. Hebe's hand is in her pubic hair. Hebe's hand is in hair soft as spun sugar. Between thighs white as ice-cream. And buttocks like meringue shells; clenched, sandwiching cream. Hebe is dipping her fingers into a delicious dessert. She doesn't need a spoon. Her hips are helpful as handles. She could do with a serviette, though. The sweet is melting fast and sticky stuff is running everywhere.

There is a small strawberry on top. This is the best bit. Hebe saves it till last.

She only has to touch it and . . .

Ice-cream.

Ice-cream.

Hebe screams.

And Celia screams.

It is a sensitive strawberry.

She only has to lick it with her fingertip and her back contracts like a brandysnap. Hebe is horizontal and grating against the textured ceiling like a lemon getting its zest off.

Juice is dripping onto the carpet.

Celia, sitting on herself in the armchair, sees it seeping. Her mouth is watering. She suspects there will be stains. Tell-tale stains.

Suddenly Celia is shouting, 'What about my family They want their dessert. I can't eat it all myself. That's selfish.'

'I'll show you family,' Hebe replies. She ducks her head and dives vertically, down among the women in the room. She weaves a passageway through their hair which waves like seaweed; but peers deeper, looking into still pools, into darker places between the bodies. Then she pauses, and sculls on the spot, and says to Celia:

'I'll show you shellfish.'

With a flick of a flipperlike foot, Hebe darts into a crevice, a chasm, all the way down to the carpet. Celia watches and waits. When Hebe comes up again, she is holding the end of the washing- line between her teeth. With a wink at Celia she kicks out for the ceiling. Her progress is slower now and the muscles stand out all over her body. After three of Hebe's powerful breaststrokes, before Celia's very eyes, another woman begins to rise up into the air. Yes! The first woman on the clothes-line gradually leaves the ground, lifted by the wrist; and when she is halfway to the ceiling another head bobs above the earthbound ones and another set of shoulders emerges from the crowd on the ground.

Hebe has gone as high as she can. Her head is on the ceiling. She levels out and launches into a speedy front crawl. She swims in ever-increasing circles, and as they get bigger more and more women come off their feet and spiral around underneath her, spaced at regular intervals like clothes on the line. By the time the last woman is lifted into the air the whole room is whirling like a spin-drier.

'Celia!' calls Hebe, as she passes over Celia's head. 'Catch hold of the clothes-line.'

Celia is standing on the carpet at the centre of the vortex snatching at the end of a piece of string. Her wiry red wig is whisked off in the wind. Her own hair, long and pale as string itself, whips around her, blinding and binding her when she reaches out for the real rope.

A window is open. Hebe, poised for flight on the sill, shouts at Celia, 'I can't stop!'

'What? What!' shouts Celia. After all they've been through, she can't believe Hebe is going to leave her in the lurch.

Celia stretches out to the light, and snatches at the loose end of the clothes-line, but the women are disappearing out of the window and out of sight faster than falling darkness.

With a death-defying leap at the last minute Celia catches hold of the wrist of the last woman on the line; and her feet finally, fantastically, leave the ground.

'Wait!' Celia cries. 'I want to come too!'

'Sorry,' says Phoebe, 'I didn't mean to make you jump.'

'It didn't look like that from where I was standing,' says Celia.

'Let go of me please,' says Phoebe.

'No way!' says Celia.

'Celia? Hey, are you okay?' says Hebe. Her voice is deep, her breath is salty, her accent transatlantic.

Celia sees Hebe.

'You waited!' she says.

Hebe smiles kindly at Celia, and simultaneously says to her sister out of the side of her mouth, 'Schizo.'

'How did you get dressed so fast?' asks Celia.

'I haven't been undressed,' says Hebe, 'not for days, I can assure you. I've been on a plane.'

'Flying?' says Celia. 'Oh fuck!'

'Sorry?' says Hebe. There's something very strange about this housemate of Phoebe's.

'No, I'm sorry, I'm sorry,' says Celia, 'I was sleeping. I didn't realise I'd stopped.'

'Oh, I see,' says Hebe.

'I *have* stopped, haven't I?' says Celia.

Hebe shrugs her shoulders.

'Probably,' she says.

'I had such a curious dream!' cries Celia. 'You two were in it too. Really, today has been altogether too queer; and now I find

222

myself dreaming about Hebe before we've even been introduced.'
She stops with a pointed look at Phoebe.

'Er, Hebe, this is Celia, Celia this is Hebe,' says Phoebe.

They shake hands.

'Hello,' says Hebe. 'Tell me about your dream.'

'It's fading fast,' Celia shakes her head.

'Tell me quickly then,' says Hebe. 'Go on.'

'Well,' says Celia, 'it all started at the top of the stairs. A Caterpillar asked me who I was. I got confused and . . . no, the White Rabbit came first. That's right. I met him on the doorstep, and he made me feel about *this* big,' Celia shows Hebe an inch between her finger and thumb. 'But it wasn't until I'd got to the bottom of the dark passageway that the adventure really started.'

'Celia,' Hebe says gently, 'that's not your dream. I'm sorry, but that one's already spoken for. Unless you're prepared to pay royalties . . .'

'No!' protests Celia. 'The dream hasn't started yet. This is the real bit. This really happened. I think.'

'It's true,' says Phoebe. 'Another one of my housemates, Cath, is having an *Alice in Wonderland* fancy-dress party, just down the corridor.'

'But it's not just fancy-dress,' says Celia, 'it's an actual-factual arty-farty yellow polka dot you know what. It's a full-scale reconstruction. With drugs.'

'Ah,' says Hebe.

'But when I left there, things went from weird to worse,' says Celia. 'Instead of going back to my own party, my engagement party, I went into Dodge's room.'

'Dodge's room?' says Phoebe. 'No one's ever done that before.'

'Right,' says Celia, 'and I know why. Now, call me old-

223

fashioned, but when I go somewhere I like to leave wearing the same clothes I arrived in. Not so at Dodge's place, oh no,' Celia compresses her lips crossly.

'Did Dodge try it on?' says Phoebe.

'Not only did he try it on,' Celia replies confidentially, 'he refused to take if off again. He left, still wearing it!'

'Wearing what?' says Phoebe.

'My frock,' says Celia. 'My special engagement dress. Blue silk,' she adds, for Hebe's benefit.

'Dodge took your dress?' asks Phoebe incredulously. 'I thought you were saying he made a pass at you.' Then she slaps her forehead with the flat of her hand. 'So it was him I saw in the kitchen! Was he wearing a wig too?'

'A wig, my shoes, the works,' says Celia, 'leaving me to end my days in this bunch of rags and this brillo pad as if I were something to be kept under the kitchen sink! Oh sorry,' she adds, catching the eye of the identically dressed Hebe.

'Well, that explains everything,' says Phoebe. 'Dodge was in the kitchen, and all is right with the world.'

'Who's Dodge?' asks Hebe.

'He lives downstairs,' says Phoebe.

'What was he doing in the kitchen?' asks Celia.

'Er . . . er, he was with your fiancé, what's his name, Ken?' says Phoebe, and spears Hebe with a look which says, Don't mention the rape.

'Dodge was with Kenneth?' says Celia.

'Yes.'

'What were they doing?'

'I'm not sure.'

'Was . . . was Kenneth cross?'

'I couldn't say,' says Phoebe.

Celia sighs. 'Oh dear,' she says, 'Dodge is in my dress. What on earth will Kenneth make of that?'

'Perhaps he won't notice the difference,' Phoebe suggests.

'That's ridiculous,' says Celia.

'I didn't,' says Phoebe.

'But Kenneth's my fiancé,' says Celia. 'I'm going to marry him,' she adds. 'Of course he'd notice the difference,' she finishes, with a terse nervous titter.

Phoebe and Hebe are sitting on the arms of the armchair, putting little plaits in Celia's wig. Celia looks from one to the other and subsides into silence.

'Well, what happened next?' asks Hebe eventually.

'I arrived here, at the surprise party, where no one knows the difference between me and you, not even your own sister,' Celia tells her.

'Yes, I heard about that,' says Hebe. 'I'm hurt, to say the least.'

'I found it quite flattering,' says Celia, then her face falls. Their different reactions to her being mistaken for Hebe show their similarity in considering Celia the inferior of the two.

'Anyway,' she adds defiantly, 'I had fun. I pulled a nun's tea-towel off.'

'Wimple,' corrects Phoebe, in an irritated undertone.

'You devil!' says Hebe. 'I would never have dared. You didn't . . . you didn't look up her skirt by any chance, did you?'

'Excuse me?' says Celia.

'You didn't happen to notice how many legs she had?' mutters Hebe.

'No,' says Celia, 'why?'

'Never mind,' says Hebe.

'No, why?' says Celia.

'I don't trust nuns,' says Hebe. 'I think they've got something

225

to hide. Loving God isn't a good enough reason not to shag a fellow human being senseless. I bet they're not the goody-two-shoes they make themselves out to be.' Then her tone changes abruptly. 'Tell me your dream,' she demands.

'It was about you,' Celia answers. 'It was a bit rude. I don't know if I should say . . .'

'Go on.'

'You were swimming round and round on the ceiling. See,' Celia points a finger skywards and winds it in slow circles. 'You had no clothes on. But you had a string, a washing-line sort of thing. All the other women were tied to it and they were all coming off the ground and whooshing along behind you as you swam. The whole room was awash with naked women.'

Phoebe and Hebe laugh.

'I was getting left behind,' continues Celia. 'I was the only one still on the ground. The rest of you were about to go through the window. Seriously, Hebe, you were in the air and out of here. And I couldn't even get off the ground.'

Phoebe and Hebe stop laughing.

'I couldn't catch up,' says Celia.

'You have now,' says Hebe, and holds Celia's hand.

Celia stares down at her hand and Hebe's, clasped in a heart shape, pinkish against the purple of the armchair. She remembers the next bit. 'There's more,' she gasps. 'Oh good grief!' She pulls her hand away.

'What is it?' asks Hebe.

'Urgh. It was sick. I mean, sweet,' says Celia.

'What?' says Hebe. 'Come on!'

'No,' Celia shakes her head.

'Why not?' says Hebe.

'You won't like it,' says Celia.

226

'What's it got to do with me?' says Hebe.

'It was you,' wails Celia. 'In my dream. On the ceiling. With sticky fingers.'

Phoebe sniggers. 'Oh yes?'

'Ssshhh,' Hebe scolds her sister. Then she says, 'Celia, it wasn't really me. It was you. Everything in the dream was your own doing. I was just a dummy, a stand-in, there on your behalf.'

'Hang on,' says Celia, 'that can't be right. I can't save myself, can I?'

'Celia,' says Hebe, 'no one else can save you.'

'But, but . . .' stutters Celia, 'you showed me something. Something I didn't know before. How could it be me if I didn't already know what I showed me?'

'You must have been keeping it a secret from yourself,' says Hebe. 'Spooky, huh? What was it then? Do tell.'

Celia clears her throat three times.

'You showed me your body,' she croaks, 'or my body. The female body. I didn't realise it could . . . you know . . . work on its own. But you single-handedly did the job of several men. Sexually. There now, I've said it. I hope you're satisfied.' She flings herself back in the armchair, flushed.

'It sounds like *you* were,' says Phoebe.

'Then you went out of the window,' says Celia.

'It wasn't me,' says Hebe, 'remember.'

'It looked like you,' Celia says.

'So do you,' smiles Hebe.

'I still don't get it,' says Celia. 'I'm sorry but . . . I know dreams are supposed to tell you something. But . . . it's nothing important, is it?'

'You must be the judge of that,' says Hebe, 'but let me just say this. Sometimes you can't see your dreams, but they can always

227

see you. It is always daylight in the depths of your unconscious mind. And it is a political unconscious. It's up on current affairs. It reads the papers. It knows what's going on.'

'Huh?' says Celia.

'Do I have to spell it out for you?' says Hebe. 'You're supposed to be getting engaged downstairs, but instead you're up here asleep and dreaming about flying out of a window with a horde of naked women. Doesn't that strike you as some sort of protest?'

'Oh,' says Celia.

It does.

'Oh, I see,' she says again.

But Celia's not that sort of person. She would never wear a woolly hat and walk along under a banner, chanting, 'Kenneth Out'. So what sort of person is she then? What would she do if, say, she had a last-minute inkling that it would be wrong to let Kenneth into her life? Supposing, just supposing, she thought it might be a mistake to marry him? Would she still see it through? Would she be a prisoner to her promises, and walk down the aisle with a ball and chain clanking under her train? Or would she have the courage of her convictions, and call it off?

Celia turns to Hebe to see what she would do, and catches her sneaking a look at her watch.

'Do you think I should go then?' asks Celia. 'Out of the window? In protest?'

'Do you?' says Hebe, staring back like glass.

'I would,' says Celia, 'if there were someone waiting to catch me.'

'But there isn't?' asks Hebe.

'I don't think so,' says Celia.

'We know the feeling,' sighs Phoebe.

'You've got each other,' Celia says. 'I wish I had a sister.'

228

'But we're orphans. What if we're both falling at once?' says Phoebe. Hebe kicks her ankle.

'Both your parents are dead?' Celia gasps.

'Mmmm,' says Phoebe.

'When did they die?' asks Celia.

There is a pause during which Phoebe and Hebe look at each other in panic.

'Sorry,' says Celia, 'silly question.'

'There's nothing wrong with your question,' says Hebe. 'It's us. We're silly answerers.'

'Did they . . . did they die together?' stammers Celia.

'No,' says Hebe. 'Our father has always been dead . . .'

'. . . And our Mum died six months ago,' says Phoebe. The sisters sound stern; it's a choice between that and sobbing.

Celia's hands fly briefly into the air, before settling like white doves on the top of her head.

'I'm sorry,' she says. 'I didn't know.'

'I didn't tell you,' says Phoebe. 'I didn't tell anyone. I hate to have people pitying me.'

'Oh, I wouldn't have pitied you,' says Celia. 'I think you're lucky.'

'What?'

'You're lucky.'

'Why?' asks Hebe, diamond-eyed.

'You're free,' says Celia. 'You can do whatever you want now, you can be whoever you choose.'

'Of course we can,' says Hebe, 'we always could. The difference is, there's no one to care now. No one to be proud of us when we do well, no one to give us a bollocking when we do badly. My face was on the front page of a newspaper last week, but no one's got a photo of me on their mantelpiece. You don't know what you're talking about, Celia.' Hebe is getting heated, 'It takes more love, not less, to release us. It takes a giant leap of love to gain each inch of freedom.'

Celia is silent. She seems to have put her foot in it a bit.

'If I shout loud enough,' says Phoebe, suddenly, 'do you think Mum will hear me and come back? Six months isn't long, she can't be that far gone.'

Celia snorts. 'If you shout loud enough,' she says, '*my* mother will come. And that, I can assure you, is a fate worse than death . . . oh, sorry . . .'

The temperature seems to drop.

Hebe shifts in her seat and swears under her breath; Celia, if she is to believe her ears, is shocked at its obscenity. Phoebe, too, is blinking rapidly and shuffling her feet and starting to look over her shoulder at the surprise party.

They are the nicest friends Celia has made all night, and now she's offended them. She can't leave it like this. Celia takes a deep breath and attempts to apologise. 'All I meant to say,' she says, 'was this. If I jumped out of the window I'd rather splat on concrete than have my parents catch me. I think there's something wrong with their love. They wouldn't set me free. They'd hand me over to Kenneth.'

Hebe slips off the arm of the armchair and kneels at Celia's feet. 'In that case,' she says, 'you'd better be sure you can fly.'

Their eyes lock together on the last word of the sentence, and bat it back and forth between them like a shuttlecock. Hebe's eyes let Celia's win. They give way.

'Celia,' she whispers, 'will you do me a big favour? Will you hold the fort here, for ten minutes?'

'Why?' says Celia.

'I've got to go somewhere. Just for ten minutes. No one will notice. You're a much better me than I am.'

'Oh. Okay,' says Celia. It's the second time this evening she's heard words to that effect. Humpty said she was more Alice than Alice; now Hebe has told her much the same thing.

'Hey, where are you going?' comes Phoebe's plaintive cry, as Hebe crawls behind the armchair and starts to sneak stealthily towards the door.

'To this Wonderland party,' says Hebe. 'I'm sorry, but I've got to see it. It sounds like it's right up my rabbit hole. Celia's standing in for me for a minute . . .'

She disappears.

Celia looks sideways at Phoebe in the silence that follows. Phoebe looks displeased. The pause persists. Celia thinks of something placatory to say, but before she can speak someone has sidled up to the armchair and done the job for her.

'I see you've got rid of Celia at last,' beams Harrier.

Phoebe falls off the arm of the chair into Celia's lap.

'I thought she would never go,' continues Harrier, taking Phoebe's previous place. She pulls a packet of cigarettes from her pocket and offers them around. Phoebe takes four and lines them up between her lips.

'Light,' she says indistinctly.

Harrier hands over a box of matches.

'All at once, Phoebe?' she asks.

'Fuck off,' says Phoebe, furiously striking match after match.

Now the other women in the room are converging on the armchair again. They are louder and larger and laughing more than before, beery-breathed and bleary-eyed. But they never really wanted to ask Hebe any questions; they just wanted her to hear their answers; so Celia need do nothing but grin and bear the weight of the still-fuming Phoebe.

Phoebe is sitting on Celia's bladder and Celia's bladder is

bursting. It was the reason she came upstairs again in the first place. She remembers waiting outside the bathroom with her legs tied in knots, but she has no recollection of untying them to use the toilet. Then, with a cold rush of what feels alarmingly like water, Celia remembers *The Dambusters*: someone was in the bathroom singing it, and it was the same sound she had heard coming from her abandoned party. The next thing Celia knew, she had made an unexpected entrance into Phoebe's room, and surprised Phoebe's party.

So Celia has been up here for hours, and still hasn't done what she came to do. Now she has to hang on longer, hang on until Hebe comes back. Celia crosses her legs, and eases the prostrate Phoebe onto a less painful part of her body. But Celia's foot is stuck on something and she still isn't comfortable.

She looks. Her heart leaps. The nun is standing dead ahead, telling the real Hebe what a fake she is. Celia's foot is caught in the hem of the nun's habit.

'Look!' Celia whispers in Phoebe's ear.

'What?' says Phoebe.

'Look!' Celia nods and nudges. 'How many legs?'

'Oh!' says Phoebe. She laughs, and one of her fags falls out. 'I can't tell yet,' she continues, 'lift it higher.'

Pins and needles prick Celia's shin as she sticks her foot all the way in and raises the nun's robes like a ruched curtain.

'Quick, quick, it's killing me!' Celia gasps. 'How many, how many?'

Two cigarettes have fallen out of Phoebe's mouth. 'Higher, higher!' she whispers, 'I still can't see.'

Celia breaks the pain barrier and her foot nearly breaks the nun's knees as it shoots past them in an upward direction.

'Two,' shouts Phoebe, 'it's two.' Then she adds, in what can only be described as a scream of derision, 'Blimey! Bloomers!'

'Sshhh,' says Celia.

But her warning comes way too late. The nun is unhooking yards of holy cloth from Celia's foot and letting it fall to the floor.

'Satan's sisters! Shameless sinners!' the nun is shouting. 'You'll be sorry for this, you just see if you're not!'

'I'm shaking in my shoes,' sneers Phoebe. Celia is shocked at her lack of repentance. But then, Phoebe is missing her mother badly and probably needs a bit of a telling-off. Celia, on the other hand, with more mother than she can handle, would rather avoid a confrontation.

'I'm sorry already,' she says, struggling out from underneath Phoebe. 'No, I am sorry,' she swears, staggering to her feet, 'but I really can't stay any longer. If I don't go to the loo this very minute, I'll do myself some serious mischief! Byeee . . .'

Celia skips out the door, up the corridor and into the bathroom. She seems a different person to the one too terrified to take a trip to the same toilet last night and the night before. Her fear of Phoebe has evaporated, and the milk of human kindness flows freely in its place.

When Celia comes out of the bathroom, the door to Phoebe's party is closed.

And at the bottom of the corridor, at the top of the stairs, stands Celia's mother, arms folded, frowning like a thunderstorm.

8. Out of hand

Celia's mother is standing on the landing, and her thunder is under control. The redheaded stranger stepping out of the bathroom is only a redheaded stranger stepping out of the bathroom and nothing to get worked up about. Wilting waif and party stray, way past her bedtime, can't stand up straight, can't stop swaying. Poor little flower.

Celia's mother sends a sympathetic smile along the wavelength of the corridor to the wire-haired stranger. Strange child seems to get a shock. Seems to stagger back against the bathroom door, seems to go slow all over, seems to stop. What is the matter with her? Is she shy? Surely not! Celia's mother is wearing her hearty party dress, a profusion of pink and purple print, patterned all over with pulsating organs of amour; she is the very queen of hearts, so who could help but love her at first sight? No, the silly girl must be shy of the light on the landing.

Ah, she takes a step; thrust of black foot at floor level, bounce of red head in landing light. At last, she is passing down the passage, coming Celia's mother's way.

But what

Slow

Progress

She makes.

How her footfalls fall behind.

Why a stranger should huff and scuff and sulk so, Celia's mother doesn't know. Why a stranger should shy away from the edge of the light, and hang her head and hide her eyes and strive to stay as strange as possible, Celia's mother doesn't know.

Until she glimpses the girl's glance, and sees the fright. Then she does know.

Celia's mother's sympathetic smile turns upside down in an instant. There is lightning on the landing. Celia's mother knows this girl.

It's her girl.

It's . . .

Celia ducks under the angry angle of her mother's elbow and finds herself teetering at the top of the stairs. But this is no escape; to descend is to surrender, to go down is to give up. If only she had avoided eye contact she could have passed herself off as a stranger. But no, she flashed the familiar fear. She let slip a fearful tear, and it gave her away.

Celia teeters at the top of the stairs and the tear is water falling downwards. Her mother is close at hand on shoulder. Celia has to think rapids. She has to paddle her own canoe.

But Mother wants to do it for her. Mother wants to push. Mother has both hands on Celia's shoulders and is bearing down, overhanging the top stair, overdetermining the direction of travel. So when Celia suddenly squats, crouching like a canoeist, Mother overtakes her. Mother takes to the air, over Celia's head, and lands four or five stairs down.

A roar breaks like a wave over the banisters.

'*Celiaaa!*'

235

Celia gets splashed. Blinking, she steps backwards. That was a dangerous thing to do. It has sent the blood and the pressure of her mother's love soaring. Now Mother is coming back up the stairs. Slowly but surely, step by step.

Celia steps backwards, as her mother crashes onto the landing again. And Celia turns around and gets the kayak out of there. Up the black passage to Cath's room she races with one brief look behind her.

Mother is not badly hurt. Only a bit bruised. She is in hot pursuit as Celia's fire-red wig goes out of a half-open door at the far end of the passageway. Without stopping to think, she follows her daughter through it.

Celia's mother has not been to Wonderland for forty years, and she has never been to a rave. There is a pain that beats the brains out of falling downstairs. Every nerve in her body stops what it is doing, turns to its neighbour and screams, 'What is that dreadful noise?'

Celia's mother fumbles for ears to force her forefingers into. In the uproar ears have erupted all over her, and if she had four forefingers on every hand they wouldn't be enough to plug it out. So Celia's mother finds her mouth and shouts, in the hope that her actual ears will answer, 'What is that dreadful noise?'

Is this music?

Yes, if that is dancing.

Is it dancing?

Possibly. If those are people.

And are those people?

Celia's mother is standing by the door. By the door is where the light switch usually is. If this is a room, if this is real, there should be a light switch about

HERE.

236

Yes. It's quieter with the light on. Now she can see it's not deafening, now it's not dark. Let there be a bright bare bulb on the ceiling, and then yes, those are people; now that there are spaces between them, and some attempt at faces, and someone running towards her shouting, 'Turn it off!'

The light is off, over and out in two seconds; but the scene is freeze-framed on the personal pull-down cinema screen inside Celia's mother's eyelids. It is not a mainstream movie. It wouldn't be on at her local Odeon. She might catch it at some struggling alternative venue, but Celia's mother doesn't go to places like that. She prefers wholesome family entertainment.

Which is why she is about to walk out of Cath's party.

Celia's mother is not prepared to put up with men dressing as animals and women going wild. She simply won't have people waving their arms and things that are not absolutely arms in the air. She can't bear to stand so close to their neuroses, psychoses, halitoses.

But somewhere in this mess is Celia. Her mother knows it. She feels the tug on intangible apron strings. She reels away from the wall. She has abandoned her anger now. She must find her child.

'It's all right, Celia,' she calls, 'Mummy's coming! Mummy's not cross! Where are you?'

There is an answer.

There is a sound which grows stronger as she gets closer to the centre of the crowd. A harmonic of it hums in her heart. Her womb moves to the boom of the bass.

Someone is plucking at her umbilical chord.

So where is Celia?

There, light in the shadows, a flick of long blonde hair. There, pretty in the apocalypse, a toss of blue taffeta. Coming through the crowd towards Mother, the patchy pink of a tear-stained face.

It's Celia. Safe, sober, single.

This seems to give Mother reason to restart the stagey machinery of her anger. Celia is safe, therefore Mother can shout again.

'*Celiaaa*!!' Mother's bellow hits the ceiling, then hovers cartoonlike below it. All around her, men dressed as animals flinch.

Celia keeps coming; doesn't stop, doesn't start, doesn't even flicker. Mother plants herself in Celia's path, red and ready, and angry as an amaryllis. They come face to face. It is too dark to see whether they are eye to eye.

'*Celiaaa*!!' Mother trumpet-mouths.

Now Celia stops. Now she starts. Now the black holes where her eyes should be suck Mother's into a singular stare. Some sort of struggle ensues. Some sort of dance. Each has the other by the shoulders; they writhe and fall. Head-banging, high-kicking, hip-hopping; shake it up baby, twist and shout.

Celia's voice finds Mother's ear.

'I'm not Celia,' Celia shouts, 'fucking let go of me!'

She is not Celia. Mother lets go of her.

'Jesus fucking Christ,' shouts Not-Celia, 'that's the second time this evening!'

'I'm sorry, dear. It's my mistake. Now you come to mention it, of course you can't possibly be Celia. She's changed. Her fiancé's father caught a homosexual with her frock on in the kitchen, would you believe. And then I saw Celia come in here wearing black trousers and red hair. If it wasn't the engagement party tonight, I'd knock her from here to next week, when I eventually lay my hands on her,' explains Celia's mother at length.

Not-Celia doesn't catch half of it, but she doesn't need to.

'Are you Celia's mother?' she shouts.

238

Mother nods, florid.

'That character she's marrying. Do you know where he is?' Not-Celia shouts.

'Kenneth?' shouts Mother. 'He's downstairs, dear. He's not very well.'

Not-Celia nods nastily. Then she nods normally, and holds out a hand to take her leave of Celia's mother.

'And your name is . . .?' shouts Mother.

'My name?' shouts Not-Celia. 'It's Alice, of course.'

She disappears into the dancing dark, leaving Celia's mother at the mercy of a sudden attack of *déjà vu*.

Four stairs? This is more like falling down forty. Falling down a rabbit hole. Falling into place.

Celia's mother forces her way out. She pushes past a Humpty Dumpty, dancing on eggshells; a balding gentleman with what seems to be a small five-bar gate strapped to his bottom; a host of precocious daisies, their fresh young flesh bare but for pink-tipped petals and dusky golden pollen.

The dancers puzzle her like pieces of a part-remembered dream, but she gets the general picture. It is fancy-dress. Whatever else this is, it is a fancy-dress party. That explains almost everything.

Celia's mother comes to a wall where the dancing stops. To her surprise, she sees a woman of her own age sitting in an armchair knitting. As Mother gets closer, she amends her description of the character; it is a sheep of her own sex. The sheep lifts a pointed face to Celia's mother, without slipping a stitch on any of the fourteen flying knitting needles.

'Feather,' it says politely.

Celia's mother smiles, and the smile gets stuck. It is funny to find that something she thought was a figment of her own childhood imagination, her own personal parody of her own maiden aunt, is out on general release. How many hundreds of people must have the same dreams? The world would be a much better place if everyone knew that everyone else knows exactly what they're thinking.

'What is it you want to buy?' says the sheep.

'I'm just looking for my daughter,' says Celia's mother, 'I wonder if you've seen her? She's wearing fierce red hair, and her clothes are completely black.'

'Blaa-aack?' says the sheep, blinking behind spectacles. Mother nods. The sheep points over her shoulder with the tip of a knitting needle.

'Thanks,' says Celia's mother, and turns around.

There is Celia, sitting in a quiet corner, deep in conversation with a big White Rabbit.

Mother draws herself up to her full height. 'What is the meaning of this?' she says, towering over Celia terribly.

Celia doesn't respond. The music is loud and she is looking at something in the White Rabbit's hand. Mother can't tell if her face, half hidden by the bargain-basement red wig, is impudent or innocent. She nudges her daughter with a tyranny of toes. It is only a tap on the knee-cap, but Celia answers it with a barrage of manic mouth-fire.

'Hello yes hello yes how can I help you?' she shouts, staggering to her feet.

Mother takes six paces backwards. She would take six more if she could walk through walls. Celia is shocking. Her face is changed.

'Overwhelming woman. What do you want with me?' she is shouting.

Celia is mad. Her eyes are different. Something has escaped

from them. 'What do you want?' she is still shouting, 'now you've woken me from my slumber. You'd better have a damn good airplane cos I want to have this conference on the way home!' Celia does not appear to have recognised her mother.

The White Rabbit makes a feeble attempt to restrain her. He places a grubby paw on her shoulder. 'Sit down,' he stammers; then, to Celia's mother, he says, 'Sorry ma'am, don't take it personally, she's out of her head . . .' As he speaks the White Rabbit pulls coyly at his waistcoat pocket like a little boy playing with his penis.

'Out of her head?' mutters Celia's mother, 'Out Of Her Head!' she splutters. 'What do you mean?' Then it hits her. It hits her hard. She screams blue murder. She screams murder in all the colours of the rainbow. She screams, 'DRUUUGGGGSSSS!?!?!'

Celia decides it's time to leave. With a stare at Celia's mother, part baleful, part flirty, she stands and starts to stroll away.

'Oh no you don't, my girl!' shouts Mother, with a swipe at the wig, the woolly, at any part of Celia that may be got a grip on. She misses; a comedy chase scene ensues. Celia crashes off into the crowd on crazy legs. Mother follows, grabbing and snatching at empty air with Benny Hill hands. Their progress is slow, and their sense of direction is non-existent. It takes them twenty minutes to find their way out of the room. By the time they leave Cath's poor party, one hot on the heels of the other, they have attracted almost everyone's attention. The dancers stop dancing and crowd round the door to watch as Celia funny-runs down the passageway with her mother bellowing 'Out of her head!' behind her. Many of Cath's guests follow. They think it's all part of the party.

On the landing Celia heads for the safety of Phoebe's room, but with some spectacular footwork Mother intercepts her. The escape route is blocked.

'Phoebe! Phoebe!' screams Celia.

Mother stands firm. 'Ssshhh!' she hisses through goose-scary lips. 'Stop running away from Mummy. Don't you know – there's nowhere to go!'

Celia backs away. She backs all the way to the top of the stairs. She looks over her shoulder. The stairs peter out underneath her.

'As God is my fitness instructor,' she says, looking back at Celia's mother, 'you'd better have a damn good reason for this!'

Mother raises a huge shaking hand. 'Get down those stairs!' she says, and prepares to strike.

Phoebe comes down the corridor from her room with her party women clustered about her like an army of angry cherubs. Phoebe is rosy-cheeked with rage.

'What are you doing?' she says to Celia's mother's back.

Celia's mother turns to face her, and Celia seizes the chance to escape, jumping and twisting in the air and landing on the fifth stair from the top, just out of Mother's reach. Celia runs. Mother topples and tumbles. They both reach the bottom at the same time. The crowd from Cath's party follows. Phoebe and her friends bring up the rear.

'Hi. How are you getting on?' smiles the Cheshire Cat.

'I've just given my mother the slip,' says Celia. 'I feel a bit bad about it. Hiding is all right. It's ... what's the word ... ambiguous enough to be laughed off as an accident later; but running away is another matter.' She slumps to the floor behind the screen in Cath's bedroom, panting.

'What happened?' asks Cath.

'She caught me coming out of the bathroom,' says Celia, 'and I couldn't face her. She's so cross it made me behave like a naughty child. I ran up your little passageway and right into your party.

I'm almost certain she followed me in, but I'm sure she won't stay long!' Celia peers round the corner of the screen.

There are bodies lying all over the floor of Cath's bedroom. Here and there, like campfires in the mountains, thin towers of smoke rise from glowing orange pinpoints to great grey obscurity.

'She won't find me here, will she?' says Celia, pulling her head back in.

'No,' says Cath, stretching luxuriously. 'So what happened? Did you blow out your engagement?'

'What?' says Celia.

'Did you break it off? When you went back?'

'Oh, I haven't been back,' says Celia.

'Where have you been then?' Cath gasps.

'Er, with Dodge,' says Celia. 'Did you know that he is a transvestite?'

'No!' cries Cath. 'Oh! So that's why he doesn't fancy me. Is he gay, then?'

'I don't know,' says Celia. 'He likes a woman. But he likes her because he wants to be like her. Or what he thinks she's like. He's not a . . . um . . . a lesbian, though. He doesn't love her. I'm fairly sure of that.'

The Cat has to think about this. After some time she shakes her head like a wet dog and says, 'Who is this woman then?'

Celia smiles.

'Who?' asks Cath, again.

Celia blushes. 'It's me, okay?' she says, 'but there's nothing funny going on.'

'Dodge wants to be you?' says Cath.

Celia nods.

Cath stretches again, arching her spine like a bow, but she

243

doesn't speak for a long long time. Then she says 'Wow!' very slow and very low and looks at Celia sideways.

Celia is looking at Cath.

'Why you?' says Cath.

Celia shrugs.

'You're the last person I'd want to be,' says Cath. She doesn't seem to mean it nastily though, so Celia opens herself up to discussion.

'I think Dodge chose me because I looked easy,' she says, 'you know, simple and straightforward.'

'My first female role-model,' says Cath, with the simpering intonation of an advertisement.

'Yes,' says Celia, 'I was living like a real woman should.'

'Only from the outside in,' Cath corrects her. 'I've never met anyone as superficial as you, Celia; your mind must be a million miles away from your body. If it's anywhere at all. That must be the attraction for Dodge. I bet he's, like, really screwed up too.'

Celia changes the subject instantly.

'Anyway,' she says, 'then I went to Phoebe's party. Phoebe's sister is a film-maker. She's quite famous. Did you know that?'

'No,' says the Cheshire Cat, stifling a yawn.

'But the funny thing was,' Celia continues, 'at first everyone thought I was her. Because of these clothes, and this hair.' She gets hold of a handful of red hair and gives it a sharp tug. The wig comes off with the same sort of pop a Barbie-doll's head makes when it's pulled off. Celia sighs with relief and scratches her scalp furiously.

'If it's so uncomfortable,' says Cath, 'why were you wearing it?'

Celia stops scratching for a second. 'Let me see now,' she says. 'It was because Dodge had sort of . . . sort of taken me over. You know, he was wearing my dress, and a wig like this' – Celia teases a tangle out of her own hair – 'so I had to put on a new personality. But weirdly enough,' she continues, 'when Phoebe's sister arrived from America, she could have been my double. And *her* real hair was just like my wig. But nicer, no really, it's in much better condition . . .'

Cath is staring in disgust at the wig, which looks more than ever like a bloodied animal corpse now that it is discarded on the carpet.

'Weirder still,' cries Celia, 'was that Phoebe didn't even notice that I wasn't her sister!'

'Pissed probably,' spits the Cat.

'I passed myself off, anyway,' says Celia, 'I passed myself off as Hebe to everyone at the party. Then I passed out in an armchair. When I woke up the real Hebe had arrived. She was ace. I told her the dream I'd had about women being tied to a washing-line; and she told me that my unconscious is political.'

'My unconscious must be political too,' cries Cath, 'because I had a dream earlier, and in it Glenda Jackson was coming out of our bathroom!'

'No,' says Celia, 'no.'

'No what?' demands Cath.

Celia is having trouble getting the words out. 'That was no dream,' she says, 'that actually happened. See. Glenda is in the house. She's one of Phoebe's guests.'

'Wow!' Cath is impressed.

In the bedroom behind the screen, there is the sound of a door opening. Celia and Cath freeze.

There is someone out there shouting 'Celia!'

Celia and Cath shiver.

'Who is that?' Celia whispers, 'whose voice is that?'

It comes again. 'Celia!' it says. It is not cross.

Cath smiles. 'I know who that is,' she says, and, slipping around the side of the screen, disappears into the room.

Celia hugs her knees and stares at the discrepancies in the alignment of two strips of wallpaper.

Cath comes back. 'Twice in one night!' she cackles. 'It was the Anglo-Saxon messenger. This is the best Wonderland ever.'

She hands Celia a missive.

Celia takes it reluctantly.

'This is one of my own napkins!' she gulps, 'Marks and Spencer! This letter must have been written right inside my party!'

'What does it say?' asks Cath.

Celia unfolds the napkin and reads aloud DEAR CELIA, I'M SORRY BUT I SEEM TO HAVE MADE MATTERS WORSE. YOUR PARTY NEEDS TO BE IN A PADDED CELL NOW. PARTS OF IT ARE GETTING BROKEN. PLEASE COME. I DON'T THINK YOU'LL BE ABLE TO SAVE IT, BUT AT LEAST I WON'T HAVE TO TRY AND EXPLAIN EVERYTHING TO YOU TOMORROW. SORRY AGAIN, LOVE DODGE. PS YOU MAY FIND IT ADVISABLE TO BE IN DISGUISE.

It is hard to talk when your jaw is on the floor, and Celia's voice is as untidy as Dodge's writing as she reads out his words. Elocution, however, is the thing furthest from her mind. Electrocution is closer.

'Advisababble 'n' Disguisababble,' she slurs, staring from Cath to the letter and back again. Cath laughs.

'Why are you laughing?' Celia asks, her hair standing on end and the smell of something singed on her breath.

Cath is laughing too much to say why she is laughing too much to say why she is laughing too much to say why she is laughing. And almost against her will, Celia starts laughing too much to say why she is laughing too.

But there isn't much else she can do. It's all been done

already. The preparations were made, the table was laid, the frock was donned, the flowers were devoured, the frock was donated to another party, and Celia vacated her engagement for six hours.

It's all gone wrong, but she can't complain. She knew she'd have to go back sooner or later, and if she's left it too late, there's no one but herself to blame. Perhaps if Celia hadn't been waiting for this evening since she was sixteen, if its purpose were fresher in her mind, she wouldn't have stayed away so long. But now it's time for the deserter to get her desserts, and serve her right if they're stale.

'Right, well, I'll be off then,' says Celia.

'Shall I come with you?' says the Cheshire Cat.

'Oh would you?' cries Celia.

'Sure,' says the Cat, 'Amoral support.'

Celia is perusing the note again. 'It says to come in disguise.'

'But,' says Cath, 'you're in disguise already, man. Aren't they expecting someone in a fuck-off blue frock?'

'Oh yes!' says Celia, and then, 'Oh no! Dodge has got the dress on. If he's in my room, they'll know not to expect me in that.'

'So you can go as you are,' says Cath, springing to her feet.

'Yes,' says Celia, then, 'No! My mother saw me like this. They'll be expecting me back in black.'

'So you've got to get changed,' says Cath, sitting down.

'Yes,' Celia nods thoughtfully, 'I've got to get irreversibly changed. Because, when I see what's going on down there, I might not want to declare myself at all. To stay on the safe side, my disguise must be irrevocable.'

Cath chuckles. 'Hey, you don't even sound like Celia any more. You're biting off big words and eating them as easily as penny chews.'

'But what can I wear?' worries Celia, 'and how can I hide my hair?'

Cath stands up and smiles down at her, and it seems as if the day's last ray of sunlight is coming through the doom and gloom to rest on Celia's raised face.

'Wait here,' Cath says, 'be not afraid. All will be well.'

She disappears behind the screen and the warmth goes with her. Celia's bottom lip protrudes and her chin is about to wobble, until Cath's disembodied voice floats back as if on the evening breeze, with the words, 'I have a cunning plan.'

Celia smiles, and doesn't stop smiling until someone else steps behind the screen, several minutes later.

It is the Duchess. Without the baby Celia saw her feeding in the dim alcove. But with the breasts.

'Oh, hello,' stammers Celia.

'You can't think how glad I am to see you again, you dear old thing!' says the Duchess.

Cath smiles warily. 'Where's Cath?' she asks.

The Duchess squats in front of her. 'She sent me,' she says. ' "Go behind the screen and get yer clothes off," she said, "and tell that Celia to take hers off too." '

'I see,' Celia sounds very brisk. 'Better get on with it then.'

She stands up, and the Duchess rises with her, staying eye to eye. Celia can smell a slight body odour and can't tell whose it is, they are so close together. But it isn't unpleasant; it is the musk of a summer meadow at dusk.

Celia clears her throat and pulls her pullover off. Emerging at the other end of its black tunnel she finds herself face to face with the Duchess again. The Duchess opens her mouth. 'Be a love and undo me hooks and eyes,' she says, 'I can't reach 'em by meself.'

'Okay,' says Celia, 'at the back?'

'Yes,' says the Duchess, and puts her chin on Celia's shoulder.

If Celia could have chosen, she would have stood behind the Duchess to unhook her. But now she finds herself clasping the Duchess in a full frontal embrace, and fumbling for fastenings she can't see. It is a slow and frustrating process.

'I dare say you're wondering,' says the Duchess after a while, 'why I don't put me arm around your waist.'

Celia unfastens faster. 'The reason is,' the Duchess continues, 'I'm doubtful about yer . . . about yer temperament.'

Celia unfastens faster. 'Shall I try the experiment?' adds the Duchess, 'or will yer bite?'

'Finished!' says Celia, and the Duchess's dress slips from her shoulders.

Celia sits down and starts to unlace her boots as slowly as possible, her face hidden in her hair. One comes off, then the other, then she lingers longer over her socks. Just when she is ready to take out her toenails rather than stand up and face the Duchess again, the Duchess says, 'Sorry.'

Celia cranes her neck up. 'No,' she says stiffly, '*I'm* sorry.'

'Shut it, you silly tit,' says the Duchess, '*I'm* sorry.'

'No, really,' says Celia, 'the fault was mine.'

'What fault?' says the Duchess.

Celia looks down again. 'I was rude,' she says to her knees.

'Fuck off, I was ruder,' says the Duchess.

Celia stands up. 'I should have made my position clear,' she says.

'What is your position?' asks the Duchess.

'I don't know,' says Celia, 'that's why I didn't make it clear.'

'Well, I could see that darlin',' says the Duchess. 'You don't know which way's up. I thought you might like to go down. But you ain't that way inclined, are you?'

249

Celia starts to unbutton her jeans. 'I've got to go down,' she says.

'Have yer?' says the Duchess.

'Yes,' says Celia, 'to my engagement party. What's left of it.'

Celia slips her jeans over her hips.

'Have you 'ad one too many jam tarts?' says the Duchess.

'I don't know,' Celia says, 'I can't remember.'

Celia climbs out at the bottom of her jeans.

'Shall I fold 'em up for you?' says the Duchess.

She takes a step towards Celia.

'I can do it,' says Celia.

Celia steps backwards and, bare but for white underwear, brushes up against the body of the Cheshire Cat, who is suddenly standing behind her.

Celia squeals. The fur feels like fire. Not quite like fire because it's hot but it doesn't hurt. The fur feels like fingers. Fingers to sink into. Celia arches her back to break the contact, but by now the Duchess is closer in front, and Celia is sandwiched. She sways, off balance. She fights to stay upright.

'Celia,' says Cath softly from behind, 'lean on me. You might like it.'

'Let yerself go,' adds the Duchess, 'yer won't fall.'

Suddenly,

Celia makes the sort of noise a cat makes when it jumps from one roof to another fifty feet in the air.

Celia is uplifted.

And she doesn't come down again.

She doesn't come down until,

Some time later, Celia and Cath tiptoe downstairs, hand in paw. They stand and check their costumes in the hall.

Celia is secure in a seamless new disguise. Celia is confident of her safety. And so, at long last, Celia sticks her strange head round the door to her own sweet room.

Her head spins when she sees the horrors happening inside. The furniture is rearranged. The chairs are rigid in rows. The banqueting table is a barricade, braced longways across the bay. Behind it, in splendid blue-curtained isolation, sit Celia's mother and father. In front of it, on smaller chairs, the elders of Celia's and Ken's families are ranged, facing the rest of the room. On the table are scattered the remains of a plate of jam tarts. Since Celia failed to serve a dessert, her guests have had to make do with scraps scavenged from elsewhere in the house.

The rest of the room is packed with people sitting like a public meeting. They are all looking forwards with rapt attention, their hush enhanced by Celia's lush carpet and discreet dark wood furniture and motionless chandelier. Round-eyed in the rectangular doorway, she and Cath spot several acquaintances from behind.

Right at the front they see Dodge, his black head as small as a pin in the great cushion of Celia's dress. There is something alarming about the angle of his posture, something that makes Celia scour the room quickly for an answer to the question marked by Dodge's pose.

Hebe is sitting next to him. It is impossible to get any clues from her as to what is going on. Her face is hidden by a burning bush. But the shock of that hot red hair sends Celia's eyes skating back to Dodge.

He is no longer wearing his wig.

And two seats away, on the other side of Hebe, and sporting the long cool blonde hair that Dodge ought to be, sits the Alice from under the table at Cath's party.

Into the chairs behind these three an assorted audience is

251

crammed. Heads, some human, some animal, bob and duck. Celia recognises some of them from her travels in the two top-floor do's, but there are strangers too. The whole house seems to have squeezed itself into her room, and she doesn't like the sensation at all. It makes her uncomfortable to see an elbow on her mantelpiece, a foot up her fireplace, and greasy hair against her wallpaper. But there are two spare seats in the back row, and Celia and Cath creep into them quickly, before they change their minds and run away again. Cath lights a fat white slug of a cigarette and hands it to Celia. Celia stares straight ahead through plumes of perfumed smoke.

Her fiancé's father is standing up at the front, holding his lapels and rocking on his heels. 'For the benefit of those who have just come in,' he is saying, 'the situation is as follows: Celia, spinster of this house, is lost.'

'Stolen!' Kenneth can be heard but not seen.

'Missing,' compromises his father, 'presumed unwed. In her place, left like a bolster under the blankets of an abandoned bed, are these' – he turns his gaze on Dodge, Hebe and Alice in the first row of chairs – 'these cast-off Celias, these fake fiancées, these decoys. Perhaps,' he continues, 'all three added together will make up one complete Celia. Perhaps, if we plot what they've got in common, we can work out the co-ordinates of the actual Celia. Or perhaps one of them is the real Celia. Double-bluffing. Disguised *as herself in disguise*.

'Clever? Too clever to be Celia? I think so. But one thing is certain: the three suspects here before me constitute the only sightings of anything remotely resembling Celia since she left her engagement dinner in the lurch. They are our only clues to her current whereabouts. We must follow the trail from one to the next and hope finally to find ourselves looking the real Celia in the eye. And it had better be a blue one!'

Ken's father stops and stares at the audience in silence, his icy orbs straining painfully in their sockets. He stays that way for some time, as if waiting for someone or something to snap under the pressure.

From a few rows back someone or something shouts, 'If you think we're wax-works you ought to pay, you know. Wax-works weren't made to be looked at for nothing. Nohow!'

Another voice replies, 'Contrariwise, if you think we're alive, you ought to speak.'

Ken's father smiles horribly at the second heckler. 'Thank you for bringing me so neatly to my next point,' he says. 'Well now, ladies and gentle animals, perhaps you can help. Perhaps you have seen something suspicious this evening. Perhaps you have been party to clothes swapping or table hopping.' With each *you* Ken's father points his finger at the assembly, like a latter-day Lord Kitchener.

'Pinch me,' whispers Celia.

'Pardon?' says Cath.

Celia looks at Cath as if she expects her to disappear or turn into a dinosaur. 'Am I dreaming?' she asks, uncertainly.

Cath shakes her head.

'Oh, go on,' Celia continues, 'I'm still asleep in Phoebe's purple armchair, aren't I? Mmmm, I can almost feel the cushions. Or is it Dodge's bed? Admit it, Cath; I dozed off on Dodge's bed and everything since then has been a dream. Please? Or was it when I fainted? Right back at the beginning of the evening, out cold on the kitchen floor. Oh how I hope I haven't come round yet. If only it has all been a dream . . .'

Cath shakes her head. 'The thing is,' she says, '*I'm* awake.'

'Yes, but you would say that wouldn't you,' Celia raises her voice crossly, 'because you're just someone in my dream.'

'Silence at the back!' shouts Celia's mother suddenly from her lofty perch at the front.

'Stand up the first suspect,' growls Celia's grandfather, whose beard has grown two inches since she last saw him, and is grey and grisly in the extreme.

The fiancé's father takes the first suspect by the slender wrist and hauls her to her shapely feet. It is the party Alice.

'It's Celia . . .' leers Ken from a corner.

'Indeed, ladies and gentlemen,' says his father, turning to the audience, 'this is the most lifelike of the suspects. This is the one we have most reason to believe is Celia. She denies it, of course; she says her name is Alice, in what we believe to be an attempt to pass herself off as a member of the fancy-dress party currently taking place in the house. It should be said that Celia's mother here is convinced of this suspect's innocence. But, ladies and gentlemen, allow me to demonstrate.

'See, the long blonde hair,' he tugs it, 'is real. The big baby-blue eyes,' he pokes them, 'are real. And look, if you please; on her pink cheeks, the tracks of real tears. Frilly petticoats, a few freckles, her fiancé's fancy: all the evidence we need to prove that this is the real Celia.'

Finishing with a flourish, he beckons Kenneth from his corner. As the fiancé staggers centre-stage his godfather stands up too, undermining the big moment with the fart of scraping chair legs. Ken's godfather reaches Father first and hands him an over-anxiously folded piece of paper. Ken's father picks the paper open and quickly acquaints himself with its contents; then he looks up at Alice and smiles like a knife.

'It has just been brought to my notice,' he says, 'that Alice is an anagram of Celia.'

The audience gasps and grasps one another, as this heavy

information sinks in. In the bay behind the table Celia's mother smacks Celia's father and sets off an alarmed electronic bleeping.

'Well, now,' says Ken's father, offering one hand to Kenneth and one to Alice, 'that wasn't so bad, was it? I don't know what all the fuss was about. You silly children.' With a fist around each of their wrists he attempts to join them together, beaming at the audience, his gold teeth gleaming like wedding rings.

'What makes you so sure that your son would recognise Celia if she stood here and punched his face in?' asks Alice.

'What?' says the fiancé's father.

'What makes you so sure,' asks Alice, 'that your son would recognise Celia if she stood here and punched his face in?'

'What are you saying, er, Celia?' asks Ken's father again.

'Well, listen to this,' says Alice. 'Earlier this evening, Kenneth attempted to rape me. He thought I was Celia, apparently. In which case, your son attempted to rape Celia too. There are several witnesses,' says Alice.

From the very back row comes the sound of someone falling off their chair.

'So if I were you,' Alice continues, 'I'd take Ken home now. He won't see Celia tonight, not even if she stood in front of him and punched his . . .'

'Shut up,' shouts Ken's father.

Alice doesn't. 'Take him home and teach him how to behave like a human being,' she says, 'but spend some of that easy-come cash of yours on a tutor, don't try to do it yourself. You too are in need of immediate education.'

'Shut your filthy mouth,' screams Ken's father. 'My son couldn't rape Celia. They're engaged to be married. She's given her consent. She's asking for it, see!'

From the second row of chairs, Alice's friend the Cook waves her wooden spoon.

'That won't stand up in court!' she calls.

'That won't stand up in *here*!' shouts Alice and pulls back her fist for the first literal punch of the exchange.

The fiancé's father steps sideways. 'Very well,' he says, 'you win. You're clearly not Celia. She'd never say unsupportive things about Kenneth. Go on then, you're free to go. Oh, and if you so much as mention the matter again you'll live to regret it – if you're lucky.'

The cook leaps a row of chairs and shoves the sharp end of her spoon up Ken's father's nose. Bull-like he steps backwards, and collides with Celia's father who is flying through the air, having been flung into the fray in an awesome act of maternal strength. There is a crunch as Ken's father's head hits Celia's; then the former father gives way, sinking to the floor with a hiss like something punctured.

Celia's father, retiring to the point of total mortification though he usually be, takes over without missing a beat.

'Hey, hey, hey,' he says, 'in the light of this disturbing new evidence, I am growing increasingly concerned for the safety of my daughter. Let us pretend to be sanitary towels, and "press on" with the next suspect. Up you get,' he nods at Dodge.

The spectators twang with tension as Dodge takes the stand. From the back there is a brief outbreak of clapping and cheering. But Dodge doesn't seem to hear it. He is grinding his teeth.

Celia's father puts his hand on Dodge's padded shoulder and forces him to face first one way, where the ring of family elders wait woodenly, then the other way, where the rows of assorted audience are ecstatic with electricity and drug abuse.

Dodge grinds his teeth.

'Clearly,' says Celia's father, 'this is not Celia. This, I do declare, is a young man. You,' he points a finger at a random member of the public in what is plainly an attempt to be dynamic like Ken's father, 'could have told me that. But, boys and girls, there is something rather odd about this young man.'

Celia's father pauses, possibly for laughter, and cocks a conservative eyebrow comedian-like at the audience. When no laughter comes, he clutches at the silk of Dodge's skirt with a desperate gesture. 'This,' he says, 'is my daughter's dress. The dress of my daughter. Watered silk, I am informed. It's been positively identified by her mother, who made it on her own sewing machine, and is something of an authority. What we want to know is; who is this young man, and how does he come to be wearing Celia's garment?'

As Celia's father speaks, Celia's fiancé is pulling himself off the floor where he fell during the clash of the fathers, hand over hand up the other side of Celia's skirt. Dodge stands firm.

'But he is shy,' Celia's father continues, 'Why? Well, he won't tell us anything about himself. I ask you, is there a member of the audience who can enlighten us as to this young man's character, and the nature of his business in the house?'

From the back row comes a cry of 'Impeccable!' From somewhere else someone adds, 'Unimpeachable!' This is followed by two 'Presidential!'s and a 'Residential!'; but by now Celia's father has realised that the audience are playing a word-association game. The muscles of his face work overtime. Worry lines his brow. He shouts for silence.

He doesn't get it. Ken is upright again and slapping himself on the forehead with the flat of his hand.

'I've got it! Oh, goody! I've got it!' Ken intones in tones which travel to the back of the room, 'Oh boy! It must have been him!

He raped Celia! He raped her, and then he put on her dress, so that if anyone asked him if Celia had been raped he could pretend to be her and say no she hadn't. Thus cunningly concealing his crime.' Ken smiles at the audience, flushed by this feat of self-defence. For a few seconds there is silence as everyone inwardly tests the strength of his argument.

Then Alice tuts like a handcuff's key turning and says, 'Look, bollock-brains, it wasn't Celia you assaulted. It was me. When will it sink into that scrotal skull of yours? It was me!'

'How do we know that Celia hasn't been assaulted as well?' says Kenneth, and starts a second sticky silence.

In the middle of it, in the middle of the second row, Phoebe stands up, sits down, and stands up again.

'Yes?' asks Celia's father.

'I saw someone . . .' says Phoebe.

'. . . Oh no!' stutters the audience.

'Who looked like Celia . . .' says Phoebe.

'. . . Not again!' mutters the audience.

'Getting sexually abused by a man,' says Phoebe, 'on the kitchen floor.'

The audience flutter. Someone in the back row falls off their chair again.

Celia's father holds his head in his hands. 'In the kitchen?' he says, '*Gott in Himmel*!' But his low moan is drowned out by the high tide of woe which washes over Celia's mother, still sitting behind the table in the blue-curtained bay.

'My little girl!' she wails, 'Oh, my baby!' And slams her head once, twice, thrice, on the top of the table.

Dodge looks at her in alarm; she looks like a glove puppet. He resists the urge to bend and see whose hand is up her skirt; she's probably working herself. Into a frenzy. Her nose is bleeding, and this makes Dodge feel so sick that he will do almost anything to stop her.

'I confess,' he says, 'It was me.' He turns back to the audience. 'It was me.'

'Ha-ha! Just as I thought!' trumpets Celia's fiancé and jumps on top of him.

The audience lean forward as one to get a better angle on the action, as Ken and Dodge sink as one to the floor.

Ken and Dodge are locked in battle. Powdery puffs rise into the air as they scuffle on the carpet; teeth rattle, limbs flail, punches fly. It is the sort of fight which would go on to the death if both participants fought like men. But Dodge has neither the time nor the inclination for that. Mid-scrap, he manoeuvres himself so that his knees are holding Ken's shoulders, and his elbows are gripping Ken's hips; it is a sixty-nine position and Dodge is fighting dirty. For a moment he pauses, poised with pointed teeth, over the dank cloth and cheesy metal of the fiancé's flies. The he buries his face and fills his mouth with heinous living trouser. And grinds his teeth.

Ken screams. Dodge stands up. His hair is standing on end and his face spasms as if he has just sucked a lemon.

'You misunderstand me,' he shouts over the fiancé's sobs, 'I was the Celia. I was the Celia on the kitchen floor. Not the man.' His gaze finds Phoebe in the audience, 'It was me you saw.'

'Can you prove it?' asks Celia's father politely; and adds, 'You bloody pervert,' too quietly for anyone else to hear.

'Only if you ask me nicely,' says Dodge.

Phoebe stands up again. The audience, who panic every time one of its number sticks their neck out, flap; all except for a couple at the back who clap.

'I can prove it,' says Phoebe.

'Then, little missy, do so at once,' says Celia's father.

'I said I saw someone who looked like Celia under attack in the kitchen. That was Dodge, in her dress. The real Celia was upstairs at the time.'

'You've seen the real Celia?' asks Celia's father.

'Yes,' says Phoebe.

Everyone holds their breath.

'Where is she now?' Celia's father gasps.

'I don't know,' says Phoebe.

'You let her go?' he lets out a long sigh.

'Look,' says Phoebe, 'she is free to go where she pleases.'

Celia's father stares at her in confounded silence, then suddenly stamps his foot. 'Well if you knew it wasn't my Celia on the kitchen floor, why did you bother to say anything at all?' he asks angrily.

Phoebe doesn't answer. She folds her arms and waits for him to work it out for himself.

'What?' he says when he can't, his voice tight with self-righteousness.

The woman sitting next to Phoebe pulls on her sleeve and whispers something in her ear. Phoebe nods vehemently and says something that sounds like, 'Go for it!' And Glenda Jackson gets to her feet and makes a short speech, a speech that finds Celia's father as guilty as a puppy tangled up in toilet roll.

'You seem to assume, sir,' says Glenda, 'that if it wasn't Celia, it wasn't sexual assault. You consider sexual assault to be a crime, not against Celia's person, but against *your* property. You imply that Celia has no right not to be raped, except for the fact of her being *your* daughter. That, sir, stinks.

'Secondly, you seem to suggest that if anyone who isn't Celia has been sexually assaulted it is none of your concern. If that

260

really is how you feel, fine. But sit down. Don't stand up there in judgement of others, when the only justice you want is for yourself.'

Pockets of clapping and cheering open up in the audience. Fingers pop out and point accusingly at Celia's father; words are thrown at him like real things. Rotten things, smelly things, sharp things. Celia's father winces and waits for the onslaught to be over, wishing that the lady were still an actress and didn't have to be taken seriously.

He looks daggers at her as she sits down. If *they* were real he would stab her with them, stab her until she cries 'Out, damned spot!' But making sad doggy-eyes at her will have to suffice. This has always been his best weapon against women and socialists alike. Celia's father lowers his head mournfully and gives the impression that his tail is between his legs. The attack of shouted sentences comes to a full stop. Then Celia's father turns to face Dodge at the same angle world leaders stand to shake hands when cameras are present.

'You weren't Celia, but you could have been. Right?' he says. Then his face changes. 'So who was it? Who violated my little . . . my . . . oooh, who violated you?'

Dodge shrugs his shoulders dumbly. He looks sick and tired. He looks as though the prospect of re-living his close shave before a jury of homophobics and misogynists is tantamount to slitting his throat. He looks at the audience, and a ruby red blush rings his neck as they all smile back in encouragement.

All except one.

The Mad Hatter has risen to his feet and is making his way along a row of chairs; treading on toes and trying to pretend that he was leaving anyway. So Dodge is spared the trauma of a dramatic denouncement; he merely says, 'It was him,' without having to point a finger or sharpen his inflection at all.

261

'Who? Him?' says Celia's father, following the Hatter's hurried progress with slow eyes.

Dodge nods.

'Madam?' Celia's father asks Phoebe for corroboration.

Phoebe nods.

Celia's father clears his throat. 'Excuse me,' he says to the Hatter.

The Hatter pretends not to notice and rushes on, with the illusory urgency of a hamster running round and round its treadwheel.

'I say,' Celia's father tries again.

Still the Hatter scurries on. Celia's father nudges Ken, who is swaying on the edge of the situation; half in and half out of it. 'Stop him, Kenneth!' he whispers hoarsely, 'Cut him off at the door!'

Once the order has been given three times, Ken needs no second bidding. He spread-eagles himself across the open doorway in the nick of time. The Hatter is trapped.

He and Ken are standing eye to eye. Slowly, recognition dawns in Ken's. 'Haven't we met before?' he asks, 'I'm sure I've seen you somewhere.'

'Yes,' says the Hatter, 'over there!'

The Hatter points to the far corner of the room, and while Ken is squinting in its direction and shaking his head and saying, 'No, I don't think that was it,' the Hatter takes the opportunity to make his escape, darting forward and diving between Ken's slack legs. It looks as though he's going to get away.

But he doesn't.

From the last chair in the last row of the audience, someone springs in a cat costume and saves the day. The Cat grabs the Hatter by the seat of his breeches and, with a furious feline scream, tosses him like a caber to the table at the top of the room. The Hatter lands at Celia's father's feet, and swaggers, staggered, on the spot.

There is a round of applause.

'Take off your hat,' Celia's father says to the Hatter.

'It isn't mine,' says the Hatter.

'Stolen!' Celia's father exclaims, raising an eyebrow at the audience.

'I keep them to sell.' The Hatter adds as an explanation, 'I've none of my own. I'm a hatter.'

A small buzz goes round the audience, like a bee looking for flora.

'What's your name?' Celia's father barks.

The Hatter takes a step backwards.

'I'm a poor man, your Majesty,' he begins, in a trembling voice, 'and I hadn't begun my tea – not above a week or so –and what with the bread-and-butter getting so thin – and the twinkling of the tea . . .'

'The twinkling of the *what?*' says Celia's father.

'It began with the tea,' the Hatter replies.

'Of course twinkling begins with a T!' says Celia's father sharply. 'Do you take me for a dunce? Go on!'

'I'm a poor man,' the Hatter goes on, 'and most things twinkled after that – only the March Hare said – '

'I didn't!' the March Hare says firmly, from somewhere in the spectators' stand.

'You did!' says the Hatter.

'I deny it!' says the March Hare.

'Well, at any rate, the Dormouse said – ' the Hatter mutters, looking nervously at Kenneth, who is unblocking himself from the doorway and striding back to the front of the room, squarer in

263

the shoulders. 'And after that,' he continues quickly, 'I cut some more bread-and-butter – '

'Who were you catering for?' Celia's father asks.

'Myself,' says the Hatter, 'and a few friends.'

'Was this one?' Celia's father draws Dodge forward.

The Hatter looks away.

'Well?' says Celia's father after a short pause, 'we're waiting. What do you say?'

The Hatter doesn't say anything.

'Have you ever seen that before?' In Celia's father's hands, the word 'that' is applied to Dodge like a cricket bat. But it gets a result.

'That is the operative word, sir,' says the Hatter in a confidential tone. 'You see, I thought he was a she.'

Celia's father nods sagely. 'Easily done,' he says.

'If I'd realised that he wasn't,' the Hatter shrugs ruefully, 'a man-to-man fight would have sufficed. But I had to do something, sir; it was the worst-behaved Alice I ever had the misfortune to take tea with.'

'Oh dear,' says Celia's father. He and the Mad Hatter are building a rapport. They talk like workmates leaning on their shovels.

'You would not believe the bare-faced cheek,' the Hatter adds.

'No, I don't suppose I would,' Celia's father sighs.

'I wouldn't either!' Kenneth's father is coming round. He sits on the floor, barely conscious, very confused, but trying desperately to get back into the conversation. He'd prefer to dominate it, if at all possible. 'So tell me more,' he says.

'Blatant deviation,' says the Hatter, 'that was about the size of it. Didn't do as he was told, didn't say the right things, hadn't paid proper attention to the details of his dress and deportment. But I could have turned a blind eye to that. I could have. I'm a reasonable man.'

'We can see that,' says Ken's father encouragingly, 'go on.'

The Hatter is approaching his punch-line. The people in the first few rows of chairs see his wrists twitch.

'Well, the little bastard only lay there and let me take him for a lady. Slap bang in the middle of the kitchen floor. In full view of him,' the Hatter nods at Ken, 'and that bird,' he waves vaguely at Phoebe. 'In full view! Now, that is what I call unforgivable.'

'It must have been very embarrassing for you,' says Kenneth's father.

Almost every member of the audience is so open-mouthed their heads are turning inside out. Rage blocks almost every throat like road-works. Only one anonymous voice from somewhere at the back manages to spit some words out: 'But he's a rapist!'

'All right, all right, we're coming to that,' says Celia's father.

'To what?' says Ken's father.

'We've got to ask him about sexual assault,' Celia's father lowers his tone.

'Why?' says Ken's father.

'Er, because it could have been Celia on the receiving end,' whispers her father, 'for all he knew. Or cared.'

Kenneth's father looks at Dodge.

'But it wasn't though, was it,' he says, 'so there's no problem.'

'Oh yes there is! It's a social problem and we're going to stamp it out,' cries Celia's father, and turns to the audience as proudly as a puppy that's learnt where not to poo.

'But if it wasn't Celia,' persists Ken's father, 'if it wasn't even a woman, how could it have been a sexual assault?'

Celia's father scratches his head. He looks stumped.

'I don't know,' he says. Then his eyes light up with a bright idea and he addresses Dodge: 'Did you do anything to suggest that the attentions were unwanted? Did you hit the Hatter, for example? Did you scream?'

Several members of the audience do at this moment.

But Dodge is silent.

'Are we to gather by your silence that the answer is no?' says Ken's father.

Dodge nods. Several members of the audience shout out; that is not the point. Ken's father shouts back that that is not the point either. This non-rape of a non-woman is sheer nonsense, and shouldn't take up any more of the parents' precious time.

Celia's father shakes the Hatter by the hand.

'Sorry sir,' he says sheepishly, 'You can leave now. Sorry.'

Grinning, the Mad Hatter skulks back to his seat. He has every intention of staying to see what happens next. But it's time for him to go. As soon as he sits down, someone in the seat behind him whips his hat off and sticks a knitting needle so far into each of his ears that they meet in the middle and make a shroud out of the wool he had for brains.

And while the Hatter is being silently done to death somewhere in the audience, Dodge is saying, 'I could have screamed until I was sick. It wouldn't have made any difference. My attacker thought I was Alice, just like Ken thought Alice was Celia. No matter what I said, it would have been Alice talking. And you know that men don't listen to little girls. His "Yes" was worth a hundred of my "No"s.'

The floor is Dodge's. But he turns and starts to tiptoe across it in the opposite direction. 'Don't blame Ken,' he says to the baying public, 'he was abused too. He was drugged, you see. By the time he found Alice and mistook her for Celia, he'd lost his grip on the hold-all of reality. All his stuff was falling out.'

The Cook points the pointed end of her wooden spoon at him. 'Whose side are you on?' she shouts.

'I'm in the middle,' says Dodge.

Ken stares at Dodge with red eyes.

'Drugged?' he says.

'That's right,' says Dodge.

'Rubbish,' says Ken, 'and how do you know?'

'You told me,' says Dodge.

'I never did!' says Ken.

'You did,' says Dodge, 'you just don't remember it, that's all.'

'Listen, you great girl's dress,' says Ken, 'I never don't remember anything! And I've never done drugs either.'

'Remember the White Rabbit?' says Dodge.

Something flickers behind Ken's eyes like old movie projection gear whirring into life in the dead of night.

'Leave it out,' says Ken.

'What?' says Dodge.

'Your poofter party pictures,' howls Ken, 'get them out of my head.'

'Say what you can see, Ken,' says Dodge, 'it's the only way to clear your name.'

'Dancing,' Ken gasps, 'dancing, with long white ears. Urgh!'

'Good, go on,' says Dodge.

'Prick!' screams Ken. 'Prick in his waistcoat pocket! But I'm a man, mum!'

Ken falls off his feet and lands on the floor.

Dodge turns to all the parents and grandparents and godparents.

'See,' he says, 'someone gave him a shot of something upstairs. It altered his perception somewhat.'

'That's his problem,' shouts the Cook, from the second row.

267

Dodge turns to her. 'Yes,' he says, 'but he shared it with Alice. And it wasn't halved.'

The Cook shakes her head at him crossly, but doesn't say any more.

Celia's mother stands up. She looks at Kenneth on the carpet. 'Take him away, someone,' she says, 'he's out of his head. Take him away and bring him back.'

Nobody moves.

'Go on,' Celia's mother says to Dodge, 'you take him away. And take that silly dress off.'

Dodge stares at her. A muscle twitches in his cheek.

'Try a pair of trousers,' says Celia's father, 'they might suit you.'

Celia's mother glares at him. 'Shut your mouth,' she says.

Dodge bends down and prods Ken. He is sweaty and shaking.

'If you touch my son again,' says Kenneth's father, 'I'll have you arrested.'

'You shut your mouth too,' says Celia's mother.

'Don't you speak to my husband like that,' says Ken's mother.

'Don't you speak to my wife like that,' says Celia's father.

'Don't you speak to *my* wife like that,' says Ken's father.

The parents have all out-parented each other, and purse their lips in a stalemate silence.

'But don't you see,' Celia's mother is the first to burst, 'the boy is sick!'

Everyone looks at Dodge.

'You can say that again,' says Ken's father.

'Not that boy, your boy!' shouts Celia's mother, 'he needs to lie down!'

'Yes, well, thank you for your concern, but I'm quite capable of dealing with the matter myself,' says Ken's father, 'Mrs Conn! Take Kenneth for a lie down.'

Ken's mother bursts into tears.

'Come along woman, what's the matter with you?' barks Ken's father.

'Don't you talk to your wife like that,' says Celia's mother.

Ken's father has got Ken's mother by the handbag and is trying to pull her to her feet. 'Take him away,' he hisses.

'I don't want to!' wails his wife.

'What?' he growls.

'I don't want to,' she sobs again.

'Why not? He's your son,' shouts Ken's father.

'But he scares me!' screams Ken's mother.

Ken's father lets go and his wife bumps abruptly back into her chair.

'Right. Fine. Sit there and let him be led away by a bloody homosexual then!' he says.

Dodge steps over the prostrate body of Ken and comes face to face with Ken's father. Dodge puts his hands on the bigger man's shoulders and stretches onto tippy-toes to lift his lips to the bigger man's ear.

And Dodge tells him something, so softly that no one else knows he said it, so bollock-twistingly explicit that Kenneth's father will never forget it. Then Dodge nods goodnight to the other parents and the godparents and grandparents, and walks wearily out of the room.

On the way he meets Celia secretly, with the eyes only. Celia winks one, and both of Dodge's grow wide at the ingenuity of her disguise. When Dodge is gone, Celia's water; he must be the only person she knows who can see through her costumes, see who she really is, and that's something worth crying for.

Meanwhile, Kenneth's father wets himself as secretly as Dodge's whisper. And the Cheshire Cat, who has been curled up

269

at the end of the front row ever since it hurled the Mad Hatter there, hooks its hands under Ken's armpits and heaves him into an empty chair. Then it sits down between him and Hebe, and the front row is full again.

Celia's mother hitches up her heart-coloured skirt and heaves herself onto the table. She crosses her legs and faces the room like a teacher whose class have finished their exams and are marking time until the summer holidays.

She smiles. At the last possible Celia left in the first row. 'You can come out now,' she says.

'Are you talking to me?' says Hebe.

'Come on, you can stop pretending now,' says Celia's mother.

'I don't know what to say,' says Hebe.

'You don't have to say anything,' smiles Celia's mother.

'I'm quite happy to speak at length,' says Hebe, 'if you could just give me an idea of what's required.'

'Well,' suggests Celia's mother, 'you could start by saying sorry.'

'Sorry,' says Hebe.

'For all the trouble you've caused,' says Celia's mother.

'For all the trouble I've caused,' says Hebe.

'For running away from your party,' says Celia's mother.

'For running away from my party,' says Hebe.

'For being rude to your guests,' says Celia's mother.

'For being rude to my guests,' says Hebe.

'For hurting your mummy,' says Celia's mother.

'For hurting my mummy,' says Hebe.

'Now mean it,' says Celia's mother.

Hebe sighs.

'But it's too late,' she says.

'Not if you mean it,' says Celia's mother.

'What? You won't go?' says Hebe. 'If I'm never naughty again, will you come back?'

'Come back?' asks Celia's mother.

'Come back,' says Hebe.

'I didn't leave you,' says Celia's mother, 'you left me.'

'Was it my fault then?' says Hebe. 'Did I go first?'

'Well, yes,' says Celia's mother, 'but if you're a good girl, if you marry Kenneth, I'll come and visit you.'

'I have to marry Kenneth?' says Hebe, hollowly.

'If he'll still have you,' says Celia's mother.

'I have to marry Kenneth?' says Hebe, 'why do I have to marry Kenneth? Is that what you want?'

Celia's mother nods, once.

'But, Mum,' says Hebe, 'I don't want to marry Kenneth. I don't love him. I don't even like him.'

His parents stand up. There is silence in court, broken only by the sound of their chairs falling over, broken only by the sound of their chairs falling onto the feet of Celia's grandfather who starts to swear and curse like Rumpelstiltskin of the Bailey.

'What sort of mother are you?' says Hebe.

Now Celia's father stands up. And Celia's grandmother. They clutch each other, then spring apart, then clutch each other again. It's the natural ambivalence of their relationship, but they look as plastic and elastic as a pair of ballroom dancers.

'Why do you want me to marry anyone at all? Aren't I all right as I am?' Hebe is coming to a climax.

Over Hebe's head Celia's mother sees the young woman from earlier stand up again in the second row.

'I'm sorry about this,' Phoebe says, 'she's not slept for two days. She's not feeling herself at all. We'll just slip away now. We

271

won't take up any more of your time.' She puts her hand on Hebe's shoulder.

'Who are you?' asks Celia's mother, icily.

'I'm her sister. I live in this house,' says Phoebe.

'Celia doesn't have any sisters,' says Celia's mother.

There is a furious scraping of chairs and half the audience stand up. They don't say anything, they just stand up and stay standing up. They are the female half of the audience.

Celia's grandfather tuts. He can't stand the sight of them, stark staring bloody women; he'd give his right hand to be holding a machine gun.

'Where are you taking her?' says Celia's mother, jumping off the table.

'Who?' says Phoebe.

'Celia!' says Celia's mother.

'I'm not taking Celia anywhere. I haven't even seen her for hours,' says Phoebe, with the patience of one who realises that she didn't know the meaning of the word until now.

Celia's mother points speechlessly at Hebe.

'She's not Celia,' Phoebe says.

'She is,' says Celia's mother.

'She isn't, she's nothing like Celia,' says Phoebe.

'She told me she was sorry,' says Celia's mother. 'If that isn't Celia, I don't know what is.'

'She's bereaved,' shouts Phoebe, 'her mother is dead. And she wants her back so badly that she'd be Celia, if that's what it takes. She'd even marry Kenneth, for her mother's sake.'

'But she looks like Celia!' shouts Celia's mother.

Phoebe kicks an empty chair over.

'Not from the outside, all right, I'll admit that,' shouts Celia's mother, 'but she looks out from the inside exactly like her. I saw the eyes on the landing. She looked at me like Celia.'

'Well, perhaps you provoke that reaction in everyone,' says Phoebe, cool suddenly.

'And what's that supposed to mean?' says Celia's mother.

'If you don't give people any space, they peer out at you like prisoners,' says Phoebe.

'My daughter does not peer out at me like a prisoner,' shouts Celia's mother.

'I bet she does,' shouts Phoebe, 'she peers out at me like a prisoner, and I don't even know her.'

*

Somewhere in the crowd, Celia stops listening. She feels a very curious sensation, which puzzles her a good deal until she makes out what it is: she is beginning to grow larger, and she thinks at first she'd better get up and leave, but on second thoughts she decides to remain where she is as long as there is room for her.

'I wish you wouldn't squeeze so,' says a Dormouse, who is sitting next to her, 'I can hardly breathe.'

'I can't help it,' says Celia very meekly, 'I'm growing.'

'You've no right to grow here,' says the Dormouse.

'Don't talk nonsense,' says Celia more boldly, 'you know you're growing too.'

'Yes, but *I* grow at a reasonable pace,' says the Dormouse, 'not in that ridiculous fashion.' And he sticks his bottom lip out very sulkily, and goes back to sleep.

Simultaneously, the Cheshire Cat is having a quiet word with Kenneth. 'Wake up,' it whispers through its whiskers.

'I am awake,' says Ken, 'but I can't keep my eyes open. I'm on drugs.'

'Can I ask you a question?' says the Cat.

'If you must,' says Ken.

273

'How come you couldn't find Celia?' says the Cat.

'I could have done if she hadn't taken her frock off,' says Ken.

The Cat shakes its head in disbelief. 'Do you mean to say you don't recognise her without her clothes on?'

'Hur, hur, hur,' Kenneth laughs a manly laugh, 'not yet. But I will when we're married.'

'You still want to marry her?' the Cat is incredulous. 'Didn't you hear her say she doesn't love you?'

'She'll come round,' says Ken, 'when she sees what I've got in my pocket.'

He's so good with words, is Kenneth, such a cunning linguist. He is referring, of course, to the engagement ring; but he'd be a fool to start slipping things on fingers and pressing lips to other lips now.

Because the closest he's got to the real Celia is Hebe, and she'd swallow him whole.

'I can prove it's her!' Celia's mother is shouting when the Cat tunes in to the mass debate again.

'How?' Phoebe shouts back.

'Easy!' shouts Celia's mother, 'easy-peasy! Pull her bloody wig off!'

'No!' shouts Phoebe, but Celia's mother has already got hold of a handful of Hebe's hot red hair.

The fire fights back. Phoebe and Alice and all Celia's sisters surge forward to release the famous feminist film-maker from Celia's mother's clutches. Some hold on to Hebe, some hold on to Mother; but the mother won't let go of the hair, and the hair won't let go of the head.

'Cut and dyed. She's cut and dyed it,' pants Celia's mother still pulling, 'that's why she was gone so long. Those lovely long locks!

274

Cut and dried. It's Celia, all right. With a new hairstyle!'

All the parents and grandparents and godparents have joined the tug of love. Celia's grandfather is having the time of his life; never has he been able to slap so many silly bitches in such quick succession. Most people are screaming at most other people. But no one is screaming as loud as Celia, somewhere in the crowd, because Celia started this crazy thing and only Celia can stop it.

'You're pulling her head off,' Celia shrieks, 'stop it or you'll pull her head off! Listen everyone, she said she didn't even like Kenneth any more, so leave her alone. It doesn't matter whether she's Celia or not now, there's nothing in it for anyone else! Oh, it's going to come off – it's going to come – off with her head!'

Nobody takes any notice. Celia's hoarse discourse is merely an apt accompaniment to the scenes of carnage as angry women fight with men dressed as animals, and people like playing-cards fly in the face of convention.

Celia doesn't know what else to do. All she knows is not to do what Celia would do. She is no longer sure what Celia would do now, anyway. So perhaps she should do what everyone would least expect Celia, or someone pretending not to be Celia, to do. Celia stutters on incoherently, somewhere in the crowd. But just when it seems that Hebe's head is about to come off with a pop like a champagne cork, there is a louder sound. It is a voice of sparkling clarity, and its chosen words are few: *Hey everyone, I'm Celia – yoo-hoo, over here – I'm Celia, the real Celia – behind you!'*

It works. Everyone stops dead. Everyone turns around and stares at someone in a cat costume standing on a chair. The Cheshire Cat opens its mouth in the ringing silence.

'Only joking,' it says, 'I'm someone else. I'm sorry,' she hurries on in a low voice, 'but you had to be stopped. You were hurting Hebe.'

The audience turn away, keen to continue with the which hunt,

275

and find the real real Celia, but the Cheshire Cat has something else to say. It stretches its arms like legs above its head, and wiggles its hips like snakes around its waist, and chimes out the following rhyme:

The time has come, the Feline said,
To call off many things:
The honeymoon, the happy home,
The golden wedding rings.
For a life of gold and honey won't be
what tomorrow brings.

But wait a bit, the Family cried,
Please don't be so rash;
Think of all the time we've spent,
Think of all the cash.
But the Feline couldn't think at all,
Because of all the hash.

'Hurrah!' cry the crowd, 'more, more!' But the Cheshire Cat gives a little bow and is about to climb shyly off the chair, until Celia's mother shushes the catcalling audience and shouts at their feline friend to hurry up and sit down. Then the Cat stands tall again and sings two more short speeches:

Celia's mum and Celia's dad
are asking for a battle;
For Celia's mum and Celia's dad
treat Celia like cattle.

Her heart bleeds for Ken, but he thinks she's a Tart,
and she thinks he's secretly a Queen:
he can't see where she's going, but that is because
he's too worried about where she's been.

'Don't listen dear,' says Kenneth's godfather to his wife, 'it's another one of those blooming feminists.'

'Don't say that word!' screams Kenneth's godmother.

'All right, all right,' says Kenneth's godfather, at the end of his fully extended tether, 'it's another one of those bloody feminists.'

Kenneth's godmother pours a bottle of wine over her head and tries to drown in it.

'Now what?' snaps her husband, 'All I said was femi . . .'

His wife throws the empty bottle at him. 'Well don't!' she shouts, 'don't say it. Flowers, feminists; they're all the same. F-words, every one of them!'

The Cheshire Cat has stopped singing. It stands on the chair and stares at the squabbling godparents, whiskers quivering.

Ken's father appears in the Cat's line of vision. He stands square at the foot of the chair and tries to be scary. 'I know your sort,' he shouts up at it, 'you're all Cat and no Pussy, that's what you are.'

The Cat smiles. Kenneth's father kicks the chair leg.

Now Celia's mother joins him, jostling.

'Come down, come down, whoever you are,' she calls to the Cat, 'we've got work to do and you're getting in the way.'

The Cat sways.

Celia's mother steps backwards and bangs into her husband. 'Oh, do something!' she says to him. 'Here's another one out of her head; we'll never find Celia at this rate.'

Celia's father clears his throat. 'Rule forty-two,' he says timidly. 'All persons more than a mile high to leave the court.'

Everyone looks at the Cat on the chair.

'I'm not a mile high,' it says.

'You are,' says Celia's father.

'Nearly two miles high,' adds her mother.

'That's not a regular rule,' says the Cat, 'You invented it just now.'

'It's the oldest rule in the book,' says Celia's father.

'Then it ought to be Number one,' says the Cat.

The audience start to clap their hands slowly. The audience start to stamp their feet.

'Well, what do you know. Maybe I am a mile high,' shrugs the Cat, and climbs off the chair. When it is standing on its own two feet it is exactly the same height as Celia's mother. It is eye to eye with her. 'Maybe,' the Cat continues, 'that's why you can't see me. Watch me walk away,' it adds, backing away down the aisle to the door to the hall, 'watch me go.'

Everyone turns to stare as the Cat disappears, tail first, through the door. Its smile is the last bit of it to leave. Everyone hears as, out in the hall, the Cat lets rip a huge howl of something that could be happiness, could be sorrow, ecstasy and agony; something that stretches like a saxophone or a rainbow of sound from yesterday to tomorrow.

Flat on her back on the banqueting table Celia's grandmother is fast asleep, and the Cat's whoop comes into her dream as the sound of the hoop she played with as a child; hurtling over the cobblestones, footloose and fancy-free.

In the back row of the audience, Humpty Dumpty turns to the woman sitting next to him. She is dressed as the Duchess, and is bent double with silent laughter.

'What's got into Catherine?' he says to her. 'What's she playing at?'

The woman in the Duchess dress straightens up and faces Humpty. Humpty jumps, so smartly that his shell cracks clean in half. He smashes his way out of it, and stares at the woman in the Duchess costume again. It is Cath!

Humpty rubs his runny eyes.

'I say!' he says. 'If you're Cath, who the dickens was that in the Cat?'

9. Celia goes global without warning due to the Dreamhouse effect

Celia

Celia is

Celia is lying

Celia is lying on the bathroom floor.

Celia is lying on the bathroom floor in the position that people who fall off roofs land in.

Celia is lying face down in a pool of her own drool.

Presumably it's her own.

She lifts her head slowly, stiff as a dick. She licks her lips, which are dry as a bone. She is alone in the bathroom.

Presumably it's her.

Celia lifts her head higher and stares at the hairy ceiling, feeling the agony of effervescence as her extremities come back to life.

But her head is heavy with some horrible dream.

Presumably it was a dream.

She lays down on lino again, and goes back to sleep.

Celia

Celia is

Celia is wearing

Celia is wearing a cat-suit.

Pet-keeping helps to relieve stress, apparently. She is stroking fur with her fizzy fingers. She is purring. The petting is getting heavy. Celia is undoing the zip which runs from throat to crutch like a child's pyjama case or a post mortem, and stepping out; leaving the cat costume limp and lifeless on the bathroom floor. She wasn't wearing any underwear under there.

Celia

Celia is

Celia is standing up.

She catches sight of herself catching sight of herself in the mirror over the sink, and nearly sits down again. Her eyes are red, white and blue. Dead weights and still, like flags on a windless day. If this is the weather forecast, the clouds in Celia's head are here to stay.

Silently, Celia stares at the reflection of this head. It has some sort of cat hat on. Some sort of motorbike helmet covered with fluffy stuff. Cat skin. Strap under chin. Celia can't see how to undo it, because it is under her chin; using the mirror for guidance only makes her pull it tighter and tighter until

Celia panics. She thrashes around in the tiny bathroom, clutching at her throat and bashing the head on the rim of the bathtub, the sink, the cistern and the towel-rail in a frenzied attempt to dislodge it.

Of course, the attempt is futile. Of course, Celia has to calm down; the only other way out of a crisis like this is the ultimate exit, the big D, and despite the drama of Celia's death-throes the cat hat strap is not in fact tight enough to kill her. So, in the course of time, Celia finds herself standing in front of the mirror again, studiously avoiding eye contact, and patiently separating the cat cranium from her own.

Her hair tumbles down her bare back. It is dark with sweat, and dense with tangles. It is a jungle, and the face looking out of the undergrowth is as bright as a bird. Celia's face is besmirched with make-up. She wets a finger and tries to wipe the colours off. When they don't budge, she compresses her lips and eyes the bathtub dubiously.

Bending over, hair everywhere, Celia turns a big bathtap on. Holding her hand under the flow, she waits numbly. The trickling, piss-yellow stream grows warm and, gradually, hand hot.

It must be morning.

While the bath fills, Celia stands still, staring into space, as if switched off. For once, nothing is happening in her head, no running commentary, nothing said; there are only clouds, their wetness shorting out her circuits. When the bath water starts to overflow she stops it coming and climbs automatically into the tub. Now she can't see for steam and can't hear for splashing and can't stand still for scalding. Celia slips and lands with a splash like a raw vegetable in a saucepan of boiling water. Celia turns pink. Some soap slides into the water with her. It isn't her soap. It's someone else's. Celia keeps hers safe in her room. She has to, or it would be covered with other people's short hairs, curling in suggestive smiles. Normally, Celia wouldn't dream of using a stranger's soap. But now, she applies it to the stripes on her face, and sinks quickly under the water to rinse it off.

Underwater, the climatic conditions change. There is a break in the clouds in her head. It's only a short break. Almost immediately a bigger, blacker cloud blows across the sky of her mind and blocks the gap again.

Celia surfaces, spluttering. She saw something in that clear space, something shocking; two words and a piece of punctuation – Cat Costume?

Cat Costume?

Dripping, Celia leans over the edge of the tub and looks gingerly at the cat-suit crumpled on the floor.

It gives her a funny feeling: the sort of feeling one might get from looking at a real dead cat. A cat one had killed oneself. And not in a very nice way.

Shaking, Celia reaches for some shampoo.

It is not her shampoo. Her shampoo is in her room, and she doesn't have dandruff. It is someone with dandruff's shampoo.

But she doesn't think it's catching.

Celia concentrates on washing her hair. It takes a long time, but she feels a little better for it. The strenuous exercise and a stimulated scalp begin to bring her back to her senses. Then she submerges for another rinsing. Underwater, the funny feeling overwhelms her again.

Cat Costume?

Was she really wearing a Cat Costume? Wasn't that just a dream?

Suddenly, the clouds in Celia's head are breaking up all over the place, but there is no sunlight coming through; only sounds and pictures all soaked and sodden with this same dreadful question: What happened to my engagement party?

The answer escapes her. Trying to confront it head-on she loses sight of it altogether. Only when her face is turned away do clues flicker in the corners of her eyes.

An advancing army of extended family.

A sudden show of friends.

Celia sits up, breaking the bath's still surface. Water rushes out of her hair and gushes between her breasts; it drips from her nipples and cascades between her shoulder-blades.

It's all beginning to come back now. The start of the evening, smoked salmon and small talk, beginning to get bigger, beginning to get unbelievable . . .

Celia blinks her smarting eyes.

Was it really a White Rabbit?

Was it nearly a rape?

Was it . . . a rattle of crockery?

Celia jumps out of the bath. There is a real rattle of crockery, coming from the other side of the bathroom door.

Squeaky-clean on slippery lino, she skates for the doorknob. It turns cold, gold and ball-shaped in her hand. She opens the door an inch, and her hot body goes up in smoke as cold air rushes into the bathroom. Celia squints through the clouds of steam.

The landing is dream-grey, faint looking, worn-out. Against its murky lines the moving figure is clearly defined. Dodge, with a tray of precarious plates and toppling bottles, turns at the top of the stairs and begins to descend.

As he takes the corner, his blue frock flicks away the rest of Celia's clouds, like cobwebs on a duster. As her mind clears, she remembers the swap, she remembers exchanging dresses with Dodge. She sees the shards of her shattered dreams: her engagement dinner abandoned on the banqueting table; Kenneth, under another table with Alice, in Celia's absence; parents and parents and grandparents and godparents, patently told to frock off; and Dodge, facing the consequences of her costume on the kitchen floor.

Celia's dreams went to pieces, and she wasn't even asleep.

She needs to talk to Dodge. Urgently. Apology.

Celia scours the bathroom for something to wear. There is the

283

Cat Costume but she can't put that on because there is something about it she hasn't remembered yet, something about Cath she hasn't remembered yet, and she isn't at all sure that she is ready to.

There are towels. They are not Celia's towels. She has a complete set of matching towels and she keeps them under lock and key in her room.

'Why do I do that?' Celia wonders, 'they're towels. Not the crown jewels.'

There are two towels in the bathroom. One is stiff and grey, the other is sickly stripey; both are in a sorry state of disrepair. Celia wraps herself up in one and winds the other like a turban around her wet hair. Tucking the Cat's head under her arm, and pulling its body by the floppy fore-paw, Celia leaves the bathroom to its moistness and mouldering and hurries along the landing after Dodge.

Passing the door to Phoebe's room, she stops dead. This is where she sheltered from the night's storm, only distantly aware that if she were not sheltering from it, there would be no storm. Not of the same magnitude, not involving so many people. If Celia had stayed where she should have been, deafened by everyone else's parties but keeping the peace at her own, the storm would have been as tiny as the tears she cried in the kitchen, a small portable depression.

Instead she hid in Phoebe's room, leaving Dodge exposed to the elements; a lightning conductor, his baton concealed by her dress.

Celia hurries on. The flat cat follows. At the top of the stairs Celia stops again and stares down the dim passageway to Cath's rooms. All is silent now but still, it seems, restless and irritable in the aftermath of the uproar. Celia is too.

'Why, oh why,' she says to herself, 'didn't I just come up and ask her to turn it down? That would have been a reasonable request. Specially since she sprang the spectacle on the rest of the household at such short notice. No regard for anyone else's arrangements. Really! If I'd been notified in advance I could have had my engagement party in a hotel. She could have paid for it.'

Celia stamps down the stairs, thinking furiously. 'Injecting people with drugs left, right and centre! That's a matter for the authorities. Trail of doped jam tarts . . . it's criminal, that's what it is!'

Celia slows to get the Cat safely around the bottom of the banisters, then creeps alongside the closed door to her room. She wants to make sure they're not still in there. But she doesn't really know who *they* are, any more; perhaps everyone except herself. She leans an ear against her door and listens carefully.

Silence. A deep unmoving volume of silence, inviting as an early morning swimming pool. Celia can't wait to get into it. But first, a word with Dodge. She walks on down the hallway, the Cat hot like a dog on her heels. Washing-up sounds splash and tinkle in the kitchen. Celia can't believe her ears. Who is washing up if it isn't her? Surely it can't be . . .

Dodge is up to his elbows in warm suds, and surrounded entirely by golden sunlight. Soap bubbles float like pure thoughts, in rings like halos around his head. At the kitchen table, also lit by a sword-edged shaft of solid sunshine, sit Hebe and the party Alice. There is a stack of paper between them and they have pens in their hands, scrawling as fast as spiders across the clean white sheets.

It must be morning.

Blinking, Celia stands in the kitchen doorway. She makes no sound, but Dodge looks round at her; suddenly, specifically, as if she had spoken.

285

'Hello,' says Dodge.

'Hello,' Celia nods.

Their voices break the concentration in the kitchen. Hebe and Alice look up slowly.

'Hi,' says Alice.

'Hi,' Celia smiles.

'Hey,' says Hebe.

'Hey,' Celia replies.

There is a pause.

'A cup of tea?' asks Dodge.

Celia shakes her head.

'Coffee,' she says.

Dodge heaves a sigh of relief. Since the Mad Hatter's tea-party last night, where all that got pawed was him, he hasn't felt the same about his favourite hot beverage. He turns aside to hide his strain from Celia, but succeeds only in drawing the wondering gazes of all three women. And all three continue to stare at Dodge in silence while he makes the coffee. But eventually Hebe's head sinks over her writing again, and Alice's follows.

'Here,' Dodge says softly, handing Celia a coffee.

'Thanks,' says Celia, taking it.

They pause awkwardly again. Celia bends her lips to the chipped mug, but the coffee is too hot to sip and now it's too hot to hold too. Celia rushes the mug onto the draining-board and blows on the burnt tips of her fingers.

Dodge plunges his hands back into the washing-up water.

Celia clears her throat. There's something she has to ask him. A fistful of memories from last night are still missing, and Dodge may be able to fill her in.

'Did you . . . ?' she shouts, and sees the party Alice send a startled streak of black biro across her page. Alice screws up the

286

paper and throws it onto a scrap heap at the end of the table. Celia starts again in a whisper.

'Did you, er, stay to the end?' she asks Dodge. She really needs to know if she did herself, because she can't remember any final outcomes, but this seems to be the best way of finding out.

Dodge is silent for several seconds, though his splashing gets louder. Eventually he looks at Celia sideways and says, 'It hasn't finished yet.'

'Oh?' says Celia, topping up her coffee mug with milk for her amnesia.

'No,' says Dodge. He looks at her again. 'Someone's left something on your bed.'

'A coat?' says Celia.

Dodge laughs. 'You're so sweet,' he says. He puts his lips to Celia's ear and his voice is quick and quiet as a knife-wound as he adds, 'Actually, it's a corpse.'

Celia sniggers. 'I thought you said corpse,' she explains as Dodge draws back and eyes her suspiciously.

'I did,' says Dodge.

Celia looks at the washing-up water, the mangy mop, the stack of clean crockery and the box of crushed beer cans, empty wine bottles, full ashtrays and spent cigarette lighters on the floor at her feet. Then she looks back at Dodge.

'Uh-huh,' she says. 'And what – exactly – did you mean by it?'

'There's a dead body,' says Dodge, 'on your bed.'

Celia is still acting casual, but her flared nostrils and flushed cheeks belie her concern.

'What's it doing there?' she says.

Dodge looks her straight in the eye. 'Nothing,' he says.

Celia swallows. 'Okay,' she says, 'how did it get there . . . how did it get . . . dead . . . in my bed?'

'On your bed, not in it,' says Dodge, 'it's not between the sheets, for heaven's sake, Celia!' His lip twitches in disgust.

'Are you serious?' says Celia.

Dodge can't be serious.

'Ssshh!' he is saying, with a conspiratorial wink at Celia and a nod at Hebe and Alice, who still sit scribbling at the kitchen table. 'No one else knows yet.'

He is loving every minute of it, but Celia can beat him at his own game.

'Listen sunshine,' she says loudly, 'I've had enough of you and your bloody body. I'm going to bed!'

Hebe slams her pen down on the table. Alice screws up another spoiled sheet and flicks it at the ceiling. Dodge says 'Sorry! Sorry!' over his shoulder, as he races out of the kitchen and chases Celia down the hall.

He is too slow. He watches helplessly as Celia opens the door to her rooms, steps inside, and steps out a split second later, her face as white and her eyes as wide as a sheet.

'My chandelier . . .' Celia says, shaking visibly, 'my carpet . . . my curtains . . . !' She is coming to a crescendo.

Dodge looks down the hallway and up the stairs. When he is sure no one's approaching, he pushes Celia back into her room and thrusts himself in after her, shutting the door quickly behind them.

Celia's sitting-room is not what it was. There is no sitting room; the wooden chairs are dismembered and piled up like a bonfire in the centre of the floor. The big table, legless now, is propped against the pile of chairs like a ramp. It is the sort of arrangement that boys with muddy bicycles would make. Celia can't imagine how it came to be created here.

There is widespread destruction of her décor. There are strips

288

torn off the wallpaper – aggessively, arbitrarily and in one place artistically, but that is beside the point. Cigarettes are stubbed out on the carpet, the curtains are in shreds, and small flakes of chandelier cover the scene like sharp snow.

'Who did this . . . ?' says Celia, turning on the spot, with three hundred and sixty degrees of despair in her voice.

She stops face to face with Dodge, who is standing firmly in front of her bedroom door, and takes a crunchy step towards him.

'Who did it?' she says again.

'Who knows . . .' Dodge shrugs.

'Don't you care?' says Celia, taking another step in his direction.

'Celia,' Dodge swallows hard, 'I do, but there's more. There really is something . . . extra . . . on your bed.'

Celia shakes her head. 'I don't believe you,' she cries wildly.

'Then you'd better see our stiff chum for yourself,' he replies.

Celia tries to sound as if she's only joking, 'Who is it?'

Dodge stands aside and shoves the bedroom door open. 'See for yourself,' he says.

Celia feels, or thinks she feels, a blast of cold air from her bedroom.

'No,' she says, 'You tell me. Is it someone I know? Is it, is it, is it someone I love?'

Dodge tries to smile, but only succeeds in sneering. 'How could it be?' he says. 'You don't love anyone.'

'That's not true,' Celia replies. 'Well it might be. But I can't help it. How can I love anyone if no one loves me? And I do know that no one loves me, after last night's display of disaffection.'

Dodge's sneer is turning sourer by the second. 'Calm down, Celia,' he says, 'come and see. Quick, before it starts to smell and we're talking about disinfectant instead.' He breaks off when

Celia's eyes show their warning whites. 'Come on,' he says in a kinder tone, 'It's okay. Really.'

He holds out his hand to Celia, and she, teetering on the brink of a blackout, takes it, and would have done even if the flesh were festering and the fingers falling off.

Dodge leads Celia into her bedroom. On the other side of the door is an infinite silence. Dodge and Celia don't say anything either. They stand and stare at the dead Mad Hatter on the bed.

After a while, Celia mouths, 'Are you sure?'

'Pardon?' says Dodge.

'Are you sure he's . . . you know . . . deceased?' whispers Celia.

'Yes,' says Dodge.

'How can you tell?' she whispers.

Dodge tuts a muted tut of irritation. 'Because he's not breathing,' he says, 'and he's got a knitting needle stuck in each ear.'

'He's got a what?' hisses Celia.

'A knitting needle!' says Dodge, 'In each ear!'

Holding her breath, Celia tiptoes towards the bed. The Hatter is lying face down in the position that people who fall off roofs land in. His head is buried in Celia's pearly pillows, but the tips of two knitting needles are plainly visible, sticking out of his bloody ears. They are size nines. Nasty.

'Oh my God,' whispers Celia. 'Oh my God. Oh my God.'

'Why are you whispering?' asks Dodge.

Celia whirls round. 'Why are you grinning?' she says.

The grin gets bigger.

'Stop it,' says Celia, a shrill edge creeping into her whisper.

The grin strains at the seams.

'Stop it!' says Celia, her tone positively sharp.

'What's the matter, Celia?' says Dodge. 'He's the one who nearly raped me. And you. I thought you'd be pleased.'

'But but,' stutters Celia, 'this man's been murmurdered!'

Dodge shrugs. 'Could be suicide,' he says. And proceeds to demonstrate; slowly inserting an imaginary knitting needle into each of his own ears, his eyes closing as their tips touch, with the smug zen smile of a sword swallower.

Celia doesn't know whether to laugh or cry at this, and in her confusion she lets slip an all-purpose vocal fart; the volume and the resonance of which is fit to wake the dead. Spooked, she takes up a new position nearer to the bedroom door, with Dodge's body between hers and the Hatter's.

'So,' she whispers hoarsely, 'when did this happen?'

'Don't know,' shrugs Dodge, looking the other way.

'Well,' Celia tries again, 'when did you find it?'

Dodge still doesn't look at her. 'When everyone had gone,' he says, 'I was . . . tidying up.'

'That's strange,' Celia says softly, 'you've never tidied up before.'

'What?' says Dodge.

'Nothing,' says Celia.

Dodge looks at her now. He is still smiling.

'You think I did it,' he says.

'No,' says Celia. But she takes a step backwards.

'You do, don't you?' says Dodge.

'What?' says Celia.

'You think I did it,' says Dodge.

'No. I don't know. I'm tired!' says Celia.

'You don't know me very well do you?' says Dodge.

'I don't know you at all,' Celia replies.

'Ah, but you do,' says Dodge, 'no one knows me better.'

'Right. Fine,' says Celia. He's only saying this to annoy her.

'Last night,' says Dodge, 'something happened between us.

291

We came together. And when we left my room, we didn't leave each other. We stayed together.' He steps towards her.

'No we didn't,' says Celia, stepping back.

'We did,' says Dodge, 'because I had entered your body. I was inside you.'

Celia holds her ground. 'You certainly were not!' she says.

Dodge sighs. 'Look, you've got hold of the wrong end of the stick,' he says.

'No I haven't,' says Celia. 'I hear exactly what you're saying, Dodge. You're trying to establish an alibi. Well it won't wash; there are witnesses; we weren't seen together at all.'

Dodge bangs his head on the bedroom door. 'Why don't you listen,' he says. 'I'm talking about our relationship. It wasn't just fashion tips we shared last night, you know.'

'So?' says Celia.

'You trusted me,' says Dodge, 'you entrusted yourself to me, and I nearly got you raped. I let you down really badly. I'm trying to say I'm sorry.'

Celia looks Dodge up and down and reaches out and gently strokes the bulging blue silk of his shoulder. Her fingers linger in the frills at his throat.

'It's a dress, Dodgy,' she says. 'Fancy, that's all. It wasn't me. I was already out of it.'

'But there was a struggle,' says Dodge.

'I don't remember,' says Celia.

'You didn't want to let it go,' says Dodge.

'It didn't want to let me go,' says Celia.

Dodge smooths the sore skin of the skirt.

'You're not kidding,' he says, 'it would have been safer if it had stayed with you.'

'Yes,' says Celia, 'but I'd have been in danger.'

292

'You'd be engaged by now,' says Dodge, flashing his petticoat-white teeth in a smile.

'It wouldn't be me,' says Celia.

'You'd be waking up with a rush of pre-marital premonition,' Dodge continues.

'What?' says Celia.

'Your sheets would be tangled round your ankles, and they'd smell of jasmine or rose; or even, if you'd played your cards right, the lovely Kenneth.'

Celia's serious look lifts at the edges.

'Lovely?' she says. 'You're mad, you are.'

They both remember the Hatter at the same time. Simultaneously, they turn to face the bed. The body is still there.

Dodge grinds his teeth and says, 'If I'd wanted to get my revenge, killing that bastard would have been the last thing I'd do. Look at him lying there, all over and done with.'

'He does look a bit pleased with himself,' agrees Celia, eager to please Dodge after his apology.

'Too right!' says Dodge. 'I suppose whoever killed him did it with the best intentions; but really, they might just as well have given him a million pounds and sent him to live in Miami!'

'Mmmm,' says Celia.

'His suffering is over,' says Dodge, 'it's tragic!'

Celia clears her throat. 'So,' she says, 'are you going to phone the police, or shall I?'

'The pardon?' says Dodge.

'The police,' says Celia.

'No,' says Dodge.

'What?' says Celia.

'No,' says Dodge.

'Why?' says Celia.

'We don't need them,' says Dodge.

'But there's been a murder,' says Celia.

'Precisely,' says Dodge.

'Pardon?' says Celia.

'That's precisely why we don't need them,' says Dodge. 'They'd only try to investigate it. Find out who dunnit. Find someone guilty and send them to gaol. And for what? For packing Mr Nasty Bastard off on an open-ended holiday, if you please.'

'Dodge, don't be silly,' says Celia, 'you can't go around knitting people to death at the drop of a hat, nasty bastards or no.'

'So you condone his behaviour?' says Dodge, his eyebrows raised like question marks.

'No I don't condone it,' says Celia, 'I can condemn without killing.'

'Well if you're such a right-on left-wing pacifist all of a sudden,' says Dodge, 'you won't want to go running to the police, will you?'

'But I want that body off my bed,' says Celia. 'I want that body off my bed this very minute, and I want men in uniforms to come with screaming sirens and fliptop notepads and do it properly.'

Without warning, Dodge pushes past Celia, knocking her sideways, and slams the bedroom door behind him as he leaves. She screams and throws herself against it, but he is leaning on the other side and it's staying shut.

'I'm sorry Celia,' his voice comes through the wood, 'I can't let you call the police. Innocent people could get hurt. And the guilty have already got away.'

Celia glances over her shoulder at the Hatter on the bed. She shudders. She's not at all sure that it can be trusted to stay dead, not now that they're alone together. For all she knows this could be an elaborate plot to get back at her for all the sex and violence enacted in her name last night. It was her they were after, this Hatter and that Kenneth, and she got away.

And she'll get away again. Celia concentrates on the soles of the Hatter's shoes and gains confidence; they're sensible lace-ups, school shoes, a well-known brand. It strikes her that the only way to get out of this situation is to pretend to be going along with it.

'So what will we do then?' Celia shouts at the door and Dodge. 'Dispose of the body ourselves? Bin-liners, that's what you use isn't it, black bin-liners? I do believe we happen to have some in stock. That's a stroke of luck.

'Dodge, if I take his clothes off and burn them,' she adds, 'will you empty the boot of my car? There's some paperwork in there; I can't have that getting covered with corpulence. Whatever would they say in the office tomorrow? No, news of my sly undertakings must not leak out. And we'll go to the woods tonight then, shall we? Just you and me and stiffy makes three. And we'll descend into the darkness with our bin bags and our bio-degradable waste and some spades, bought in disguise from a shop twenty miles away. And we'll dig a deep grave under a yew tree. Oh yes, I can see it now. I'll probably take a flask of coffee and wear my wellingtons. And the hole won't take all night to dig, and the owls won't hoot and the wind won't howl, and the plastic bag won't slip from his face as we're putting him in, and his dead eyes won't look lively at us in the moonlight; and I'll be able to breathe all right ... oh yes, Dodge, I'll really be able to breathe ...'

Celia breaks off. She can't breathe. To be more specific, she can breathe but she can't stop. She is hyperventilating. She is starting to sound like the screaming sirens that Dodge is so keen to avoid.

Dodge opens the door and gets her out of the bedroom, breaking a toe in the process. In the living-room, he holds her up against a wall with one hand and picks an empty brown paper bag off the floor with the other. Single-handed, he shapes the lucky bag into a balloon and tells Celia to blow into it. Cherry-red and panting, she can't comply. 'Blow into the bag, Celia,' says Dodge again, his voice extra stern to compensate for its shakiness, 'come on, snap out of it.'

Celia doesn't hear him, she is making so much noise herself. Desperate to shut her up, Dodge slips the rim of the bag over her slippery lips and holds it there. Celia sucks the bag in and almost swallows it; she blows out again so hard the bag bursts with a resounding bang.

'Whoa there!' shouts Dodge, jumping involuntary inches into the air.

Celia doesn't stop. The paper bag was no match for her panicking lungs. They pound on like horses. Dodge grabs her by the bath-towel, and reins her in. 'Celia,' he says, 'if you don't stop, I'll stick my tongue so far down your throat you'll think you're growing a penis.'

Celia stops. Her eyes register surprise. She places the flat of her hand in the centre of Dodge's chest and shoves him backwards. Then she heaves the contents of her stomach into the newly-opened space between them.

'Whoops,' says Dodge, watching.

Pasta-faced, Celia looks at him in silence. Only her sick, sizzling like a pizza on the carpet, makes any sound.

After a minute, Celia turns on her heel and walks out of the room.

She steps unsteadily into the kitchen. The first thing she needs is a glass of water. The last thing she needs is Alice getting up from the table and greeting her in grim glee: 'I suppose you've been aborting your bottom drawer.'

'Sorry?' says Celia.

'Aborting your bottom drawer. Now your engagement is over. You look a bit shaken,' says Alice.

'I want a glass of water,' says Celia.

'What?' says Alice.

Celia is already at the sink with the tap turned on. 'I want some water,' she shouts over her shoulder.

Alice is standing right behind her. Celia jumps, and drops the glass in the sink. Alice lifts it out, fills it up, and takes it away to the kitchen table.

'Come on,' she says, 'come and sit down.'

Celia follows Alice and her chalice and collapses into a chair. She sips the cold liquid slowly, swishing it around before swallowing, but it lands like something solid in her stomach.

'We've nearly finished,' says Alice, shuffling a sheaf of papers, 'if you don't mind waiting a moment.'

Hebe is still scribbling fast. Her lips are moving and her toes are tapping and her hair is on fire in the sunlight. Every so often she laughs out loud, and once she curses and kicks the leg of the table. Alice watches her every movement with shining eyes.

'What are you doing?' says Celia.

'Pardon?' says Alice. There's something wrong with Celia's voice.

'What are you doing?' Celia tries again.

'Oh,' says Alice, 'we're making a film. Well, I say we, but Hebe's done most of it. I've been helping her with the end, because everything got a bit confusing. It's about last night.'

'What about last night?' Celia says hotly.

Alice draws back from the blast. 'Well, you know,' she says, 'about you, and your folks. Ken, and me and Hebe. And Cath and Dodge. Everyone.'

Before Alice can say more, Hebe's right hand screeches to a standstill and her pen goes sailing into the air. She leans back in her chair and trumpets triumphantly at Celia.

'You've come in the knickers of time,' she says, 'hold on to your hat!'

'Is it finished, then?' asks Alice, eagerly.

'It's rough,' says Hebe, sorting her tower of paper into several smaller piles, 'but it's ready to read. Shall we go from the Cat's exit?'

Alice drums on the table.

'Yes!' she says, 'The Cat's exit! The Cat's exit!' Then she picks up her script and finds the place. 'We don't really know why Cath did this,' she tells Celia, 'but we'll ask her about it when she wakes up. Anyway, it was brilliant. She looked beautiful and she backed down the aisle between the rows of chairs, saying "watch me walk away" or "see me go" or something like that. She was speaking to your mother, Celia, but everyone else did as she said too. Without asking why, we all waited with bated breath till she got to the door. And in the film version, the camera will follow, staying on her until she is quite, quite gone.'

Alice gives a small bow, smiling hugely at Celia. Hebe claps. Celia shivers in her skimpy towel. It seems that these two are about to fill in the holes in her memory with all the subtlety of a trowel.

'Now,' says Hebe, 'all hell breaks loose. We need some help here, Celia. Will you read a part? And look, here's Dodge! Hey, Dodgums, do you want to play?'

Dodge is standing in the doorway, arms folded, legs crossed. He doesn't look much fun. 'What are you doing?' he says.

'I thought you knew,' says Hebe, 'it's my new film. About last night. Do you have a problem with that?'

298

Dodge glances at Celia. 'Very possibly,' he says.

Hebe catches his eye on the rebound. She sees that there's something going on between him and Celia, something she's failed to spot so far.

'There is a happy ending,' she says, with a lame laugh.

Dodge doesn't look convinced. 'Tell me more,' he says.

Hebe stands up and studies her script.

'Okay,' she says: 'Interior (Celia's living-room). Night. The old lady lying on the table starts to laugh. That's your grandmother, Celia, you can do that.'

Celia's top half is already on the table anyway. Hebe helps her bottom half off the chair and heaves it up too.

'Laugh, Celia,' she says, 'Thank you. And Alice, you're Celia's mother. You're crying. You sit down on the chair that the Cheshire Cat's just vacated, and you cry your eyes out. And the laughing and crying must be in harmony, or at least in the same key. But not like that. No. Stop. Celia, stop laughing now. Celia, you're going to strain yourself. Celia! Stop!'

'Let her be,' barks Dodge. 'She's feeling a bit funny.'

'Funny?' says Hebe, 'You could have fooled me. But let's go on with the show. Right; Interior. Night. It's a long-shot: we've got Grandmother laughing in the background, Mother crying in the foreground, and me in the middle, not knowing whether to laugh or cry. I stagger to my feet, feeling to see if my hair is still there. It's coming out in handfuls, but it isn't a wig. I am clearly not Celia. That's in close-up, I think. Big close-up.

'The music swells and the camera pulls back and Celia's mother holds her hand out to me. I take it. And Celia's mother says . . .' Hebe stops and looks expectantly at Alice.

'So you're not my daughter,' Alice says.

'And you're not my mother,' says Hebe.

'It's not too late, you know, to own up,' says Alice. 'I won't make you marry Kenneth.'

'I don't see why you wanted to in the first place,' says Hebe.

'Celia needs somebody to love her,' says Alice. 'My husband and I aren't very good at that sort of thing. And now we've lost her.'

'She's alive,' says Hebe, 'and where there's life there's hope. Hey, even where there isn't life there's hope. I'm still thinking that my real mum will turn up to take me home tonight.'

'Have you lost your mother?' asks Alice.

'Yes,' says Hebe, 'but only in body. If you want to find your daughter, look for her spirit.'

'Hebe and Celia's mother hug,' says Alice.

'And . . . Cut!' says Hebe, demonstrating her familiarity with the film world's technical terms. 'Moving, huh? Now, Dodge,' she continues, 'while this womanly wailing and wringing of hands is going on, Kenneth has come over all manly. He's stood up, and he's said that there are still some tables left unturned.'

Hebe stands with her hands in her pockets and her voice drops an octave in a rough impression of Ken, as she says, 'If Celia won't come to me, then I'll go to her. Who's this Dodge I've heard so much about? Where does he hang out? I bet he knows where I can find my fiancée.'

Hebe hurries on, her voice getting higher again as it picks up speed. 'There's some conferring in the crowd and then someone shouts out that Dodge was the chappie in Celia's dress and the door to his room is just across the hall. Ken says right, that's all he needs to know, and off he goes.'

Hebe whips round to face Dodge with a creamy smile.

'So,' she beams, 'the scene shifts to your room, and only you can tell us what happens next. Did Ken arrive safely? Did he find you at home? Was Celia there too?'

Her questions hang dangling in the air between them. Dodge stares at Hebe with his mouth shut. He isn't going to take the bait. Slowly, Hebe takes a pencil and a piece of paper from the table and holds them out to him.

'You could write it,' she says, 'if you wanted to.'

'Write it yourself,' says Dodge.

'Call me boring,' Hebe replies, 'but I'd like to know what really happened.'

'So would I,' says Celia, still flat on her back on the table, and sinking fast.

'So Celia wasn't there!' says Alice. 'Ooooo!'

'Sshh!' says Hebe. 'Go on Dodge, what did you do with Ken?'

Dodge is standing with his back to the open door, but he looks cornered. He looks at the floor.

'Nothing,' says Dodge. 'We talked.'

'Terrific,' says Hebe, licking the tip of the pencil, 'what did you say?'

'Nothing,' says Dodge.

'What did Kenneth say?' says Hebe.

'Nothing,' says Dodge.

Hebe sighs.

'So you'll have to make it up,' Dodge adds.

'Dodge?' Celia says feverishly, clinging to the table as if to a raft at sea. 'Was I there? I don't remember it. I was there. Wasn't I? But Kenneth wasn't, was he? Did we come separately? Did I come back later? Did I ever see him again?'

'Come off the table, Celia,' says Hebe, gently, 'sit down. You're not feeling very well. Oops, steady on, that's not a chair!'

But Dodge is forced face to face with Hebe as they struggle to get Celia seated.

'We had a few drinks and watched the telly,' he says to her

over Celia's head. 'We talked about the meaning of life. We talked about love and marriage. We talked about him and Celia. We came to the conclusion that there is nothing attaching his horse to his carriage, as it were.'

Hebe has left Dodge holding Celia up, and is writing down his monologue, word for word.

'What did he say about attacking Alice?' she asks abruptly.

'Plenty,' says Dodge.

'That's exactly how much paper I've got,' says Hebe, pencil poised.

But Dodge is out of patience. 'Kenneth regrets his indiscretion,' he says. 'Can I go now?'

He drops Celia into a chair and pats her head perfunctorily.

'Typical!' snaps Alice. 'That is so fucking typical! Did you see that?' She turns to Hebe. 'They close ranks, don't they! When it comes to the crunch, they're all boys together. Even the ones who wear dresses.'

'Especially the ones who wear dresses!' says Hebe. Then she screws up her piece of paper and puts it in her mouth, saying, 'I'm sorry Dodge, I didn't mean that.'

Dodge doesn't acknowledge the apology, but he seems to accept it for he doesn't flounce angrily out of the room. Instead, he takes the towel off Celia's head and starts to dry her hair.

'Ow!' says Celia, 'Dodge, is that you? Is that my hair?' Shock has set in. Celia doesn't know what's what.

'Yes, it's me,' says Dodge.

'Dodge, what became of the Kenneth?' Celia continues. 'Didn't he find me? Did I want him to? Will anyone ever love me enough for it not to be too much? Tell me what happened, do!'

Dodge dries her hair harder. 'His parents picked him up on

302

their way out,' he says. 'I expect they took him home.'

'Well, wasn't he lucky,' says Alice, 'the one that got away. You wait till you hear what happens to Max Hatton. Then maybe you'll stop seeing sexual violence as violent sex, and start believing that there's not one woman in the whole wide world who wants to be raped "really".'

'What are you talking about?' says Dodge.

'Just watch,' says Alice, 'the final scene of the film. Hebe let me write it because no one took any notice of what I said last night. It's between me and Max Hatton. I give him what-for.' She thrusts a sheet of paper at Dodge.

'What's this?' says Dodge.

'You're playing Max Hatton,' says Alice, 'I'll be me.'

'But Hebe said this was about last night,' says Dodge. 'Who's Max Hatton when he's at home?'

'Ah,' says Alice, 'by day he goes by the name of Max Hatton. But by night, he is known as the Mad Hatter.'

Celia's head drops out of Dodge's hands and onto the table with a thump. Celia appears to have become unconscious. If Dodge were not still standing up with his eyes open, the same might be said of him. The colour has drained from his cheeks.

'Come on then,' says Alice, 'you start.'

Dodge doesn't.

'Dodge?' says Hebe.

Suddenly, there is a scream from Celia's bedroom. Alice, Dodge and Hebe start. They look at Celia slumped across the table, then at each other as if to say, 'Who's that screaming in Celia's room if it isn't Celia?'

Someone is staggering out of Celia's room and screaming in the hallway. Alice, Dodge and Hebe look at the kitchen door, in something approaching horror. Cath appears in the doorway, in a pink dressing-gown two shades lighter but three degrees dirtier than her hair, her hand on her heart.

'Heavy!' she says. 'Heavy, heavy, heavy!'

Dodge tries to stop Cath coming into the kitchen, but she looks straight through his unwelcoming expression. She looks at Celia.

'Celia?' she says uncertainly, 'Celia!'

Celia, face down on the table, doesn't stir.

'What's the matter with her?' Cath asks in alarm.

Alice, Dodge and Hebe look at Celia too. There is a pause.

'She's tired?' suggests Alice, eventually.

'Has she been to bed?' asks Cath.

Alice shrugs.

'Has she seen the body?' asks Cath.

'What?' says Alice.

'Has she seen the body on her bed?' asks Cath.

Alice shrugs again.

'Look, forget about Celia,' she says, 'Watch our film instead.'

Cath sits down and lights a cigarette with shaking hands. She makes eye-contact with Hebe through a screen of smoke and confusion.

'Did we meet last night?' asks Hebe.

'I was the Cheshire Cat,' says Cath.

Hebe smiles. 'You were fantastic,' she says. 'I loved what you said on that chair. It's in the film. I hope you don't mind.'

'Huh?' says Cath.

'I'm Hebe,' says Hebe, 'Phoebe's sister. Did you make those songs up as you went along, or had you prepared them earlier?'

'That wasn't me,' says Cath, 'that was Celia. We'd swapped costumes.' She waves her cigarette at the cat-suit which Celia left in a heap by the skirting-board near the sink. It looks like the victim of a hit-and-run.

304

'It was Celia?' says Hebe. 'It was Celia standing on the chair?'

'Yes,' says Cath.

'Godsbollocks!' gulps Hebe. 'So she was raised up right in front of her family and they still didn't recognise her. Nobody will believe this!'

She snatches a clean sheet of paper and starts scribbling again.

Alice tugs at her sleeve like a small child.

'Please can I do my bit,' she says.

'Absolutely,' says Hebe, only half listening.

'At last!' says Alice. 'Right, Cath, are you ready for this? Watch closely. Max Hatton is in a meeting with his maker, and there's only one thing on the agenda!'

Cath chokes on smoke.

'Anyone of a nervous disposition,' Alice continues, 'should avert their gaze now.'

'Alice, man,' Cath stands up suddenly and sends her chair crashing to the floor, 'can I ask you a question?'

'Quick,' says Alice.

'Is this film real?' says Cath.

'Yes. Why?' asks Alice.

'Well, because Max Hatton,' says Cath, 'is, like, dead on Celia's bed. With knitting needles in his ears. He's been murdered.'

The film isn't meant to be *that* real. Without another word Alice leaves the kitchen, Hebe hot on her heels.

Cath tries to give Celia her out-size cigarette.

'Come on, Celia,' says Cath, gently shaking her shoulder, 'hair of the cat that scratched you.'

Dodge leans across the table and dashes Cath's hand away.

'She's sick,' he says, 'you stupid hippy.'

Hebe and Alice come back. Without a word, they gather up every sheet of paper on the table and shove them into the kitchen sink. Hebe lights a match and sets fire to her morning's work.

'What are you doing that for?' says Cath.

'It's evident,' says Dodge.

'What?' says Cath.

'Evidence,' says Dodge.

'Everything's different,' says Hebe. 'I'll have to go back to the beginning. Someone really did kill the Hatter!'

'It wasn't me,' says Alice.

Dodge points a finger at the film script burning badly in the sink.

'Max Hatton meets his maker?' he says. 'Alice gives him what-for?'

'I was making it up!' protests Alice.

'It's true,' says Hebe, 'if she'd really shown him to the pearly door, she wouldn't have needed to write about it.'

The kitchen is dark with smoke; it hangs whole in the air, as corporal as the body on Celia's bed, and as incriminating.

Cath shuts the door to the hall, and leans against it looking dazed. 'What are we going to do now?'

Hebe is looking up at the high window.

'Does that open?' she says.

'I don't know,' says Dodge.

'I've never tried,' says Cath.

'Well,' says Hebe, dragging a chair across the floor and clambering onto it, 'this is its lucky day.' She reaches the window and wrestles with it.

'Where's your sister?' Cath calls to her.

'Upstairs. Asleep. In bed,' grunts Hebe. The window won't open.

'I wish I was,' a sob comes from Celia, who has quietly regained consciousness. 'Then maybe I could wake up.'

306

'Ah, Celia,' says Alice. She clears her throat. 'What do you know about the body in your bed?'

Celia lifts her head off the table.

'I know it's there,' she answers plaintively, 'because if it wasn't, I would be. Can someone get me some water please? I can't speak properly. Oh, the sink's on fire.'

Alice kneels down next to Celia's chair.

'Celia,' she says, 'this is serious. When was the last time you saw the Mad Hatter?'

'Do-don't ask me,' stammers Celia. 'You're Alice, ask yourself. Ask Tweedle-Hebe and Tweedle-Phoebe. Ask the Cheshire Cat. But do-don't ask me. Dodo. I'm extinct!'

'Don't be silly,' says Alice. 'Where did you sleep last night?'

'What? Do you think I did it?' says Celia. 'Why? Because I was disengaged from Kenneth? Cor, blame me!'

'Leave her alone, Alice, she's not up to this,' says Dodge sharply. 'Celia, take no notice, just have a little nap.'

He puts his arms around Celia, but she slips out of them.

'Dic don'tate to me, Dodge!' she cries. 'I might be asleep already. I might be a murderous!'

Hebe gets her by the towel and holds on tight.

'No one is accusing you, Celia. We just need to know if you know how Max Hatton got in your bed,' she says.

Celia slips out of the towel and out of Hebe's clutches. She slips off her chair and onto the table. Celia is crying like a baby. All over her bare body, blotches and scratches and ancient bruises are brought back into existence, as the bucket of her tears reaches the very bottom of her well of woe. Sobs jump like frogs from her throat.

'Whose bed?' she gulps. 'It's not my bed. I'm not in it! It's his bed now. That robbist has raped me of everything!'

307

Cath approaches the table cautiously. Celia is standing on it, stark naked, and she doesn't seem to care.

'It's all right, Celia,' Cath says, 'It's all right. Come with me. You can sleep in my bed.'

She holds out her hand to Celia. Celia doesn't take it. She is growing furiouser and furiouser.

'I don't want to sleep,' says Celia. 'I've been asleep my whole life. I want to wake up now. You lot can stay in Wonderland if you want, but I'm going to phone the police.'

Alice screams and falls flat on her back on the floor. Alice screams like a steam train screeching to a halt, and then she screams again; and though no one knows what she's screaming about, they catch the gist of her fit and start running in hysterical circles around her, screaming too.

'I've just remembered something!' Alice's scream starts to have words in it. 'I've just remembered something!'

'What?' everyone screams back.

'What Max Hatton is in real life,' shrieks Alice, 'when he's not busy being the regional Mad Hatter!'

'What?' the others holler.

'*He's a policeman*,' Alice screams, 'he's a policeman. We can't call the police, they're already here!'

The Mad Hatter is a policeman. Hello, hello, hello. What's all this then.

The frenzy grinds up a gear. It's now in fifth. The circles run faster around Alice. Everyone is screaming fuzzy at the back of the person running in front. Except for Celia. Celia is still starkers on the table, singing opera. It's the climax of something, almost out of control, with foul-mouthed fuck-me fuck-me lyrics; and she is managing to do all four parts of the vocal score and much of the orchestral accompaniment.

308

Celia hits a high note. She rams her hands between her legs and her voice reaches the ceiling as she screams, 'Come, my head's free at last!'

Cath recognises this bit. It isn't an opera. It's Alice in Wonderland. She stops running and looks up at Celia.

Cath looks up at Celia. Her body is so white she can see right through it. Her breasts are like those optical illusions which could be either hills or hollows.

Cath looks up at Celia,

and up

and up

and up,

because Celia's neck seems to go on for ever.

There's a ten foot stretch between Celia's shoulders and Celia's head, which is touching the ceiling.

Cath rubs her eyes. 'Excellent,' she says, 'an authentic hallucination. You don't see one of those every day.'

Hebe runs into her from behind.

'Look,' Cath laughs, 'there's an hallucination on the ceiling.'

Hebe looks. Hebe sees something too. Hebe sees Celia starting a fire with two fingers rubbing like sticks against another part of her anatomy. Sparks fly electric blue and petrol green from the pure white of her thighs and the black of her pubic hair. Hebe sees Celia singing higher and higher until her straining neck snaps like an elastic band, catapulting her body up to join her head on the ceiling, and bringing them both abruptly back down to earth.

Hebe doesn't enjoy seeing Celia fall through the air like that. She looks away before her hallucination hits the deck.

'But that's it!' She grabs Cath and spins her round in their own private circle. 'That could be the end of my film! There's no such thing as the real Celia. She's just a cartoon.'

'Far out.' Cath can't give it her full attention. The kitchen is whirling too fast.

Alice appears beside them, then disappears, then appears again, like a stationary parent viewed from a playground roundabout. Alice is standing up now, but still panicking. 'Someone's killed a policeman,' she screams, 'and we'll all have to pay!'

Cath and Hebe stop spinning.

'Pardon?' says Cath, striving to keep her dizzy gaze directed at Alice.

'We're all going to prison,' wails Alice.

'Prison? We've never been out of it!' says Celia.

'They'll have to prove it first,' says Hebe, putting a supportive arm around Alice.

'Proof? Pah! It's as easy to turn upside down as a pudding,' Celia interrupts again. No one takes any notice of her.

'They'll torture us,' Cath says, taking the opportunity to lean on Hebe too, 'they'll torture us till we tell them everything.'

'But we don't know anything,' says Hebe, big sisterly.

'I do,' Cath says, 'I do. I know the names and addresses of everyone at my party. They'll all be, like, suspects.'

'Maybe there were gatecrashers,' says Hebe.

'There were two,' says Cath. 'Namely, Mr Dodgson and Ms Celia Small. Both of this address. Oh wow!' Her head sinks heavily onto Hebe's chest.

'It won't take much torturing to make you talk, will it?' Hebe smiles.

Cath sniffs. 'I even know who the knitting needles belong to,' she whispers into Hebe's warm woolly jumper.

Hebe laughs.

'You'll be laughing on the other side of your face,' shouts

Dodge suddenly, 'when it's your precious Phoebe's turn to be interrogated.'

Dodge is sitting cross-legged on the floor, crumpling stray sheets of Hebe's film script, and cramming them into his empty bra. He meets Hebe's gaze full on, and holds it coldly.

'Phoebe doesn't know anything,' says Hebe.

'Oh no?' says Dodge. 'But her sister is an international feminist, a militant extremist whose films encourage women to turn into gorillas and turn on men. There was a whole roomful of the virulent viragos in the house last night, and Phoebe knows every single one.'

Hebe lets go of Alice and Cath, propping them up against each other instead, and sits down with Dodge on the floor. Reaching into her pockets, she brings out handful after handful of soft pink tissues and two-ply toilet paper, and fills Dodge's cups to overflowing with them.

'There are two kinds of women,' she says as she does so, 'women's women and men's women. It's nothing to do with sexual preference, more about order of priorities, who you're living for. All that time spent trying to look like a lady could be in vain, Dodge. Because you're talking like a man's woman. You're talking like a man.'

Dodge looks down at his well-shaped bust. Hebe is tweaking the tissues into twin peaks. He has never sculpted such nice nipples himself.

Dodge blushes. 'Thanks,' he says to Hebe, hot as a beetroot, but playing it cool.

'The pleasure was mine.' Hebe stands up and turns away to hide her smile. 'Now do your dress up. We've got a body to dispose of.'

'We're not going to do it ourselves?' gasps Cath.

311

'We can't!' says Alice.

'Let it rot,' rasps Celia.

'Sorry Celia?' says Hebe, not bothering to look at her, but cocking amused eyebrows at Cath and Alice instead.

'The Mad Hatter is a policeman,' says Celia. 'What's Wonderland then? A teapot dictatorship?'

'Sit down, Celia,' says Hebe, 'you're in shock.' She looks over her shoulder, but Celia isn't standing on the table any more. Hebe swivels, trying to find the source of the strange tirade.

'I should have got that frock off sooner,' Celia continues, 'I never should have put it on.'

'Where is she?' Hebe whispers to Alice. Alice starts looking too.

'Generations of little girls have sat at that tea table and been told to shut up and listen,' Celia's tones are terrible, 'and all they hear are nonsense crimes, but the Hatter's word is the law.'

Hebe and Alice look at Dodge. He's sitting on the table now, shamelessly admiring his shapely new bust.

'Search me,' he shrugs, 'I don't know where she's coming from.'

'We must get out of Wonderland.' Celia drones on, 'There's only one way to make dreams come true, and that's to wake up!'

Hebe drops to her knees.

'She could be under the table,' she says, 'and that's why her voice sounds so wooden.'

Cath joins her at floor level, followed shortly by Alice.

'Fucking hell,' says Cath, 'she's not there.'

Hebe, Alice and Cath get shakily to their feet and dust themselves down.

'Well, she's got to be here somewhere,' says Alice, and starts looking in cupboards, and under the sink, and behind chairs, and

312

outside the door to the hall. Hebe picks up the limp cat-suit and shakes it, then comes to her senses and stares at the ceiling which is where she last saw Celia, thinking hard. Cath stands still and looks at Dodge.

A minute passes in silence, then Hebe clears her throat and calls, 'Where are you, Celia? We can't see you.'

'Disillusioned? I know I am!' Celia replies.

'It was Dodge,' shouts Cath.

'What?' says Hebe.

'It was Dodge! His lips moved!' Cath points an accusing finger.

'They didn't!' says Dodge.

'You tell them, Dodge,' Celia booms. 'Big bang boy.'

'There he goes again,' shouts Cath. 'Did you see that?' she adds, turning to Hebe and Alice. 'He's a ventriloquist.'

'He'd better be,' says Alice, 'because if he's not, I'm bloody scared.'

'This is ridiculous! Why can't we see her?' says Cath. She pulls the plug out of the sink and peers down the plughole in desperation.

'No Cath, that's ridiculous,' says Hebe, shoving her aside and filling a glass with water from the tap. 'This is the solution,' she continues, carrying it carefully across the floor to Dodge on the table.

'What am I supposed to do with it?' he snaps.

'Drink,' Hebe says. 'We'll see if you're a ventriloquist or not.'

Dodge takes the glass in silence and puts it to his lips. As he starts to swallow, Hebe lifts her head and shouts at the ceiling, 'Speak to us, Celia!'

For several seconds they hear nothing but Dodge slurping.

Then Celia says, 'This is the last thing I will say.'

Hebe gulps. She looks at Cath and Alice who have been staring at Dodge's glass of water and Dodge's adam's apple respectively.

'Is he drinking?' she whispers.

Cath nods white-faced. Alice falls to the floor in a faint.

Hebe looks at the ceiling again and waits with bated breath for Celia's last words. She is hoping for a speech of world-shattering significance, a speech to finish her film.

She waits.

And she waits.

And her neck aches.

Then Dodge gets to the bottom of his glass of water and burps rudely to attract her attention.

'Finished,' he says casually, as her gaze meets his; but Hebe works in Hollywood, and knows an actor when she sees one. She sees through Dodge's eyes. She sees that he is looking harder for Celia than anyone.

Hebe steps over the unconscious Alice and gets closer to Dodge.

'If you were a talented ventriloquist who could make us think that Celia is still in the kitchen, invisible and altogether wacko, when in actual fact she left ages ago without anyone noticing,' she says, 'you would tell me, wouldn't you? Because if you were a talented ventriloquist, I'd like to offer you a job. On my production team. In America.'

Dodge isn't fooled by veiled flattery. 'I believe you only employ women,' he says coolly.

'That's right,' says Hebe, 'I do.'

Actually, Dodge is fooled by veiled flattery. He glows from top to toe at this compliment.

Cath gets him while his defences are down.

'Yes,' she adds desperately, 'you would tell us if this was a trick, wouldn't you? Because then you could stop sitting around doing nothing but your nails all day like some bored suburban housewife.'

314

Dodge does not reply. Because at this moment, the kitchen door bursts open and Phoebe appears in a billowing purple nightdress. 'Well, bugger me twice before breakfast,' Phoebe bellows, 'who's done all that washing-up already?'

She waits for an answer, but none is forthcoming.

Phoebe tries again. 'Someone's been busy,' she says.

Still there is no response.

Phoebe can't believe it.

'Am I not really here, or what?' she says louder.

'Sorry?' says Hebe, tearing her eyes away from Dodge on the table.

'Nothing,' Phoebe shrugs, 'I just wondered who'd done all the washing-up.'

Cath too looks at Phoebe now. She is cross-eyed, Phoebe notices, and wonders why she never noticed before.

'Dodgy did it,' Cath croaks.

'Dodge! Well bugger me thrice! I thought it must have been Celia,' says Phoebe.

This harmless observation has an alarming effect on her housemates. Dodge starts to hammer on the table with his head, crying, 'Come back! Come back!' Cath pushes past Phoebe and storms out of the kitchen, slamming the door hard behind her. Hebe turns in a slow circle, looking at her sister all the way and laughing like a dalek.

Phoebe knows from years of experience that hangovers move in mysterious ways. She is not disturbed by these displays of internal damnation and hell-fire. Instead, she smiles serenely and sets about squeezing fresh fruit juice for everyone. Phoebe is feeling fine this morning, rested and peaceful.

As she is pouring small, pithy portions of her cure-all into clean glasses, the kitchen door opens again.

315

'She's not here,' Cath delivers her message of doom from the doorstep, 'she's not anywhere. I've looked in every room in the house.'

With a great groan, Dodge falls off the table and buries his face between its legs.

'Who isn't here?' says Phoebe, handing around glasses of fruit juice. 'Who are you talking about?'

'Celia,' replies Hebe, 'she's gone missing.'

'No she hasn't,' says Phoebe.

'Yes she has,' says Hebe.

'No she hasn't,' says Phoebe.

'Yes she has,' says Cath.

'You lot are shot to pieces,' says Phoebe, and downs her drink in one.

'What?' says Hebe, sipping slowly.

'A good time was had by all, I assume,' Phoebe smiles.

'Except Celia,' says Cath quietly, and tips her fruit juice straight down the sink.

'What is all this about Celia?' asks Phoebe.

Dodge raises his head from the floor.

'She's disappeared,' he says, and his voice is deep with distress.

But Phoebe doesn't take him seriously. 'Pull the other one,' she laughs.

'Phoebe, it's true,' says Hebe. 'We're not being funny. One minute Celia was here, having some sort of major identity crisis. And the next minute she was gone.'

Phoebe looks at Hebe hard. She knows when Hebe is having her on.

'You mean you really can't see her?' she says.

'You mean you can?' says Hebe.

Phoebe nods speechlessly.

Dodge gets to his feet, his head spinning. 'You can see her?' he asks.

'Of course I can see her,' says Phoebe.

Cath comes up behind her.

'Where is she?' she whispers.

Phoebe snaps. 'What's the matter with you?' she cries. 'She's right under your noses!'

'Where?' whispers Cath.

'There!' Phoebe points in front of her.

'Where?' Hebe wheels round.

'There!' says Phoebe again.

'Where?' Dodge is staring into thin air.

Phoebe strides across the kitchen to the table.

'Here!' She points at the woman lying motionless on the floor next to it, her hairband askance and her long blonde locks slanting across her face. 'See!'

Dodge screams a dismal scream.

'That's Alice,' says Hebe.

Phoebe bends over and brushes the hair back behind the blue band.

'So it is!' she gasps, as the familiar countenance appears. 'I thought it was Celia. Silly me!'

'That's Alice,' says Cath. Her voice echoes.

'Celia's not here,' Hebe adds.

'So?' Phoebe looks confused. 'What's it to you? She's probably gone out. Perhaps she went home with Ken after the party.'

Cath coughs. 'I don't think so,' she says. 'I've just seen Ken. I had to look everywhere, you see. For Celia.'

'Ken's still here?' Hebe says incredulously.

'I've just seen him,' says Cath.

'Where?' says Hebe.

'In Dodge's bed,' says Cath, 'but it's all right. He *is* still breathing!'

'Well Celia must be here too,' says Phoebe, 'perhaps she's . . . I don't know, perhaps she's in the garden.'

'But we haven't got a garden,' says Dodge, round-shouldered and red-faced from Cath's revelation of Kenneth's final resting-place.

'Yes we have,' says Phoebe.

'No we haven't,' says Dodge.

'Yes we have,' says Phoebe, 'we've always had a garden. You can see it from my bedroom window. But it's a jungle out there. The grass is as high as . . .' She looks around for inspiration and catches sight of Cath, who has somehow found the wherewithal to light another of her alleged cigarettes, 'as high as she is.'

'Oh,' says Dodge. Then he pulls his shoulders back. 'Well, let's go and look in the garden.'

Everyone pulls back their shoulders, throws out their chests and rocks on their heels, in readiness for the rush to the garden door.

There is a pregnant pause.

'Hang on a minute,' says Dodge, when the pause has already lasted much longer than that, 'are you sure about this garden, Phoebe? I've never even seen a door to it.'

'Oh yes,' says Phoebe, 'there is a door. But it's very, very small. Follow me.'

Leaving Alice out of it on the floor by the table, Phoebe leads Dodge, Cath and Hebe to the door to the garden. It is in a quiet corner of the kitchen, and the others can be forgiven for never having noticed it before. It really is very small, not much bigger than a cat-flap.

Everyone kneels down in front of it. Dodge gives it a tentative tap, and the door opens outwards on rusty hinges.

318

'Hmmm,' ponders Phoebe, 'maybe Celia couldn't have fitted through here.'

Dodge elbows her out of the way. 'Maybe she couldn't,' he says, bending to put his eye to the door, 'and maybe she could.'

Dodge looks through the miniature aperture and there is a garden. There is a garden with grass as tall as trees and trees so high their heads are in the clouds. Dodge blinks and a butterfly flutters by.

'Wildlife!' he whispers.

'What? What?' say Cath and Hebe, right up against his ears in their eagerness to see into the garden. 'Is it a garden, man? What can you see?'

Dodge's look has got stuck on a flowerbed, where a host of primitive penises and prototype vaginas lift their glowing colours to the sun and shout their smells triumphantly at the air. The air is alive and laughing, laughing gas; and everything that breathes it – every apple, every beetle, every chrysanthemum, every dandelion, every earwig, every fungus, every grasshopper, every heather – everything that breathes the air gets the joke and giggles inwardly.

The stones aren't silent for nothing. They know it's better that way. The moss and the ivy are secure in the knowledge that they are beautiful too. Earth and water are absorbed in each other, so together they don't know which is which, too moist for words. A bee comes and hangs humming in the air, an inch from the tip of Dodge's nose, and his sinuses buzz in harmony. Out of the corner of his eye, a spider runs across its web like a hand across a harp, or a shiver down Dodge's spine.

Something touches his bottom, and he pulls his head in sharpish, knocking it on the top of the tiny door.

Cath is tugging at his skirt.

'What?' he snaps.

'Is there a garden, man?' says Cath. 'Is Celia out there?'

'There's a garden,' Dodge replies, 'there's a garden. I never thought I'd say this but, oh Wow! Hallelujah! Hip-hip-hurrah!' Dodge smiles. Dodge hardly ever smiles.

'Let's have a look.' Cath dives at the door on all fours, but Dodge grabs her by the collar and holds her back.

'No,' he says, 'I'm finding Celia.'

Cath has got her eye to the door, nearly strangling herself in the attempt.

'You can't see her from here though, can you?' she chokes.

'No,' says Dodge.

'Shall we go out there, then?' Cath coughs.

'Yes,' says Dodge. He releases his grip on Cath. 'I'm going first,' he warns.

'Keep your hair on,' says Cath.

'Sorry?' says Dodge.

'Mellow out, man,' says Cath, 'ease up!'

Dodge shakes his head in exasperation. 'Celia's lost,' he splutters, 'and all you can find is crass platitudes!'

Cath's head is out of the door now, but her disembodied voice comes back into the kitchen:

'Crass platitudes, cross plotitudes; maybe I'm closer than you think. Now let me see . . .'

There is the sound of straining.

Cath is trying to enter the garden.

Dodge, Phoebe and Hebe look on in embarrassed silence as Cath grunts and groans like a camel attempting to pass through the eye of a needle. Cath tries for a long time to leave by the short door. When she withdraws, there are tears in her eyes.

'I thought I saw something,' she says, 'but I couldn't get through. I think I've broken my bloody shoulder. Ow!'

'What did you see?' asks Hebe.

'I thought I sawyer . . .' Cath is clearly in agony, 'I thought I saw her. Under a tree. I thought I saw Celia.'

'What was she doing?' says Dodge.

'I don't know,' says Cath. 'There was this . . . this aura about her. Like a peacock's tail, all azure and emerald and sapphire shimmering white and gold at the edges. I can't explain it. Someone else had better look. Hebe?'

Hebe shakes her head. 'I'll never get through there,' she says modestly.

'Someone will have to,' says Dodge. 'Come on, try; we got Celia out of this and only we can get her back in.'

'If she's in the garden, she's there of her own free will,' says Hebe. 'Maybe we should leave her be.'

'She'll be freezing,' says Dodge firmly, 'and her will will have fallen off. Go on, out you go,' he brings Hebe to her hands and knees in front of the door. 'Goodbye. Go and find Celia. Fetch!'

'Oh fuck it,' says Hebe, and sticks her head through the hole. She stops when she gets to the shoulders.

Cath, Dodge and Phoebe watch as Hebe's breathing deepens. They see the small of her back get bigger as her lungs expand lengthways to take the air as low as it will go. They see her spine straighten and her shoulders soften. Before their eyes, Hebe gets longer and thinner.

'She's using her mental powers,' whispers Phoebe proudly, 'mind over matter.'

Hebe is practically a snake. Each breath ripples from top to tail, rolling out her body's contours like waves on a sandy beach. Each breath rattles. Then, just when it seems that Hebe is all set to slip like a serpent into the garden, she gives a gentle sigh and passes out.

'Oh no!' says Phoebe, grabbing Hebe by the heels and dragging her back into the kitchen, 'she's fainted! Someone bring some water.'

Dodge is getting desperate.

'I'll do it!' he cries, 'I'll look after her. If you could just try your hand . . . or your head . . . at getting through the door.'

Phoebe looks at him with a tiny child's disproportionately large dismay. She opens her mouth wide, to get it round her massive passion.

'I'm not going anywhere,' she says, 'without my sister.'

Dodge sees at once that it's useless to argue. And the last thing he wants is for Phoebe to start shouting for her mother. Luckily, at the very moment Hebe fainted, Alice started to come round. She is sitting up now, half under the table, muttering something about having had such a curious dream. Dodge sees her swaying there, with something that looks suspiciously like sick in her hair.

'Ah, Alice,' he says, 'just the person. You get bigger and smaller, don't you?'

Alice stumbles to her feet. 'Huh?' she says.

'Come here,' says Dodge.

She starts to stagger towards him.

'Could you go through this door?' Dodge demands.

Alice considers the little opening. 'I could,' she says, 'for a bit of cake. Or a swig of drink. Or a nibble of mushroom.'

'Anything,' says Dodge. 'Please try. We must find Celia.'

'Celia?' says Alice, distantly. 'She was in my dream.'

'We think she's in the garden,' says Dodge, 'only none of us is small enough to see.'

'Oh,' says Alice, all right then. Shrink me.'

'I think that's Cath's department,' Dodge says, standing back.

322

'There's a couple of jam tarts left,' says Cath, 'will they do?'

'Your jam tarts?' asks Alice.

'Yes,' says Cath.

Alice shakes her head and looks pityingly at Cath.

'When will you realise that your tarts don't work?' she says. 'They don't really make you smaller. They just make you think you are.'

Alice's legs buckle beneath her, and Cath catches her, and they both fall down together.

Dodge sighs. 'Well, that's that then,' he says, 'I'll have to do it myself.'

He gets to his knees in front of the door and adjusts his dress. 'Don't look,' he mutters, his face pink with embarrassment.

Phoebe, Cath and Alice don't look away.

Dodge puts his head through the tiny hole. His shoulders are too broad to go too. His blue silk dress was Celia's once, and the shoulders are artificially padded.

Everyone hears Dodge clear his throat.

'Celia!' he calls, 'Celia! Can you hear me?'

There is a pause.

Then Dodge pulls his head back in. His face is bright red.

'Well?' says Alice.

'Was she there?' says Cath.

'What did she say?' says Phoebe.

'No,' says Dodge.

'No what?' says Alice.

'No she wasn't there?' says Cath.

'No,' says Dodge. 'No is what she said. I think.'

'She said no?' says Phoebe.

'I think so,' says Dodge. 'Well, someone did.'

'No what?' says Alice.

'No she couldn't hear me,' says Dodge.

'Celia said no she couldn't hear you?' says Cath.

'Yes,' says Dodge, 'I think so.'

'So she must have heard you,' says Alice.

'But Celia wouldn't lie,' says Dodge. 'If she said she couldn't hear me, she couldn't hear me.'

'That doesn't make sense,' says Phoebe.

'Listen,' says Dodge, 'Celia said no. She said no, and she meant no. So we're just going to have to take no for an answer.'

There is a knock at the front door.

And another.

And another.

And the knocking doesn't stop.

Dodge leaps to his feet and runs out of the kitchen and down the hallway. He stops dead at the door, and looks over his shoulder. Cath and Alice are hovering behind him. Phoebe is still in the kitchen, trying to shake her sister awake.

'Shall I open it?' he whispers.

Alice shakes her head.

'Find out who's there first,' she mouths.

'Who is it?' Dodge calls cautiously through the key-hole.

'*Police!*'

'Pardon?' says Dodge, taking a step backwards.

'*Police! Open up!*'

Dodge takes another step backwards.

'*If you refuse, we'll force entry!*'

'I know,' says Dodge, and takes his third step backwards, knocking into Cath and Alice.

There is the sound of boot on wood.

'What do you want?' Dodge shouts.

'*Some missing men!*'

324

'There's no missing men here,' shouts Dodge, 'sorry. All the men here are here.'

A truncheon comes through the letter box.

Dodge, Cath and Alice look at it.

Dodge, Cath and Alice look at each other.

Dodge, Cath and Alice decide not to do anything hasty.

'*We wish to pinpoint the whereabouts of a Mr Kenneth Conn and our own constable Max Hatton; both known to have been at this address last night. Both reported missing this morning! Have you seen these men?*'

Dodge approaches the truncheon on tiptoe.

'I am one,' he says.

'*What?*'

'I am one,' Dodge speaks to the truncheon, 'of those men.'

'*Ken Conn?*'

'Er, yes,' says Dodge, 'hello.'

'*Open the door!*'

'But you know I'm here now. I'm not missing any more.' Dodge is talking into the truncheon like an experienced broadcaster with a microphone.

Cath and Alice laugh.

'*Stop laughing. Open the door. In the name of the law!*'

Phoebe and Hebe come running up the hallway hand in hand. Hebe is back in the land of the living.

'What's happening?' whispers Phoebe.

'It's the police,' says Cath.

'Looking for Max and Ken,' adds Alice.

'Mayhem!' says Phoebe, 'what are we going to do?'

'Well,' whispers Alice, 'I've been thinking about this.' She clears her throat quietly. 'We could let them in.'

'No!' squeaks Phoebe. 'They'd find the dead body.'

'Well,' whispers Alice, 'we could tell them Celia did it. She'll never . . .'

'NO!' shouts Cath.

'*Right! We're coming in!*'

The police begin to break the door down. Luckily, the door is substantial; designed to have old-fashioned families raised behind it, designed to keep strangers out and secrets in.

So Alice, Cath, Dodge, Phoebe and Hebe have a little time to decide what to do.

'We can run around like headless chickens,' says Alice, 'but we can't hide.'

'Celia has,' says Hebe. 'Why can't we hide with her? Like sardines.'

'We don't know where she is,' says Dodge.

'But she must be somewhere,' says Phoebe.

'I had a dream,' says Hebe, 'while I was unconscious. Or it may have been my film. Anyway, Celia was in the garden, asleep under the lullaby leaves of a splendiferous tree, a book open on her lap. And we were all standing at Phoebe's bedroom window, with the blind up. That was the way out; a strong length of washing-line was stretched between the window and Celia's tree. Like a death-slide, you know?'

'Did we zoom down it?' asks Cath, enthusiastically.

'No,' Hebe looks a bit embarrassed, 'we strapped the Mad Hatter to it and sent him down instead.'

Alice applauds this idea.

But Dodge doesn't. 'What a horrible thing to do,' he says, 'you ought to be ashamed of yourself, Hebe.'

The front door begins to splinter. Boots and truncheons appear. Dodge tries to force them back, with the hoover and the hatstand. He is sweating like a pig, but now that the others know

326

he is a woman his strange smell makes perfect sense. It's perfume.

'Ken and Max aren't missing!' Dodge is shouting at the pieces of policemen, 'They're here! Stupid bastards, you don't even know what missing means! Try looking for our Celia! That would show you a thing or two! You'd never say the words lost property in the same breath again.'

'Oh, why didn't she tell us she was going?' sighs Phoebe, watching Dodge's fight with tears in her eyes.

'Why should she?' says Alice. 'None of you liked her.'

'Shut up, you!' says Cath, grabbing Alice and using her, much as Dodge is using the hatstand, to hold the police at bay.

'And why didn't she tell us where she was going?' More tears pour out of Phoebe. Nothing upsets her so much as not saying good-bye.

'I don't think she knew herself,' says Hebe. 'At the end she went completely cartoon. She was standing around with no clothes on for ages. The cold may have gone to her head.'

The entire upper portion of a policeman has come through the door. Cath hits him on the helmet with Alice.

'But she could have left a forwarding address,' cries Phoebe. 'She could have given us a clue.'

'She probably did,' Cath calls back from the front line. 'Once she'd got that boy's wet dream of a frock off, Celia was quite a girl. And she was well into being chased.'

The half-policeman takes advantage of Cath's momentary lack of concentration to become three-quarters of a policeman.

'So what was it then?' panics Phoebe, 'what was the clue?'

Dodge takes his hatstand to the boy in blue.

'I'm not in Wonderland,' he grunts. 'You couldn't riddle-me-ree if my life depended on it. Ask Alice.'

'She's otherwise engaged at present,' says Cath, as the first

327

policeman becomes a huge whole in the hallway, with handcuffs. 'But I'm working on it. What was the last thing she said?'

'Yes!' Phoebe jumps on the idea. 'What was it?'

Can anyone remember? Dodge doesn't. Cath can't. Alice is already being taken away. Phoebe turns to her sister. She'll know.

'What was the last thing Celia said?' Phoebe asks.

'This is the last thing I will say,' says Hebe. 'Sadly.'

By the time the postcard pops through the letterbox, the door is mended but the house is empty. It lands on top of a mountain of junk mail on the doormat and doesn't slide off. Fingers of light alone stir the refined atmosphere of the hallway.

It is not a pretty postcard. There isn't even a picture on the front. There are just two words, big and black on white.

READ ME.

On the other side is a stamp, a postmark from Khartoum, and a final reminder from Celia Small:

DEAR ALL, I'M CROSSING THE THRESHOLD BUT NOBODY'S CARRYING ME, I'M STANDING ON MY OWN TWO FEET. NEXT STOP CALCUTTA, WHERE THE HOLE IS GREATER THAN THE SUM OF OUR PARTIES. I'M IN A NEW WORLD, BUT IF MY PARENTS CALL, PLEASE JUST TELL THEM I'M OUT.